THE THIRD TESTAMENT
FOR THE THIRD MILLENNIUM

UNITY

Kevin Carey

Sacristy Press
PO Box 612, Durham, DH1 9HT

www.sacristy.co.uk

First published in 2012 by Sacristy Press, Durham

Sacristy Limited, registered in England & Wales, number 7565667

British Library Cataloguing-in-Publication Data
A catalogue record for the book is available from the British Library

ISBN 978-1-908381-02-6

www.perpetua.tv

MISSION

Gregg scanned the 270 yards from the god4u offices to the underground station and chose the darker side of the street. He moved as quickly as he could without appearing to hurry. He didn't want any witnesses to remember anything. Out of character with his training, he checked that he still had the memory stick in his pocket.

He swiped his merit card and got into an empty lift rather than using the escalators, caught a train South for two stops where he could cross to the opposite track from the same platform, and went North until the underground intersected the overground. He used cash to buy a ticket from a machine and headed North again until he reached an unmanned station with an extensive car park. It was badly lit which rendered the CCTV cameras useless, but still he identified an area where the camera had been vandalised. He took a small tool from his money belt and opened the door of a grey Fiat Uno and with the same tool he started the engine. There was a minute risk that the owner would see him, but this was minimised as the exit was at the opposite end of the car park from the station. The tank was almost full. He made his way towards the M1.

◆　◆　◆

The paramedics said that there was no doubt that Jim was dead. They could find no immediate cause. There would have to be a post-mortem and a Coroner's Court.

Only when they had left could Trina and her followers discuss Gregg. Because Stacey had thwarted Gregg's attempted escape with a brief case of god4u documents she spoke first, but didn't have much to say. When Jim had pronounced his condemnation of Gregg as a danger to the movement she had watched Gregg closely. He had a poker player's face and he looked round without seeming to look. All his slight moves were in the direction of the inner office and when he came out with a brief case his moves were towards the outside door. Stacey had gone to the lift to meet the paramedic team and when she was letting them in she sensed Gregg behind her. He made for the lift as the paramedics came out. The doors, as they often did, got stuck half-closed. As he struggled with his head between them she slipped behind him and down the dimly-lit, unused stairs. With luck she could beat the lift to the bottom. She was gaining, there were no sounds from the lift cage. She was two flights from the bottom when, on the turn, she saw him. She did not know whether to run or stay. He might hit her or he might just run past, but if he ran past he had something to hide. On the last landing before the ground floor she put her back to the wall, facing up the stairs. He came on down, also looking indecisive, not knowing whether to hit her or give her the slip. When he was four steps from the landing she sprang forward and grabbed his knees. They fell in a heap with him on top, but the brief case was wedged between her and the wall. he got up and ran down the remaining flight of stairs and out into the street, leaving her with the brief case.

"It's as near a complete set of Perpetuan documents as we have got," said Max, the god4u Secretary. "I don't know why he wanted them, and I certainly don't know why he thought he needed to steal them. All the time he worked for us he was told he could read and copy anything he wanted. The only conclusion I can draw is that he wanted them without us knowing."

"Interesting," said Father Bill, the group's external adviser, "but the main thing to think about is Jim."

"I don't want to seem callous," said Trina, "but there is nothing we can do about him except help the civic authorities if they ask. Perpetua said nothing about death ceremonies."

"But what about Gregg?"

"Jim said that Gregg was evil. He died saying it, but unless the post-mortem finds poison or something like that, there's nothing to be done. Our code prevents us from guessing motive or making assumptions about the stresses people suffer. We are not to judge, are we, Bill?"

"Quite right," said Father Bill, "but Perpetua did ask me to look after him and I did grow to love him so."

"Yes, he was a wonderful boy/man," said Trina. "He was very stoical about his Downs syndrome except that he so wanted a girl friend, and he had very special powers as a seer. He was the only one who saw Perpetua dance in her own sacred light on the night she died. The only one to see the light when her body was taken up to God our Parent. So sad to lose Jim after Dexter and Miles. Three martyrs in nine months, but we must carry on. I will wait here until everything is cleared up."

"No you won't," said Max, emphatically. "The body won't be released until after Christmas, so you go on your planned retreat to that little cottage you've found near Silicon Ridge and I will look after things here."

They were all convinced by Max's good sense. The Paramedics had taken the body and informed the police. Except for saying a few more prayers for Jim, led by Father Bill, there was nothing for them to do. They left quickly to make a start on their journeys to different mission stations.

◆　◆　◆

Once he was comfortably in the inside lane Gregg turned on the radio for the 8pm news summary. There was a tail end of traffic news and then a furious argument about a threatened airline strike, which the court had suspended because of ballot rigging. As the union representative talked in impenetrable jargon and as nobody seemed to have read, or understood, the judgment, the item was pointless. After the jingles and the reading of a clutch of pointless emails, the summary came. The Opposition was attacking the Government for nationalising Southern Gem and doing nothing about the economy. Hypo shareholders were mounting a campaign to dislodge Sir Pluto Millman as its Chairman because of a 2% "slump" in profits. "War" had broken out between climate change advocates over carbon trading; Melanie and her newly acquired third husband were splitting up. The new religion of Perpetuanism had just received another blow with the death of Jim, it's chief visionary, worship designer and musician. There would be more details as they came in.

When Jim was mentioned Gregg did not so much as twitch although he was surprised that the news had broken so quickly. He did, however, flinch when a red Toyota travelling at well over the speed limit almost swept him onto the hard shoulder. Automatically he registered and memorised the number.

He thought he must have dozed temporarily as everything around him was a bit dim: the radio sound was fuzzy; his headlights seemed to be dim; onward coming vehicles seemed ill defined; but as he drove on everything became darker and fuzzier. He was frightened and began to sweat. He wondered if it was some long delayed after effect of torture. He had given much more than he had taken, but, still, he wished he could forget Syria. It was Syria that had ignited the damp tinder of his Christian faith and ignited his Perpetuan fire. You never knew with the after effects of torture, which was good in general because he had not had to tell a deliberate lie to a congressional committee. He wasn't against lying on moral, but on pragmatic, grounds. You never knew when and what would be found out by whom, and he knew operatives who had simply forgotten the fine details of a well constructed lie.

Again, without thinking, he slowed as the light grew worse and came to a halt on the hard shoulder. Gradually, the light turned from darkness, tinted with burnt orange, to an indescribable golden light which did not hurt the eyes.

"Gregg!"

"What? Who's that?"

"Gregg!"

"I don't believe it!"

"You better."

"Is it really you?"

"You know it is, Gregg. Why resist reality? I am real to you now. Why are you fighting against me?"

"It's the inner war in me between a heart that cannot resist you and a head that thinks it must."

"The head is a means to the heart, and without that leaning towards, the head is the source of pride. I know of your inner turbulence and your past wickedness in the name of the good."

"But you always said that it was not for any one to judge any one else. Only God could judge."

"Gregg, remember, I am God. I know it will be difficult for you to stay true because of your terrible, tortured past, but I will help you. In the meantime, drive very slowly to the nearest services and wait for one who will come."

The golden light faded back to orange tinted black and although he felt that he could barely see enough to drive he knew that She would be guiding him. As it turned out, it was only a few hundred yards to the services slip road. He parked next to what he could only just make out as a red Toyota near the well, lit main door and edged his way inside, using all his training to calculate likely obstacles.

"Forgot your white cane, have you?" said a serving lady in a kindly voice. He looked confused, but that only made her kinder. From her healthy, 30-year-old perspective, old and disabled people were confused.

"What can I get you, ducks?"

He calculated. "A triple espresso and a packet of chocolate chip cookies, please." He didn't know how long he would have to wait so caffeine, sugar and chocolate were the best thing. As he sat at his corner table the light grew ever dimmer as the last customers left until he was in complete darkness. He was totally blind. He was frightened. He could hear the staff tiding up before the arrival of the night shift, talking about Christmas shopping and parties. He had a sudden rush of sentimental affection for the light and colour of Christmas.

"I thought I would find you here!"

Gregg automatically raised his head towards the new arrival but saw nothing.

"You look in a poor way. Still, I've found you as She said I would."

"Who?"

"Perpetua. She told me to come here and find you."

"Who are you?"

"O'Helly. Joe O'Helly, former Roman Catholic Priest and Perpetuan Guide. Former hell raiser, recently 'come out'."

"And what did She tell you to do about me?"

"She told me to get a move on and find you as you were in distress."

"Red Toyota?"

"How could you have known that?"

"You passed me before my encounter with Perpetua."

"Before! You, too?"

"Yes. But if you passed me, why did you arrive here after me?"

"I was so anxious to reach my final destination that I, well, I must admit, I discounted what she said, like Jonah, you know. Anyway, she gave me hell so I had to get off at the next junction and come back!"

"She seems to be everywhere in spite of her apparent 'ascent'."

"You never can tell in matters spiritual. Anyway, you look as if you need a bit of help."

"I seem to have lost my sight."

"She's getting awfully corny in her tricks. Saint Paul all over again."

"Yes, but I don't much like the implication for me."

"I think you better tell me about it as we drive North. Give me your car keys and I'll hand them to the manager with a note that you've taken ill and the car may be there for some time."

"I'm afraid I can't find them. I'll tell you more later."

"Well I'll tell the manager you took ill and can't find them, then."

He put Gregg's left hand on his upper right arm and led him out to the car. On the journey North, Gregg told O'Helly everything he could have found out for himself from a phone call, including Jim's "strange" condemnation and the struggle with Stacey. But he didn't tell him about Syria, the memory stick or the car theft.

"So why were you trying to steal Perpetuan documents?"

"I want to be a missionary, but they don't trust me."

"You can see their point."

"Yes, but it doesn't make any difference. I have this compulsion, I'm drawn to Perpetua even though part of me feels revulsion."

"A strange admission, but I know what you mean. I had an intense love/hate relationship with mother church which ultimately resolved, thanks to Perpetua, into self-affirmation and a gentle denial of her claims. We must pray that something similar happens to you to free you from your torment. I'm not a psychosomatist, but perhaps your blindness has something to do with the inner struggle."

"I don't know whether Perpetua was trying to claim me or reject me."

"We will try to find out."

When they arrived at Stumpy Knoll, Joe and Wayne had a quick conversation, agreeing to sacrifice the joy of their reunion by giving Gregg the only bed in the house while they respectively slept on the sofa and the floor. Wayne phoned Max. "Gregg is here."

"The police are interested in him."

"Why? Was it something to do with Jim?"

"No. We played that down. There was no purpose in it. It was something to do with a stolen car. The CCTV pictures at the station car park and the motorway services matched. So did the number plate." Gregg barely flinched. "What are we supposed to do?" "Nothing. We will sort it out. The owner is a Perpetuan sympathiser. So what did you call about?"

"Gregg has been blinded and Joe has rescued him and brought him here."

"A pretty amazing story, but I can now believe almost anything. Keep him calm and report progress."

Except for sparse meals, Gregg stayed in his room for two nights and a day, keeping the curtains shut and accepting little food, clutching the memory stick. On the third morning he could not bear the tension any longer and asked Joe and Wayne to sit with him. It wasn't the blindness. His training had helped him to adjust relatively quickly. What obsessed him was the thought of what was on the memory stick. The power. But he could do nothing about the memory stick without their help. He would have to tell them something to get something.

After lunch on the third day he said, "I didn't tell you, but I need to, right now. I had a memory stick with all of the Perpetuan documents on it, or I think all of them."

"As a back up for the brief case?" asked Joe, interested.

"Yes. I wanted to keep it pure."

"It's not really any of our business," said Joe, carefully, "but some people might think that you wanted to publish your own version before anything 'official' got out."

Gregg winced, but said nothing. Wayne looked at Joe and then brought his lap top and Joe plugged the memory stick into the USB. It was totally blank. Gregg began to cry. He was blind and his power had gone from him.

Wayne who had more than half suspected the result, tried to sooth him but Joe, the experienced pastor, signalling to him to be still, took his hand and Gregg's, and waited for the storm to blow out. Within minutes, Gregg's tears of frustration turned into tears of humility. It was obvious that the deeds of men were puny beside the power of God. It was just that, in his pride, in his need for action, in his compulsion to justify himself, he kept forgetting this basic truth. Here he was, discovered to be a thief, blinded on the road, robbed of his treasure, and still he found it hard to adjust to his creatureliness. Joe laid his hands gently on Gregg's head and signalled Wayne to do the same; and through his tears Gregg became aware of light perception and then of the shape of the window. It was all so matter-of-fact, no invocation, no drama, just a sense of perfect peace. Joe took his hand away. Gregg wanted to leap out of the chair and shout but he stayed calm and waited as smaller objects took on shape and colour.

"I can see," he said very quietly. Joe smiled and said: "I thought so. Somebody up in heaven has been reading Acts."

Joe wondered what sort of Paul Gregg would be.

At the same time as the memory stick was plugged into Wayne's lap top, there was an inexplicable small fire at the god4u headquarters in which the Perpetuan paper archive was destroyed, including the sole copy of Hawthorne's Perpetuan statement of doctrine.

◆   ◆   ◆

Trina had meant to leave on the evening of Jim's death, as Max had urged her, but the fire had finally told her to go. If Perpetua wanted to intervene, there was nothing left for her to do. She arrived at her tiny rented cottage near Silicon Ridge on the Saturday before the Forth Sunday of Advent just as the sun was setting. She unpacked her sparing provisions, lit the fire and a candle, put out the electric lights, and sat in an armchair. She soon fell into a light sleep of the sort experienced on long air flights, following an inner line of thought while being vaguely aware of the external environment. She saw the playground of her school and her peers teasing her because she worked hard. She saw her parents' disappointed faces when she failed Oxbridge Entrance Exams. She saw university students making fun of her when she would not go out drinking because she had to work hard to keep up. Nothing came easily to her. She saw the Job Centre woman telling her that she would no longer qualify for benefits because she kept turning down suitable jobs. She felt, rather than simply seeing, the Grunge Park bed-sit she had taken to "escape" her Excelsior Gardens home with all its external loveliness sanitised by obsessive tidiness and, she had to admit, to escape the unremitting pressure on her to take a job, any job, with "prospects". The combination of parental pressure and the need for a basic income had led her into the office of Annie Price who had intended to give her a five-minute interview. "There's a silly convention," Annie said, "that says that some people are over qualified for jobs. You can never be over qualified. If you do your simple job well, there will be opportunities. I will be happy to recommend you to our graduate training programme once you have proved yourself here. You have a lot to offer. Your colleagues will welcome the leadership and understanding which you can provide. Some employers want the bodies and souls of their employees 24 hours a day. I want them to read and watch movies and think about the world, and be happy." Reassured, she took the job as a shelf stacker and became a pillar of the bipolar leadership with Dexter. he sorted out the physical side and the logistics, shielding the weak from censure, she helped with form filling, liaison with the Floor Manager, and emotional support. For just under a year after university she worked happily in Hypo and then, just as she was beginning to feel the stirrings of ambition, Perpetua came into her life. During the recruitment process each follower had been given a personal "interview" which, in her case, was more of a pep talk.

"I saw you hanging back, not out of fear, but out of what you think of as modesty. Some of the others tell me that you are a leader, a comforter, but you seem to deny it in yourself. Leaders are not people who bluster and bully, they are people whom others are willing to follow. I want you to be a leader of our new family, to continue in the way you have in Hypo with Dexter, but there is something else. I know you are a very skilled communicator and, although it will frighten you at first, I want you to handle the media for us. I see great challenges ahead for you, but also great happiness."

Great challenges; great happiness. The weeks on the road with smiling faces and cheering crowds, the wondrous acts, the stirring speeches, the utter humanity of the God made Woman. Then the weather changing, the sky darkening, the twisted conspiracy to humiliate them all but particularly her, and the terrible denials and the running away and the gruesome death. And the "resurrection".

She saw Miles, grim in evangelism, strong when she failed. Shot. She saw Dexter. Shot. She heard Jim's flute. No more, dying with a strange prophesy on his innocent lips. She saw Gregg and almost flinched awake. She looked at the candle with its German Gothic lettering and nativity scenes. It seemed to belly, its flame filling the whole room, not frightening her into thinking there would be a fire.

"I really must not go on doing this. I really must leave you to your own choices. That is what I always said, that I came to strengthen you to make your own choice for God, but I cannot help it. I cannot bear to see you sad and bewildered. I had to die, like Jesus My Brother I had to die, I had to show you that there is nothing humanity can do to impair God's infinite love for humanity. Even if you kill God that love is not impaired. How many times must God show this to you? Humanity killed God in Jesus and then in me, but the world is still full of worry instead of being full of love and hope. I want to see you, of all people, choosing to smile. I know it was hard for you to lose me, I know it was even harder i some ways for you to lose Miles, and Deter and Jim too. The bigger picture does not change. You were made to be happy in loving God. That is your nature.

"Theology lecture over. Now, look, Trina, the challenge is still before you. It will not come from a wicked person, nor even a militant atheist. It will come from a tortured soul. You will have to combat Gregg and love him at the same time. Our Sister the Spirit will be with you and so, strictly, I should not come back; but perhaps once more. I just want to see you smile."

The candle flared and then shrank back to its normal dimensions and she was fully awake. She put on a CD of Christmas carols, poured a glass of red wine, cooked some pasta and vegetables, and then looked at some pictures of Perpetua. There were so few left. For reasons she could not understand, Perpetua had caused most of her heritage to be destroyed. There were only a few photographs and Trina wondered how long these would be allowed to survive. Then she saw that the reality of Perpetua must be in her heart as a living presence, not an archive nor a doctrine. No amount of theology and memory, of adoration and nostalgia, can be a substitute for pure love.

◆　◆　◆

Gregg continued to stay in Wayne's room until Christmas Eve, causing anxiety and generating massive tension not only because of his brooding, but also because Wayne and Joe could not develop their partnership as they had planned. Wayne had expected some improvement in Gregg, a sense of gratitude, not to them but to God, reflected in an effort to improve his behaviour, but Joe knew better. Gregg's relief did not express itself in softness, but in an excruciating adjustment, an attempt to put himself back in control of himself and those around him. The blindness was a supernatural blow, as was the cure, but Gregg could not help resenting the human agency of his hosts. They were now, they realised, deeply in love but whereas Wayne was extrovert and prepared to take some risks, Joe was deeply reticent and physically inarticulate. His Catholic upbringing had made the thought of intimate relationships with girls pretty unthinkable, but the dark anathema over relationships with other men was all the more effective in dealing with the completely unimaginable. So the three men edged round each other, waiting for something to change. They called Max in the hope of some advice that would get them off the hook, but he told them to hang on. There was nothing to be gained by pushing Gregg to talk or to move on.

Even though they knew that Gregg's coarseness of manner was a front to ward off intrusion, its effect escalated. He was aware that he was an intruder, but he felt mentally grid-locked. He did not want to stay but he could not leave. These people, whose lifestyle was so repulsive, were a direct link with Perpetua. He was drawn compulsively to the figure of Perpetua, even though she was black and female, but he felt an equal compulsion to purify Perpetuanism of its all too obvious liberalism, exemplified by these men. He saw her life and death as a new start, a genuine sign from God of equal status with the life and death of Jesus but, as with Jesus, he was deeply suspicious of the departure from the YHWH of the Old Testament. It was not that he did not understand generosity or sacrifice, as he was personally capable of both, but he knew that the world could not be built on altruism. There was a terrible contradiction which his fundamentalist Baptist elders had never resolved between economic liberalism and moral conservatism and that tension was now living inside Gregg. Then there was the memory stick which should have contained all the major Perpetuan documents, his key to making a major revision before the originals were published, if they ever could have been. He had learned from a one line news item about the small fire at the god4u offices and surmised that it had something to do with the papers—Perpetua was playing some strange tricks with her heritage—so he had come close to being the only person left with any record of what she had said. That was a useless thought because she had sought him out and found him.

On the morning of Christmas Eve, once he had made the decision to act, he emerged from his retreat and moderated his manner just enough to signal a change of heart. He did not want to do anything suddenly as that might cause suspicion, but his task was made easy because the two men were in a mood to be cheerful as they went down their shopping list, intending to take part in Christmas like any good Christian family. They had bought an optional Perpetua figure for their portable crib, a small tree, a set of lights, a packet of tinsel, and a box of red candles, and were now discussing food and presents. They broke off to ask Gregg how he was and to say they were pleased that he had emerged from his isolation. He, in turn, thanked them for looking after him and said that he was sorry he had occupied Wayne's room. From now on he would be happy to sleep on the sofa. Joe wondered whether to refuse, but Wayne intervened and said that he was grateful. He had not found it easy to sleep in the living room. They went out cheerfully, looking forward to the bustle, with a short list of requirements from Gregg. Outside, Wayne phoned Max. Gregg gave him a spooky feeling. He didn't have anything to hide, but still he didn't want to be overheard. "There's nothing we can or should do to restrain him, but I hope you will not mind if he stays with you for Christmas and then we will consider what to do next. Our real problem is working out what his relationship is with us. Trina insists he is special. Yes, I know, it's a Saint Paul kind of story, but the first leaders of the Christian church were properly cautious about the convert Paul.

We don't have to like everyone we love and, again, although we are supposed, by Perpetua, to trust everyone, trust must in some way be proportionate. It's not the same thing as respect which is to be accorded equally and universally. Apart from that, Wayne, you will recall that I've got a funny feeling. I know we shouldn't base decisions on that, but I can't help it. When I first saw him at the American Embassy I thought I'd seen him before and I thought the same when I bumped into him again on the flight from Washington DC. I still can't shift the idea that he's part of a totally different picture that I can't properly re-assemble. Is he ours or not? Merry Christmas!" The three men sat together companionably with a bottle of red wine to listen to the Carols from King's before going out to Pastor Drone's Crib Service.

◆　　◆　　◆

Jezebel's beauty salon was packed and there was a steady stream of harassed looking women going into The Eye of the Needle dress shop, replacing a scarcely less harassed stream of women emerging with smart carrier bags. Trina looked at her watch. It was 2pm and she wanted to get home for the Carols. This was no time to preach moderation and delayed gratification, let alone the futility of worldly goods to these women. They had problems enough. For most of them Christmas would be a challenge to their self-esteem based on competition, their cuisine based on slavish adherence to recipe books, their diplomacy based on blandness, and their stamina based on sheer "professional" doggedness. They would not enjoy Christmas, nor its food and clothes, its dinners and its parties, its services and functions. This was not the right time to say anything, so she walked across the threadbare fields in the pallid sun whose warmth was neutralised by a cutting East wind, saying a little prayer for them and promising to see them in a few days. She made a cup of tea, lit her German candle, and listened to the Carols. This was, by any measure, an unusual experience. The largest concentration of Scripture broadcast, the majority of the music was not easy and, therefore, not popular, and the whole event took 100 minutes, supposedly way past the contemporary attention span. She suspected that the occasion was much more widely known about than known. What she liked most was the wide variety of musical styles. True, there were some nineteenth century carols which tended towards the sentimental, though Darke redeemed Rosetti in a quite miraculous way, and there were Bach organ pieces to frame the occasion, but what struck her most forcibly was the bond between Medieval and contemporary carol writing which seemed to bypass the baroque and the classical. There was a crunchiness and directness in the new writing that echoed the very old in both words and music. There was the Medieval world of grim dependence on the almighty, underlined by high infant mortality and the inability to store and plan, superimposed upon by a contemporary world increasingly aware of

its own mortality and a feeling of helplessness in the face of violence and uncertainty. Looked at objectively, you could see why the Jews in the time of Jesus
were so obsessed with preserving their identity against imperial incursion and
why, today, people were worried about their identity in the face of metropoli-
tanisation. It wasn't racist to seek coherent self-identification as a necessary precondition for corporate well-being, but the shallow bourgeois bureaucracy had
used its quite proper abhorrence of racism to smother the bigger question. How
can we have identity outside creatureliness? She listened with renewed love and
attention to the story of how God made good his promise to mankind (humanity) and wondered, as the organ played its first recessional, how long it would be
before a Perpetuan Carol was included as a King's Commission.

◆　　◆　　◆

Stella and Lucia, dressed demurely in warm, woolen dresses, were handing
out carol sheets and miniature candles at the door. As more families arrived,
the noise level rose in a soccer-style crescendo. Pastor Drone, who had never
seen so many people in his church before, not even for the celebrated visit of the
Rev. Myron T. Skraun Jr, looked with something approaching wonder at his re-
roofed, building with its new coat of whitewash, sparkling windows, and lively,
vivid scenes from Scripture, including a photograph of Perpetua conducting a
choir of children of all races and a somewhat grim portrait of Dexter in whose
memory Max had made a restoration grant. Pastor Drone had initially resisted,
but could not deny the miracles performed in his church and as it was a con-
gregational organisation in which everybody knew somebody who had been
"cured" by Dexter, it was made clear to him that his continued tenure depended
upon respect for the miracle worker and martyr. Pastor Drone never quite regretted the old days, but his temperament was better suited to tiny, wizened congregations than to churches packed with lively worshippers of all ages. He was
particularly frightened of children who were volatile and careless (carefree). He
still worked hard at his own spiritual life as well as holding services for his traditional core, but he had, inch by inch, accepted Wayne's ministry in spite of his
absolute detestation of homosexuality—he could not bring himself to use such
a pleasant word as gay—which he could not imagine, let alone understand. But,
he reflected, to know something is to escape prejudice. Wayne was good with all
ages and kinds of people and they seemed not to notice, let alone mind, that he
was—he began to learn the jargon—of a different sexual orientation.

There was only mild disappointment when the carol sheets ran out, but a
potential crisis when there were no more candles for distribution. Anticipating
this shortfall, Joe walked in briskly with another box, followed by Wayne.

"Stella, I've never seen you with so many clothes on, even on a Winter's
evening! I thought Max had arranged for proper heating in here. Yes, it is quite

warm. You don't have to be wrapped up to be a Perpetuan, you know. Not being a lady of a certain kind doesn't mean that you have to hide your natural beauty and Lucie, I don't think grey is your colour, darling. Bring back the good old lilac, I say!" Both, initially minded to take offence, smiled at this obvious banter.

"Speaking of which, your friend Joe looks very nice in that shirt which is more towards lilac than ecclesiastical grey, and how nice he looks in those much tighter than clerical trousers."

"Touche! Merry Christmas!"

It was like any other Nativity Play, where relentless parental competition was overlaid with a veneer of adult sentimentality and child piety. Yet for all the confusion brought about by secular competition and an outrageous amount of shameless up-staging, everybody knew that the main point of the exercise was to celebrate the birth of the Baby Jesus and so there was genuine, if temporary, joy when his likeness, or, rather the likeness of a Nordic boy, was gently placed by the blue-eyed Mary in the manger. Then the play took a surprise turn when Mary turned towards the back of the church and said, "Joseph, look, his Sister Perpetua is coming to welcome Her new brother into the world," at which point a tall, slim early teenage girl with big Afro hair, dressed in skin tight blue jeans, a matching bronze crop-top, and sandals walked down the central aisle through the throng of actors. She walked slowly and purposely until she reached the crib and then, without saying anything, knelt between Mary and Joseph and held the hand of the baby. For a moment there was intense silence, and then the children let out a mighty roar of approval. This baby was no longer the centre piece of an anachronistic ritual drama, but was loved by the sex goddess most of them respectively wished to be or to acquire. When they arrived, the kings tried to look down her still-forming cleavage and forgot their lines. There never was, in anyone's memory, such a joyful and noisy Nativity Play. How the older Perpetua was the sister of Mary's first-born was a mystery too far, but it was no more arcane than the virgin birth. Pastor Drone said the closing prayer with more liveliness than he had ever before mustered and almost beamed at the departing hordes.

"We are going to have to do something about the theology of the Holy Quartet," said Joe, amiably, as he said his farewells. Drone looked troubled.

"Don't worry, it took us Centuries to work out an internally consistent Trinity. No hurry."

Joe sat at the dining table trying to work it out:

1. Contrary to Islamic misunderstanding, the Godhead is not a numeric phenomenon of three in one, or three or, strictly speaking, one. However, one is the closest we get to the idea of the *form* of God. ("One is the loneliest number!") in metaphorical terms, God approximates to one.

2. The Trinity as a way of understanding God in metaphorical language refers to an entity which is itself unchanging and it is not so much a noun as an economy.

3. God can be described as having the attribute of Creator and by creating matter God created time.

4. As this God is in and of itself "normally" or normatively not human, nor consisting of matter in the same category as created matter, we think of its attribute as being Spiritual.

5. But for whatever "mysterious" cause (Joe liked the mysterious aspect as it explained so much or, rather, meant that there was much less to explain) the Creator had chosen in the shape of Jesus to participate in what had been created. Christians accepted that Jesus was as timelessly part of the Godhead as the Creator. The Credal phrase, "born of the Father before time began", is contradictory and takes the metaphor of fatherhood to be actual. There is no logic in "only begotten" as the Godhead is infinitely everything. It would be odd for an article of faith—which this is—to limit the options of the Godhead.

6. Likewise, giving the Holy Spirit a history was seriously problematic as, from the human standpoint, the Godhead always had possessed an attribute of Spirit. The Lucan and Johannine ideas of the Spirit being created successively to Jesus "proceeding from the Father and the Son" could not be upheld because any such proceeding contains within it a temporal element. Judaism had never got its head round God as timeless. God first appeared creating time.

7. If Christians hold that Jesus is God, but that the Godhead is not a numerological phenomenon, it is difficult to see why the Godhead should only break into history in human form once. There is no reason why Perpetua should not be part of the Godhead. There is, too, no reason why the Godhead, which created all, should not "intervene" in other places at other times. This leaves the problem of the formulation of the death of Jesus as the "full and final sacrifice". It might be full, but it need not be final and the fullness of subsequent sacrifices, such as that of Perpetua, does not compromise the fullness of the Jesus sacrifice; they contained the same fullness at different times and places.

8. The critical point, given that all humanity is created by God to be re-enfolded back into God's perfection, is the nature of the difference between humanity as part of the Godhead and Jesus and Perpetua as part of the Godhead. This lies, thought Joe, in the nature of the difference between Creator and created. Christianity had veered too far in its view of Jesus away from his intercessory, mediating role, to that element of his Godhead, his timelessness, which had tended to obscure the primacy of creation as the quintessential attribute of Godhead.

9. If humanity is part of the Godhead, but, as created, distinct from the Creator function, it is of little importance how many or of what kind are the God/humanity hybrids or intermediates;. As all humanity is, to some extent, though different in nature from Jesus and Perpetua, a God/humanity hybrid, the vital attribute of Jesus and Perpetua is that of intermediary. The nature of the required level of intermediary activity is dictated in some way by the exercise of humanity's free will.

10. Our chief concern with intermediaries, therefore, is to express our gratitude for them to the Creator attribute of the Godhead.
11. In a circular phenomenon, the idea of "one" is helpful, but the idea of the Trinity is unhelpful, as would be the idea of a Quartet. The only key ideas are God as creator, humanity as creatures and the necessity of intermediary "intervention" to mitigate against the necessary errors of behaviour made by creatures as a result of their free will which enables them to love the Creator freely, or not.
12. Love is at least supererogatory, if not infinite, but the Godhead could not confine itself to anything that is not infinite. Creation is supererogatory, but for the created to be so they require a framework within which choice is possible.
13. Therefore, the necessity of error requires the necessity of intermediary correction so that the purpose of creation, of creatures choosing to love the Creator, can be properly fulfilled.
14. Created and preserved supererogatorily.

Joe reviewed his handiwork with pleasure, but without pride. Perpetua seemed to be doing her best to erase records of her own direct communication, leaving only life incidents for god4u, but no theology. Well, that might be her way and she could easily subvert anything he did, but theology was a well developed muscle in his professional physique and it needed constant exercise to keep it in good trim.

They ate a simple supper, in anticipation of tomorrow's festivities, and slipped into the back of a Roman Catholic church for Midnight Mass.

"I suppose we should have done something Perpetuan," said Wayne.

"It isn't worked out yet. They have to make some theological and liturgical decisions about Christmas. Obviously it's a big Perpetuan festival, but we need to decide how to commemorate her and celebrate the two. Re-aligning Good Friday when both Jesus and Perpetua died is, if anything, more tricky than remembering the births because they happened on different dates, but imagine changing the three-hour Liturgy of the Cross! There is this terrible fallacy which corrodes Western culture that if you add something it necessarily means subtracting something else, so if you give Perpetua's death a place on Good Friday you are diminishing the role of Jesus. Admittedly, in time allocation that is true, but there is a kind of richness that can be achieved with more elements—polyphony, counterpoint, the sonata, as opposed to the solo partita—but pride and partisanship in the matter of intellectual property, ideas, emotional investment, all play their part in this woeful zero sum game."

The Priest did not mention Perpetua—there was no reason why he should—and this made the Mass feel somewhat anachronistic but nostalgia went a long way at Christmas and Joe felt something lurch in his heart when he went up to kiss the effigy of the baby for the first time since his final year before Priestly Ordination; and it was so nice to sing *Adeste Fidelis* instead of *O Come, All Ye Faithful.*

◆   ◆   ◆

Trina walked over Silicon Ridge, past the familiar shops to the unfamiliar Parish Church. The choir were singing as the pews steadily filled, even on such a festive occasion, from the back.

She was greeted by a smartly dressed lady who said, "I've seen you before, haven't I. We see all kinds of people at Christmas."

"I've never been here at Christmas before."

"I know, I was taking a dress back that I didn't like. You were with that charismatic girl, weren't you, the one who died and did something funny to the television."

"Yes."

"You've no idea what an impact that has had. That Girl—Perpetua wasn't it? Could have been a model—talked to us about responsibility and setting up a scheme to listen to children reading at Slatethorpe Primary. I can't really talk now as there are other people coming, but our lady vicar is very much in favour."

The lady in question, Rev. Monica Broad (she somehow didn't like to be called "Mother" matching the male priest "Father"), was another of Perpetua's companions on the first visit to Slatethorpe. She had been ordained as a priest (she loathed the verb "priested") six months ago and was acting as Priest in Charge while her boss was recovering from surgery. She had asked her parishioners about the role of Perpetua in the Church and had met a surprising degree of enthusiasm from the ladies who usually confined themselves to the social and fund raising committee. They even had a few photographs of her standing outside the Eye of the Needle! Monica, who seemed to be somewhat ambivalent about Perpetua, had consulted her boss who said that nothing was cut-and-dried; although he didn't hold with people kissing a doll, for example, all kinds of things happened at Christmas which tangled up the superstitious and the secular with the sublime mystery of incarnation. As long as she was sure that anything she did would not upset the Bishop, she could proceed. Knowing that the Bishop, Reginald Crowther, had other matters on his plate and was about to move from the Diocese, she felt that she might do just about anything she wanted, but her radical plans were made even more radical when the sideswoman, during a slight lull, pointed out the Perpetuan follower to her colleague, who identified her as Trina from the coverage of Miles' martyrdom and therefore told Monica that the Perpetuan leader was among them.

Monica was deeply scarred by the controversy over the ordination, first of women priests, then of women bishops. She understood why a handful of traditionalist men were opposed, but she did not see how these should be considered equally with the thousands of women clergy, most of whom were being forced to serve as non-stipendiary. She was lucky, but that luck made her more, rather than less, radical because she fully realised what her sisters were missing. Her year as a Deacon had coincided with Perpetua's mission and out of a theological world of male authority figures this amazing woman burst onto the scene. She had—it was difficult to separate the emotional from the spiritual—totally out of character, fallen in love with Perpetua. She had persuaded her supervisors to allow her to study the current phenomenon as her special subject and so she had spent much of her study watching god4u and finding reports or transcripts of her speeches. During the lead-up to her final ordination she had had less time, but she was aware of the emerging Perpetuan heritage problem and she was determined to put herself at the disposal of the movement. She had planned to make an approach after Christmas, but now, here she was, standing in the pulpit in front of Trina.

"A blessed Christmas to you all! It is nice to see so many of you here in spite of the more relaxed pub opening hours. In fact I rather miss the traditional Midnight Mass drunks!

"Unusually for a sermon preached in front of a large congregation, I'm going to explain some theology. I don't know why it's usually reserved for the few. Perhaps if we preached richer sermons, more of you would come to church between Christmases!

"Incarnation was a much more mysterious word than it is now that so many of us go to Spain. It literally means flesh. God became flesh. I know, you've heard it all before, but the question we need to ask ourselves is how serious are we about this baby? I mean, if we just want to have an excuse to enjoy ourselves, buy presents, eat and drink too much, and go to a pantomime, why don't we just do it? Why do we go through the motions of pretending this is a religious festival?

"I know, I've offended you. I meant to. Being nice is never going to get us into the place where we need to be. We are here because we care about this baby's special place in our lives, this baby who was born in obscurity. This man who lived almost all of his life like the bloke next door, but then changed the course of world history in one or three years, depending on which Gospel you read.

"Now the main indicator of how serious we are about this baby is whether we care what happened to him when he grew up. You don't buy a biography of Churchill or David Beckham or Mother Theresa or Kylie Minogue and stop reading after the first chapter on childhood. So the big indicator for me is how many people turn up at our services on Good Friday, at the Easter Vigil, and at the Eucharist on Easter Sunday. No. not many.

"But here's the big news! It isn't our fault. We can all understand what a baby is, but we're totally alienated by the Crucifixion and Resurrection, not because we don't care, but because we don't really understand. Now the obvious answer to this is that we shouldn't need to understand, we must simply have faith. But faith has to have something to hang onto, something it can come to terms with. The Jesus life is just too far away from us in time, temperament, and custom for us to take a hold of it as our means of faith.

"But we, in our own lifetime, some people say, have seen another incarnation of God, god taking on flesh, in the person of Perpetua. She was, like Jesus, born in obscurity, but because of the media times we live in, her mission received world coverage whereas Jesus was only famous in his own tiny country. We saw her teach and perform mighty acts and we saw her die at our hands. Unlike the Apostles, who were terribly confused by the Resurrection of Jesus—a confusion which has come down to us today—Perpetua's appearances after her death have been vivid and, to some people, totally credible.

"So the reason that we celebrate this baby is that it tells us that God is with us and will never abandon us until we rejoin her. We know that because when most of us thought that the world had completely turned away from God, Perpetua came in what some people call 'the second incarnation' to restore our hope and to reinforce our failing understanding. Why God should do this is not the mystery some people say it is. I will talk about that on another occasion. In the meantime, I want us all to see this baby, not just for itself, but standing for the whole, brilliant, life affirming idea of God's incarnation.

"Now before I finish, I just want to say that Trina, the leader of the Perpetuan movement, is with us. She looks as if she doesn't want to speak to us at the moment, but I'm going to ask her to put on this white robe and celebrate with me at the altar."

As most people assumed that Trina was an ordained priest this caused no stir. People had not really worked out how Perpetua fitted in with Christianity, but they generally classed her as an inspiring and important figure. Trina was well known by the kind of serious people that made up the bulk of the congregation. Silicon Ridge was well educated and prosperous, if a little self-indulgent and self-regarding. It read its gossip studiously, pretending that it was in the public interest rather than simply of interest to the public.

Trina saw the sense and generosity of what was being offered and approached the altar as modestly as she could. At the end of the service, just before the blessing, Monica put the effigy of the Baby Jesus into Trina's arms to present it to worshippers and she pulled the draw string on the crib, nestled beneath the nave altar, to reveal Mary and Joseph on either side of Perpetua, with the shepherds in the background and the kings on the road outside. When the baby had been duly kissed, it was put into the manger. Monica gave a blessing:

"May you be blessed this Christmas by the all-loving God who gave us Jesus and Perpetua in the New Testament and the Third Testament for the Third Millennium; By Jesus and Perpetua who have shown us, through their incarnations, deaths and re-manifestations, the bridge between the Creator and humanity; and by Our Sister The Spirit. Amen."

Trina didn't want a lot of attention so she stayed in the vestry while Monica stood at the church door talking to parishioners. Trina needed to make a rapid assessment of Monica who would not doubt want to form a close relationship with her and the movement. Monica was clearly bright and brave, but a little impetuous. She had taken a large risk with her sermon. Perpetuans were not against risk and were open to bravery, courage, and adventure, but Trina found herself thinking like the leader of a movement instead of a follower of Perpetua and she checked herself. What she really meant, when she thought carefully, is that she didn't want a close relationship with Monica right now because she didn't want a close relationship with anybody. She wanted to be alone. She realised from Monica's sermon that the baby had made Perpetua's absence acute. Such a short and tragic incarnation in her own lifetime. She wanted no more cribs or carols.

Monica was helping to tidy up. Trina took one last look at the crib and saw it bathed in a beautiful golden light. She said nothing, but walked towards the door and greeted Monica.

"I was sorry to put you on the spot like that, but it was too good to miss."

"It's all right. I'm not a preacher, but I enjoyed standing with you at the altar."

"I presume you are here for Christmas. You are always welcome at my house. I'm alone at the moment."

"I am staying in a rented cottage and, quite frankly, for the next two days I want to be alone. Your sermon rightly talked about incarnational gain, but all I feel at the moment is incarnational loss."

"Perhaps next week. Many of the core congregation are very anxious to become involved."

Monica locked the side door. They shook hands, a little awkwardly, and went their separate ways. Trina missed Perpetua terribly. Monica had mixed feelings.

◆   ◆   ◆

It was Bill and Stacey's first Christmas together. Bill had decided, in the spirit of Perpetuanism, that they would celebrate Christmas at Saint Simple's in the usual way, with minor additions to the texts to acknowledge the Godhead of Perpetua. The house groups, the core of the movement, had worked hard and faithfully and deserved a good time. The morning Eucharist was packed, with many strangers. Bill asked as many of these, as they left, why they had chosen his church. "It's her shrine," most said in one way or another. "It's where she danced with Jesus and was taken up into heaven." Bill wondered what each meant by that kind of statement. How literally did they mean it? That was an un-Perpetuan question. Only God knew.

◆   ◆   ◆

Kylie had sat at the back of the church during Mark's Midnight Mass so as not to disturb his careful choreography and she would have done the same at the morning Eucharist (the strange clash of terms still persisted), but Helen noticed her as she came in and felt sorry for her because she looked so lonely. Here was a leader of the Perpetuan movement with no liturgical function on the birthday of Jesus. She caught Mark at the side door and pointed Kylie out to him. He could be prickly, but he could also be impetuously generous. On this occasion he hardly gave himself time to think, but said, "She should preside. She's the equivalent of my bishop." He rushed down the aisle to the back. "You must preside."

"I don't know how."

"I will sit in my stall just behind you. You will be fine."

After the traditional, Yorkshire *Christians Awake!* Mark said, "I want to welcome our new leader, Kylie, who is responsible for Perpetua's mission in our part of England." Everybody knew her, so there was no stirring. Mark went on, "but she isn't used to all the details of th way we celebrate God's presence with us, so don't worry if I occasionally act as the butler."

Kylie thought that this was sweet and it rather overcame his exaggeration of her role.

Lady Marianne Gowers thought she might write to the "legitimate bishop" and then decided it would be pointless.

◆ ◆ ◆

Max sat at the merrily littered table with Marta, little Perpetua, and Brian, head of god4u media. "I have become so used to being an administrator that I still find it difficult to think of myself in any other way," he said, filling a glass with red wine and neatly arranging four tiny biscuits on a patten-like plate. He blessed the elements in the name of the Parent, Jesus, and Perpetua and called upon the Sanctifier to make God truly present with them.

◆ ◆ ◆

Gregg watched himself watching himself. He always invoked this meta experience when he sensed danger. All through Christmas Day when Joe and Wayne were almost childishly happy he did just enough not to spoil the party. He chopped vegetables and helped set the table, ate a modest Christmas dinner, did the washing up and commented positively on their choice of a classic costume drama DVD. What he was watching was the turmoil within which needed to be kept under control. If he opted to stay with the orthodox Perpetuan movement, then there would be a right time to say something. If he decided to leave and strike out on his own, then they would know soon enough. In the meantime, it was best to keep his torment to himself.

The issue was not one of belief, but of tactics. Gregg profoundly believed that Perpetua was an incarnational phenomenon, but he thought that her ultra libertarian position had already been seriously compromised by weak-minded European socialism. She had stood for a new start to the human relations project, putting the individual at the centre of society, renouncing the victimhood and oppression that comes with bureaucratic dominance, but there was already a distinct whiff of corporatism in the air. What started out as family and peer solidarity so easily turned into collectivism. So his decision was whether to reform Perpetuanism from within or to establish a new pillar. The first course would be difficult because he had alienated himself from the core group and although he knew that they were ultra tolerant he sensed that Max in particular knew the difference between loving and trusting. If he struck out on his own he would be cut off from the cultural core of the movement. Although he was poor at showing his affection, he genuinely admired Trina and Stacey and the paradox was that although he was poor at human relations he was even worse at being alone and was dangerously vulnerable to violent mood swings when he felt lonely. Ultimately, his decision wasn't the outcome of this rational process, but an abhorrence which he could not overcome of Wayne and Joe's gay relationship. Perpetua had chosen gay followers, but there was no follower who had not sinned, and because she had been careful not to condemn, that did not mean that she condoned. As he lay awake on the sofa, he could not stand the thought of his two hosts sharing a bed. By the time they left it, he had left them.

When he received the news, Max was confirmed in his view that Gregg would mean trouble. Just as a self-conscious drunk takes extra care not to stumble, his very self-control betrayed his inner instability. He was, thought Max, a repressed obsessive who was walking an emotional tightrope between loving and hating Perpetuanism; or was it Perpetua herself? Was the inner contradiction caused by a white supremacist falling in love with a black woman? In other words, was his own personal emotional turmoil at the root of his strange affair. During his period of his social isolation, Max had come into contact for the first time with domestic violence. He could not understand the oscillation between love and hate in some of his male neighbours but, seen close up in Gregg, he began to understand. Lovers were frustrated and turned violent because they thought they were giving love to the beloved when what they were actually doing was trying to exercise power; their version of love was obedience. What Gregg wanted was to take the highly attractive ideas of Perpetua and impose himself upon them. The danger was not any views which Gregg might promote but that he would force Perpetuanism into excessively sharp positions. In European culture controversy produced dichotomy, so the danger was that if Gregg said one thing, opponents would be tempted to adopt precisely the opposite position. There was, in turn, the danger that the debate would be conducted by proxies. Trina would be measured, but not all of her followers would be. Fidel might well fall back into his former, somewhat abrasive, mode. Living Perpetuanism at the beginning of the twenty-first century would be as difficult as living Christianity in the middle of the first.

◆   ◆   ◆

Bishop Reginald Crowther was in every way a self-made man; there was no aspect of him that he had not created. He was reared in a cocoon of privilege, affected working class manners, demotic speech with a penchant for flat vowels, wore jeans, and had adopted a sharp edge of Evangelical rhetoric. The only person who did not see through the artifice was Reginald himself. His peers knew where he had been educated, noticed when he forgot to flatten his vowels, could easily ascertain the price of his designer jeans, and regretted the theological muddle in which he operated. Everybody except Reginald knew that the Church had been his fall-back career after an early catastrophic failure, against the trend, to hold a safe Conservative seat in the 1970 General Election, and everybody, not least Schuhorn, the Prime Minister's Appointments Secretary, remembered that he was a Conservative. There was only one factor which had frustrated his ambition to be translated to Canterbury, but it was significant because the Prime Minister held to the "One of us" philosophy as tenaciously as its founder. There were practical reasons. Crowther's cosmetics had led to the belief that he was not to be trusted and implementing the fragile buildings settlement which Varnish had reached with the Petrans would require extraordinary trust. His theological equivocation had made it impossible to weigh him in the balance as either catholic or evangelical, so on both counts he was found wanting. Above all, he was seen as the epitome of the triumph of style over substance. As far as anybody knew who mattered, he knew nothing about anything that mattered. He had been so busy ingratiating himself that he never had time to develop and deepen an idea or a useful relationship and, only listening for correspondences which would further his purposes, what he heard never broadened his mind.

On the Thursday after Christmas, Schuhorn telephoned Bishop Hall of Alchester. "James, I am sorry to telephone you on the day after Boxing Day when you are no doubt taking a well earned rest after your Advent and Christmas exertions ..."

"... That is all right, Theo, I suppose you have to take soundings as quickly as possible."

"Yes, James, I think I can say that I have been unusually expeditious, as was the Committee which graciously agreed to meet between Gaudete and Advent 4."

"Well then, Theo, I do not see how I can help."

"Just like you, James, to be so modest, but I have been asked by the Prime Minister, on behalf of Her Majesty ..."

"... Don't say it, Theo, pray don't."

"I fear I must, James, I fear I must. Or, rather, I feel I must. The Prime Minister, I say, on behalf of Her Majesty, has asked me to inform you that you are to be offered translation to Canterbury."

"Oh dear, Theo! Oh dear! This does put me in an awkward situation. I cannot but think that I am unworthy and it would be wrong to say that I feel 'called'. I am touched by the confidence placed in me and am deeply aware of my duty to the Church."

"I understand, James, but I must press the latter consideration. I know that the culture—er, theology—of the Church requires a degree of reticence—er, humility—and that the preference—requirement—is in favour of deliberation—discernment—so that the Holy Spirit can be consulted, there is no reason to believe that the said Spirit is necessarily in favour of delay. While I respect the reticence it can be taken too far, James. Hawthorne was always, if I may use a slightly odd phrase, standing on his reticence."

"Without wishing to be pompous, Theo, I do think I am entitled to some explanation. I do not want you to sing my praises and I certainly do not want you to comment on other candidates, but my heart cries out, 'Why me? What could you possibly want me for?' Let's face it, Theo, you would be better off with the Dean."

"How long have we known each other, James? Forty years?—Remember the time we got stuck at Grantchester—I think I am entitled to say that I know your strengths as, as a matter of fact, I know the Dean's. You know better than anyone else how he has burned his Anglican bridges and gone over completely to Perpetuanism—and that is fair enough, it's a free country, thanks more to officials than politicians—and we were quite properly obliged to choose a theologically sound Anglican. We know that you have been somewhat equivocal—strongly against Perpetua and then mildly in favour—but we are assured that you are quite properly in a state of open enquiry which is where Hawthorne wanted the Church to be."

"But if Hawthorne could not get the Church to be open-minded, I do not have a hope."

"But the Church has changed so much since Perpetua's death, James. We believe that you are the only senior Bishop sensitive enough to implement the buildings deal which Varnish concluded with the Perpetuans. I know that your natural strengths are in pastoral care and its associated theology, but this Church cannot move on until the buildings issue has been resolved."

"I take your point, Theo, but why did Varnish have to go? Why could he not stay to implement his own buildings settlement? He is, after all, the buildings man par excellence."

"I would have thought that was obvious, James. A Primate needs faith and hope, not to mention charity, to underpin what can often be tedious and sometimes harrowing, administrative duties. Varnish would not mind my saying that his heart was not in it and you, James, are a a modest man with a big heart. So, James, in conclusion I repeat my offer. The Prime Minister would like you to know that he does not respect the convention by which two names are forwarded with his marked preference for one being indicated. There is only one name in the frame."

"I certainly do not wish to be ungracious, Theo, but I do say that I accept the Prime Minister's kind offer with the greatest reluctance."

"That is well understood. Now I am sorry to worry you immediately with an urgent matter."

"Well, Theo, if I am to take on this role I had better be sanguine."

"Thank you, James. I do not think that I am betraying any confidences not proper to the Archbishop of Canterbury when I say that one of the disappointed was Bishop Reginald Crowther of South Yorkshire who, I believe, had high hopes of translation. He was not found suitable and, indeed, there were some of the Committee who thought—who think—that he is not suitable to be a bishop at all. He was, as you know, appointed when—how should I put this?—there was an unfortunately small field of Conservative episcopal candidates and it was thought that maintaining the balance was even more important than applying the strictest possible selection criteria."

"Yes, Theo, I get your drift."

"Sorry James, but in sharing confidences one cannot be too careful."

"I fear one can, Theo. If you are to share a confidence that sharing should be complete, which involves directness of speech. An elyptical style will not make the confidence any more or less safe."

"I am properly rebuked, James. Well, as I say, the Committee think a grave error was made in appointing Crowther to South Yorkshire. He should be kept as far as possible away from matters pastoral and theological. On the other hand, contrary to appearances and his own self-image, he combines a deep interest in liturgy with considerable administrative capability. We therefore wondered how you would feel about appointing him Dean of London Minster."

"Very apt Theo, very apt. I have been told that it needs a firm hand in the office and a tidying hand in the chancel."

"Very good, James. May I proceed?"

"As long as that is in order from your point of view."

◆　　◆　　◆

"Reggie."

He could hardly speak.

"Theo."

"I am calling, as you have probably guessed, in respect of an ecclesiastical appointment."

"Yes."

"I am authorised, on behalf of the Archbishop of Canterbury designate ..."

Finished! It was like the dreadful night of the count at Silicon Ridge when a maverick Liberal stole enough votes off him to let Labour in.

"The who?"

"Archbishop of Canterbury designate—is the line bad, or something?"

Then Schuhorn realised for the first time that Crowther actually, no matter how unrealistically, thought he was going to be translated. He had gone in too directly, but he thought that the nice phrasing of the sentence would allow Crowther to know that something good was coming.

"No, I can hear you." He was recovering his poise. He was a shrewd man in spite of his self-obsession and he knew that Schuhorn had not called him simply to break bad news. His sentence had an ending which needed to be heard.

"As I said, I am delighted to inform you on behalf of the Archbishop Designate that he is pleased to recommend you to be appointed Dean of London Minster."

Crowther was almost overwhelmed with relief. Whereas his insatiable ambition had driven him to want Canterbury all his other weaknesses favoured the relative anonymity of London over the perpetual prying of the Diocese, let alone the exposure as Primate. In South Yorkshire he had worked so hard to please without obviously giving pleasure and he had deprived himself of many pleasures in order to please. Canterbury would bring much more of the same but London Minster would bring influence and power and a pleasing liturgical aesthetic. It would also bring sparkling champagne, glittering society, daring women, and risk. He was a prince bishop, more a prince than a bishop, and if becoming a Dean enabled him to live more like a prince, he would gladly change his situation.

"How kind of the new Archbishop. Of course I will be terribly sad to leave my wonderful South Yorkshire flock."

""Tosh!" thought Schuhorn. "Very commendable, Reggie, but needs must."

"And I will miss the lovely variety of parish churches and my few days of country pleasures."

"Naturally, Reggie, but surely London will have its compensations."

"Ah, Theo! Its temptations, more like. After my modest state in the country I will find London a much more trying environment."

"Never mind, Reggie there will no doubt be consolations."

Schuhorn let Reggie go on. He, and only he, was party to the whole of Crowther's file. Not even the Nominations Committee had been allowed to see that part of it which related to Crowther's pleasures. He had had a very narrow squeak indeed over the matter of a Lady Mayor and representations had been made that a move was in order, but because moving him to another diocese would be as unethical as moving paedophile priests to new parishes without warning the parishioners, a creative solution was required which had been furnished by Clement Sutcliffe, recently appointed to the Archbishop's staff, and supported by the gloomily inscrutable Crozier, Chair of the Archbishops Council. The Dean of London Minster was offered a low level diocesan appointment rather than the suffragan appointment he could have expected and so there was room for Crowther.

"Reggie," said Theo, adopting an altogether more serious tone, "never forget that I know more than anyone else knows, so spare my time. I am bound to warn you, on nobody's behalf but mine, seeing that I am the only person who is in posession of the whole of your file, that you would be exceedingly unwise to grow careless in the apparent anonymity of London. It is a big place, but its social circles are surprisingly small and tight. We would not want a second municipal-type incident." Crowther bit his tongue.

◆   ◆   ◆

Clement Sutcliffe found himself in the oddest of positions. He had applied to be a member of the Archbishop's staff shortly before Easter, but in the turmoil which followed the death of Perpetua and the consequent resignation of Hawthorne, recruitment had been put on hold. In the latter days of Varnish interviews had taken place by which time Clement was a confirmed Perpetuan, but such an ass was the employment law from whose tentacles the Church was trying to disengage itself, over the gay issue, that the external interviewer from the Public Appointments Panel insisted that not being an Anglican was no reason for barring a person from appointment and that even being from an allegedly hostile denomination or faith was no reason for barring a person from appointment. Sutcliffe was well qualified in strategic thinking and media handling which were the essential points of the job specification. He even fulfilled the desirable requirements of holding a theology qualification and having been a minister, if only lay, of the Church. He had accepted his appointment conditionally upon its being approved by the in-coming Archbishop who turned out to be his old adversary, James Hall, who was gracious and said he would trust Clement if Clement would trust him. He had disagreed with Clement in many things, he said, but had always held him to be sincere to the point of fearlessness. He could now be as fearless in private as he had been in public. Even though he was a Perpetuan, Hall knew that he would not be partisan. He was sure that Clement knew his duty.

His first duty was to operate a coherent office through the interregnum. Once he had taken the decision to resign, Varnish had been anxious to leave as soon as he decently could. He, Max Silver, Sir Felix Crimp-Walker of the Church commissioners, and Sir Justin Peal who acted for them in the House, soon reached agreement. They had read the evil omens in the fall of Southern Gem and property prices were falling in every sector and region. Varnish had departed leaving an empty desk and cabinets stuffed with unfinished business. In the five days before the new year Clement appointed Janet Burns, recently fired by *Bad Morning* for not being aggressive enough, as the new, anachronistically titled,

Press Officer, drafted terms of reference for an enquiry into the implications of Perpetuanism for Anglicanism, regularised the retirement papers of the bishops who had left with Hawthorne, regularised the papers for the new appointments, proposed a ranking of salient, unresolved issues and, most difficult of all, in spite of his conversion to Perpetuanism, marshalled the arguments against the ordination of women bishops, substantially improving on the notes sent up from the Legislative Committee but, never mind, he would do even better when the notes came from the proponents.

◆　◆　◆

Trina and Monica met on New Year's Eve for dinner in Monica's little house next to a former church which was now an exotic carpets warehouse. Monica was dressed in a Rajastan skirt with mirror work and a far too flimsy, skimpy satin scarlet top. Like her, the house was a lively jumble of bright, clashing colours. "I have passed the point," she said, "when I can tell whether I am an optimist or whether all this brightness is concealing a deep depression. I think I am an optimist in spite of the years of struggle, but it's impossible to say. I mean, do I dye my hair red to be bright or to hide the grey?"

While Monica opened a bottle of New Zealand sauvignon blanc, Trina looked at her shelves. You could always tell most about people from their shelves. There were no ornaments and only a gathering together on a glass shelf of pebbles, shells, driftwood, and pieces of non-commercial coral. Next to them a clutch of Celtic worship books. The theology section was sharp-elbowed and smaller than the religion and feminism section, which in turn was smaller than the section on "left wing" politics. The books were arranged in sections rather than alphabetically. There was a lot of Joni Mitchell, a substantial representation of Bob dylan, pre- and post-throat, and a complete set of Leonard Cohen. She wasn't an optimist after all. The Celtic books seemed to be an attempt to escape from an otherwise troubled world. Everything else—the books, pictures, rugs, music, decor—had an edgy, restless, snatching quality. There was no symmetry, there was no traditional poetry, no classical literature, no Renaissance pictures, and, from Trina's perspective, most significantly, no systematic theology.

"Oh those," said Monica as she came in. "I suppose we all liked Joni Mitchell, Bob Dylan, and Leonard Cohen—there is something strangely bleak about Canadian pessimism—when we were students, particularly when we lost a girl friend or a boy friend. I seem to have spent my life losing them. There was always something more important—study, protest, campaigning, priesthood. The campaigning was the best. There was real electricity. There was never enough time for other people and they just faded out."

Trina wondered if they had ever really faded in.

"I suppose I should say that the most important thing in my life has been the priesthood, but I have to admit that the protest has always been the most important thing. I mean, being a priest was itself a kind of protest."

Trina waited. It was only a matter of time. This lonely, somewhat self-obsessed woman, needed to justify herself and, given a bit of time, might ask for comfort.

"And now it's so busy: church, fund raising, visits, youth club. I haven't got time for personal relationships. I don't even have time to say my prayers most days. There is just too much to do."

She went into the kitchen to finalise the preparations for the meal. Trina wasn't a Freudian nor a psychologist, but she knew at an organisational level that Monica's temperament was at the opposite end of the spectrum from Perpetuanism and, at a personal level, she knew that Monica was a suppressed lesbian. She passed over this second conclusion, knowing that Monica would have to find her own way to self-knowledge, but she needed to work out the first conclusion.

What was it, wondered Trina, in this obviously passionate and compassionate woman that was so at odds with Perpetua who was both passionate and compassionate. The presenting cause was that Monica suffered from a severe case of victimhood, more inclined to complain than control. For her, society, not herself, was responsible for society, so the way that she chose to change society was to change other people. Behind the victimhood was the lack of self-knowledge. She was not sure of herself and not sure in herself, so she could not take responsibility for herself. Perpetuanism began with choice and responsibility as the chief creaturely attributes. Without these you could not be fully human. This was not the same as American fundamentalism where the purpose of choice was self-affirmation. The ultimate point of choice for Perpetuans was exercising the choice to love. Monica's love would be active, interventionist, directional, whereas Perpetuan love was ultra permissive, simply creating space for the beloved. So did this mean that Perpetuanism could not accommodate people like Monica? It could because by making room it helped people grow in self-assurance. Paradoxically, Monica would not need to intervene and control if there was greatly increased scope for it. Like water issuing out of a pipe, the narrower the outlet, the more directional and forceful the jet. A few novels would be a good start! Then a few, low key, non-competitive, ambling relationships.

Monica came in with a vegetarian risotto and a green salad. Trina, whose reflections had been somewhat rarified, suddenly realised that one of Monica's chief disadvantages was that she did not know how to enjoy herself because she did not know how to enjoy self. This really was human psychology 101. She decided that making room, Perpetuan style, was the best way forward.

"This is lovely," said Monica.

Trina wondered whether Monica should have said that.

"I like simple food. I think that Western society eats and drinks too much."

"That was Perpetua's starting point, encouraging people to reduce their consumption and that is one of our main campaigns now, being led by Hypo's boss

Sir Pluto Millman. It's not all that easy because the money you save from reduced consumption has to be directed back to the people who suffer from the
reduction. Diet for the body's sake isn't good enough, and diet for the planet's
sake isn't even good enough. It's like Christians in Lent giving up chocolate for
the sake of their figure. We don't write these off, but the chief purpose of reducing consumption is to improve the life chances of others."

"Yes, it's about time the main political parties took the green agenda seriously."

"Which one are you in?"

"I wouldn't join one! They're all the same and they're all corrupt."

"I'm reluctant to get into controversy during my first visit to your house, but
as this is more your territory than mine, I feel that I can venture, but say if I go
too far. I can't speak to the charge of corruption as the word is used to mean
anything from the careless and trivial to the gross misuse of power and wealth,
but even if our political parties are all rather in the centre, wherever you stand
it matters which way you face. Any institution abandoned by principled people
will suffer damage. You can't expect other people to effect change simply at your
prompting, can you?"

"I've been on plenty of demos to protest against our corrupt system."

"But we are all necessarily part of our system, Monica. It isn't somebody else's
system, it's ours."

Monica looked shocked. "But I don't want to have anything to do with it."

"But you have no choice; you are it."

They sat in silence for more than a minute before Trina picked up the topic
tentatively. "It seems to me that the major problem with life is knowing what you
want. If you know what you want then getting it is the much easier part. Most
people only seem to know what they don't want, what they're against. Look at
those on the 'left' who characterise themselves as idealists. They have no time
for any Labour government because it is too right wing. It has sold out. It is full
of traitors. Yet what they are really saying is that they would prefer a Conservative government which they could then dislike even more. That, surely, is self-
indulgent because it takes no account of how different governments affect people, particularly poor people. Now take people on the 'right' who characterise
themselves as idealists and think that Conservative governments slide towards
the centre. Do these people support a free market in agriculture and banking?
Do they support a free market in property development? Certainly not. They
want agricultural subsidies—although they attack the EU—bank bail-outs and
no new houses near their own properties. Again, they are focused on themselves. Perhaps the best way to describe our politics is that the 'left' are intellectually self-indulgent and the 'right' are materially self-indulgent."

Monica was growing restless. "I'll stop in a moment, but this is New Year's
Eve so we should make a couple of simple, feasible resolutions."

Monica, keen to be ahead in the game, said, "Brown out and a new green
policy for the Council."

"All right, but what about resolutions for you."

Monica looked puzzled. "But they are mine."

Trina wondered whether to let the subject drop but felt that she was too far in to turn around. "But, Monica, only a rebellion by Labour MPs can bring Brown down, and only a majority of Councillors can bring in a greener policy. What we need to focus on is what you can do yourself."

Before Trina saw it coming, something gave way in Monica. "It's obvious, isn't it. I can't do anything. That isn't self-pity. I am paralysed by self-doubt. I know what other people should do, but I don't know anything about me. I seem to have spent all my life reacting."

"We mostly do, Monica, but let's see if we can find you a tiny foothold, a starting point. Have you tried to start a Perpetuan-style house group?"

"No. We do have three house groups, but I don't go to them. One is very tedious, taking the Bible verse by verse and reading a commentary, one is full of holy people who sit silently for an hour, and the third is a bit intellectual."

"It sounds to me like most of the people in them are mixing with their own kind. One of the best ways to understand yourself is to be with people who aren't like you. Most of the people on a demo think the same way, and most of the people in self-selecting groups think the same way. Other kinds of people give us sharper profile and enrich us with their difference. The idea of the Perpetuan house group is that it's like a form of 'bussing'. People from different backgrounds—even classes—work together so you are not campaigning for better conditions for the poor, but are with them."

"But that exposes another problem, Trina. I am an ardent campaigner for the poor but, if I'm honest, I don't like being with them. In fact I don't much like being with anybody, I'm frightened and lonely."

Every time she tried to get them out of the miserable impasse they seemed to get back into it. Trina wondered how such an extended ordination discernment process did not detect and try to deal with problems like this.

Monica said, "I love you."

Trina said, "I'm the wrong person but you've made some kind of breakthrough in recognising the kind of people you might love, but you will have to work that out."

Monica began to cry. "I loved her and now I love you."

Trina said, "There's no easy way to make a breakthrough but once you have, it gets easier." And, like the good Perpetuan she was, she sat silently, giving space.

The church clock struck midnight.

"The year that you find yourself and find what you want," said Trina. She put a pebble into Monica's hand, kissed her on the forehead, put her calling card on the table and left, quietly closing the door.

Monica did not move for another eight minutes. She forced herself to sit still, holding the pebble. She didn't really love Trina in the way she had said. She loved her because of Perpetua and because she saw in her, for the first time, the possibility of beginning to love herself. She was grateful for the calling card, but resolved not to use it until she was able to call not wanting something, but offering. She would use the day's holiday to weed out her books and music and make a new start.

◆　◆　◆

As the sun began to rise, Gregg, watched by Adam, one of Sir Pluto's minions, watched two men making black pudding in half of an oil drum in a narrow street at the centre of Castries. Although no special measures were required as he had no criminal record, he still called in a couple of favours to ensure that his movements would not be recorded. He had a diplomatic pass which got him out of Heathrow, through Bridgetown to Vigie without any questions. Now, dressed on the verge of scruffiness, nobody would take him for anything other than a redneck tourist.

The question was, how and when should he begin? He had to start somewhere, soon. He had chosen the Caribbean because he hoped to dominate small islands relatively quickly, giving him a base for wider operations with an ultimate US destination. Most of them only had one or two little radio stations glad to give air space to guests when there was so little going on. There was plenty of conventional and a smattering of unconventional Christianity, but he suspected it did not go deep, being British rather than American-born.

He walked down to the town beach knowing what he would experience, but unable to resist. The all but naked girls fired him with rape and revulsion. He had hardly removed his trainers to walk on the sand when he was hurrying away, trainers in hand. He went back to his cramped, scruffy guest house and threw himself on the bed. He needed to make a public statement, to launch his project, but he was frightened. He dozed off and saw Perpetua's face, uncharacteristically out of focus, as

She said, "You have to make a start. The energy of my mission is leeching away…"

◆　◆　◆

GREGG TO THE WORLD—BLOG ONE

Fellow Perpetuans,

1. I have been appointed by Perpetua to bring her good news to the world. I am doing so on her direct authority. I need no permission from her other followers. I am who I am by virtue of her making herself known to me.
2. Some of you may have heard that I worked for a short time with her fol-

lowers, but that I left them. I did so because they seemed to be losing the essence of her message of individual responsibility. I had scarcely left them when Perpetua appeared to me and called me to follow her. As a sign of my calling she temporarily blinded me and my sight was restored by Father Joe who is not an official Perpetuan follower.

3. Perpetua wants you to know that almost before her mission has begun it is already being subverted. What she advocated was personal responsibility for choice and the rejection of victimhood. She wanted people to make their own choices, no matter how slight, and she said that everybody could make decisions, no matter how slight. She believed and taught that the best form of social advancement is the house group entered into voluntarily for mutual support, but this does not mean social engineering. What she was trying to break away from was the hierarchical power plays of the Christian establishment, and her London followers are already falling back into that trap.

4. You have heard it said that man was born free. Everywhere you look people are trying to curtail that freedom.

Firstly there is the whole governmental system, starting with the United Nations, continental economic blocs, and national governments loading us down with resolutions, laws, regulations, and directives.

Secondly, there are hordes of regulators, busy-bodies and do-gooders with their codes of practice, tying us all up in a whole mesh of restrictions under the benevolent titles of:

» Best practice, which is simply a lazy way of following everybody else.
» Bench marking, which only requires you to be as good as everybody else.
» Diversity, which spares all judgment in making decisions about people.
» Equality, which means box ticking.
» Audit, which means going through ever more complex processes to dilute responsibility.
» Risk management, which means writing everything down but not differentiating and then taking action.
» Health and safety, which means finding excuses to be static.
» Political correctness, which means pretending that people are what they are not.

You can see from this list that the whole regulatory framework stifles the kind of freedom of choice for which Perpetua stood.

Thirdly, there is the whole nexus of social custom and unwritten rules about behaviour. These, too, exist to keep everybody in line, making the lowest common denominator ever lower.

Fourthly, there are innumerable social organisations which give themselves power or which are given power to control us. Schools tell children how they can and cannot wear their hair. If the emerging fashion is for long hair, that is forbidden, and if the emerging fashion is for short hair, that is forbidden. What is always forbidden is what people want. If you want to join a club to take part in perfectly innocent and, you thought, non-controversial activities, like playing golf, there is a fat club rule book.

When you put all of these forces of conformity together, you can see how difficult it is to realise the Perpetuan dream of freedom.

5. Yet we cannot live in a state of complete freedom because, as Perpetua always reminded us, we are, as part of our human condition, necessarily flawed. We must, therefore, submit ourselves, not to a whole host of secular authorities, but to the authority of the Godhead. One of the extreme paradoxes in our society is that it is so repressively governed and yet license is rampant. Girls flaunt their naked flesh on public beaches, salesmen bellow down mobile phones in public places, teenagers go on drunken binges... every kind of sexual practice is tolerated as legitimate self-expression. The planet is being suffocated in junk. Obesity is widespread, language is coarsening, and foul language is commonplace. It is as if, having given up on the important things, we wish to regulate a plethora of trivialities.

6. Although her ideas differed from those of contemporary Christians, there is no doubt that Perpetua intended to leave behind a core of authority. As she was so committed to freedom, she would not stipulate a rigid system. She would not have wanted the kind of tight governance network that the Perpetuan movement is in danger of establishing. What we need is dispersed authority so that we can adapt to different conditions. What is suitable for one place might not be suitable for another, just as different climates require different clothes, even though they should be equally modest in all places. There is no doubt that all sensible people can easily identify general rules which can subsequently be locally applied, but that application must be set out in terms of what is acceptable to the Godhead. I have been sent to establish such local arrangements to ensure that the writ of the Godhead runs wherever Perpetua's name is honoured.

7. Now all this will be denied by the metropolitan Perpetuan elite which is trying to take hold of the whole Perpetuan movement when it was designed to be a loose federation and so I am not bound by it. I am as much a Perpetuan leader as any of them can claim to be and so I speak in her name. When I claim that she appeared to me in a vision, let them deny it! When I say that they are methodically destroying the evidence of her teaching, let them deny it! When I say that I am Perpetua's future, they will deny it! But do not be misled.

8. The apparent conflict between the exercise of authority and the exercise of the will is not difficult to resolve. Authority maintains the framework within which the will can be exercised. Take, for example, the damning accusation levelled at Perpetua that she condoned, or even encouraged, homosexuality. She certainly did not. She admitted that she had homo-

sexuals amongst her followers, but Jesus had Judas and the denying Peter who went on to be his successor. By admitting that we are all sinners and by entrusting certain functions to sinners we do not condone the sin. At no point did Perpetua support or encourage homosexuality, she simply admitted that her human followers could not be perfect, just as I am not perfect.

9. And so I speak with the full authority of Perpetua in saying that the liberal elite of her followers in London should not be allowed to mislead themselves and you into thinking that Perpetuanism has changed the moral code of Jews and Christians. It has not. What Perpetuanism has done is to inject a massive dose of freedom and the exercise of God-fearing liberty into Christians gone limp, prepared to go along with a lazy, liberal consensus.

10. I therefore call upon Trina and all the high ranking Perpetuans to come clean and admit that they have gone too far. I call on them to return to the Perpetuan spring which is the fountain of liberty and individual conscience within God-given limits. I call upon you all to exercise your God-given liberty against all kinds of oppression, taxation and imposition.

◆   ◆   ◆

Like something you always knew would happen, but hoped it never would, Gregg's message came as no surprise to Trina and Max. They decided to call a meeting of the whole core leadership: Wayne came from the North with Joe as an adviser. Kylie arrived from the South, and Stacey made the short trip from South London with her new husband Bill as adviser and Cara, also from South London, the newest member. Brian popped across from the god4u Network. Q and Smoother, their media advisers, stood by. It was terrible that so many of the original group were no longer there. Heather and Jo had apparently died at their own hands after betraying Perpetua. Andy and Bob had departed, disillusioned. Dexter had been killed, along with Miles and the journalist Will Dignot. Jim had died in strange and tragic circumstances.

Opening the meeting, Trina said, "We meet in strange and sad times. The repercussions of the Southern Gem crisis seem not to be abating and people are becoming more pessimistic. The Christian Churches seem to be turning defensive instead of gaining new vigour from our movement, and now we have been attacked by Gregg, briefly an employee here, who seems to have a love/hate obsession with Perpetua. In affirming what it means to be Perpetuan we should be able to work out how to respond, if at all to Gregg."

"I know what the pure position is," said Max. "I say 'pure' as opposed to 'purist' because I'm not being pejorative. The pure position is that we should not respond to Gregg at all that, as Perpetuans, we say what we say and he says what he says, but that we do not get into a confrontational position. Although I see the merits of the pure position I recognise that people who, accidentally or deliberately, subvert the truth, put those who stand for the truth into the awkward position that they either remain pure and say nothing, risking the survival of their cause, or respond, entering the fray and equally risking the survival of their cause. It is part of the human condition that, as corporate people, regardless of our individual virtue, we have to live in a corporate world and corporate imperfections necessarily wreck corporate purity. I conclude nothing, I simply put the case."

"As the person responsible for education," said Wayne, "I would naturally want to believe that what we need to do to combat Gregg is to educate people, but that would miss the point altogether. One of our problems as a culture is that we have become dutiful Christians lacking in faith and love, just plodding on with it like Balaam, you know, with the donkey. Philosophy helps with faith, but an extensive exchange of letters isn't going to get us there. We must try to put our point across but not respond directly to Gregg, avoiding a show-down and all the dangers of dichotomy."

"I agree with that," said Brian. "You learn in media that you have to be in control of your own story and that if you are not, it will only be a matter of time before somebody else controls it. I don't think, at a pragmatic level, that defending your position in terms set by somebody else, is effective. People turn off if the argument turns to definitions. To counter Gregg you would have to get into arguments about the meanings of words. We should just go on telling our story."

"Yes," chimed in Cara, "and we need to be careful that the story is practical instead of being theoretical. People want to know how Perpetua can change their lives and they don't want some long statement with difficult words."

"True," said Stacey. "Looking back on it now, I think that when I was a missionary I just said lots of words and handed out things to poor people. I didn't feel Jesus so I don't see how they could."

"Kylie agreed with the position. Bill was content to say nothing. Q and Smoother agreed with the line.

Joe looked twitchy. It was difficult for him to contain his pugnacity.

"It's a sad thought," said Trina, "but it seems to me that the issue is how pure can we stay for how long. Sooner or later, whether it is pressure from Gregg or somebody or something else, we will have to descend to a less pure position. Over time we will repeat the climbing down, ever lower. That's why Perpetua came, to lift us back up, but we are like those with inordinately high white cell counts, the chemo knocks the count down and then over time it rises. The only wonder is that the Godhead waited so long to succeed Jesus with Perpetua. I don't believe it will be 2000 years before the next incarnation.

"So, for now, nothing. Get on with the work of spreading the good news. Pray that the Spirit will be with us and that we will not have to start the climbing down too soon."

◆   ◆   ◆

Gregg's letter did not make the headlines on the major information channels but it was viral on the secondary, specialist, sites so that by the time that he entered the square in Castries, the waiting crowd knew what he had said.

"Brothers and sisters, you have all heard how Jesus came to earth and was crucified and died for us and was raised from the dead. You have all been witnesses of the good news which the sacrifice of Jesus brought about, and you have been made aware, too, of how Perpetua was also sent from God in the selfsame manner to perform the selfsame offices for us all. In spite of the power of the Spirit humanity fell away from Jesus so that Perpetua came to bring us all back to God, and you know how the strength of Jesus within us, the power of the Spirit, has been weakened by luxury and ease, by the corrosive dictatorship of the civil state. Knowing all these things, I call upon you now, to denounce luxury and to turn back to God, renewed in the Spirit, in the persons of Jesus and Perpetua."

There was scant direct experience of ease and luxury among the crowd who largely dispensed these desirable items to tourists in exchange for scanty wages, but they got the drift.

"And so, brothers and sisters, Perpetua has appointed me as a special act of her grace and favour, to be her representative in these parts."

The audience had no clue about the Perpetuan succession and they quite liked the lively worship and gentle social life of their churches, but they needed some excitement and, as accepting Perpetua—one of their own—did not mean rejecting Jesus, they could afford just a little enthusiasm. They recognised the American preacher type from their newly acquired cable televisions, but this man had a different message. He wasn't ranting about the kind of sins they particularly favoured—a little over indulgence in alcohol and intimate relations—and, what is more, he was not asking for money, but they were not sure what to do until a couple of the younger women attracted by one of their sisters being so prominent, hit on the idea of a chant: "Perpetua is our sister!"

They chanted, drawing more of the crowd into the chant. A desperate mother thrust her tiny, mortally ill baby into Gregg's arms, but he was so awkward and frightened that he almost threw it back at her. She was about to remonstrate when the baby nuzzled her breast for the first time since its first week of life. The woman shouted, "Miracle! He's cured my baby!"

Gregg, who was looking straight into the sunset was momentarily blinded so that he could not move. He thought he heard Perpetua. The wavering golden glow made him unsteady and he fell to the ground.

Sir Pluto walked steadily against the rapidly retreating crowd until he reached Gregg who was being attended by an off-duty nurse and a trainee paramedic, assisted by Adam.

"He needs somebody to look after him," said the nurse to Sir Pluto. "It's some kind of nervous exhaustion."

"I will look after him. Can we get a taxi down to the marina? Or better still, can either of you help. Taxi drivers talk too much."

"I have a beaten-up old car," replied the paramedic. So they went down to the Marina and when they arrived Pluto tipped the paramedic handsomely and made sure that he was well on his way before he signalled to Annie ensuring that he did not see which boat Gregg was taken to. In the ways of men of influence like Sir Pluto, the boat slipped out of the Marina and Saint Lucian territorial waters as easily as it had slipped in. His extensive economic interests, particularly in the revival of the Windward Islands banana trade, guaranteed him a warm, but still profoundly respectful, reception. By the time Gregg came round, they were well on their way to Barbados.

Gregg came to suddenly, but instead of making an impulsive movement or saying something he might regret, his old habits kicked in automatically and he took in his surroundings. The size of the almost certainly single, windowless cabin meant that it was probably a 40-footer that would need two competent crew. He put his feet gently on the rug and felt for the light switch. He walked carefully to the door. Locked. He did not panic or pound his fists on the door. He went back and sat on the bed. He had been preaching, he had apparently performed a miracle, and he had swooned. He was on a luxury yacht with some rather fine, as far as he could tell, pictures in the cabin, but no evidence of the personal. The drawers and cupboards were empty, except for the standard hair dryer, note paper, and small bowl of mints. He could not dismantle the lock with the special tool in the inner zip pocket of his denim jacket because his outer clothes had ben removed. There was no point being hostile until he knew a bit more. He couldn't sail a boat without the collaboration of the crew.

He heard feet coming down the ladder and he put himself as far out of the entrant's eye line as he could, keeping behind the door as it opened.

"Well done, Gregg. I would have expected nothing less. It's hard to kick the habit, isn't it, in a strange environment, even on a friendly boat like this. Just Edge round the door, please, if you would. I'm not carrying any weapons, but I do know how to take precautions. Yes, we have met, although you might not remember."

"I never forget."

"I thought not, it's the training."

"Why do you keep going on about the training? What do you know about it?"

"Oh Gregg, Chilean Tile, Vietnam Mechanical, The Colombian Emerald Corporation, Baltic Mills, those sort of things. Need I go on?"

"Yes, I remember your face now, but we didn't say anything. So who are you?"

"Just call me Pluto. Let's go and have a drink."

Annie poured three large glasses of chablis and three glasses of iced water.

"I want you to know that this is freelance," said Sir Pluto. "You see I take an interest in everything, so I took a particular interest in you when you left Stumpy Knoll on Boxing Day. From Max's scanty details I managed to get a fix on you and called in a few favours to gather a complete dossier. I was not sure what to do until you sent your message to the world. My people traced it to Saint Lucia and I thought that a belated honeymoon—I've just married Annie—would be very pleasant. We've been here just over a week. I knew where you were and I have a log of your daily activities, but we were on the verge of leaving when you made your pitch. I'm not inclined to do anything in particular. I just thought you would be better off the island. Medical facilities in Barbados are better than on Saint Lucia and I thought you might need a bit of anonymity just in case people, particularly the mother of the baby, feel let down."

"I can handle most of my strange relationship with Perpetua, but I get totally freaked by the idea of performing miracles."

"Well the local radio stations are still saying it's a miracle twenty-four hours on. As I said, I have nothing in particular in mind, but as I'm not a pure, passive sort of Perpetuan who simply believes that love is creating space for the otherness of the beloved, I tend to want to be a little more proactive. I can't object to what you write and say—and I've been told that that's the Perpetuan party line—but I have some evidence to suppose that it's only your rigourous training that prevents you from descending into violence and I am extremely anxious that that does not happen, particularly in respect of my friends."

"You looked very strange the other day at the beach," Annie said, "as if you were a preying mantis that wanted both to rape me and kill me."

"You were almost naked."

"So, if you hadn't run away in a panic would you have been? I told Pluto that I thought you needed help. We were still trying to work out what to do when you preached yesterday evening."

"I'm aware of your behaviour pattern," said Sir Pluto. "I know that we can find you a place to rest and recover where you can think carefully about what Perpetua means, and then you will again feel the need to run away and suffer the torment of a divided mind."

"Very clever."

"Now come, Gregg, you are our guest. There's no need to be unpleasant. I am only going on your behaviour so far."

"What business is it of yours?"

"I've been in business long enough not to expect gratitude, but you might have been in a bit of a fix after your swoon. Heaven knows whether they might have thought it a divine trance or a symptom of poor mental health. I do not know, but you might have been manhandled in a very unpleasant way. Now I know you're accustomed to that and that is, in a way, why I think you are my business. I have chosen to be interested in—I say that advisedly as I don't think I could characterise my commitment as one of faith—Perpetuanism and so, for a very different set of causes, have you. I have been fortunate enough to be able to learn more about you than you have learned about me. Doubtless, if things had turned out differently and you had had the head start, it would have been differ-ent, but here we are. I know enough about your apparent self-control and sup-pressed and actual violence to be concerned. The goodly Perpetuan leadership would leave you to yourself but, you see, as I am neither part of the leadership nor committed to the Perpetuan notion of sublime passivity, I will continue to take an interest in you. We need say no more. It is time for dinner."

Gregg had always preferred being the hare rather than the hound. It took more skill, it involved greater risk, it induced more adrenalin, and the terms of trade meant that violence was permitted and forgiven. As he walked through the garish streets of Bridgetown he wondered whether he needed to give Sir Pluto the slip and decided that there was no strong case for it, but he anticipated his moment with great pleasure. As he would not be able to take a boat or a plane without detection, the game would have to wait. For now, he would take a rest. The papers were full of the story of the baby that had been healed, but there was hardly anything said about the healer. Perhaps people expected "miracle" men to simply appear and disappear.

Once he had recovered, he flew down to Grenada. Not entirely surprisingly he was met at the airport by Claris Henry, a leading socialite and Elder. "We heard of your marvelous oratory in Saint Lucia and the cure of the baby, and because my brother is a LIAT pilot we have been looking at the passenger lists in case you might come. We thought we had lost you, but we did not give up. Somebody said they had seen you in Barbados, so we went on hoping. We are very pleased to see you because we are in some turmoil at the moment because although we are very small, there is a split. Most of the men say they are in Dex-ter's party while most of the women support Perpetua, and now there are even a few people—forgive me—who say that they are Greggites. We need your help to resolve our problems."

They gathered in a church hall in Saint George's. Gregg listened as the dif-ferent factions made their respective cases. This was not what he was in busi-ness for, but he would have to be patient. Put simply, the Dexterites said that he had been the leader all along and that Perpetua—who was only half afro-Caribbean—had simply been the "pretty face" of the movement. The Perpetuans said that Dexter was a great leader, but he was only Perpetua's successor. She had been part of the Godhead, and he was only a martyr. The Greggites said that Perpetuanism needed to adapt to the local customs to be "relevant" to the people. They were the descendants of slaves and their needs were very different from English people.

Apart from his natural inclination to take a high profile and his substantial doubts about Dexter, Gregg immediately saw that his best chance of power lay in sticking to the orthodox line, at least for now.

"Sisters and brothers: let us remember why we are here, to be children of God. Let us remember that Perpetua proclaimed herself to be a very special child of God. Let us remember that Dexter died for Perpetua and for God, and that I am nothing."

Murmurs of assent and dissent.

"Above everything else, we must be united. We cannot afford to be divided. Look, I am no orator. My words will not be able to persuade you. I am only stating the obvious so that you can remind yourselves. Look how many Christian sects there are, even on this tiny island, and imagine how strong Christianity would be if they were all united. The same goes for us who are even smaller."

There was a call for a vote, but Gregg sensed that this would be divisive—and muddled as it was between three "candidates"—and that reaching a rather vague consensus would be better. But a compromise would break down as soon as he left. So he thought that taking a poll, to test how things stood, might be better. There were 23 Perpetuans, nine Dexterites and three Greggites. He begged the three to abandon their cause and they split so that there were 25 Perpetuans and ten Dexterites, split almost entirely along gender lines. This was awkward so, in his rather clumsy way, he had another go at it and detached another three from Dexter.

"What shall we do now?" he asked. "Perpetua would not like what we have done, but you have to draw a line as she was part of the Godhead and he was not."

After a little whispering, and Without any fuss, the seven remaining Dexter supporters left. Gregg wondered what to do now. He wasn't a preacher and he didn't think he could try any of Perpetua's Sacraments as he only had a sketchy idea about them, so he hit upon the simple idea of getting them to sing some songs and hold hands. Some of the Christian songs where Perpetua was substituted for Jesus sounded a bit awkward, but it all went well, that is until, knowing that the meeting was coming to an end, people began to bring their sick relatives and friends to the front for Gregg to touch. He dare not refuse and, with a rising sense of panic, he put his hands on each head and mumbled a few words which he hoped would pass for a blessing. After that, everybody was reluctant to leave, wanting to see what happened. He begged to be allowed to sit in a side room to "recover", but his respite was shattered by chanting and cheering as one old lady was proclaimed cured. The room was in uproar as people from the surrounding bars heard the news and got on their mobiles to get other sick people into town as quickly as possible. Gregg found himself calling for more songs as he laid his hands on a seemingly endless procession for, with uncanny timing, every time the enthusiasm began to wane, another "miracle" was proclaimed. He promised he would hold another ceremony tomorrow, but he was pressed to go on. The new sect was gaining new adherents with every cure.

Meanwhile, the group of Dexterites which had left held a very quick meeting. Even though five of them were powerful young men, they could hardly use violence. They dispersed, one to the Catholic priest, a second to the Anglican Vicar, a third to the Baptist Minister, a fourth to the Lutheran Pastor, a fifth to the Church of the Latterday Saints and a sixth to the Assemblies of God and the last, more significantly, sought out his uncle Templeman, the Minister for National Security.

"Look, Job, as the competent Minister, I can hardly sanction violence." "And anyway," he thought to himself, "our masters the Americans are curiously interested in this Gregg and have hinted that he's one of theirs." "But there won't be much that I can do if he's given a bit of a warning."

At last all the sick had been "blessed" and he allowed himself to be escorted ceremonially to his hotel. Slumped on his bed, he was relieved to have got through the ordeal without the golden light and the swooning. Perhaps it would wear off. He needed some time to develop ritual and a basic sermon if he was to succeed. As he could not sleep, he climbed the few steps from his balcony onto a tiny beach and walked towards the water. Two men suddenly appeared, following him none too carefully, but before they could do anything, three men sprinted up behind them, knocked them to the ground, picked up Gregg and put him into the back of a car at the top of the beach steps. "Room key," said one. He handed it over. Minutes later he came back with Gregg's small suitcase. "The bill?" said Gregg, mechanically. "Compliments of Uncle Langley and Pluto."

"Welcome aboard," said Sir Pluto, amiably. "I don't much care for your brand of missionary work, but you are apparently performing miracles, so you can't be ignored at any rate. I don't know what we might do with you."

"It's the miracles that are the trouble."

"I wouldn't know, but here we were, hoping for a bit of a honeymoon and here you are turning this into a—pardon me—cheap thriller."

News of the Grenadan Christian Solidarity Movement spread throughout the Windwards, but so did the miracles.

"The trouble is," said Sir Pluto to Annie over a late breakfast, "We can't keep hold of him and we can't let him go, not just because he's not a genuine Perpetuan, but also because he's not safe from himself, from others, and for others."

Without any argument, Gregg, almost graciously, accepted the offer of a retreat in an "exclusive" resort near Sandy Lane. Its inhabitants were elderly, which would save Gregg from becoming inflamed when he went for a swim, and a couple of the residents were from his own trade a generation earlier.

Time to think about theology. Why did he really object to mainstream Perpetuanism? Or might it be, as he had the self-knowledge to see in his lucid moments, a kind of psychosis. As he was inescapably in the hands of Sir Pluto, he would use the time as best he might.

◆　◆　◆

Bishop James Hall sat in his London club on an unseasonably early and cold Shrove Tuesday reading about himself in *The Times*.

It is only fair to say that in the past we have been somewhat critical of the uncertain stance on Church matters taken by Bishop James Hall of Alchester. There was a time when his name was a byword for Catholic Anglican orthodoxy, but that reputation took something of a knock when he—possibly under the influence of his controversial Dean, Simon Prior—perceptibly wobbled and showed some sympathy towards Perpetuanism. Now, however, in spite of any shortcomings—to which Bishop James would himself admit—we believe that the humble and fair-minded Bishop is precisely the person the See of Canterbury requires to provide the Church of England with a period of stability. Although—indeed, perhaps because—Archbishop Hawthorne was egregiously holy and high principled he made a grave error in meeting the emergence of Perpetuanism with a proposal for an Anglican Commission to study its theological significance. Although Archbishop Varnish was proposed for the best of reasons—his knowledge of church architecture being beyond dispute—his tenure demonstrated that the position requires a combination of holiness and practical skills which he, and Hawthorne, in their different ways, possessed, but did not combine. The task before the Church now that Varnish has achieved a settlement in respect of its real estate is to achieve a modus vivendi between Anglicanism—and, in time, Roman Catholicism—and Perpetuanism which recognises the more modest reality of the Church which, nonetheless, must continue to be respected as established."

"I suppose that the whole of my life—well, my adult life at least—I have been damned with faint praise. What, Reggie, are you still here?"

"Yes. The Deanery is being refurbished—about time too—so I am dividing my time between here and the Palace."

"Why not join me for some coffee. Don't take it too hard, Reggie, I know you wanted the job and, believe me, I would be very glad if you had got it. I don't know what it is about Canterbury, but all its recent incumbents seem not to have wanted it. I very much doubt I would have taken it if the Dean and Schuhorn had not pressed so hard. The Dean said that I was exactly the right man to keep what's left of the Church intact and to bring it into a proper relationship with Perpetuanism. Schuhorn was less complimentary, the faint praise again, saying he couldn't think of anybody else. Oh, sorry Reggie!"

"It's all right, James. I know that I was the wrong person, really. Not enough theology. By the way, How's that new man of yours, Sutcliffe, doing?"

"Oh Clement, he's doing very well. He is the most fair-minded person you could wish for, seeing all the different sides of everything but, unlike me, when he's seen all the sides he steadily weeds out the weaker cases, like Radio 3's *Building A Library*, until he comes up with a clear recommendation."

"So what does he, or, you, think about the Perpetuan question? He is one of them, after all, which must make him suspect."

"Not in the least. He says that if there is to be some sort of settlement with Anglicanism it's important that it doesn't fracture into its constituent parts because, he says, once you start doing that it never ends. The established Church of England has a responsibility of coherence whereas sects have no such responsibilities, so there is a mutual interest between Perpetuans and Anglicans to keep our Church together."

"Very pretty. So what does he think about the Catholics?"

"Well, he doesn't think anything about the Roman Catholics. According to him they are locked into a crippling debate about authority which will keep them turned inwards for as long ahead as he can see. As for the Anglo-Catholics, he says they will have worse psychological than theological problems with a female component of the deity. After all, if they won't let women be bishops they won't let a woman be a component of the deity. He thinks that, not for the first time, the Church of England will be an ecumenical locomotive, but matters will take a long time, even if the Romans cut loose. He also says, interestingly, that the outcome will crucially depend on what happens to Perpetuanism as it faces up to its medium-term future. When the glow of Perpetua's 'real presence' begins to fade there will be pressure to organise in opposition to the pressure to remain pure. Then there's the Gregg factor..."

"Yes. I can't really work out what he wants."

"Clement says that the problem is that nor can Gregg."

Although by the usual standards the timing of the ceremony was rushed, it was well attended and perfectly choreographed. James preached a theologically sound sermon that was neither inspiring nor dull, but might best have been described as "useful". The only slightly daring note was struck when he remarked that, "We have to be careful to see the presence of God where it is", which some commentators took to be a reference to Perpetuanism.

Next morning it was Dean Reginald who sat at his club table reading *The Times* report on the ceremony. All things considered, the Schuhorn appointment was both generous and sensitive to his needs. It was ash Wednesday, a day which made him properly penitent. For although there was nobody who loved the good things of life more than Crowther, and not many who were as self-deluding as he was, like the medieval adventurers he was deeply aware of the idea of personal sinfulness. He wished he had the self-control to be less of a sinner, recognising that to practice virtue was the only way of achieving it. He was deeply moved by the poetry of Hildegard of Bingen, Gottschalk, and, above all, Notker and he accordingly loved ceremonies like the ashing and really meant it when he vowed to be less carnal. If only he could control his wine, women, and wit. One factor which ran in his favour was his genuine commitment to his new job. He loved the administrative machinery and the liturgical rhythm of the Minster. He might have many personal weaknesses, but London Minster brought out his strengths. He had immediately been able to revert to his traditional stance, abandoning his Northern twang and casual clothes, at last living comfortably within himself. Local papers had cared about his every move in South Yorkshire, but only a very select and tight-knit part of London cared about what he said or did. So although his relative obscurity was a temptation in one direction his love of the job pulled in the other.

As he walked down the nave, deeply aware of his own insignificance in the sight of God, he saw Clement stand at the end of his valedictory private prayer.

"How are things, Mr Sutcliffe?"

"Clement, Your Grace."

"Reggie. Or, if you must, Dean Reggie. How are things?"

"Very complicated, really. I am sure that Archbishop James will be a wonderful leader but everything in the Church of England is so complex. Synodical Government has inevitably led to bureaucratic excess. The one thing that legislators cannot resist is legislating. The bishops then get hold of a law and smother it with guidance, regardless of the cost. It's strange that an institution founded on love can't be more trusting of its clergy and people."

"I didn't really mean that, though of course what you say is very interesting. Occasions like tonight remind us of how poor and insignificant we are."

"I presume you are interested in my dual role."

"Yes. What you have just said is very relevant in that context."

"Well, Dean, if language about God is metaphor, how important is it, given that we are all God's children and will all be re-enfolded back into God's infinite love, whether we think God has three or four or many more 'persons'? How much does it matter how we distinguish between you as a child of God and Jesus as a child of God? Put that way, it might sound blasphemous to a Christian, but it forces us to think. Was the creation of Jesus in some way fundamentally different from the creation of you and me? The Nicene Creed is a masterpiece of creative equivocation. Jesus was 'created' before time began, but we were created after. So what? I saw your face when you were returning from the ashing and hope that mine looked as yours did. We have made life more difficult for ourselves than we need. I see my job as giving Archbishop James the help he needs by focusing on simplicity and trust."

"Very well put, Clement. I wish you well. Next week, God help me, I may not, but now I sincerely do."

As Clement was about to leave the Minster he was approached by what he recognised to be an African Bishop.

"I know this is hardly the place, young man, but am I not right in thinking that you are a luminary of the Perpetuan movement."

Clement smiled as the best way of providing some encouragement while admitting to nothing.

"There is a great interest in Africa in Perpetua."

He smiled again.

"Well, I wondered if you could help me."

"I will try. You probably know that I work for Archbishop James, so I am in something of a difficult position, but he has kindly told me that it would be wrong of me to build a 'Chinese wall' between my faith and my occupation. He says that I must live my faith and simply keep to the terms of my contract which says nothing about my private behaviour. He says my loyalty to God is more important than some notion of loyalty to him to which he is not, he says, entitled except in a strict employment sense. That is very good of him, but I do not wish to exploit what I regard as a privilege rather than a right. I think him therefore very generous and wanted you to know of it before we go any further."

The Bishop nodded appreciatively. "In my part of the world we have become so obsessed with the entanglement of homosexuality and anti-imperialism that it is just so refreshing to have something more interesting to talk about. Admittedly, the starting point of sharing racial identity is not ideal but no earthly religion is. I wondered whether you might put me in touch with people who could help. So English not to have started in the right place, I'm Bishop Ignatius of Pokot."

Clement gave the Bishop a card and said, "Although Archbishop James gives me a certain latitude I do not like to abuse it. Please excuse me, but my friends will help you."

Bishop Ignatius courteously took the card, said that he quite understood and made his way to the door where he said goodbye to Dean Crowther.

Crowther, who was so fond of the light and movement in the Minster, sought the quiet of the Lady Chapel as vergers closed the building down for the night. He remembered how naively devoted he had been to the Blessed Virgin during his early teens and how he had abandoned her. Clement had set him a problem about the creator and creatures, about the difference between himself and Jesus as created beings. Where did that leave Mary? Perfect in every way and a child of God, why wasn't she part of the Godhead? It was the time thing again. He sighed. It was all too much. he dedicated Lent to Mary in the hope that he would at least moderate if not reform his ways.

When Bishop Ignatius presented himself at the Perpetuan headquarters Max was waiting for him. Clement had told Max of his conversation with the Bishop and this had sparked off a lively debate which involved the whole leadership.

"The question is," said Trina, "should we think of ourselves as an evangelical organisation to realise Perpetua's mission or should we wait upon Our Sister the Spirit?"

"God will not fix what he created us to fix," said Kylie, who had been growing in confidence as she spent more time praying and reading. "The Christian Apostles waited for the Holy Spirit in Luke, but they didn't wait for it in John. We have had an abundance of the life of God living with Perpetua. The question is, perhaps, whether we should be Evangelical or not."

"It's so easy to get it wrong," said Stacey. "I have been an Evangelist, but I don't think I communicated anything. What do we have to say?"

"That Perpetua, like Jesus, is a child of God," said Wayne.

"That's theologically right," said Cara, "but what difference does that make to real people? It sounds rather abstract. So you go down the street and say to people, 'the good news is that not only is Jesus the Son of God, but Perpetua is the Daughter of God.' 'So what?' they will say, 'what's in it for me?' I think we have to avoid making the Christian mistake of thinking that the proposition is what is important. What is really important is that we were created out of love to love and that Perpetua has given us that power back. For what it's worth I believe she was a child of God in a very different way from that in which I am a child of

God. Cleverer people than me might understand that she has parity with Jesus, but it's the message of love that counts."

"So what does that mean," asked Trina, "in the context of our starting question about Evangelism?"

There was silence for a long time. They were comfortable in the intimacy of their collective rumination. Max, momentarily distracted by the thought of Bruckner, suddenly saw something that he had never seen before.

"All the time that Perpetua kept telling us that she was our Sustainer and God's Sacred Vessel created to contain within her all humanity's wrong choices, eternally iconised in the way she died, we kept thinking of her as a category. She categorised herself in the Godhead category and then in the Jesus category and, of course, in the human category. This was easy for us because Christians had done the same thing. What if that is just language to break down the reality into pieces we can understand? What if the real truth is that in some way we were all created before time began? Then, to go back to Clement's question, where does that leave the difference between Jesus and Trina?"

"Interesting," said Trina, looking a little distracted, "but where does that leave the question about evangelism?"

"Well, said Max, if we believe that Perpetua shed some new life on the sacred nature of creatureliness, we can place greater emphasis on humanity as children of the Godhead. I know, I know," he said, looking at Wayne, not wanting his stream of thought to be broken, "but the thing is, Christians have lost the idea, not of what God is nor that we are children, but they have lost the idea of what children are. Health services, safety, storage, planning, schooling, and, God help us, sexualisation, particularly of little girls, have stopped us thinking about what it really means to be a child. It means being weak, dependent, and only capable of growing in the full ardour of parental love. Christianity, in essence has lost its humility, it's unconditional trust."

"So?" said Trina, trying to be a competent chair, but failing.

"So, if I may," said Father Bill, "we must go out into the world to take the message that in spite of all our great power and wealth—even in Africa there is infinitely more power and wealth than there was 100 years ago—we are totally dependent on God and that this is wonderful news."

"I can see how being children of God is wonderful news, but I can't quite get my head round the idea that dependence is wonderful," said Wayne.

"The idea is this," said Trina, who had made her own breakthrough. "There is so much stress in thinking that you are responsible for running the world, so when it gets too much—indeed, before we do anything—we should turn to God for support."

"So how close is that to fatalism?" asked Stacey.

"Fatalism is asking God to fix everything. It's like waiting for fate but, be careful, Muslims aren't really fatalist in that way, Stacey, it's a bit of a Christian caricature. All they are saying is that no matter what you do, it's insignificant compared with what God does and can do.

"The thing we have to hold onto is that being humble does not mean being idle. I think that is where we lead right back into the evangelical question. There are so many unhappy people out there and God created us to be happy as children. If we think that really is good news, we must spread it. I must say I have some difficulty with Christians who say that they can't evangelise competitively with Islam because that's like saying the two faiths are equal. If we believe that the faith we hold is simply a matter of birth place, rearing, and temperament, where does that leave all the theology of Christianity's uniqueness? Well, we don't have to bother about that because we've gone on from there. What we say is that the Godhead has renewed humanity in the person of Perpetua. We can say that in any and every place and if we are challenged we simply have to affirm that that is how we see things, that is what we believe, and that it is so wonderful that it can't be negotiated away. We all believe in the same God but we have seen God in Perpetua in a way that others have not seen God. It is easier for us in many ways which gives us an extra responsibility. This might not be very coherent theology, but it's the best I can do for now."

They then went on to discuss how to proceed in a practical way. Anticipating questions, Trina said, "If we lay hands on people they are our equals. Even with email and webcams we have to trust them within their own sphere. We do not want to turn into a never-ending virtual consultative assembly. This, in turn, means that those on whom we lay hands in turn have that power, although I think we should retain Archbishop Hawthorne's original idea—it was his, wasn't it?—that there need to be three Guides to create a new Guide through the laying on of hands. I suppose we need a corpus of the leadership to lay hands on a new member of the leadership."

Bishop Ignatius said that he had heard about Perpetua first on his short wave radio and then from colleagues in Nairobi. It was so often forgotten by Westerners that Jesus was not blonde and blue-eyed and that he was racially near to many Africans.

"I am only concerned to bring the news of God's love to people and if Perpetua makes that easier than a Jesus who has been culturally Westernised and a God the father who has been culturally imperialised, then so be it."

"So do you believe in Perpetua?" asked Stacey.

"Well, I'm not really sure what that question means," said the Bishop. "I believe in her to the extent that she existed. I believe that she was a child of God as we are all children of God. The question arises whether she was a child of God in the way that Jesus was. What matters here is not a theology of parity but a theology of bridges. Let us say that the purpose of bridges is to cross impassable spaces. Jesus was a bridge between God and humanity. Perpetua was a bridge between God and humanity, but not all bridges are identical. There are different kinds of banks and different kinds of spaces. In the case of Jesus I have always thought that the Old Testament was getting the Jews ready for Jesus and until they could get the language right in their heads Jesus could not come. The Jews of vengeance could not have understood the Jesus of the Gospels.

"In the case of Perpetua the situation is rather different. It should have been that the evolution of Christianity in the power of the Spirit did not need another bridge, but Christianity has evolved away from God's love to God's supposed judgment, and in the course of that evolution, the Church has lost most of its adherents because we are bound to lose out in disputes about moral codes. So Perpetua's bridge, for me, the bridge between the human and the divine, was not the result of accumulated wisdom, but the result of a terrible breakdown in communication between God and the world. People will warm to her because they understand how broken we are, individually and collectively."

"Yes," said Stacey, "I can relate to that, thank you Bishop. I see the organic nature of Jesus and the traumatic intervention of Perpetua."

"Well, Bishop, this was not supposed to be an interrogation," said Trina, feeling slightly uncomfortable.

"Never mind," said Bishop Ignatius. "Theology is a never-ending tangle of questions which concern me, but will not really concern my Pokoti people, not because they are not capable of high thought, but because their life is necessarily concerned with essentials. As the climate changes they are finding it harder to live. I need to bring them hope and I firmly believe that Perpetua's story will bring them great hope."

They laid hands on Ignatius and he affirmed himself both as a Perpetuan Guide and a member of the core leadership, the first from outside the land where Perpetua had lived, taught, wrought her mighty acts and died.

"While we are discussing places outside the United Kingdom," said Trina to Ignatius, "what do you think we ought to do about Gregg?"

Ignatius looked puzzled. "Why do you have to do anything about him?"

"Because," said Stacey, "he is subverting Perpetuanism."

"But much of the world will subvert it as it has subverted or denied Christianity. The problem, Stacey—and I can see why you ask the question as you have travelled—is our love of conformity, of what Christians call 'orthodoxy'. At the heart of our existence there lies a mysterious paradox which we need to embrace with love rather than fear. We should do everything in our power to bring people to God but, ultimately, only God brings people to God. It is not our doing as nothing we do is really our doing. Now we all know this in our hearts, but we are so bent on doing good, of seeing that people do not go astray, that we end up with rules of orthodoxy. The problem with rules is that they are, ultimately, useless in the commerce between God and humanity. They only apply to our way of seeing that we can conduct ourselves with each other. There is a terrible confusion between the moral life, as defined in different societies, and the holy life. I should know, I have studied and worked here as well as in Africa. I can tell you that Africans are no more impressed with Western morality than you are with African 'corruption', but that is not the point."

'Maybe," said Cara, "maybe that is why Perpetua seems to be against a theological core document."

"You will find that most such documents are written 'against' people and organisations, to define differences and to justify exclusions."

"Should we let anyone in, then?" asked Wayne.

"Yes, unless they affirm that they have no sympathy or commitment to the Godhead in which case they are really wasting their own time. Even then, don't waste your time with it. God knows about our commitment and the Holy Spirit will bind us together."

"But where does that leave Gregg?"

"Well, of course it is very annoying that he claims to speak in the name of Perpetua and he says things on her part which you say Perpetua would not have approved of, but Perpetua didn't strike me as approving or disapproving anything. I recommend that you remember Gamaliel. Truth will emerge in the end."

"But you said that Perpetua came to us precisely because truth did not emerge in the end," said Wayne.

"She came to strengthen the hands of the truthful," said Ignatius, "and the Spirit will sift us all in time. As you have not laid hands on Gregg, which involves a certain amount of trust and loyalty, I do not see that there is anything you can do."

◆   ◆   ◆

"Remember Gamaliel," said Archbishop James to Dean Crowther as they sat just inside Black Rod's entrance waiting for the recently ennobled Lord Griswald of Warpley.

"Gamaliel's all very well," said Crowther, "but there are decisions to be made about property that can't wait. Either we accept Perpetuanism and lose our place or we root it out at once."

"Clement told me that you were not so definite as that."

Clement said nothing.

"He caught me at a rather unusual moment. However, we won't go into that." Crowther looked threateningly at Clement who had, it must be admitted, tactfully withdrawn when the Dean's attention wandered from their conversation to a very pretty new lady curate at a small reception to celebrate his arrival at the Minster. "The point is, James, we have a vital strategic decision to make and Gamaliel isn't going to help us. Let's face it, by the time that the Palestine Jews had worked out that Christianity was a mortal threat, it was too late. Even without the destruction of Jerusalem it would have triumphed."

"But what if God wants us to accept Perpetua in the way that he wanted the Jews to accept Jesus?"

"Well, James, I'm rather sympathetic to the High Priest on this point. You can only do what your upbringing and temperament train you to do until such time as God vouchsafes a breakthrough of some sort, but it's got to be a breakthrough personal to you like that which Saint Paul underwent. If the Holy Spirit had wanted to change the mind of the High Priest, that is precisely what would have happened. So unless you get the call from the Spirit, James, I believe you should go on holding on to what you believe."

"The problem with that, Reggie—I know bishops aren't supposed to say this— is that I know what I believe in, in the conventional way—I can say the Creed with a good conscience—but I am not sure what believing is, in this context."

Lord Granville Brompton heard the Archbishop's last phrase as he came towards them, but tactfully chose not to take it up. Since his resignation from the Government he had been content enough in his study, but the Prime Minister had wanted some help in Their Lordship's House with matters ecclesiastical and had asked Granville, as a personal favour, to oblige.

"I know you gave up your job at the Department to protect another," the Prime Minister said, "and that's admirable, Granville. However, you're too bright to leave us and it's that very principled stance that you take on affairs which is what we need. We're always being dismissed as mendacious when what we actually are is muddled by the huge complexities that face us, the conflicting priorities. I don't know whether you're seen to be principled because you can untangle things or the other way round. Either way, you're sorely missed as a Minister in the House and so I hope you will accept the invitation to go upstairs."

Granville had agreed. It wasn't the flattery, but his realisation that he had probably pulled away a little too quickly. What he had intended to be cover for his junior, Strider, had been hailed as an act of principle bordering on the saintly. Frankly, it embarrassed him. If he could take on a little work and make the occasional compromise, perhaps the gilt would wear off.

Crowther looked uncomfortable. He certainly didn't want the pious Lord Brompton to know that they were meeting Lord Warpley. He needed to get him out of the way as quickly as possible and was considering going to the excessive length of inviting him to the Deanery when he was spared by Granville's almost legendary tact. He didn't know why Reggie was so uncomfortable, but he knew he was and so Granville said his farewells crisply, but without abruptness, and passed through the revolving door.

Scarcely had he disappeared when Lord Warpley appeared.

"Ah Griswald," said Crowther, beaming broadly. "It's nice to see you in these magnificent surroundings. A nice change from Brickton."

"I don't need to be reminded of Brickton, Reggie. In fact I'm trying to write it out of my history in much the same way as you've re-written your history, Reggie, the only difference being that you do it more often."

This was a bad start and Crowther, remembering just in time why he was there, said, "Well, Griswald, we're not the sort of people to pretend, are we?"

They sat at the corner of a large table in a committee room.

"Come to the point, Reggie, you never go anywhere without wanting something."

"No, and I'm wise enough never to ask anything without offering something in return. What we want to discuss is the prospect of entrenching the Establishment of the Church against the inroads being made by Perpetuans, Polish Catholics, Muslims, and the like. You know, the sort of nonsense about the Coronation Oath talking about 'faiths'."

"Good idea in principle, Reggie, but look what happened to Old Rufus."

"Tartan! He was just a poor tactician. Being an Ulsterman he had no idea how these things are done."

"Now you and I ..."

"... Not so much of the 'you and I', Reggie. I don't understand 'how things are done', but I am beginning to. In Brickton you found a seller and a buyer and made a price. Here's it's all in a code I don't understand. I soon discovered, for instance, that I was better off pretending I went to a grammar school than owning up to my third-rate public school."

"All right, Griswald, there's no need to get prickly over a compliment. I know how things are done, but you are in the right place."

Clement wondered if the Archbishop should be present, even if he said nothing, but he judged that, for the time being, the risk of being tarnished by these two plotters was outweighed by the intelligence he would gain from these two self-made men who, like all aggressive Tories, assumed that everybody, except the very poor and mad, were natural Tories.

"I agree we shall have to be a good deal more subtle than was Sir Rufus Tartan, but that won't be difficult. In any case, he did have a bit of bad luck with those three shootings which had nothing to do with him. All the same, a xenophobe shouldn't run away to his house in France when things go wrong!

"The point is, Griswald, you and I know that in spite of Perpetuanism's superficial charm for liberals, and in spite of a bout of aggressive atheism, we are moving into an era of puritanism. It's only a matter of time before the Tories get back into power and they, like the Republicans in America, will be increasingly influenced by the 'religious right'. In America they still believe that they can control their own economy so they have more energy for moral issues, but over here we know all too well that we have lost control of our economy to Brussels and the global market. We need a more determined moral effort; but it's in the nature of legislators, even right wing legislators, to want to legislate; and if they can't have the economy, they will settle for morality."

"Yes, Reggie, very convincing, but there's another side to it which we need to consider. As you say, there is a move from the 'right', but if a Republican or Tory is asked to choose between morality and money which does he choose? Is there any real evidence that the Republicans want to close down the American porn industry when they can hide behind 'freedom of speech'? Here's another thing. The recent campaign to move the watershed on TV from 9pm to 10pm will soon create a fissure between vacuous innocence and pernicious pornography, tearing the troubling centre ground out of our discourse. Pornography, separating the scenario from reality, and romanticism are just two sides of the same coin, but it's the stuff that battles to understand the self that counts rather than the

Waltons or Supercock."

Clement was enjoying this. It was Griswald, the self-made peer who had risen from the post room to the board room of one of the UK's biggest insurance companies who had a better grasp of theology than the Dean. As long as the discussion went on at this level, James need not fear.

"Anyway, that's all very interesting, Griswald, but what about the business in hand."

"I'm a very straightforward man," said Lord Warpley.

"Oh, don't give me that tosh," thought Crowther. "I know the games you played to get to the top of United Mutual. I took the funeral of one of the suicides." "So you will have to come clean."

This is where Crowther found himself at a disadvantage. The last thing he wanted to do at such an early stage was to come clean. Getting your own way in a big matter was best accomplished by moving in a co-ordinated way over small matters that made the outcome increasingly irreversible.

"As I said, Griswald, I want to give the Church a more secure position by enacting a little Parliamentary business. There's an education bill going through the Commons at the moment—when isn't there?—which includes some provisions on the National Curriculum. All that we need to do is to make orthodox Christianity compulsory on the curriculum and outlaw all other religious teaching from state funded schools. It's not that radical. It's difficult to admit they're better than us, but it's roughly what the French do."

"No it isn't," thought Clement, "but it's best to say nothing."

"And how do we get that through?" asked Lord Warpley, a shade peevishly.

"We hold our fire until the Report Stage in the Lords and slip it in. There's a tidy majority which will accept it as long as we get our people in and make sure the other side is unprepared. We might even do a deal on gay anti-discrimination as liberals are obsessed with that and will give up almost anything for it."

"What about the Commons?"

"They won't like it, but the Prime Minister needs the bill now because it won't give him any electoral advantage inside two years and if it gets delayed then the goodies will be delivered too late to influence the vote."

Archbishop Hall stirred as if to speak, but Clement put his hand gently on his arm.

"We will look forward to seeing the text of the amendments," said Clement, betraying nothing. "I am sure that the bishops in the Lords will want to be fully acquainted with your plans so that they can vote accordingly."

Crowther, who took this to mean acquiescence, smiled as benignly as the ingrained habits of his physiognomy permitted.

"But isn't Warpley a bit mad?" said the Archbishop as they walked past Saint Margaret's Church.

"No," said Clement. "He's a very wily man who has made his way in the world, but hides his cleverness like the exiled King David. "That way he always gets a great deal more than he gives. That was one of his more forthcoming appearances, from what I hear."

"But the bishops in the Lords will never vote for amendments like that."

"They will have to be very careful. Imagine Anglican bishops voting against compulsory Anglican education and in favour of comparative religion. I know that is our official policy and we get on quietly with our multiculturalism, but the new zealots will not rest."

"So what is Lord Warpley's angle?"

"Although in secular matters he is a man of impenetrable calculation, in religious matters he has been consistently Toran, using his money and influence to very good effect. His only calculation will be the chances of success."

"But on its own this will not do that much damage to Perpetuanism, which seems to be their aim."

"The Dean never does anything on its own, Archbishop. I gather from Lord Brompton that he has already approached Strider at Trade and Tittle at the Treasury to alter the tax system in favour of the Church and against all other denominations and religions."

"They can't do that."

"I think they can, if they see advantage in it. The sacred cow here is multiculturalism, but the Treasury has a mind of its own and almost unbreakable power. It's sadly amusing to see the Prime Minister smarting under the scourge he made. Before we get back we have to be clear on what we say if we are asked about any of this, particularly if one of them says that you were present and agreed with them."

"I said nothing."

"Commendable Archbishop. We simply went to be briefed and said—well I said—that we would study the text."

"But they might say anything."

"So they might, but in extremis I would give the recording of the meeting to Sneer. I am reluctant to do that as it would make subsequent meetings more difficult to tape."

"How did you do that?"

"Most people only notice that there's a camera, MP3 player and radio in most mobile phones, but many have a memo recorder. I have two such phones."

In their different ways, Clement and Archbishop Hall contemplated the level to which they had sunk, dragged down by the two noble Lords. They were both deeply sorry, but saw no alternative.

"Well," thought Clement, "if good people don't take the risk of being corrupted by power then bad people will step in. Jesus said we would never be asked to do anything for which we would not be given enough grace."

James thought, "I can see why so many good bishops—not that I am one—have turned down this job. I wish I was back in the Palace at Alchester gently settling matters with the beloved other Dean."

◆   ◆   ◆

"I think," said Max, "that we have dealt with the problem of whether to evangelise or not to evangelise. The Spirit doesn't do our work for us; so let us now move onto the next question. How do we view our work in places with strong religious traditions, Christian or otherwise?"

"It seems to me," said Trina, "that much of the discussion about this subject has become entangled with imperial history, not just our own in Western Europe, but also the history of the Ottoman Empire. Europeans, for example, took Christianity to south Asia and now it is suspect there, seen by the adherents of Islam and Hinduism as an aspect of imperialism. This explains why the initial religious imperialists, the Christian churches, have adopted an apparently absurd position by agreeing with indigenous secular authorities that they should not proselytise, particularly when ministering to people who are weak. I understand the history, but that is terrible theology. If you really believe that the Good News of Jesus or, in our case, Jesus and Perpetua, will give comfort to the weak, why would you withhold it to please a secular authority? The only reason is that your resolution to say nothing allows you to provide humanitarian assistance, but that is to put the cart before the horse. God comes first. Much worse, we do not wish to collude with the secular assumption that the humanitarian assistance is good, but the message of Jesus and Perpetua is bad. The contradiction between what Christians tell themselves and what they are prepared to tolerate from others is startling, a real manifestation of post-imperial guilt. I am sorry, I have said far too much as the supposed Chair."

"Fine," said Max. "As the supposed Secretary I will try to condense it. I am anxious that we proceed as clearly as possible, not making compromises by accident. So what about Islam?"

"This is the most difficult," said Stacey, "because, for a variety of reasons, it oscillates between tolerance and intolerance, primarily symptoms of political and psychological security and insecurity. We ought to consider the theology. The three Abramic religions worship the same God, it is said, but it actually means the God with the same history. The Jews, Christians believe, are saved regardless of whether they turn to Christ. Their behaviour does not often demonstrate this, but that is the official Roman Catholic line. Just because of Jesus, God will not go back on his Covenant. Islam is an altogether more difficult matter because of the imperial element. It's difficult to have a rational discussion from something as serious as the Christian Trinity down to the fact that Muslims invaded the Holy Land which in turn triggered the Crusades. If we spread the Word in Islamic countries we will be taking risks with our lives. From our perspective, should we be taking any risks when the general view is that they simply worship the true God in a different way from us?"

"I thought I had escaped from my banking roots," said Max, "but there is a Perpetuan principle at stake. She believed, above all else, in exercising choice and taking control of your own life. Put crudely, there's a market in ways to finding God. Some people will find the upheaval of changing religions—or banks—too great, but others will derive great benefit from it. People may want a monopoly, but it never works in the end. The question might be more a matter of timing. For me the priority is to care for those who have no sense at all of the reality of God."

"That's my view," said Trina. "I know we have to deal with all these cases logically, but the question does not arise practically at the moment."

"Then," said Max, "what about Christianity?"

"We all agree," said Wayne, "that the big Christian mistake was to entangle the church with political structures. Perpetuans will be politically active but make a sharp distinction between what God demands in pure love and what we must accept as the result of necessary human imperfection."

"Next, then, what about spreading the Word in Christian communities?"

"This is the easiest," said Cara, "as we know from our own communities. I've never tried to persuade Muslims to be Christian or Perpetuan but we have been working with Christians. The idea is that we add in the way that Jesus added to Judaism, but was able then to extend the new synthesis to non-Jews. Don't you remember the story of the Parsees who landed in India to be told that there was no room for them. They asked for a full glass of water and put a pinch of salt—or was it sugar?—into the cup. Won't it work like that, Joe?"

"I doubt it will be that simple. Religion has a lifelong habit of making compromises and then retrospectively justifying them with theology. Christianity is a tough nut."

"But we don't want to crack it," said Trina. "I don't know anything about plant life so I can't do the appropriate metaphor, but isn't it like cross breeding for strength?"

"Yes," said Father Bill. "There's a kind of Christian in-breeding which has been damaging, always looking inwards, but we then made the mistake of trying to reverse everything too quickly and we were accused of having 'trendy vicars'. There was then a strong Evangelical backlash. I think what I advise is that we stick to very simple principles. It looks as if Perpetua's habit of removing our doctrinal formulae might be good, at least for the time being. I mean, what's doctrinal about loving God and each other? In any case, it's not really up to us. We can try to discern what God wants but we can only be friends—I say 'only', but it's essential—with people of other religions and walk along side them. There isn't a choice between evangelising and not evangelising. We will offer friendship and the Spirit will sort out the rest."

Warm smiles all round.

"So finally, said Max, "the less fundamental, but more immediate, problem of Gregg."

"I thought this was going to be contentious," said Trina, "but I don't think so really. Gregg is misrepresenting Perpetua and we must do our best to represent her fully, accurately, and passionately, but we don't need a civil war with Gregg about it. If anybody reads what he says and what we say, from the two messages, put side by side, it will be easy to see which is genuine or, rather, which better represents what she stood for."

"Does that mean we are going to write. I thought we had just said that we only had a simple message that didn't need a creed," said Joe.

"We will write, but we will write simply in as many different ways as it needs writing. As an English graduate I am persuaded of the power of careful and beautiful words to reach the heart."

"For the time being anyway," said Max, "the Christian Caribbean is hardly our problem, but we will have to think again if Gregg, as I think he will, takes his mission to America."

Max did not mention the operations of Sir Pluto over whom he, conveniently, did not presume to exercise any kind of advisory role. This was, to an extent, venal and hair-splitting and took the Perpetuan doctrine of free choice into rather strange territory because he knew, if he wanted, he could gently ask Sir Pluto to pull out of the Caribbean, leaving Gregg to get on with it, but the intelligence was useful.

◆　◆　◆

TRINA'S MESSAGE TO THE WORLD

Dear Friends in Jesus and Perpetua,

I intend to write neither at length nor often, believing that the power of words to change a life must be accompanied by an underlying culture which makes that change possible, and that means that the teaching of Perpetua should largely be spread through the human agency, carrying written words only when they are a helpful tool. Neither will I write in order to contest what others say about Perpetua as her own message is her own best witness. I am conscious that what she said and how she lived presented a profound challenge to our culture and that, consequently, many will feel threatened for good and for not so good reasons. To ask a culture to move from defining love as active care to providing unconditional space for the other is a huge shift, and to put believers at the centre of religious life with Guides to assist them instead of hierarchical clergy, is another enormous shift. Taken together, to ask society, individually and collectively, to be more humble requires an enormous shift of consciousness and practice. Not that as Perpetuans, we do not care, but we must always be careful to distinguish between necessary and rewarding caring and the ultimate act of love.

The primary purpose of this message is to remind you of Perpetua's imperative of love. No matter what other people might say about Perpetua, the only thing we need to hang onto is her imperative of love. She died, like

Jesus, to show us that as long as we try, there is nothing we can do, even killing God, which will impair God's love.

In recognising the love of God our Parent as children, we put ourselves into a position of proper creaturely humility. The problem of thinking that caring is love is that we take the credit for what we do.

Humility is true happiness.

◆ ◆ ◆

Lord Griswald of Warpley who usually had no time for such nonsense as religious journalism, was drawn by a lurid headline.

RELIGIOUS WAR BREAKS OUT

War has broken out between orthodox Perpetuans and a breakaway movement based in the Caribbean. Perpetuanism's claim to be non-re-active and non-aggressive has been blown apart by its leader's two-faced message claiming Perpetuan virtue while laying into the breakaway movement.

The Perpetuan official spokesman, formerly a Fleet Street hack of the worst sort, refused to comment.

Dean Reginald Crowther, a rising star of the revival of the Church of England said that Trina's outburst was a warning that Perpetuans were "Like the rest us with no special claim to virtue. They will soon find," he continued, "that their quarrels will be like our quarrels but like all arriv-istes they will also find that their claim to special piety will be seen for what it is. It's the kind of dodge that Liberal Democrats have been practising for years, but people see through it."

Sneer found it very difficult to control himself, not because of the personal reference, which was par for the course, but because, in a strange way, Trina had made the mistake she was accused of in the article. She had somehow thought that she was immune from the assaults of a hostile media.

She saw it before he pointed it out. "I know. I'm sorry. I thought it was in-nocuous."

"Let us understand each other. Even if you tell the absolute, perfect, com-plete, honest truth in language which can be understood by a child with a read-ing age of eight, with no room for misunderstanding, you will be maliciously misunderstood, traduced, distorted, attacked, and insulted. That's only the usual treatment. If we stand for love in the name of pure principle, rather than in defence of an institution, the venom will be more powerful because behind the aggression is the worry that we might be right."

"So can't I say anything at all?"

"Frankly, not unless the imperative is so great that you have no alternative and only then with help from people like me. In this nasty world you have to be as far as you can in control of your own story and that means the god4u channel. Then, if material is picked up and mangled, you can at least re-run the original. In the case of text this is never so effective because people don't bother."

Lord Warpley, who was as shrewd as Sneer when it came to his handling of the press, read the original Trina statement to put him fully in the picture, to assess as accurately as he could how hostile the press was. Where there was any take-up at all, the press with the predictable exception of Ranjit at *Humanity*, was hostile to Trina's lack of hostility, underlining the truism that although it routinely calls for moderation in others the media is incapable of it.

Griswald Smythe had been raised in an atmosphere of suffocating virtue which he had grown to hate, not only because it cramped his life, but also because it made false claims about human beings. He was a strict solefidian who lived his life at a practical, nuts-and-bolts level, claiming that there was nothing spiritual about it and that God would decide in due course whether he was to be saved or not but, in the meantime, he was as clear as he could be without presumption that he was saved because he had an unshakeable belief in the absolute power of God. During his rise to prominence and wealth he had supported a variety of Strict Evangelical causes, but had accepted that, human nature being what it was, there was nothing he could do to limit the pluralism of Christianity. His money and time would only go so far.

Then came Perpetuanism in the form of the woman herself interfering in a primary school where he was Chair of Governors by walking in without permission. When he found out about her view of humanity which was, he thought, ultra-Pelagian, he was enraged and had tried to eradicate her influence, but the other Governors, keen to meet targets both to obtain more Government money and to improve its position in the league tables, had gone against him and agreed to retain the group of ladies who came, at Perpetua's urging, to listen to the children's reading. Had Griswald applied his usual careful method of checking, he would have found that the ladies in question knew no more about Perpetuanism than they knew about poverty and that their duties had become a pleasant social habit which gave them cachet at diner tables, but Griswald's dual rage at the attack on his status and his core Christian doctrine had got the better of him.

Part of his reaction was to take counsel with his school contemporary, Reggie Crowther. They had never precisely liked each other, but their sparring gave them both pleasure. When Reggie had become Bishop of South Yorkshire he naturally turned to Griswald as one of that class of people who might fill vacancies and when Griswald had been given a peerage Reggie naturally turned to him for political favours. Griswald had always known about Reggie's weakness for the finer things of life but, true to his religion, he neither condemned nor condoned what he knew. He had found his youthful behaviour embarrassing but now he only thought it tasteless. He thought that a Bishop should no more commit adultery with a debutante than he should himself commit adultery with a factory worker. Likewise, he took a grim, pragmatic view of gambling. A bishop should know how to calculate the odds as nearly as his own accountant. While there was nothing wrong with the occasional drink or two a bishop, like a factory owner, ought to mind what he said. So Reggie had his two sides as he always threatened a degree of reputational contamination, but he had given Griswald some local status and now wanted to cash in his chips. As it was, he need have done nothing as Griswald was committed to destroying Perpetuanism anyway, but Reggie need not know that.

He had been on the point of making his first move when Sir Rufus Tartan had blundered in and ruined the show, but this time he hoped for better luck and better judgment.

◆　◆　◆

Gregg lay on his bed, sweating in spite of the fierce air conditioning. His retreat was becoming oppressive, but he did not know how to escape from the intense theological war within him, fuelled by the nearby presence of beautiful female sunbathers. In lucidly intense periods of contemplation he knew that the problem was one of human nature. Perpetua had talked about unconditional space made for the beloved, but the only space he could think of was inside the micro bikini bottoms or g-strings that were the women's only covering. Could she really have meant what he thought? Clearly not, so he must resist. So what was this unconditional love? A kind of mental rape, the risk of being exploited? Yes, surely, if she really meant what she said then making unconditional space for the beloved was going to lead to abuse.

She surely meant freedom within rules. We were to offer unconditional space for benevolent actions. That didn't work.

When he was sure that all the sunbathers had gone indoors to dress for dinner, he walked along the jetty where Sir Pluto's yacht was moored. He looked at the sea and the sky, the two great metaphors of space of, he thought, unconditional space. You took out your boat or you flew your plane without asking permission as long as you were prepared to take the consequences. The sea could be ruthless without warning, the sky was the most exacting of examiners, punishing minor errors with catastrophe, but that was disembodied space. How could embodied space be unconditional?

He remembered something he had read in an old *Herald Tribune* that Max had said about Bruckner. He wasn't really a classical music fan, but he couldn't help checking out what was on Max's mind. "There is the silence of nothing," said Max "and there is the silence that is only made possible by the notes. There is a space which is nothing and a space which is only made possible by what we do. Unconditional space is a construct. We make it. We don't start out that way, we start by being closed and wanting to make all the running. We think of ourselves as storehouses and we only open the door to bring in new materials that we have grabbed from the outside, then we slowly widen out and make more space, sending stuff out as well as bringing stuff in, but it never becomes infinite, perfect. As human beings there will always need to be notes to enclose the silence."

Notes. Rules. Markets. Behaviour tokens. Gregg supposed that a boat was a kind of use of limitless space, but that did not hep him. He kept coming back to the same questions. Are there rules? If so, who makes them?

In the Service the answers had been easy. There were rules and the bosses made them. In Christianity the answer was only a little less easy: there were rules and although there was a bit of a fight about who made them it didn't make much difference as the makers came out with more or less the same rules. Was Perpetuanism fundamentally different on rule-making from Christianity? Or should it just pick up Christian rules? That would not work because although the rules were roughly the same there was a fight over rule making.

Start again. The main body of rules are about what we do and do not do. These are the active rules, associated with caring and not caring. These can be religious or secular. You can view them as moral and/or utilitarian. What Perpetua was asking us to understand was a rule on humility or meekness, a rule about making space for the other which the other might abuse. If you believed that Perpetua was part of the Godhead, then she could make a rule on behalf of it which developed the Jesus theory of meekness which developed from the YHWH very mixed views on meekness. Making progress.

In order to protect this openness and meekness there needed to be a rule about abuse which the abused did not set, but was set on behalf of the whole community of openness so that it was protected from the charge of setting its own limits. That was what authority should do. That was what authority did when it told him he could not abuse a woman's space. She might want to make it available unconditionally out of some conviction but the rule said he could not abuse it. The rules were not about the meekness, but its abuse.

◆　◆　◆

GREGG TO THE WORLD—BLOG TWO

Fellow Perpetuans,

1. I have already written to you so that we can explore together the implications of Perpetuanism for the way that we live.

2. As I said then, in my first blog, I am directly responsible to Perpetua who appeared to me in a vision and gave me my instructions and so I am writing on her behalf and on behalf of the life she laid down so that we all might be renewed in God.

3. I tell you in her name, just as a child needs protection from paedophiles, just as a woman needs protection from the advances of a predatory man,

so Perpetuans who believe in leaving themselves open unconditionally to the other need protection. The protection is not imposed by the lover on herself or himself, but is imposed on the beloved. In real life we play both roles. At one time we are the lover, at the other the beloved, so this rule of life applies to all of us when we are acting in the role of the beloved. We are to obey rules of restraint and respect which all share.

4. This is why, although Perpetua has revolutionised the culture of love, we still owe our allegiance to the Christian heritage of restraint governed by authority.

5. The pagan world in which we live is striving in every sphere to cast off authority, whether church, state, judicial, or regulatory. The response of the state, followed by others, is to impose ever more inspectors, but it will not work. Only the recognition of sacred authority will work.

6. We must recognise that without authority to help us curb our corrupt nature we will fall. There was much, justified, sunny optimism in Perpetua. How could it be otherwise? We were created in optimism and, in spite of our murder of two incarnational manifestations of the Godhead, no doubt we are in no different a relationship with the Godhead than we have always been, but we have been given new hope in Perpetua. That should not allow us to be mislead by our own false optimism. As secular society pulls away from moral values, it becomes even more important that religious entities insist more strongly on them.

7. What this means for us is that we must combine much more individual freedom with much greater moral sanction by religious authorities. This will clarify our position. People who behave properly in case they are caught out by regulation are not behaving well at all, and people who behave badly, but do not understand that they are behaving badly need to be brought to full recognition. The greater the liberty, the greater the sanction. Perpetua really only explained fully the first part of this dual proposition, but she has left us to work out the second part.

8. As the tide of licence rises we will need ever greater resources to bring people to their moral senses. Perpetuanism will be a new, purified, puritanism. Do not be misled by the rotten decadence of Western Europe. There are many parts of the world which are morally clean, which are examples of hope. You can see this in the fascinating revival of orthodox Anglicanism in Africa. Nonetheless, let us not be diverted by the minor successes of Christianity. It has failed. It has given itself massive moral authority, but has nothing to say. It has sunk into acquiescent liberalism.

9. As I look into the future I see an impending catastrophe engulfing the decadent world. There are already straws in the wind and it will soon become a whirlwind. Bankers and investors are so busy making money now that they have lost their bearings. They do not know when they will pull us down, but they know that they will.

10. When the disaster strikes, I will be with you in the world, to comfort and

encourage. In the meantime, I am thinking of you and am building up my spiritual strength for the struggle.

◆　◆　◆

"He doesn't mention prayer," said Trina.

"But he's right about the crash," said Max. "Southern Gem was only the beginning. I don't want to go into asset prices, but it is coming to a head and we will need to think pretty quickly what to do."

"But the worst thing of all," said Trina, "is that he has cast Perpetua as a Puritan. She was just the opposite. She was totally non-judgmental. She wanted house groups so that people could encourage each other, with a few Guides to keep the show on the road. She never said anything about sanctions or authority. What are we to do?"

"Well, we have been through this before in a slightly different context, so why don't you take us back to the beginning and see where we get."

Trina looked troubled but started slowly. "We are here to help people into a personal relationship with the Godhead. The Old Testament charts the way that relationship became less barbaric, making the incarnational advent of Jesus viable. Jesus changed the world, but his influence seemed to be waning. Perpetua came to revive it so that, to repeat, more people are in a direct relationship with God."

"So far, so good," said Father Bill.

Trina smiled. "But," she said, "if Gregg wants to strengthen 'old fashioned' religion that is fine. He's entitled to do that. It's subverting the name of Perpetua that is at issue."

"But," said Max, "it isn't like tarnishing somebody's brand. Think of how often Christians have had to endure the subversion of Jesus. Growing resentful or getting adversarial is both unhelpful and, in the end, not what she would have wanted. So everything we do must be constructive."

"This will take some special praying and communicating," said Trina, "if we are to be successful. This is what Perpetua really meant when she said how hard it would be to live this life of openness to the other without complaint. We should make big plans for Easter, the first anniversary of her death and re-manifestation."

◆　◆　◆

Gregg was growing bored as his struggle subsided. He felt safe now from his demons. He could walk along the beach without being attracted or repelled by the women. He even bought a pair of swimming trunks. The accommodation was good and he was well looked after. If you had to have a prison, it might as well be luxurious. As for the theology, there had only been a few wisps of comment against him on the blog. Most of the reaction had been favourable and, as he expected, there had been nothing from official Perpetuanism. It wasn't their way. Although he didn't have a very clear plan, he knew that the ultimate prize was not the reform of Perpetuanism in England but the capture of the United States.

An hour before sunset he went to the beach for a swim and then walked along the shoreline. The tide was out so that he could walk round the spit of rock at the end of the popular beach and found himself in a tiny cove with its own tiny beach. He saw a girl standing there, silhouetted against the gold of the rapidly descending sun, and when she moved out of the direct line of the glowing light he could not bear the intensity of the detail of her as she stood, thinking herself alone, in the pride of her thonged nakedness. He withdrew with a splash from the shallow water, hurriedly dressed, and returned to his room.

Later he walked along the jetty and heard the music thumping at a nearby night club. The silence between the notes was non-existent. There was no room for it in the sexual frenzy that it did not so much represent as promote. This was what the forces of religion must contest. He supposed his conclusion was that Perpetuanism, as a new force following the example of a young Afro-Caribbean woman, had a better chance than any other force.

◆ ◆ ◆

Myron T. Skraun Jr held the *Wall Street Journal* as if it were a flaring match, necessary for lighting a candle, but threatening to burn his fingers. It told him so much that he needed to know and so much that he wished he did not know. His church needed the data which only it could provide to ensure that its investments were sound, but it could not help being an emblem of the smug and smart Babylon "back East". Speaking in the management jargon of Babylon, Myron did not recognise that under his leadership his church had passed from having a purpose to itself being the purpose. The congregation, swelled by a never ceasing influx from the colder states, had reached a comfortable size and expansion would involve a level of investment which could only be supplied by the continuing influx showing more generosity than his current flock, most of whom claimed the relative poverty of seniors. The price of land in Miami showed no sign of stabilising and the Coral Gables Church of Christ would see him to his own senior status as long as long as the Elders continued to turn in a performance considerably above bench mark.

Dolorez glided meekly into the room and refreshed his coffee and then withdrew. His eyes followed her furtively over the top of his paper. Not quite a wife, not quite a servant, an accomplished, demure and pretty hostess. Myron and his Elders were able to accommodate her within their world picture without any qualms. Had she been white, fornication would have been on their minds; had she been black, her role would have had to be purely private, much nearer to the slave than the hostess. The church could accommodate these two racial polarities. A man of Myron's stature should only marry a white woman and might be served by a black woman, but this intermediate phenomenon required an adjustment. Clearly, he could not marry her but, equally clearly, she was "higher" than a slave, or even a servant. Her competence in the bedroom and the kitchen were a blessing. Her poise in the board room and the drawing room were greatly admired, and her example of quiet faithfulness at church and in its outreach work were exemplary. Myron was proud that his church had a small number of Hispanics to ward off any accusation of white supremacy and these women made outreach credible, bringing in more money than it cost. For her part, Dolorez was content, after a makeshift life where waitressing was a pinnacle. She had learned her English from television and movies and had then refined her viewing, seeking out European costume drama because she was attracted by its glamour, radically deeper than American chic, and she soon realised that the acquisition of some of its mannerisms might be to her advantage. Her quiet finish attracted the better customers wherever she was and she steadily graduated from a local bar to the dining room of the Coral Club where she served Miami's finest and practised her ever more refined English. Over the two years that she was at the Club, Myron had seamlessly metamorphosed from appreciative guest to uncle and would have gone no further, at least not on his home patch; but Dolorez saw her opportunity, researched the man and his church and decided that she would never get a better chance of a contented, if not a happy, life. She might have a child, but she doubted it. She might enjoy sexual ecstasy, but she doubted it. She might be swept away by a new romanticism, but she doubted it. Myron would always be meticulous in his demands. She was correct on all counts. Myron did not want children to compare with the two he had reared with his wife, who had died of breast cancer and they had fled to Babylon. His sexual requirements were routine, and even pleasant. More importantly, they apparently gave him much more pleasure than they gave her. He was scrupulous in the matter of presents, preferring the elegant trifle to the ostentatious bauble. Above all, the domestic and church routines were a blessed contrast to the chronic improvisation with which she had grown up.

Myron was attracted by a foreign stamp among his envelopes—he was neither opposed to nor in love with email, but he liked his letters, not least because they frequently contained cheques—so he put this to the bottom of his pile, delaying gratification to the last. He methodically worked through the letters, dividing them neatly into piles for re-cycling, for shredding and re-cycling, for the attention of his office, and for his own personal attention. He made a note of the three cheques and consequently adjusted his opinion of, and obligation to, the three senders.

The letter was from Pastor Drone

Stumpy Knoll
Ash Wednesday 2008

My Dear Pastor Myron
   I have never forgotten your kindness to me in agreeing, all those years
ago, to hold a revival meeting at my humble church before its sad decline.

Myron remembered the mission to unchurched England but not the church,
the Pastor or the place. Clearly the impact on the Pastor had been greater than
on him. The only recollection he could readily call to mind was how the English did everything on the cheap. It was hardly surprising, then, that they also
did church on the cheap. They never tired of praising their "English breakfast"
as if it was superior to a full American. He longed for a power shower instead
of a cramping, chipped enamel bath. He was often hungry because they often
thought that the main point of a sandwich was its bread, whereas Americans
knew that bread was the necessary container for wholesome food. For sure, they
did everything on the cheap, but everything was expensive. He had hoped, as
a junior member of the mission team, to assist at massive rallies in soccer sta-
diums, but his hosts, who never stopped talking about mission, scheduled the
team to talk to worn-out congregations in their own worn-out churches.

   Those were bleak years when we feared that we would not have the
   means to keep a roof over our heads, when our stalwart people passed
   away, not to be replaced by their children in the ranks of the faithful. Ah,
   Pastor! There are few men today like yourself who can command a congregation's attention for more than an hour.

"True," thought Myron, "but there are few men who recognise that the brand
is only burned into hard material with patience and application. We shall get
nothing significant out of them until we have convinced them, and they have
convinced themselves, that gaining security in their eternal life means giving up
a little of it here."

   But now, Pastor, I come to the purpose of my letter. We, in our very
   own church, have witnessed a remarkable occurrence of miracles wrought
   by Dexter, the martyred leader of the Perpetuans who now work alongside
   me in Stumpy Knoll.

Myron's antennae twitched. The great churches of the United States had been
trying for decades to lay their hands on a reliable miracle worker. They all knew
that healing services were a risky business and that a great many of the "cures"
would not stand up to immediate, detailed, and certainly not to long-term, scrutiny. Litigation was on the rise and revenue was on the way down. Anybody who
could get himself a real miracle worker would make a fortune. Pity that this
Dexter—he vaguely remembered the story—had died, but maybe these Perpet-

uans—enthusiasts of some sort, no doubt—could produce another.

I am writing to share the joy of the Perpetuan experience with you.

"Joy! That's it! I remember now. Drone. It must be full of miracle workers if it can make him smile, let alone talk about joy."

My friends tell me that you can find all the information you need on the internet, details below. Once again, thank you for your kindness all those years ago in coming to inspire us. I hope this letter will go some way to repaying your kindness.

"Repaying. Well, it just might."
Again, consciously delaying gratification, Myron took his silver fountain pen, a relic of more spacious days, and wrote:

My Dear Pastor Drone
I well remember my visit to you and can only hope that the sad decline you mention was not a result of it.
I have read your letter with very great interest and thank you for the information and the leads which I will follow.
If you ever find yourself in these parts, the Coral Gables Church of Christ will always be pleased to welcome you.
In God's name ...

Rather than going to the official Perpetuan website which Drone had indicated, Myron thought he would check the popularity ratings by making an open search. The whole of the first page of results concerned the blogs of a man called Gregg. He put "Gregg miracles" into the search box and came up with a story from Grenada.

MIRACLE MAN

A tourist miracle man known as Gregg healed scores of people at a church service before mysteriously disappearing from the island. Amid scenes of biblical turbulence and emotion he laid his hands upon all-comers in a Perpetuan service that surpassed any of our Christian Services of Healing. Rumours circulating in Saint George's say that he was chased off island by jealous Christian leaders.

There was more, but he hurried on to read a shorter and equally interesting story from Saint Lucia. Working miracles and disappearing was an intriguing combination.
Myron telephoned a friend in Homeland Security in Washington who passed him on to a colleague in the office of the Secretary of State who was polite but unhelpful.

◆   ◆   ◆

Sir Pluto did not know what to do for the best. He was keeping Gregg out of harm's way, but it did not stop him writing his highly provocative blogs. He was not the man to give way on a point simply because his wife had made it coherently, nor did she expect that he would, but Annie, who was still on the edge of the Perpetuan core group by virtue of Will's death, had taken an intense dislike to Gregg because of what she called his "stunts". Perpetua had always said that any acts she undertook were on behalf of the Godhead and she only did them on very special occasions for good reasons. This Gregg, from what she could gather from the Eastern Caribbean media, seemed to be claiming credit for himself.

"I know," said Pluto, "but what can I do?"

"If I were you, I would let him loose. He is bound to make a mistake."

"But that 'mistake' could be self-harm or murder."

"But you're not really his keeper. You have done your best for the best of reasons, but it's time to let him go."

"He isn't objecting. He isn't a hostage."

"Just let him go, Pluto, or there will be more trouble."

He saw the sense of it, not least because they planned to return home in a few days and Pluto knew that without him the surveillance would grow sloppy. He went to Gregg's "cottage".

"How are you?"

"I think I'm cured of the aberrations."

"Well, you do look calmer and the sun has helped to take away that rather pasty look. What are your plans?"

"America."

That was the problem. Once Saint Paul got to Rome, Jerusalem didn't count, but there was nothing he could do.

"Can you manage?"

"I have money and I'm a US citizen.

"When will you go, then?"

"The day after tomorrow."

On his last evening, he was drawn to the tiny beach. He had to see her once more. She was standing on the shore line, looking out to sea. He walked silently up to her and put his hands on her shoulders. She gave a sharp scream of surprise which made him grip her even more tightly. As he felt himself growing hard inside his trunks, he moved his hands upwards towards her neck.

He was struck on the back of the head and fell, unconscious.

◆   ◆   ◆

"I don't know whether you were going to rape her or kill her or both, but I can't do any more without colluding. You should consider yourself very lucky indeed that your friends from Langley have agreed to look after you."

Gregg had to stop himself smiling. Wise though Sir Pluto was in his own sphere he knew nothing about Gregg's friends from Langley. They looked after friends and foes in all kinds of ways from lavish provision to extermination, but there was always a deal to be done.

◆   ◆   ◆

Archbishop Hall was growing restless. It seemed to him that he could do anything he liked except be the Archbishop, or even a bishop. His duties were too many, his advisers were too helpful, and, although he was out of sympathy with both of them, he spent an inordinate amount of time trying to heal the widening breach between the African and American churches. On the Monday morning of the Winter meeting of the Grand Synod he read through the annotated agenda gloomily. There was another round in the bout over women bishops, another spat over gay Christians, three weighty reports on social matters with attendant pious resolutions about which the Church could say nothing credible; and a Private Motion on Perpetuanism which could not be legitimately kept off the agenda. He wondered why people wanted to be on it. Then there was his Presidential Address which would inevitably be compared with the elegant complexities of Hawthorne.

"Clement, what am I to say?"

"I am sure that I am advising you unfashionably, Archbishop, but I think, as an archbishop, you should tell the truth. The general custom, as I understand it, is to nuance what you say, to speak in code for the cognoscenti, but you are not a politician. Naturally, you would not wish to give offence in any way, but the point of an address is to say what you think it is most urgent, or pertinent, in the context of the present situation or the Synod agenda."

"I don't think I can say anything helpful about the Anglican Communion or most of this agenda."

"Well then, pick a topic to speak on."

"I suppose it's my duty to speak on the Perpetuan issue."

"It would be difficult to contest that conclusion."

"And what else?"

"Well, if I were you, rather than going through a list and taking a dart at each item, I would shape your address round the big subject and embroider it with smaller observations as they come to mind. Now, I will play Janet for a moment. What is the major point in your address, Archbishop?"

"If we can have dialogue with other faiths and with other Christian denominations, we have to have a very good reason not to have a dialogue with Perpetuans."

"Which is precisely the point which floored Hawthorne."

"Not quite. He wanted a Commission to see how Perpetuanism impinged on Christianity. I want a dialogue to see what we can do together."

"In other words, you will respect Perpetuanism, but you do not think that it changes anything in Christianity, in the way that the Jews did not think that Jesus changed Judaism?"

"That's a bit harsh, Clement."

"Janet. I know, so let's work it out. I'll go back to being me."

Clement made himself comfortable. He liked this sort of thing more than any of his other duties. "Let us start at the widest point. Let us say, following Karl Rahner, that God self-communicates indiscriminately with everyone what, then, is the key characteristic of faiths?"

"That they in some way enhance the ability to tune into, receive, interpret that self-communication."

"And what might be the core message of that self-communication?"

"Creatureliness conceived in love."

"That's extremely helpful, Archbishop."

"And that creatureliness intrinsically involves worship, communicating back to God. There is, then, a two-way process of listening and worship."

"And if we in the different faiths are involved in listening and worship would it be reasonable to think, as we all believe that we are listening to and worshipping the same God, that we might learn from one another how better to listen and worship?"

"That is why we have inter-faith dialogue and ecumenical dialogue."

"I wonder whether we do the first to avoid conflict and the second partly to do that, but also partly to strengthen our influence. So let us take the two separately."

"Inter-faith dialogue does teach us a great deal about different approaches to God."

"But it hardly alters what we say and do. With the exception of the moderation in the Christian attitude to Judaism, reflected in its prayers, I can't think of any instance of how the world's other great faiths have changed Christian belief and practice."

"Again, Clement, that sounds a bit harsh, but I see your point.Ecumenical dialogue is different because we do influence each other in the way we listen to God and worship. As for the point you made about extending influence, as our chief purpose is to establish a friendly relationship with God, then we should mirror that in a friendly relationship with each other, with people of all faiths and none."

"So no proselytising, then?"

"Well, no."

"So what about the missionary societies?"

"Good point. I mean, if we believe it's good news we ought to spread it."

"So what's good about Christianity's news?"

"The incarnation which makes it possible for us to say, because God in Jesus has told us, that we are God's creatures and will enjoy eternal life with him."

"Well, I often think of it as the moment living forever than a never-ending string of moments and I don't like the male pronoun. I do go along with you there, Archbishop. So let us stick with this train of thought for a moment. If our religion is fundamentally incarnational—we are Christians not YHWHists—does that make Perpetuanism a religion more like ours than, say, Islam? In other words is it a kind of Christianity or another faith? Would it be in your inter-faith class or your ecumenical class?"

"I suppose in the ecumenical class."

"So you might, then, as you do with other religions, wish to learn from it?"

"You're very clever, Clement, I can see where you're taking me."

"I'll be open, Archbishop. Whatever my personal feelings as a Perpetuan where I might have wanted Archbishop Hawthorne to establish an Anglican Commission to study the implications for it of Perpetuanism—a very handsome compliment—it was a serious error of judgment. The intention of taking Perpetuanism very seriously was good, but the Church would not have reacted that way to other faiths or denominations, it would have called for a dialogue. That is within its tradition and practice. People would understand that."

"Well done, Clement, I see it now. We should have an Anglican/Perpetuan Commission."

"Something like that. This isn't my area of competence, but you will find others who can help you with the fine detail."

"Yes. I'll ask Damian. He knows those kind of things."

◆　　◆　　◆

Isac Fuller had never felt so elated or so nervous in all his life. He had piloted his Private Members Motion to the top of the Grand Synod list and was preparing to make a fifteen-minute presentation. This had been beyond his wildest derams when he was elected eight years ago, but his seriousness and persistence had gained him a following near the end of his first term and he was now a luminary in the Fundamentalist Toran firmament who sat on the committees of all the major campaigning groups with their euphemistic titles a throw-back to supposedly democratic Marxist states, such as *Reform* and *Mainstream*, which were respectively ultra-conservative and ultra-fringe. Fuller was no orator, but his utter conviction went a long way. If he was confronted, for example, with the conflicting accounts of the death of Saul respectively at the end of the First and at the beginning of the Second Book of Samuel, he would not argue, but would just look at you as if you were mad.

Understandable as it was for Fuller to think that he had brought his Motion to the top of the list by virtue of God's power and his own sincerity, it could not have been done without the financial muscle supplied by Lord Warpley who, in turn, was able to call upon the resources of North American allies such as My-ron T. Skraun who was a hard nut to crack, but still worth the effort. Griswald was not on the Grand Synod, but he sat on influential financial committees and was always present at its big occasions. It was he who had helped to hone the Private Members Motion down to a manageable proposition:

> That this Synod regrets the conduct of a previous Archbishop in pro-posing a commission to examine the implications of Perpetuanism for Anglicanism, affirms its commitment to the orthodoxy of the Church of England as set out in the Thirty-Nine Articles of Religion and the Book of Common Prayer, and charges the Archbishops Council to use its best ef-forts to combat the heresy of Perpetuanism.

At his first meeting of the House of Bishops as its Chair, Hall had opposed the proposal to insert an amendment, deleting all the words after "That this Synod" and substituting a different proposal. He said that this was a wrecking amend-ment which asked the Synod to debate a different proposition. Synod should be allowed to vote for or against Fuller's Motion. What was the position of the House on this motion?

There was an animated discussion. Nobody wanted particularly to condemn a previous archbishop in the proceedings of Synod and most thought the term "heresy" a little old-fashioned but, robbed of their usual device of formulating bland, almost meaningless, amendments to strong motions, they floundered. James concluded that the House should have no agreed position, not least be-cause he had not come to a conclusion himself.

By the time that the Synod opened, matters had become more clear. James was to make his address, based on his dialogue with Clement, on Tuesday after-noon, and Fuller's Motion was to be put on Wednesday.

Janet Burns naturally asked the Archbishop for a press briefing and an embar-goed copy of his speech, but on Clement's advice he politely demurred. "It isn't that I don't trust you Janet, but I don't trust your erstwhile colleagues. Clement advises me that, based on his experience with Ranjit at *Humanity*, an embargo should mean that the speech can't be used at all until the time line, but now it only means that it can't be attributed, but can be used as background which al-lows journalists to twist their predictions even before the speech is given. I don't want what I have to say trailed and subverted in advance."

Janet was grim. Clement was firm. Crozier was silent. James was soothing. The lack of advanced briefing and text being unusual, the small section of the media that was interested in these things was intrigued.

James spoke evenly, without rhetorical flourish and undue elaboration. Since he had become Archbishop he had worked extremely hard at making his state-ments clear and simple. He believed that Hawthorne, motivated as he always was by generosity, had, for the most honourable of reasons, faced with the unusual circumstances of Easter 2007, gone further in proposing a Commission than the situation warranted. He now wished to bring the Church back to its usual custom and practice by proposing the establishment of a process of dialogue between world Anglicanism and the Perpetuans as it would with any other faith or denomination.

Isac Fuller momentarily shook at the prospect of contradicting the Archbishop, but then stiffened in the knowledge that God was with him.

Griswald was furious that he had been out-manoeuvred and would be forced to organise open opposition to Hall.

Damian identified a liberal lawyer and a progressive stalwart on the floor of the Synod and signalled to them to follow him. They drafted an amendment to Fuller's Motion echoing the Archbishop's remarks, checked it with the Synod's legal draughtsman, and identified half a dozen speakers.

When the news reached Isac he was unmoved. God was with him, and while all those around him fumed and plotted, he simply concentrated on his text.

In only consorting with his own kind, Fuller and his circle made a grave error. Their case was that dialogue with the Perpetuans was not only a waste of effort, it was unbiblical. Liberals gleefully argued that strict Torans, like Fuller, conducted dialogue with Petrans whose Eucharistic practises they thought to be unbiblical. This hurt because the Petrans and the Torans were in an uneasy alliance to prevent the consecration of women bishops, but they still frequently insisted that they would only hold dialogue with their own kind. Liberals pointed out that even in the Church of England they had, with the exception of the alliance against women, stopped dialogue and had set up their own enclaves. Just because they didn't want dialogue they should not try to stop others having it.

The more passionate the Torans became, the more sympathy they lost among the waverers. The liberal wrecking amendment—Damian did not feel bound by the archbishop's strictures to his bishops—was passed by a large majority:

> That this Synod instructs the House of Bishops to agree a process for dialogue with the Perpetuan movement as part of its mission to explore the realm of faith.

Griswald was furious. He had spent a considerable amount of his own money and some of that which he had received through Skraun and he had lost credibility.

"Never mind," said Dean Reggie. "It won't do any harm nor any good, for that matter. You made a mistake in not being nicer to people like me on the Petran wing, but it wouldn't have made any difference in the end. The Torans have got a near majority in the Synod, but they've also got a near monopoly of arrogance masquerading as sincerity."

"You should know," said Griswald, "having been among us when it suited you."

"True enough, Griswald, but although I pretended to be a Toran, I never pretended to be part of the Puritan Papacy, which is Fuller's mistake. It's a strange kind of Protestantism that promulgates dogma."

Griswald knew better than to go on. Crowther was at his very worst when he affected humour.

Sitting in the gallery, Cardinal Podric weighed the merits of the Synod and the Papacy. He supposed that the Holy Spirit could work through any agent she chose. If God could work through the Babylonians to punish Israel, then the Spirit could work through a tyrant, so there was nothing intrinsically problematic about the Spirit working through a Synod. However, he didn't like theology by majority vote and he hated to admit it, even to himself, but he didn't like the laity having the same voting power as the bishops and clergy. At least with the Papacy you knew where you were except, of course, that you were often where you didn't want to be. Look at the issue of child abuse. He felt in his bones that there was an indirect link between a celibate clergy and paedophilia in that any celibates remained so because they were incapable of adult relationships. He also thought that with an equality of women clergy none of this would have happened, and while there were some theological problems with women, there were none such with married priests. His mind came back to the matter in hand when the motion on dialogue with the Perpetuans was approved, as amended. At least they were sending it back to the bishops.

He was thinking of slipping out for a cup of tea and a sympathetic chat with some of his Petran friends, who were chronically pained by the issue of women priests and had suffered yet another reverse, when Clement greeted him quietly and asked whether he would mind joining the Archbishop for a few minutes.

"I know this is a bit tricky, Podric, but you and I worked on ARCIC long enough to be frank. Is there any chance that Pope Benedict will agree to take part in the dialogue with the Perpetuans?"

"I doubt it, James."

"I thought so. You won't mind my saying, Podric, that I sometimes get the impression that Rome is more comfortable talking to non-Christians than other Christians. I've just been reading a book by your Theological Adviser which says that salvation is for all humanity except, it seems, Christians who are not Roman Catholics."

"It's something I have to put up with more than you, James, so I'll go this far. I'll ask the said Theological Adviser to be an observer at your dialogue."

Clement took a note, smiled at James, and escorted Podric to the refreshment room where he found some ecumenical colleagues.

"We still have the problem, Archbishop, of deciding whether this Commission, which Damian got so nicely together, is ecumenical or inter-faith."

"Clement, you sometimes drive me almost mad."

"It isn't me, Archbishop, I'm just following the rules."

"But what's the point of being an Archbishop if you have to follow the rules."

"Because you're not the Pope, Archbishop. You've got the Synod and all the paraphernalia of an established Church. If I were you, I would bring the matter

before the House of Bishops and bring them round to thinking they want a colloquium rather than a Commission, then you can do what you like. There are
rules of representational balance for Commissions, but you can have anybody
you want on a colloquium. It's lower case, you see."

◆   ◆   ◆

Max was no longer puzzled by the god4u archive phenomenon. He knew
that they would soon have nothing left, but some pictures of Perpetua. She did
not want to leave any record behind of what she had said, but wanted them to
transmit it. She had started with the record of her own death, then the fire, and
now the leaching away of the records. They had even lost Hawthorne's theological draft and Hawthorne had said that the file in his computer had disappeared.
They could assemble the basic facts, but that was all. Then there was Gregg making all kinds of claims they could not refute with documentary evidence.

"That's the point," thought Max. "She doesn't want us to get into disputes with
documentary evidence. We will just have to keep the tradition alive in what we
say and what we do."

"I know," said Trina, looking over his shoulder at his notes, "We are living
under a requirement of terrible purity. We are being tested to see how far we
can live out what she said without resorting to structure and doctrine. Sooner
or later we, or our successors, will be forced towards both and this will be the
beginning of our decline and the beginning of the need for a fifth person, a
Third Incarnation. It will be a mark that we, like those who went before us, have
failed."

"Doesn't Incarnation get devalued if there's too much of it?"

"I don't think so. It may well be, for all we know, given the half a millennium
between the events and their committal to writing and the authorial agenda,
that Moses was incarnational. Samuel too, and maybe there was incarnation
before writing."

"But can you have incarnational events at ten-a-penny?"

"I'm not sure that the number matters, it's the nature of the event. I can understand that we as children of the Godhead are different from Jesus and Perpetua as children of the Godhead because of their creatorship and our creatureliness, but I'm not sure where that gets us. I can, however, see the argument
about doctrine and structure. Both become sclerotic when the world moves on.
You know the idea of Vico's that words change their meaning through time, and
we know they change their meaning according to place, the problem of Antioch
and Alexandria. Structures that mean something in one generation mean nothing in the next, but we hold onto them. Look at the strange words of the Nicene
creed or the College of Cardinals."

"This is all very well, but what are we going to do about Gregg?"

"Max, we've been there before. There's nothing we can do about Gregg and, anyway, he seems to have gone quiet."

"Funny. Annie Millman, as we must now learn to call her, said something about Gregg, blushed, clammed up, and hurriedly changed the subject. We know he went to the Caribbean because of those strange and rather disturbing miracle stories, but it would be very strange if his path crossed with Sir Pluto on his posh yacht."

"It makes no difference, Max. We just have to stay pure as long as we can. The one thing we can and must hang onto is Perpetuan Sacramentality. I've been thinking about it lately because Ignatius encouraged me to read some material on the early Christian Church. It seems to me that they got it wrong with the big Eucharist on Maundy Thursday, nothing very sacramental on Good Friday, and initiation and perhaps confirmation at the Easter Vigil. I mean, it seems to be the wrong way round. So I plan to do it this way on the first anniversary of Perpetua's death.

» On Thursday we can celebrate the Sacrament of Reception, remembering how Jesus washed the feet of his disciples and how Perpetua made a similar gesture; it means the key element will be water

» On Friday, we will celebrate the Sacrament of Response, emphasising our brokenness in the shadow of the Cross of Jesus and the Hollow of Perpetua; the key element will be fragments

» Then on Saturday we will be ready for Affirmation, to make our promises as to how we will direct our lives; th key element will be fire

» And on Easter Sunday we shall have the most joyful sacrament of all, that of Union, remembering the Resurrection of Jesus and the re-manifestation of Perpetua, the Sacrament at Emmaus and the first Sacrament of Union performed in triumph by Dexter; the key element will be things of the earth

"I don't want to cause unnecessary offence to Christians by doing it this way round, but it just makes more sense to me, particularly for the hundreds of people who have applied for Reception and also those who want to be Guides. So we want a large sacred space for four days, and that is difficult because the Christians will want all their spaces."

"Well no, they haven't retained all their large spaces. In the deal we made with Archbishop Varnish we took on some pretty big buildings that the Church of England didn't want. Still, what about Saint Simple's where her body was taken and from where that body was taken away. It's a huge Victorian church, as you will remember."

"Good, that will please Father Bill and Stacey particularly. We also need to have some kind of ceremony to remember Jim."

◆　◆　◆

On the Monday of Holy Week, Lord Warpley, Dean Crowther, and Horace Strider met for lunch in a private room at the Goring Hotel.

"You seem to have fallen on your feet, Horace, after that run-in with Sir Granville."

"It wasn't really a run-in. Looking back on it I can see that he fell on his sword to keep me afloat, if I can mix my metaphors, and although I didn't get his Secretary of State at Trade—I didn't expect to—the move in the Department was certainly upwards, with more duties and more patronage."

"None of which explains why you're here," said Reggie, wanting to get on.

"Oh, that's easy enough," said Horace. "We've finally run out of patience with the Perpetuan campaign to reduce individual consumption and although HMG can't be seen to do anything official about entities that class themselves as faith-based, anything we can do unofficially to clip Perpetuan wings will be helpful. It's a pity that this will mean inconveniencing my old friend Sir Pluto, but we'll just have to accept that as collateral damage."

"Oh, him!" barked Griswald. "A precious piece of humbug. Properties and interests all over the world and he's now gone pious. All very convenient when you've got as much money as he's got. I'd like to see him pious on £20,000 a year rather than £20 million."

"True," said Crowther "but he doesn't figure in our calculations, or does he?"

Griswald looked at his notes. "We'll see. Let's check where we have got to. Last time we were talking about the current education bill and whether we can alter the National Curriculum at the Report Stage in the Lords to enshrine orthodox Christian teaching and get rid of the rest. Well, unfortunately, we can't do that. It isn't the Human Rights Act or anything silly like that, it's hard politics. The other Christian denominations, particularly the Papists, would cause a fuss, and then there's the Moslems. We might be able to bash Christians, but we certainly can't bash Moslems. Christians are fair game, but Moslems present a sensitive issue. It's not that strange. It's well known in all spheres of corporate life that trouble makers get rewarded and those who quietly do their job get nothing. Instead of being more exacting since 9/11 and 7/7 we've gone all soft."

Even Crowther felt a little uncomfortable. "You don't say this sort of thing, do you, Griswald?"

"Only amongst very close friends, Reggie, don't worry. But there are a great many people who think this way who don't say anything. It's going to change, though. I think you'll find that in a few years there will be none of these offensive attacks on Christians for wearing crosses or bans on nativity plays. There is a new breed of Evangelical Christian militant in the Tory Party and there will soon be enough of them to exert pressure. Well, Horace, what have you come up with?"

"I'm not promising anything specific," said Horace, looking uncomfortable.

"Typical of you socialists," said Warpley, with a slight sneer.

"Careful," said Crowther. "We're all on the same side."

"I'll overlook that," said Horace, a little stiffly. "The reason I can't promise anything is that my proposal is somewhat tricky to turn into action, but I think it's worth considering. I think that there is enough support in the House for some kind of ban on sects, you know, like the Moonies, and it wouldn't be difficult to get Perpetuans scheduled. Catholics and Moslems might just go along with that, but you can't tell with Hall. Then—and this is more interesting—the recent raft of terrorist legislation leaves a lot of room for harassment, if you know the right people."

"I don't know," said Crowther. "If believing that there are four persons in the Godhead makes you a sect, are we going to pursue Unitarians?"

"Of course not," said Strider.. "You don't suppose, do you, that Government is consistent? Part of it is currently, as Griswald says, trying to assuage Muslims under the banner of 'Community Cohesion' while the security services and some police forces are giving them as much hell as they can. So if we had it in for the Perpetuans it wouldn't affect some much more eccentric Christian denominations. We just have to pick out Perpetuans and a couple of other fringe organisations and schedule them. Getting them declared a sect would be a good start, not so drastic as getting them to swear some kind of oath of loyalty, but strong enough to leave them out of public life. That is not so feeble as you might think. Most people hold their religion relatively lightly. If it's the choice between being a Christian and sitting on the local council and being a Perpetuan and virtually banned from doing so, most people will stay where they are. There are exceptions, but martyrs usually spill their blood in vain. Contrary to popular sentiment, repression works for extended periods."

Crowther was still looking uncomfortable. "But my Archbishop has just agreed to establish a colloquium with the Perpetuans."

"Look Reggie," said Griswald, "it's a well known fact that Archbishops are odd people who do precious little good or harm when left to themselves. People expect Christians, forgive me, Reggie, to have odd ideas about prisoners and refugees and all those kind of things."

Crowther knew that this was his moment either to pull out and report to Sutcliffe, or stay in to the end. He wanted to pull out, his experience told him to pull out, but he just didn't have the will power to do it, and—like a girl who doesn't want to get married, but doesn't have the nerve to say "no"—the moment passed.

"Are there any other measures?" asked Warpley.

"Well, we promised that, sooner or later, we would come to Sir Pluto," said Strider. "We can't, under freedom of trade, pan him for running his experiment at Hypo in reduced personal consumption, but we can try to alter the terms of trade in favour of his rivals, Jambo and Lakshmo, and we can rain all kinds of inspectoral inconveniences down upon his head."

"But that won't do unless he knows why," said Griswald, irritably.

"If I may," said Strider, again stiffening. "I can get that message across to him without getting us into trouble."

"Is that all?" asked Lord Warpley.

The other two stayed silent.

"Well then, to sum up. We can more or less outlaw these people which will keep them out of public office, out of the religious curriculum, and make a laughing stock of them. We can study ways of applying terrorist legislation to them, and we can give pious Pluto a hard time."

◆　◆　◆

The Holy Week and Easter celebrations at Saint Simple's were a source of great spiritual strength to the Perpetuan core group. Enmeshed in the daily problems of securing buildings, raising funds, puzzling over the disappearance of their archive, and worrying about Gregg, they had lost sight of what was happening on the ground. They had kept core meetings to a minimum and the leaders—they disliked the word, but could not think of anything better—had spent most of their time on the road. Kylie had done great work in Alchester and the South of England. Wayne had produced some excellent, new material and he and Joe—who had been made a Guide—were reaching out from Stumpy Knoll to the whole of the North. Stacey and Father Bill had taken responsibility for London. Cara was looking after all house groups. Brian was still at the god4u Network, but divided his time between that and the Midlands. Max was tireless, with Sneer and Smoother, who had formed an effective media partnership. Trina, occasionally subject to doubts about her competence, was planning visits to Scotland and Wales.

On Maundy Thursday almost 500 people who had never been baptised Christians were admitted to the movement by the Sacrament of Reception. Trina, in memory of Jesus, washed the feet of those who were about to be admitted and, in memory of Perpetua, cleaned the shoes of those already part of the movement. On Good Friday more than 700 crammed into the church for the Sacrament of response, acknowledging their brokenness. There was the customary "creeping to the Cross", but the cross was made of the fragments that people had brought as offerings of their own brokenness and it was followed by a second procession as people took different fragments away. Trina preached on the parallels between the deaths of Jesus and Perpetua, and Bill said the Solemn Prayers. At the end, people in small groups went into the vestry to pray at the spot where Perpetua's body had been lain. On Saturday there was an outside celebration of of Sacrament of Affirmation in which each person wrote down their commitment and placed it on the altar. While prayers were said, the commitments were sorted by Cara and the results announced to give people an idea of the range. There were new Guides, engagements, volunteers, philanthropic commitments, and promises of better behaviour. The highlights were the commitments of Wayne and Joe, and Q and Poppy to each other. Then the crowd, after praying at the lighting of the new fire, went into the dark church where the Easter candle was lit and the Resurrection of Christ was proclaimed. The customary readings and Psalms were completed by some words of Perpetua and a newly-written quasi-psalm. Father Bill presided at the Eucharist and Trina preached on the Resurrection of Jesus and Perpetua's re-manifestation just a year ago. Again, as they left, people went into the vestry to pray at the spot where Perpetua had risen.

"I suppose," said Father Bill, "that we will have to re-order the church so that the spot where Perpetua was lain and from where she was taken up becomes the focal point."

"I don't know," said Stacey. "She might not want to take the focus off Jesus her brother. We will have to work this out."

On Sunday morning the church was at the centre of a sea of people served by large screens. There was a truly joyful celebration of the Sacrament of Union where Trina and all the core group concelebrated, with Father Bill preaching the sermon on new life. It was the most joyful day since that Sunday a year ago when Perpetua had appeared to the world.

◆   ◆   ◆

When Dolorez opened the door to prepare breakfast in the front yard, she found what looked like a corpse on the door-step. It was a man, scruffily dressed, with the shallow sun-tan of a holiday maker. When she came closer and knelt down, she found that he was breathing unevenly. Careful not to touch him, she went unhurriedly back into the house. She did not call Myron, but allowed him to dress at his usual speed before reading his Bible and saying his morning prayers. On her way to and from the breakfast table in the bower she checked that the man's position had not changed. It never crossed her mind to ring the emergency services. This was, first of all, a family affair. Myron would know what to do.

"Myron, I had rather a shock when I opened the door this morning. There was a man slumped next to the steps."

Myron barely reacted. He loved the story of the Good Samaritan, but he didn't want to be in it. Neither, as Dolorez had guessed, did he want to involve the emergency services. The man was too heavy for the two of them to move him but, as he was in the shade and still breathing, Myron phoned his family physician.

"Injury on the back of the head a couple of days old. Drugged!"

"Will he need to be hospitalised?"

"He should be, to be on the safe side."

"Somewhere very, very private."

Gregg woke up in the late afternoon. He could see the sunlight at the edge of the window blinds. He had a terrible headache and felt woolly, but that part of him which meticulously assessed his situation did not let him down. The blinds were different, the walls were meticulously painted, and there was a picture on the opposite wall that must be something from the Bible. The bed linen was spotless. Except for a bottle of water and a glass on his bedside table, the room was bare, like a prison cell. He could not see his clothes. He must be in a high class, high security prison. If that were so, there was no point doing anything until he had got some more sleep.

He woke again, he guessed, the next morning. The water had been changed and there was a note under the glass which told him to press the button behind his head for attention. His head ached and he still felt fuzzy, but he also felt hungry. He had nothing to lose. He rang the bell.

A smocked nurse appeared. "Good morning, sir, what can I do for you?"

"Where am I?"

"I have been advised not to disclose any information of that nature, sir. Is there anything I can do for you?"

"I think I need to see a doctor."

Without saying anything else, she disappeared and a few minutes later a doctor came in.

"Where am I?"

"We can come to that later."

"Is this a prison?"

"Good Lord, no. It's a Christian medical facility."

"Where?"

"Well, I think I can go as far as to say that you are in the United States of America."

"But I was in Barbados."

"Is that a fact?"

He considered. Was that a fact? Which bit of him was fact and which bit of him was dream? He had been in Barbados, for weeks on end. Then? He decided to leave it for a while.

"What's wrong with me?"

"I think you can tell me that."

"I've got a headache and I feel fuzzy."

"We can deal with the first but will have to investigate the second. Are you hungry?"

"Yes."

"OK, we'll deal with that and the headache first, and then we can see where to go next."

As he ate a breakfast of fresh orange juice, fresh fruit salad, freshly baked bread, and coffee, Gregg tried to assess his situation. He had been in Barbados; he was sure of that now. The memory of the girl on the beach could have been a recurring dream, but something about the quality of the flesh beneath his hands convinced him that that had not been a dream. He had been told that he was in the United States and although he had no evidence for that, the nurse and doctor were white and they and the room were spotless. He turned his plate upside down; Taiwan. He thought of getting out of bed to have a look in the drawers, but he didn't bother because he knew they would be empty.

The doctor returned with a sleek, grey-haired man.

"Now then, how did you get that blow on the back of your head?"

Gregg had already decided not to say.

"I don't remember."

"And how," said the grey haired man, "did you end up on my front steps?"

"I don't know."

"I think," said the doctor, "that we better take a look before we go any further with the interview."

After the examination the nurse took blood samples and he was instructed to provide a urine sample. Around lunch time the two men came back.

"As far as we can tell, Mr Brewer, you were hit on the back of the head, maybe three days ago, and heavily sedated." Gregg adjusted to being Mr Brewer, but wondered what his Christian name was.

"You arrived on my front steps like a man off the streets except that you had an American passport, which isn't all that usual. I mean to say, most people don't carry their passports around, and this one has the most curious selection of stamps, the last one being Ecuador, a very picturesque country."

"Oh yes, very. The turtles."

"Quite."

This was going nowhere which, from Gregg's perspective, was helpful because it gave him the chance to pick up scraps of information. He had been hit over the head and sedated, brought to the United States and given a false passport. He wondered who had the real one. It must be someone from Langley. He wondered whether Sir Pluto was, improbably, tied up with Langley but, then, Sir Pluto was probably tied up with almost everything.

"So here we are," said the grey haired man, "with a stranger, recently arrived from Ecuador, with no money and no luggage. What are we to do with him?"

"That depends on where he is," snapped Gregg, one side of him getting tired of the game that the other side still wanted to play.

"I think we can go so far as to say, Mr Brewer, that you are in a Christian medical facility in Miami."

That figured. From Barbados to Miami in life, from Ecuador to Miami in his passport. Well, at least he was in the United States, but he supposed that somebody knew where he was. He would have to wait.

Myron got up from his chair at the side of the bed and went down to Gregg's feet and stared at him, full on.

"You wouldn't be Gregg Brewer, by any chance, would you? I only saw a rather blurred picture on the internet, taken by a mobile phone in bad light, but the resemblance is striking."

Here was a dilemma. He could say "yes" to Gregg but "no" to Brewer.

"It's a puzzle because the internet only ever uses the name Gregg and never gives him a surname; and your passport says you are Jefferson Prevett Brewer, and you can't get Gregg out of that.."

Gregg gave nothing away as the key data was transmitted. Prevett had been his controller during operations in Syria.

"An unusual name, Prevett."

Gregg waited.

"In fact I've never heard it before. So, Mr Jefferson Prevett Brewer, what are we to do with you? Once you are better, of course. I do not wish to be unkind, Mr Brewer, but it is such a pity that you are not Gregg. I have a very great interest in him."

The doctor returned once he had, apparently, escorted the grey haired man off the premises.

"Who is that?"

"Oh, I think I might be allowed to tell you that that is Myron T. Skraun Jr, noted preacher and philanthropist of the Coral Gables Church of Christ and your Good Samaritan."

"So when can I get out of here?"

"To be honest, it is not that simple. Here we have a body, supposedly dead, on the steps of a private house, bearing wounds and evidence of sedation, carrying a mysterious passport but no driving licence, and, you know what, nobody in the whole of Miami is looking for him. He might as well not have disappeared at all. Our contacts in the outreach projects have talked to the people of the streets and they do not recognise the name or the picture. He carries no money and no receipts, which makes it unlikely that he came here from another city where he might be missed. The question which my esteemed patron asks is, is this man an asset or a liability. This may, you feel, be a somewhat harsh, even two-dimensional way of looking at things, but if we hand you over to the police or just let you out into the street, you might say any number of things which bring your erstwhile Samaritan into disrepute. My patron is, quite properly, very careful. However, let us not be too gloomy. Although your sedation was extremely, I might say near fatally, heavy, it is wearing off nicely and your skull is undamaged. You should eat a modest lunch and then I think you should see if you can walk around for a few minutes."

The nurse brought him a chicken salad, a bottle of apple juice, underwear, and a track suit. He dressed before eating and then waited to be escorted on his walk, but nothing happened, so he carefully opened the door. It might as well have been a prison. His door was the only one in the short corridor which led to a small courtyard surrounded by high walls. He sat on the stone bench next to a melancholy fountain and longed for a cigarette and a drink. The nurse came out of the only other door in the courtyard.

"Enjoying the afternoon air?"

"It is somewhat confined," said Gregg, trawling for polite language.

"Yes, but our most exclusive patients value the privacy. You look a little anxious."

"I need a smoke and a drink."

"Oh dear! Not the kind of, er, pleasures we usually allow here, but the doctor has advised me to be lenient, as you are in such a private place, so I can find you a cold beer and a packet of cigarettes."

Gregg was grateful. Myron knew he would be.

Myron had not told the doctor anything more than was necessary. Discretion with respect to the mysterious patient and appointment to a more senior position were never discussed in terms of a bargain. Myron had briefed the nurse while the doctor was examining Gregg. He had time on his side, and he needed it because extensive genealogical searches found no Prevetts. He was also studying the fuzzy old and the sharp new pictures he had of the man and he was becoming ever more convinced that he was Gregg. Had a miracle worker really fallen into his hands? At what risk? Myron was a cautious man who wished he was courageous and, indeed, as a boy he had shown a high degree of initiative and bravery but over time he had become cautious for Christ. His problem now was that there was no way of being cautious. He could not imprison the man, but letting him loose could be a risk. He had a few days before the excuse of illness would wither.

Gregg told the nurse that he was tired of wearing a track suit which was nice in its way, but was the equivalent of prison clothes. He asked for his own clothes which had been removed on his arrival at the hospital, or whatever it was. Satisfied that no harm could be done, he was given the clothes which had been folded neatly. He minutely examined the shoes and socks, the underwear, jeans, and t-shirt. Then he took up the jacket and felt the inside lining. There was an anomaly with the lining. He removed what was obviously temporary stitching and his black speedos fell out. Between the two layers of the front panel there was a folded scrap of paper: "3 strikes—Pluto".

◆　　◆　　◆

Myron talked to his contact in Homeland Security.

"We don't know anything about a Jefferson Prevett Brewer but we can confirm that his passport is a forgery and that he is almost certainly your Gregg."

"Odd," said Myron. "You would have thought that such a rare name as Prevett would be easy to trace."

The voice at the other end did not react, but said, "his behaviour in recent times has been decidedly unstable. In fact we think he's dangerous, but we have nothing we can nail him with. If I were you, I would lose him as quickly as you can."

"But he might keep on coming back for money."

"Well, the more you give him, the longer he may stay away; or the more you give him, the more often he may wish to return. Please don't contact me on this again. Two calls constitutes a cluster, three's a trend."

The contact rang off and put through a call to Langley. "Prevett! Gregg is in a medical facility in Miami whose patron is the man whose steps he was dumped on. Was that deliberate?"

"No, he just needed to be in the shade and out of sight of the street where he would be discovered well in time for his life to be saved. He's trouble, but we don't dispose of old friends unless we really have to."

"But he's dangerous."

"So are a lot of people, but the main point from our perspective is that he won't give his background away, so we are in the clear."

Myron's agony had intensified. He was in possession of a dangerous miracle worker. Ambition and caution warred within him but his hand was forced when Dolorez came into his study quietly and closed the door.

"Myron, you remember that real estate that the Church invested in to provide social housing? Well, there has been a collective default. It started with one person who talked to the others and they've all disappeared."

"Well, it's a setback, but we will find replacements."

"You might find the people, but that is not the point. We under-wrote the loans, taking our cut every time an instalment was paid. Now they have gone, we are liable for the loans and we don't collect. Worse, any new loan would charge such a high rate of interest that none of our kind of people could afford to borrow. I don't understand economics, but there's something sick in the realty market."

The Church investments had been made on Myron's sole signature. He was so certain that he could do well by appearing to do good. He dare not tell anyone. Dolorez, watching him closely, saw all the options pass across his face, from disgrace to rectification.

"Myron, until now you've not really treated me as your wife. I understand. we both, implicitly, understand the contract we made. I might be your wife in name, but I'm your mistress and servant in fact. I accept that, Myron, it was the best I could ever hope for and you have been good for me, but I think that from now on you will have to treat me as your wife because you have nobody else to turn to. Ideally, the wife should be first, but I don't mind being last. Just tell me the story."

He only hesitated for a moment before seeing the good sense of what she said.

When he had finished she said, "Whether you tell the Elders is your choice. I would, but I know you won't. That leaves you with this Gregg. we will visit him so that I can see what kind of danger he is."

"I don't want to put you at risk."

"You won't, but if he is dangerous then two pairs of eyes and the panic routine are useful."

"I want to start by telling you," said Myron, "that I know you are the Gregg that was in the Caribbean. I don't know anything about Ecuador, but that's a red herring. I've matched your picture and unless you've got an identical twin who wears the same t-shirt as you, then You're Gregg."

"So?"

"Well, it's like this, Gregg. I saved your life."

"How do you know that I wanted it saving?"

"Well, you've shown no signs of wanting to die since you came. So you owe me a favour and, as it happens, you can repay me and I will keep quiet about what I know."

"Blackmail."

"How unpleasant you are. Not at all grateful. You don't seem to recognise the position you're in."

"And you don't recognise the position I'm in. If I can get out of here I will sue you for kidnap."

"We will all enjoy learning more about you in court, but it need not go that far. The doctors here are very good, but even they make mistakes."

Gregg looked angry and his face betrayed a slight spasm which all his self-control could not quite suppress. "Threats as well as blackmail!"

"Come, come, Gregg. We both hold mixed hands. Let us play! Ha ha!"

Dolorez watched, just out of his eye line.

"This isn't helpful," said Myron, "so let's do as I say and play some cards. We need each other. You need some way of building your life again. I don't know if you have any savings, but I doubt you could get your hands on your own money simply by producing a passport which is, in all likelihood, suspect and on a black list."

The suspicion of a spasm again.

"I have reason to believe that you have skills that I need."

Gregg now looked genuinely puzzled.

"Miracles!" said Myron, unable to moderate his desire, as a negotiating tactic.

Gregg looked shocked.

"I've read the reports and we need some miracles round here," Myron said, without intending irony. "Our religious life is a little flat at the moment."

"And the donations," he thought.

"So some healing would come in very handy."

"I suppose your church is Christian, but I'm a Perpetuan."

"I don't think folks mind what you are if they get healed. They can be awful shallow. Look, don't get mad at me. Sit down and write me a letter. Tell me what's different between Christianity and Perpetuanism and we can talk again. What really matters here is that we get some healing done."

Gregg was still frightened of his healing experiences because it was these that had temporarily de-stabilised him.

"I will bring you some coffee, and later on you can have a beer and a cigarette," said Dolorez, trying to look sly.

Without thinking about it, Myron went to his study and Dolorez brought

Gregg's coffee. As soon as they were alone, she knew everything she needed to know as he fixed his eyes on her and began to tense. Unhurriedly, giving nothing away, she put the coffee on a small table inside the door and left.

"He's got some compulsive disorder," she said to Myron. "I think they call it psychotic. He'll either rape or murder someone, or both."

Myron should have been shocked, but for the first time since he began his mission for Christ, he felt excited.

◆ ◆ ◆

GREGG TO THE WORLD—BLOG THREE

Fellow Perpetuans,

1. Cynics, wreckers, atheists, and those with sectarian interests are trying to throttle Perpetuanism at its birth by claiming that there is no difference between Perpetuanism and Christianity. The difference is profound, but that does not mean that we do not value Christianity for it was the fertile ground out of which it was possible for us, in the Spirit, to discern the incarnational status of Perpetua, stamped in identical typology to Jesus. Nonetheless, the differences are so important that they must be clearly understood from the start so that we may strengthen ourselves for the struggle against our assailants.

2. It is obvious that the primary difference is that we believe Perpetua to be an incarnational manifestation of the Godhead but I do not want you to be entangled in dogmatic complexities. What matters is the difference in the way we lead our lives. A few Christians in various places, notably in the United States, have set high standards for the way in which Christians should live but the overwhelming majority of Christian leaders have failed us: Christianity's centre is soft and liberal, caving in to the pressure of secularism, conceding that their commitment has nothing to do with legislation. The Popes, from whom we have the right to expect so much, may hold the correct views, but their inability to communicate convincingly has been a disaster and now there is growing evidence of clerical child abuse which is spreading like an oil slick across the Holy Sea.

3. It has been said that Perpetua preached a gospel of total freedom, of moral relativism. It has been claimed that she was an ultra liberal. These claims are pernicious. Perpetua believed above all in individual moral responsibility, but she also recognised the reality of human weakness. Indeed, she said that imperfection is intrinsic to our condition of choosing, but if she had meant to leave such hazardous choice to individuals she would not have established a new institution to promote her teaching and bear witness to her life, death, and re-manifestation. There are those who say

that what she left was a core group in London, but I am as much an Apostle as they. Perpetua said that it was not for an institution to claim that it could second guess the Spirit, that people would know when they have a vocation, and I have been called, called to lead Perpetuans to their true witness.

4. To those who say that I am not what I say I am, I must point out that I have performed miracles in the name of Perpetua's almighty power. Christianity has grown bland with its weak prayers and healing services, but what Perpetua offers is a vibrant church of morality and miracles. Those who want firm leadership, and those who need their faith strengthened and their minds and bodies restored through Perpetua's power, shall not be disappointed. Those who are Christians, even if they have denied God's healing power and moral force, will be in a better position than the unchurched to understand what is being offered, but the offer is open to all.

5. There will be no healing without the moral force. Liberals argue that Christianity has no judgmental element, but it claims to accept the Old Testament as part of its Scriptures. As such, it must accept that God is our judge and that, even though justice will be tempered with mercy, that does not mean that there will be no justice. If mercy meant withholding God's wrath from all sinners, where would justice be? What would be the point of it? If some Christians are sinfully equivocal about the Old Testament, look to Jesus. Again, liberals argue that Jesus is non-judgmental, but that ignores the depiction of the last judgment and the separation of the sheep from the goats. Look at the story of the rich man and Lazarus. Look at the eye of the needle. To claim that Jesus did not promise eternal damnation is to traduce his message. Look at the punishment that Peter meted out to Ananias and Sapphira. Look at the warnings of Paul about such matters as homosexuality (I refuse to use the preposterous word "gay") and Lesbianism. Even the gentler James warns us. Because Christianity has forgotten these lessons with, as I say, some exceptions, the Godhead has withdrawn its healing power from what was Christ's church. Christianity, except for the few elect, has lost its claim to be the perpetuator of God's Word on earth. That torch has been picked up by Perpetua.

6. I therefore call upon the elect, upon Christians who are strictly orthodox in their beliefs and in their lifestyles, to join with the new star of Perpetua to establish God's kingdom on earth. We should not assume that, no matter what factors are in their favour, all Christians should comfortably assume the Perpetuan mantle. We will have to deal with many Christians in the way that we deal with the un-churched because they have travelled so far from where they need to be. If the elect of Christ and the elect of Perpetua join together, then God's healing powers will be set free in the Spirit, acting through God's holy ministers.

7. We must therefore re-align the forces of God, taking advantage of the new vigour injected into man's spiritual ecology by by the life, witness, death,

and re-manifestation of Perpetua. We shall know how well we are doing by the salience of God's mighty power working among us. The presence of the miraculous will be our index. Throughout Scripture, it is easy to see that God's mighty power operates in direct proportion to the faithfulness of mankind. When the Chosen People turned away from God, they were defeated, but when they believed in his word, they were victorious. Naturally, as Jesus brought God's word to the people and they expressed their faith to his face, God's powers worked through him. It is also the case that the Apostles performed wondrous acts. As the Word of God was brought to all kinds of places, new faith was rewarded with miracles, from Ireland to China new faith brought new physical as well as spiritual life. Naturally, as there has been a falling away, God's healing powers have been withdrawn. Miracles are an exception in our time; even the superstitious activities of Rome in conjuring saints has come up against a scarcity of miracles.

8. I should, however, warn against false ministers. It will be easy for people to pretend that they are Perpetuans, claiming miraculous powers. Remember the scandal in England of Fidel. We must be on our guard so that only those who are genuine are allowed to serve. This is why the London Perpetuans have let us down. They are too relaxed. They are happy to appoint what they call Guides who are, in effect, old fashioned priest/administrators. They seem oblivious to the need to vet those who will exercise mighty powers. We know that some of them have exercised such powers, but unless they steel themselves to their responsibilities, those powers will wane. I therefore call upon the elite in London to take up their responsibilities to set up a system which authorises God's true ministers to teach and heal. If that does not take place, then other apostles of Perpetua will need to take up the challenge. We cannot wait. The whole of the world lies before us.

9. You may ask why I am not publicly working towards this end. The sad answer is that I have been a prisoner of the London elite. My steps have been dogged by spies and guards sent out by Max and his London henchmen. I will prosecute what I advocate as soon as I can break free from my current imprisonment.

10. I am not discouraged. I know that with God's help I will overcome the constraints from which I suffer. I am prepared for the fight.

◆　◆　◆

Myron was so overcome by the theology of miracles that he scarcely looked at the closing paragraphs. He was blown away by the possibility of controlling this extraordinary man whom God had placed in his hands. He recognised himself as one of the Christian elect, called upon to ally with orthodox Perpetuans who would, together, exercise such healing power (and therefore psychological and financial power) that the world would marvel at their achievements.

The question was, how should he handle this spiritual dynamite? He looked across at Gregg who was tightly controlling himself while Myron read on, ever more rapidly, ever more excited, until he skimmed the last page. Gregg regretted the final two paragraphs because he thought that Myron might veto sending the letter, but once he saw that Myron's mind was focused entirely on miracles, his priority was to get the message out. He waited for Myron to speak first.

"I believe that we have an understanding. You and I can form a partnership to change the world through miraculous powers. I understand that you have such powers and I expect to acquire them in recognition of my position as one of the Elect."

Gregg considered and saw that he had the stronger hand.. "As you say, Brother Myron, I have miraculous powers which I can impart to you. As a good Perpetuan I do not want to impose any conditions—God chooses whom God chooses—but my status must be changed. I need access to communications and I need to plan my work in freedom."

Myron saw the sense of this, but he did not want to lose his grip Gregg might disappear. Gregg had no intention of disappearing. He needed Myron's money and influence. He understood Myron's insecurities. He also understood that there might be a crisis if he could not transfer his powers, but he would have to deal with that if it arose. In the meantime, he confirmed the fiction that he still required medical surveillance and was supplied with a laptop. Later that day, reading more at leisure, he was sorry about Gregg's final remarks, but he could overlook them. The blame was with London, not himself, and he still had the miracle man!

◆　◆　◆

Max looked gloomily at the print-out.

"So, Pluto, what do you know?"

"Well, Max, you might think that I went beyond what you, as a purist, might have done, but I three times saved Gregg from disasters of various sorts. He was in danger of being harmed for his activities, but we also saved him from damaging other people."

"We?"

"I have contacts in many places Max, some of them connected with Gregg, but I would rather not go there."

"Fair enough, but where did you leave him? Where is he?"

"I agreed with his friends that we would get him out of harm's way, out of the Caribbean. They said they would deposit him in a safe place and I gather that their intention was to deposit him at a medical facility. In North America."

"Oh no, Pluto! Perhaps I should not say this, but I did not mind him so much while he worked in the relative obscurity of the Caribbean, but I hoped that we would have a clear run in the USA and Canada. Let me call Trina."

"It seems to me," said Trina, "that while we want to broaden and deepen the spiritual life of Christians and while we need them working with us to expand the house group movement, we do not wish to be entangled in Christian factionalism. Gregg might take sides with Baptists and other Torans, but Christianity will be increasingly difficult territory for us as it becomes more politicised over the Perpetuan issue. Let us see how our message is accepted at London Minster."

◆　◆　◆

Dean Crowther was a champion choreographer. Where cunning could be combined with elegance, he was supreme. Not for him the messy compromise of retro-engineering bolt-ons. If he was to practice a deception he would plan it from the beginning; not otherwise could a work of art be executed. His plan on this occasion was to invite the Perpetuans to the Minster and to ambush them so effectively that they would abandon the attempt to subvert the Church of England.

He found that his artistry was wasted on the key figures in the movement. They took no persuading. It was they who pointed out to him that they might be entrapped but, they said, it was up to their Sister the Spirit to guide them. They actually needed to know whether they should continue to spread the word among Christians or whether they should go to the unchurched. Their dilemma was acute because they did not want to cause the kind of rift that had been fatally opened between Jews and Christians, but if that was the will of their Sister, they would have to comply.

On the "Low" Sunday after Easter a large crowd gathered to hear what Trina had to say. She was nervous and had made many drafts of her speech until Max reminded her that she was better to leave matters to the Spirit who would speak through her. Dean Crowther, who had his pick of the Church's finest theologians, had opted for the polemic over the academic.

"Many of you will have heard what I have said before but it is important to state the obvious, to remind ourselves, particularly in view of recent communications from Gregg—which I am not going to meet in a series of confrontational rebuttals—about what Perpetuanism is all about.

"Let me start with the fundamental point which will cause trouble to most Christians. We believe that Perpetua is the fourth person of the Godhead, as much God as Jesus Christ. Next, we believe, like Christians, that we were created in love to love God and each other. Unlike Christians, our understanding of love is distinct from the Christian concept which we would call care. Love is the facility to the beloved of unconditional space. Christians might call it humility. It is a facility totally apart from morality. Thirdly, like Christians we believe in the individual imperative to choose to love God and each other because that is the essence of our creatureliness. Such a choice is impossible, without imperfection, but, unlike Christians, we believe that intrinsic perfection as part of our creatureliness is a good thing for which we will not be punished.

"Finally, therefore, we believe that all humanity will be enfolded back into the Godhead's perfect love, without exception. God cannot create out of love members of humanity who fail. This is our good news which is so great that we must see that all humanity learns it, making their lives on earth more meaningful and infinitely more hopeful."

People listened in silence but, at the end, there was an almost imperceptibly low, menacing roar. Dean Prior looked pointedly at Dean Crowther and saw his barely disguised malicious smile.

"But who are you," asked the first questioner, "a motley band of shelf stackers from Hypo, to presume to define the Godhead?"

"And who are the great leaders of the Christian Church to tell God that only three 'persons' are allowed? Having answered briefly, however, I came for a friendly dialogue, but your tone leads me to think that I am in hostile company."

"Frightened?" asked Crowther, taking a roving microphone.

"No, I am not frightened, but we believe, as I thought Christians believe, that you do not bring people to a faith in the Godhead through intellectual argument and certainly not through brow-beating."

"So you don't believe in reason?"

"I do believe in reason but, again, in line with Christianity, it is a servant of faith. We bring the Word of God to people and we provide them with material for thought consonant with their capacity to absorb it, but let us not think for a moment that we effect the 'conversion', that is the work of My Sister the Spirit."

"What a silly phrase that is. Why can't you stick to the usual terms?"

"You know why not. The Godhead has no human gender, nor the Spirit. I use the female gender to describe the Spirit because it has good Jewish roots and to jolt people into thinking."

"Jolt! Isn't it all show? Wasn't Perpetua just a self-appointed B-List celeb?"

"She believed and we believe that she was not self-appointed. The argument you deploy is that which the religious authorities deployed against Jesus. I want to ask a question in a totally non-aggressive way, not to question your integrity, but to learn and understand. How do you account for the decline of the potency of Christianity in Western Europe and, to a certain extent, even in the United States?"

Crowther kept the microphone. "Because it has been subverted by liberal materialism with which you apparently collude. You don't say, like Jesus, give all you have to the poor. You seem to belittle what you call 'care' and we call love.

Instead you offer something, literally vacuous, called space. It is these sort of ideas, that say that religion is easy, that have seduced so many liberals."

"I believe," replied Trina, still very calm, "that to provide unconditional space is far more difficult than either to impose a moral code or to provide care which can never fully escape from the power relationship."

"That is an insult to us all," said Lord Warpley, who could contain himself no longer. Crowther moved over to sooth him. He did not want his choreography ruined by an ill conceived, too obviously aggressive, intervention.

"Let us be civil," said Reggie. "Let us consider these claims carefully. Is it not true that what we have to rely on, apart from what she said herself, are a few technology tricks and a bit of healing?"

"We have never understood, nor tried to, the technology incidents involving Perpetua but, contrary to what Gregg says—and it is the only time I will mention his arguments directly—Perpetua only invoked the power of the Godhead to put things right so that people could start again. It was a precondition, not a substitute, for self-determination. We do not believe that there is a correlation between miracles and the presence of God. If anything, we think something like the opposite, that mighty acts, as Gregg calls them, might be needed to right the situation enough to allow a new relationship with God."

"You keep talking glibly about relationship with God."

"I hope I am not talking glibly, but I am talking in the context of a mystery."

"Good get-out," shouted Griswald. "All that Papist rubbish about mystery!"

"It does not seem appropriate to me that you should charge me with being anti-Christian when you have just attacked one of its principal leaders."

"What we want is orthodox Christianity, and nothing else," bawled Lord Warpley.

There was a certain amount of hubbub during which Dean Simon Prior of Alchester, Perpetuanism's first senior Church of England adherent, escorted Trina from the pulpit. They walked slowly, as the noise died away, down the central aisle of London Minster, without looking to right or left, and quit the building.

Dean Crowther was not sure whether he had achieved his objective and he was furious that Griswald had stolen and then wrecked the show.

◆　◆　◆

After a hurried meeting, Sneer booked a round of television interviews for Trina and issued a statement.

> The Perpetuan movement has made every effort to establish cordial relations with the Christian churches. We were pleased with the agreement reached over the best use of church buildings and we welcomed the call by Archbishop Hall for a colloquium.
>
> Perpetuan leader Trina, commenting on today's discussion at London

Minster said, "earlier today I was subjected to insulting remarks. I am not thin-skinned, not least because I speak in the power of My Sister the Spirit, and so we are not changing our stance for personal reasons.

"For some time," she continued, "we have been discussing the perils of dialogue deteriorating into confrontation, and so we have agreed to focus on the un-churched. We look forward to the colloquium and, in anticipation of media speculation, we will not set any preconditions, but we will not subject ourselves to ambushes. Perpetuans welcome dialogue with all people."

On balance, Crowther was pleased with his work as the first editions appeared on newspaper websites, but he was stunned the next morning to find that the story had completely changed. Ranjit in *Humanity* was a fair representative of the coverage.

GOD4U TURN

In a remarkable u-turn late last night, Trina, the head of the Perpetuan movement, admitted that she had been wrong to allow herself to be escorted out of a theological debate at London Minster when she was faced with some hostile comments.

"It just shows how difficult it is," she said, "to live the love which Perpetua taught. Instead of accepting what was going on I reacted negatively, making my love conditional."

Critics were divided last night as to whether the apology would weaken or strengthen her position, but she said, "that's a question about power and politics. I've done the right thing."

In tactical terms, Trina had played into Dean Crowther's hands, for although the media are always asking leading figures to apologise for their mistakes so that the slate is wiped clean, once the apology is made the celebrity is slaughtered not just for being in error, but for being weak. Trina was therefore attacked relentlessly by the press and 7/24 news channels. Viewed as a political vignette, it was classic disaster but viewed as a piece of religious example it was powerful. It gave ammunition to her enemies and encouragement to those who would be her friends.

Sneer tried to come to terms with the humble u-turn, but in spite of Smoother's best efforts he could only see it from an intellectual, abstract standpoint. He thought they had made a bad mistake.

Encouraged by his success, Crowther took up a more aggressive position, openly claiming the leadership of the anti-Perpetuan forces. He might have held back, to be on the safe side, but he could not bear the thought of Griswald taking control. Strider was content to let him get on with it as the economic storm clouds gathered. It was no longer a matter of whether the world economy would implode, but when. Beside that, the Perpetuan question was trivial but, still, he said he would continue to be supportive. Politicians find it much easier to plunge their fingers into pies than to take them out again. The education proposal was gaining ground again, the idea of out-lawing sects had been taken up enthusiastically by the Conservative "right", and Sir Pluto's experiment in voluntary cuts in consumption would be smashed by the economic down-turn when it came.

Crowther was therefore in high spirits when he came across Max in the atrium of a City office block.

"Hard times," said Crowther in a way that might have referred to anything, including Trina's humiliation and the state of pension funds.

"True enough," said Max. "Looked at from one perspective, times are always hard: always hard for the poor, always hard for the power hungry, always hard for the innovator."

"That's a strange trio."

"Well, the point about the poor is easy enough. I was only thinking about it because of where we are standing. When this lot crashes, as it surely will, there will be outrage at the sight of unemployed bank executives, but within a year they will all have jobs. Failed regulators will become bankers and failed bankers will become regulators and both will presume to tell elected politicians what to do, but the poor will be poor. Bankers will go on receiving bonuses, but poor office workers and office cleaners will be thrown out. When the depression really bites, politicians won't have the courage to raise income tax. They will raise sales taxes which disproportionately hurt the poor. Whatever goes wrong, the poor will pay, with their hard-fought little nest-eggs, with their pension pots, with their working hours. When Southern Gem is nothing but a tiny firecracker in an atomic explosion, this place will stand while the houses of the poor collapse. Sorry, but you did ask about the trio.

"The other two are much easier, Dean crowther. It's hard to be powerful because you can never get enough. It's as bad an addiction as heroin. As for the third, it's hard for innovators because we look at the present in terms of the past rather than the future. I say these two things just to let you know that although we admit to the hardship we are not down-hearted. We recognise that last Sunday's occasion in London Minster was a power play. Don't look like that, Dean, I would never say it except between ourselves just so that you know that I know. There is one last thing—and I say this as a banker—destruction doesn't pay half so well as growing your own brand. If you manage to wreck Perpetuanism— which you won't—it will not be of the slightest long-term benefit to Christianity. Do you think that if you manage to recruit from our wreckage that this will give you new vigour? If you crush us it will give you more status and perhaps even more power, but how Christian is that?"

Crowther was about to break into a tirade when Max bowed slightly and stepped into a lift whose doors closed before he could say anything.

"I should not have done that," said Max to himself, "but it was more for his good than my pleasure, honest, Max, it was."

He got out on the top floor and was greeted by Annie. "Not the usual lovely view of the river which Sir Pluto so enjoyed," said Max.

"No," said Annie, "but we didn't come here for the view."

"I don't know why we came here. Sir Pluto's message was enigmatic."

He was ushered into a room full of computers and large screens. There were a couple of dozen people, mostly men, drinking coffee.

Sir Pluto said, "I have been doing some research, Max, and have found out that this is the room where Perpetua brought some of her followers to witness what we might call a technological transfiguration. I thought this would there-fore be a good venue to launch The City for God. As you know, I am not quite attached to Perpetuanism, but I see its merits and I have one short-term and one long-term aim. In the short-term we need to protect Perpetuanism from attack. I know, Max, you are not in favour of combat, that is why I said 'protect'. We will try to halt legislative and other attempts to hobble Perpetuanism. We already know of the plans of Strider at trade to attack our experiments in volun-tary consumption cuts, and we know that there are other moves in education. I know, Max, don't look at me like that. It is not my purpose to be aggressive, but listen to the end, my friend.

"When the economic down-turn comes—it might be the shape of a helter skelter or a ski jump, we don't know yet—we will need to be useful to the poor, not only practically, but also at the theological—if I might call it that—level. The poor will need defending, as you know, but they will also need hope. They will need to believe that they can take control of their own lives. The problem with conventional conservative politics is that it believes in personal control while depriving people of the means to exercise it. There is the danger that Perpetu-anism will be entangled with the irresponsible choices of bankers. The whole idea of responsible autonomy will be suspect because of irresponsible dealings. I won't mind if banks—and even supermarkets—are regulated, that is the price we will probably have to pay for the crash, but I do care if hope is squeezed out of people, particularly if the rhetoric is hope, but the reality is oppression. That is why we are here now, to affirm the centrality before God of human dignity and autonomy. We won't collect money—well, not unless you want it, Max—but we will use our influence to keep Perpetuanism in the field and to allow you to operate in your naive way while we do what we do best. And, by the way, the owners of this building have agreed that this room where Perpetua brought her followers should be a chapel. I don't think it would be idolatrous to name it for her."

This was so opposite from the words of Dean Crowther that Max could do nothing but admire. It was all very well for Perpetuans to believe in love as the creation of unconditional space but that had to be distinguished from the poor's powerlessness to protect what they had from invasion. Max might find the strength to be humble but that must not be confused with being down-trodden. In a way which he was only now beginning to see, the idea of love as space was most easily represented by erotic imagery in which the female wel-comed the male rather than the male imposing under the guise of loving. But how far could anybody leave themselves open when they exposed themselves to the danger of rape?

Max, Pluto and Annie left the building together and walked towards the god4u headquarters.

"How is Trina bearing up?" asked Annie.

"Well," said Max. "She was deeply ashamed that she allowed the Dean—our Dean—for the most honourable of reasons, to lead her out of the firing line. Once she had seen how wrong she was, and had admitted it publicly, she felt stronger than she has felt since she became leader."

"And has that led to anything?" asked Sir Pluto.

"Yes. She will tell you herself in detail if you care to drop in for half an hour but the overall summary is that she thinks she has been too introverted, sticking too much to the safety of the London headquarters. She wants to travel around and talk about Perpetua. She doesn't think of it as preaching or conversion, she thinks that it is the story that counts and, of course, the sign."

Trina looked more animated than Annie had ever seen her. "There is a time," said Trina, "when we have to do what Perpetua taught. We have to make a choice for going out onto open ground, to take what people of no faith would call a risk. Remember how the Jerusalem Church, with the exception of a few forays (like Peter's unfortunate spat with Paul in Antioch, and his wonderful encounter with Cornelius, and Philip's amazing encounter with the Eunuch) sat in its enclave while Paul roamed. I'm not for a moment likening Gregg to Paul—I'm not going out to combat Gregg—but I have let the other members of the group do all the work while I have been waiting for the right, or rather the safe, moment. There's no such thing as the right moment.

"If Perpetua has decided to withdraw all our documented resources, what she is saying to us is that she wants us to proclaim the message, in person. That is the only conclusion I can draw. Doctrine can get in the way of proclamation. If you give people a book—even a prayer book—and you let that be a substitute for saying to someone, 'I know, from my experience, that the best thing in human life is a relationship with God Our Parent, you haven't done your best. So I am going to go out and simply tell the story. For the past months we have been dangerously close to becoming a seminar. Quintus is staying here with Max to hold the fort and I am going on the road with Chris."

◆　◆　◆

Dean Crowther knelt in his private chapel. It was after midnight, but he could not sleep and he could not bear the thought, even of a candle. "Broken!" he said to himself, "Broken!" This was not a sudden, traumatic experience like the experience of pain as the result of a heavy blow, a cut or a burn, nor was it the culmination of a process of sliding, nor yet was it a kind of depression cloud falling and suffocating him. The sensation was, rather, of an eruption blasting its way through his urbane carapace, staining the patina of his self-image with the ash of his human weakness. "Broken!" he said again, not with self-pity nor in self-indulgence, but to get the idea into his head as the basis of penitence. Perhaps, he thought, the Perpetuans were right after all about the nature of creatureliness and, equally, if he was going to be rigourous, Martin Luther had been as wrong as he ever could be. Luther was so aware of his own human frailty that he had found his life jacket in Romans, telling him that he was saved quite regardless of his human conduct, of his weakness. He was saved because he had faith in God. This had later been caricatured to portray Luther as a man who thought that human conduct was indifferent to salvation—solefidianism—but although it was never quite that—Luther was a polemicist, not a theologian, and was therefore opportunistically inconsistent—his wilful behaviour, in the light of his salient fear of damnation, was a strong indicator of the marginality he assigned to his individual conduct. Perpetuans, on the other hand, thought that their brokenness was the intrinsic nature of the human condition and that one could not be punished for it. To that extent they were similar to Luther in their foundational proposition, but they drew precisely the opposite conclusion, that brokenness was a necessary precondition for making choices. The obligation to control our own life, our own conduct, our own wilfulness, was overwhelming. He had failed to control his wilfulness. He could never resist the witty line, no matter how cruel. He could never hold back the anecdote that capped another speaker. He could not help recounting anything he thought was to his credit but, much worse, he could not resist the power game. That was why he was kneeling in penitence. He did not think for a moment that what he did could mend the harm he had done, nor did he believe, although he was absolutely sincere in his sorrow, that his new resolve would last. The eruption of his inner bile would cease, the carapace would heal, the patina would be restored, the tarnish wiped away. He had experienced the cycle so many times that he marvelled at the depth of the pain he suffered and the forgetfulness of it afterwards. All his life, the outer polished, shiny Reggie had denied the inner, turbulent, volcanic Reggie.

He knew that he should make some kind of amends, but he knew that he would not. He did not think himself worse nor better than his peers. He certainly did not think himself or any other cleric, morally superior to lay people. His only consolation was that he believed that he knew himself better than most people know themselves. He knew he was a sinner and that was what pained him.

Without being able to see it, he knew that there was a simple line drawing of the parable of the Pharisee and the Publican above the simple altar. He wanted the finest pictures in the public part of the Minster but he had chosen this simplest of unattributed, late fifteenth-century Italian drawings, which had apparently never produced a full painting, as his only visible aid to prayer in his private space. Perhaps in a perverse way, he did not want people to know that he really was agonised and that in some way he might even be holy. The world knew him to be a useful scoundrel and he was disinclined to deny it. If he was agonised, or holy, that was his business. To that extent he was more like the Publican than the Pharisee but the world knew otherwise. He had chosen the picture because he knew he was both. It was absurd not to think that most human beings were both. He took a lighter from his pocket and, feeling slightly better, lit a candle and looked at the picture. The Pharisee, at the top right of the picture was looking up and to his left, back arched, legs straight under his flowing robe. The Publican was crouched in the bottom left-hand corner, head on chest, back bowed, knees slightly bent. There was no eye contact between them, but the way that the drawing was composed forced the eye to travel from the one to the other, uninterested in the almost blank bottom right and top left quadrants. Yet here was something even more striking which was why he really loved the drawing. The Pharisee in left profile and the Publican in right profile were superficially different because of the different ways they wore their hair, but they were the two profiles of the same face!

He blew out the candle and walked into the cloisters whose outlines could just be seen in the early dawn.

◆　◆　◆

Becalmed, Gregg thought on his own brokenness. After the strange events of the Caribbean, resentment at the enforced "medical" supervision had stopped him thinking straight. He had imprisoned and been imprisoned and he knew that both made him unstable. He only enjoyed real stability when he was alone in unlimited space, far away from cruelty and imposition. If he had been a farmer he would probably have been well enough, but disastrous parental financial management had forced him into the armed forces and the only decent niche there was in security which, necessarily, meant cramped conditions of all kinds.

Apparently generously but prudently, Myron had agreed that Gregg could visit one of the tiny quays owned by one of his congregation. He received supplies for his room and his fridge and freezer every day, but was otherwise left to himself.

The first thing that he recognised was that he had a fatally unstable relationship with his own power. The thing about the girl on the tiny beach was that it had never occurred to him to hold an ordinary conversation with her, to seduce or be seduced. He needed power over her and, worse, and contradictory in the extreme, that power might have led to murder where all power ends. Considering what he could remember, he knew that it really had nothing to do with desire in the ordinary way, only the desire for power.

That explained where he was with Perpetuanism. He needed a religion of power to curb his power. He understood the theology of brokenness, of imperfection, but his imperfection was so great that he needed drastic measures to be taken to save him. He was not so self-deluding to think that all the harm had been done by the armed forces rather, he thought, his temperament had drawn him to where he ended up.

So why Perpetuanism and not a strict Christian sect? He thought that fundamentalist Christianity was hollow. He knew that the extreme Evangelical Republicans were greedy, that their private lives would not bear scrutiny, that they would always put profits above everything else, but that was not the worst of it. They had, as a class, totally ignored the human psyche and what had been learned about it in the twentieth century. Their women visited therapists, but the church elders would not allow psychology to be a factor in the behaviour of the rest of the world. What attracted him about Perpetuanism was its fit with real human need—well, human need in the round, in the abstract—but his problem was that normality was not his need. He knew that he should not, therefore, subvert it to suit his own ends, to meet his own needs, but he knew that he would. The inexorable rise of income and wealth, the proliferation of hand guns, the availability of cheap and plentiful pornography and sex and, above all, social sanction for self-indulgence, called for a new start. Christianity had lost its credentials.

Myron had no such doubts. Gregg was calming down nicely on his little quay. His supply girl said that Robinson Scruffo was getting calmer every day. Myron needed Gregg to be calm so that he would consider the proposition to be put before him rationally. Myron had the network, Gregg had the supernatural powers. Myron needed money, Gregg needed to exercise his powers. There was a deal to be made. If everything went wrong, there was a bank account with enough in it to see them through. Yes, he'd take Dolorez because she would be useful and would not complain. As for Gregg, he would leave him to his own devices and the shadowy friends who had brought him and, from what he could gather, would no doubt take him away.

◆   ◆   ◆

Clement viewed the Archbishop's itinerary with resignation. Poor James would be subjected to a week of undiluted hostility for no gain. The churches of East Africa saw the issue of gay clergy as a touchstone for liberated orthodoxy against decadent imperialism. James would try to promote Anglican Communion solidarity by presiding at youth Eucharists, planting trees, saving the elephant, establishing a commission in Kenya to mend the tribal rifts opened up by the (he could not say) rigged election, opening a new seminary, but it would come to nothing. Somehow the idea of the Anglican Communion had turned sour. He could not hope to reconcile the North Americans with the East Africans because the argument was still being waged on narrow, moral grounds, quite distinct from Christian solidarity. Clement knew that James would suffer pain for nothing, but the pressure to be seen in action was insatiable.

It was, thought Clement, a tension between the structural and the organic. The legacy of Empire had pushed the Church towards the Anglican Communion and it had inevitably borrowed from Rome, but the reality was that this kind of centralism did not work. It had reached the point where East Africans and North Americans had lost the capacity to imagine the other as Christian. They had, through polemics, forgotten what Christianity was. Instead of its being a liberating, living force it had descended into Pharisaic hair splitting.

The problem for James was that there was no escape route. He dare not propose to the Grand Synod that there was no such thing as the Anglican Communion. He dare not say that the post-Second World War faith in global jurisdiction was over. The United Nations was an expensive shell and even the Vatican was only hanging on by a thread. To Africans, globalisation looked like a new form of imperialism. Africa had no permanent member of the Security Council even though it accounted for so many wars. It now had to contend with BRIC as well as the "western" powers. In the consumer market, people wore Levis and Nike, drank Coke, ate McDonalds and subscribed to English Premier League soccer, but they insisted that this was the individual exercise of preference and had nothing to do with global market forces. They confused power in the market with power over the market.

When it came to Anglicanism Eucharistic fellowship was less strong than McDonalds. There were African bishops a-plenty who refused to share the Eucharist not only with some bishops in North America, but also with some of his own. A bishop was no longer a bishop. He was considered in the same light as a race horse, his ordaining pedigree set out for inspection. He could not ordain some men if he had ordained women or gay clergy, or if he had been consecrated or ordained by women or gay clergy, or if any of those who had consecrated or ordained him had been consecrated or ordained by women or gay clergy.

When they landed at Jomo Kenyata Airport they were pushed into the VIP lounge. Clement dealt with the officials while James sat patiently. The Anglican Church of Kenya had not filled out a form correctly so there was a discrepancy between the Archbishop's documentation and that of his hosts. Clement, wearily, dropped some US Dollar Bills onto the floor in the eye line of the immigration official sitting intimidatingly high up. The official asked a colleague to come out from the fortress to assist the dignitaries. The Dollars were retrieved, the passports and forms stamped, and the so-called VIPS were released into the arrivals hall.

There had been no advance briefing papers, so they were surprised and pleased to be greeted by Bishop Ignatius. "Aren't you supposed to be a Perpetuan?" asked the Archbishop, mildly ironically.

"I suppose so," said Ignatius, "but Africa is not very doctrinal. Not at all like Latin America. We are, primarily, interested in the morality and dynamics of community living. We don't do liberation theology, we do community theology. The big problem in Africa with Perpetuanism will not be the doctrine of the Godhead, but the gender of the fourth person. This is not true everywhere in Africa, but here most of our tribes are highly patriarchal. So, let us say, that for the sake of our mission to bring God to the people it is best for me to be an orthodox Christian here while I enjoy my private relationship with Perpetua. It's a pity really, as she could be an anti-imperial figure, and she might make some headway in South africa, but not here. By the way, there is a small demonstration outside but the police are keeping it well under control. The authorities don't like demos of any sort."

There were no more than a dozen standing outside in complete silence with small placards reading:

GAY SIN

GAY HELL

WHITE SIN

In spite of a restraining hand from Clement and a nod in the direction of a waiting car from Ignatius, James went over to the demonstrators. "It's kind of you to take the trouble," he said. "We might not always agree but, it's more important to be passionate."

They seemed, unlike Western demonstrators, far from being passionate. They had not expected to be noticed and they were slightly embarrassed by receiving such attentions from the man they were supposed to be demonstrating against. "Come and see me," he said. "Bishop Ignatius will make the arrangements."

Ostensibly because Archbishop's House was not considered good enough for Archbishop Hall, he was put in the Nairobi Club. If he felt the insult he said nothing, not even to Clement. "I feel the divisions more sharply here," he said, "than I do when listening to the Grand Synod. There it is a matter of doctrine— what they quite improperly call theology—whereas here it is a matter of faith. I often feel that when English Evangelicals insist on taking the text of the Bible literally, as if it were the spiritual equivalent of an engineering manual, that they are somehow in denial, that they are playing a mind game that keeps everything simple whereas here I feel that people are deeply attached to the Bible as their way of life, the way perhaps we were before Jane Austen. You know, Clement, I don't think there's really very much I can do about it. The gap is too wide for any documented stitch-up. I can see why English parishes twin with African parishes and I believe our officers when they say that the learning is genuinely two-way, but that's quite different from a Covenant or a concordat."

"So what will you do, given that your main purpose for being here is to 'sell' the Covenant?"

"I will listen and teach, as a bishop should, and at the Grand Synod in July I will say that I am not convinced that the Covenant process will work. Look, Clement, what happens if any province signs up to the Covenant on a split vote? The supporters say that the arrangements for adhesion are benign but you know as a matter of history that nobody is ever given a power that they do not end up using, in spite of protestations, because it's only ever a matter of time before occasion arises for the last resort."

The visit went better than Clement had hoped. Although some of the arrangements were haphazard, there was genuine warmth. The ritual was a little untidy, but the fire of faith burned bright, and although the Archbishop had resolved from the start to be formal and cool on all occasions, his private and public conduct soon converged. It was a hard man who could resist James' humble, self-deprecating charm, and Ignatius and his friends were not hard men.

"Look brother James," said Ignatius, as they sat in a small sitting room in the *Pig and Whistle* with the rain lashing down, "I can see how the Americans and some of your people have got where they have. I can see why my people have stayed where they are. I can also see that global communication is biased against localism. Sooner or later, different people in the same sphere of activity look at the world and respectively opt for change and no change, although change is often justified in terms of going back to a golden age. There is a bias in favour of change because keeping things as they are doesn't make exciting news or stimulating entertainment, so stances are not judged on their merit, on their usefulness to the person or the institution, but on their usefulness to media revenues. Conversely, the conservatism of Localism is just a quaint curiosity, of peasant traditional costume, exotic dances, and plangent folk music (almost always, "my goat has fallen off a cliff, oh what a disaster!"). So if two Anglicans on different sides of the world see its future in different ways, there is a premium on conflict and the North American will be seen as universal whereas the African will be seen as local. It is only a matter of time before one of them wants to dominate the other, but the odds are stacked in favour of the universal radical. I wish we could have been left to ourselves, but we have been pushed into controversy by the American factions who finance us as proxies. We are more at home with the fundamentalists and they are more at home with us and, not incidentally, they have been prepared to invest more in us directly. Perhaps it would be bad religion, but good politics, if one side won a decisive victory, but the protagonists are evenly matched so the issue cannot be brought to a swift conclusion. Look, we have a polarised Church just as we have a polarised United States and a polarised Thailand, and here, with the tribal forces more or less equal, we have a polarised Kenya but, in spite of its failure to deal with polarised conflict, Western people are so obsessed with the ideology of democracy—which is not an integral part of Christianity—that they don't see the necessity for strong rule. It all looks so complex and impossible, with a terrible bias in favour of change and power, based on an ideology of personal autonomy and majoritarianism that It would just be better if we left each other alone at the institutional level and let the Mothers Union and Parish twinning do the Lord's work."

When the two archbishops parted amicably at the airport, there were no official statements, no press releases, and only the briefest of press conferences at which both men said they had enjoyed learning from and teaching each other and that they trusted that God's faithful people would continue the dialogue and fellowship.

The church press was taken aback by the lack of a story, but soon picked up on Archbishop Hall's disenchantment with the Covenant process. Before they could fully develop that story, a much bigger one appeared.

◆   ◆   ◆

Dean Crowther's penitential pain, intense though it was, was as short lived as he had foreseen. Assessing the situation at the end of May, he felt himself strong enough to open a second front. While the secular politicians were working away quietly under the promptings of Griswald, he decided to launch a Church offensive. For a start, he was fed up of fencing with Griswald and was prepared to let him get on with the politics as long as he had his own role as a leading churchman. Secondly, he wanted to show that you didn't have to be a Bishop to exercise influence and power. Thirdly, he enjoyed the game. Surveying Grand Synod, he thought he detected some valuable room for manoeuvre. While the conservative Evangelicals and the traditionalist Catholics were still involved in clause-by-clause, hand-to-hand fighting over the issue of women bishops, the majority of Synod was bored with the whole issue, just wanting to get it over with and into the dioceses for consultation. It was coming to the end of its five-year-term with precious little to show for its long hours of deliberation except for the chronic downward adjustment of financial plans and interminable adjustments to the pension fund, for which which it would be thanked by no-one. Crowther would help it to go out with a bang by saving the Church from sleep-walking into a modus vivendi with Perpetuanism. He knew that to characterise it as another faith would have no impact at all, but if he were to describe it as "a parasitic sect, extracting its life blood from the Church", he would make a great impression. All he needed to do was to throw in references to the Christian heritage, true religion, the *Book of Common Prayer*, *The Authorised Version*, and the quiet and unassuming devotion of the English people to their established Church and he would pick up a tidy number of people who did not think too much, but felt deeply, if quietly, about these things.

His principal problem was procedural. There was no way in which he could accelerate a Private Members' Motion to the top of the list so that it would have to be taken. He did not think he could sway the House of Bishops from outside and he knew that he would not move Clement and, therefore, the Archbishop. But a concerted campaign, spear-headed by the *Toxic Times*, might just do the trick. Accordingly, he went to see Sneer's Editor successor, Rupert Snarle who had taken the chair in spite of his Oxford pedigree, not because he was particularly well thought of by the new owner who had bought the paper at a highly competitive price from Sir Pluto, but because Sneer's sudden departure had caused a vacuum as Sneer had always been careful to decapitate pretenders.

"I am not sure," said Snarle. "From my personal point of view it's a very interesting development, but it takes some skill to turn the Church of England into news, outside the women and gays thing, of course."

"But you have those skills, Rupert, I know you do. I remember telling Sneer, who improbably appeared at a Church House reception, that you were the up-and-coming star."

"That could have ruined me."

"Nonetheless, Rupert, you have the skill and we'll keep this exclusive to you. It isn't the sort of scoop you would like, such as the discovery of Little Phil Mac, but it would be a good one for you to start with. A lot of very sweet church-going ladies read your nasty paper when their husbands have gone to work with nicer fare."

"That's a point. I've often wondered why women are so devoted to our rather, let us say, grudging style. We aim to stir up discontent and quite reasonable, balanced women start mouthing our somewhat unpleasant, even toxic, agenda. It only goes to show how shallow is virtue."

Crowther refrained from comment. He knew that Rupert would soon settle the matter himself. He needed to make his mark after Sneer's departure, he was still technically acting up and he was becoming fed up of the way rival papers made fun of him. "All right, then, Reggie, we'll give it a go."

◆　◆　◆

Clement warned James of what was coming. "They are going to characterise Perpetuanism as a Christian parasite not a faith in its own right, which means that it is fair game. It's not a standard ecumenical partner, but a heretical organisation sucking out our life blood, though how you distinguish between a heresy and another denomination is a mystery to me. For instance, does the Pope think that Anglicanism is heresy or another, respectable denomination, symbolised by its deep affection for Archbishop Hawthorne?"

"And me, too! I wish people got as worked up about poverty as they do about dogma, or is it doctrine?"

"I don't usually obtrude my own personal concerns into our discussions, archbishop, but my continued presence at your side might weaken your ability to withstand Crowther's pressure."

"I understand the point, Clement—and thank you—but Crowther's big mistake is to think that the newspapers matter. He can try to force us to put Perpetuanism on the agenda, but that's the limit of his power."

The Archbishop was wrong. With Strider's help, Griswald had managed to yoke the doctrinal discussion with the final ratification of the deal between Christians and Perpetuans on sacred buildings, producing the surreal paradox that the Church of England could only get its compensation for buildings it didn't want from the Perpetuans and the Government acting as under-writer and broker if it agreed to table a motion on the status of Perpetuanism as a dangerous sect. The Perpetuans, on the other hand, had to pay to be vilified. Griswald was overjoyed with the neatness of the device and even Reggie smiled. James, in a moment of panic, pressed by Crozier who was beside himself with worry over the Council's budget, put his name to an emergency motion and Clement resigned. A day later, James saw the terrible error he had made, but he could not put the bile back in the bottle. He could have resigned, but resolved to pay for his own weakness by suffering in office. When he came to clear his desk, Clement sympathised, but would not reverse his decision even though James had shown his sorrow.

"It was going to happen sooner or later," said Clement. "I knew I could only be of limited use. Try not to worry—er, James—I will become a full-time worker for Perpetua. We will surely meet again."

Meanwhile, out of the reach of Trina and Max who might have imposed some limitations on their range of options, Sir Pluto and Sir Granville sat in Pluto's secluded house near the canal.

"Not a very strong hand," said Pluto. "Griswald is nasty but doesn't have all that much leverage. Crowther is above himself, as usual. James, poor fellow, doesn't know what he's doing. They might get us under the Prevention of Terrorism but would lose in the courts. They might get rid of comparative religion in schools but it would be unenforceable. They could get the Grand Synod to declare us—what was the phrase?—a parasitic sect, but nobody much takes notice of the Grand Synod except when it makes a collective fool of itself, which it frequently does."

"You are, I think, a little too sanguine, Pluto. We need to have a plan to check these people before they go too far."

"Remember Sir Rufus Tartan? We gave him enough rope and he hanged himself."

"But you can't count on it, Pluto. You never know in politics."

You never do. For reasons which might only appear when his memoirs are published, The Prime Minister caught the whiff of battle and decided to weigh in on Strider's side, hoping to blunt the impact of Conservative Evangelical support. It wasn't a big issue but, was just big enough to merit his attention.

◆　◆　◆

A man appeared and said he had been cured by a follower in the name of Perpetua. Another man came and said the same. It seemed discourteous to trouble them when they had so recently been cured of distress, but Max thought he must. Neither had been "cured" by an official Guide or known follower. Was this a threat or a new opening? Did the core group somehow need to "control" everything undertaken in Perpetua's name?

Max convened the core group and asked Clement and Pluto to join them. He knew that Pluto was doing a certain amount of freelancing, but he couldn't help that, and he certainly couldn't stop him.

"Not for the first time," Max began, "we seem to have got two very different issues entangled: miracles and authority. If people say they are performing miracles in Perpetua's name, do we say they have no authority? If we do, this helps because we can then go on to say that the miracles are nothing to do with her, which is what we would want to say as we must avoid being associated with a miracle cult when the Godhead was so sparing in using her as an agent."

"Hold on," said Wayne. "We may be in danger of promoting a post-Perpetua ideology which isn't entirely accurate. I don't know what you would count as 'sparing'. You might use that general description for most of her mission, but you couldn't use it for the last Sunday before her death when she cured thousands of people."

"True," Max said. "I suppose what I really mean is that they were almost always quiet acts. Even the thousands were cured quietly, without fuss, quite different—sorry Cara—from the Fidel episode, the promises, the fanfare, the stage, a kind of entertainment. So, on the whole, we don't really like the miracle cult. It goes against the idea of people fixing their own lives. Perpetua only used God's powers to put people back on their feet to start again. She said as much."

"But what point is there in saying something like, 'well, on the whole we don't like miracles but'?" asked Wayne.

"We're reacting," said Trina, looking at Sneer. "We are also becoming overly complicated. We should say that we see miracles—I prefer to call them divine acts—as Perpetua did, as a way of giving people a new start, but not as a substitute for taking control of our own lives. We do not know these people who have reportedly performed acts and we certainly don't know whether they are acting in Perpetua's name. How can we? We could have a discussion about whether they should be saying that they are acting in her name, but that really does pitch us into a discussion about authority. Perpetua definitely chose us, but there's nothing to say that God Our Parent has to stick to our assumed rules."

"If we're asked about these freelancers," said Sneer, "and all we say is 'don't know', it will look weak."

"Well," said Trina, "it's the truth, so we don't really have any choice. We are going to have to settle the authority question."

"That's yours," said Max. "Don't look at us."

"As I see it," said Trina, "we know what Perpetua said and did. We are the people she blessed and left behind to carry on the work. The only instruction she really gave us was to go on founding diversity house groups. Since she left us we have been holed up here far too much which is why I'm about to go on the road. That's our only authority."

"And to celebrate the Sacraments," said Father Bill.

"Yes, sorry, I was getting too emphatic and astringent," said Trina. "To form diversity house groups, to celebrate the Sacraments, to appoint Guides. The last is stretching it a bit, but when we are no longer here we will need people to celebrate Sacraments which needs some grounding, some faith, some training. I think, looking back, that we were probably wrong to ask Archbishop Hawthorne to draw us up a theological code, but Perpetua saw that off. As I see it, she was set against doctrinal codification and authority and we should be too. The word 'guide' is the right word and I suppose I'd have to call myself the primus inter pares amongst the Guides, and nothing else. We have, however, been laying on hands in a way that is reminiscent of Christianity's bishops. What do we think of that?"

"It's probably necessary in the short term," said Stacey "but it's so easy to get into the habit. On the other hand, if we say that we're the only 'bishop figures' and as such the idea will die with us, that sounds drastic. We still have to face up to the idea of what we do with this movement. So far it has been England, but there are groups in America and also Gregg claiming to speak on our behalf in the Caribbean. There's Ignatius in Kenya and scores of people in little pockets all over the world."

"I suppose if we are to keep the faith of Perpetua, to be purists, we must just let Our Sister the Spirit go where she will," said Trina.

"But she won't fix what we were made to fix," said Cara.

They sat in silence, each praying in an individual way, but the prayers somehow came together so that they could feel collective prayer drawing the Spirit towards them.

"We are servants of the Spirit," said Trina. "As long as we choose to be servants, everything will be fine. The danger is when we stop serving and begin bossing. We will serve. We will make it clear that that is our intention and that those we seek to serve should always tell us when we are in danger of becoming too proud. As for the miracles, I'm sorry, Quintus, but we really have to say we don't know."

Again they fell silent and allowed the Spirit to work within them and between them.

"As for miracles, as for Gregg, as for Dean Crowther who is mounting some sort of campaign against us, we will simply refuse to be drawn. They do what they do, and we shall do what we do. We cannot control them nor stop them. We learned from Perpetua, that we must resist the temptation to control. We have all been reminded here by Our Sister the Spirit to proceed quietly and humbly, not trying to do what we were not meant to do?"

"What about our broadcasting?" asked Brian.

"And our educational materials?" said Wayne.

"As long as these activities exist to help us to carry out Perpetua's wishes, that is fine. She did not mean us to carry out our work with our hands tied or for us to be a primitive people, going back to a non-technological age. She loved technology. That is perhaps why she had power over it from God."

Cara looked troubled. "I've never sorted that out. You say she had power from God and that she used that power to perform mighty acts, as if, without that power given to her, she could not have done anything, but she was God so was not the power her own?"

"This is a language problem, really," said Trina. "In Christianity, because God created everything, including, in some way, Jesus, the 'son' figure, the power that Jesus displayed was attributed to that Creator, but the attribution, particularly in John, was because the Evangelists weren't sure whether Jesus was God in the way that God was God. The language is rather unhelpful, so let me put it this way. The Godhead has revealed itself in creation, in Jesus, in Perpetua, and in the Spirit. Jesus and Perpetua are as much the Godhead as Creator and Spirit. Leave out Perpetua and that's what Christians believe. Our language diverges at this point from Christian language because we say—and, forgive me, I was falling into Christian formulae, it's so easy to do—that Perpetua and Jesus were acting in the power of the Spirit. It isn't that they couldn't act without that power because that power was not being doled out or withheld; rather it's a constant. I think that's what Christians mean, too, but they fall into the trap, because of language in John, of formulating ideas about power being 'given' by the Father as if it were not a constant within Jesus, but a transaction. Jesus actually says that he can't do anything without the Father but the truth is he is never without the Father. I can see why the idea of a dynamic Godhead is so attractive, but it loses the dimension of the constant."

They sat in silence for almost ten minutes.

"We will go out refreshed, humbled, simpler people," Trina said.

Max looked at Pluto. He wasn't sure how far that message had been taken on board by the quiet tycoon.

◆　◆　◆

Myron's plans were complete. A becalmed Gregg was preparing himself spiritually. He had told myron every day that he did not know whether he could repeat what he had done in the Caribbean, but Myron would not listen. His enterprise was well on the way and building strongly. You could not offer miracles in exchange for money, but you could collect from the grateful. There was a nice distinction between charging and collecting.

Myron's fastidiousness—and perhaps a tinge of prudential caution—steered him well clear of stadium or television evangelism. He had hit upon the idea of inviting a select gathering of those needing help and their carers to the elegant conference centre at the hospital. Professionals would be on hand if anything went wrong. As an insurance policy he also put out strong statements linking healing—not specifically physical healing—with faith. If you were not healed it wasn't the healer's fault.

Some thirty people gathered at the centre. Myron said some prayers as Gregg had indicated that this wasn't his strong point. Then, nervously, Gregg laid his hands on a dozen people. There was silence. Then, smoothly, without a twitch or a start, a lady in a wheelchair put her feet to the floor, stood straight and walked over to Gregg. A blind man saw. After ten minutes during which Myron's grip never faltered while Gregg sat, limp, there was not a word. Then Myron said a prayer of thanks. Nine had been healed, three showed no sign. Myron put this down to a lack of faith. Being human, he wanted to focus on the failure rate but, being a philosopher and an accountant, he worked out that a 75% success rate was more than acceptable. The uncured would cause trouble for not being given what they thought was a right rather than a gift, but he would have to face them down. If you had a portfolio, they couldn't all go up together.

The unhealed were taken to private rooms and the healed were de-briefed. "Just remember," said Myron, "It's God through the power of Gregg who is the Patriarch of the American Church of Perpetua."

Gregg lost consciousness.

All the planned measures were immediately activated. The healing gift certificates were printed, the ACP bank accounts were activated, the testimonials were recorded and broadcast, together with low-key adverts for an exclusive healing audience with Gregg.

No amount of discretion nor exclusivity could ward off a population which was almost self-identified by its actual or feared ailments. The seniors of Florida rose up as a body and made their way, in "Biblical" numbers, to Myron's door. One miracle in Stumpy Knoll might make a paragraph in a local newspaper, but nine in one session was world news. The low-key commercials were drowned by the rantings of shock jocks who variously said that the end of the world was at hand, that God had vindicated capitalism, that atheist decadence was at an end, that the New England traitors would be punished, that if the people had listened to God 9/11 would never have been wrought to punish them, that no gays or lesbians would ever receive healing, and that gays and lesbians would be cured of their perversions by Gregg's power. He was invited onto every news channel in Florida and many further afield, but Myron warded off all enquiries. Gregg seemed to be in a coma and so Myron's triumph was tempered by the fear of the death of the goose. He wanted to bring in the best doctors he could find, but Dolorez advised him to stick to the doctors in their pay. High profile clinicians did not feel bound by confidentiality. Myron felt a little sorry for himself as he always seemed to be trapped in quandary. He put out a statement saying that the holy man wished to be close to God in thankfulness and to regain his strength.

After three days, Gregg came to his senses and had to be told by Myron what had happened. Myron scrupulously told what Gregg could check, but said nothing about the transactional yield. Gregg knew that money was involved, but he somehow didn't care. He wondered how his future would work out if he went on performing these strange acts, and as he gained strength again, he thought about power.

Myron's problem was how to control the supply of Gregg's gifts and he reluctantly concluded that he would have to consult Gregg. You might want to imprison the goose but it was not possible; and, anyway, it might stop laying golden eggs.

Gregg's second session, in the same place, for a slightly bigger gathering, was almost equally successful, with the rate only dropping to 66%. Myron wondered whether this was a blip or a trend but, still, you couldn't argue with 66% and this second time people had come prepared to be grateful. Then Myron's greed got the better of his prudence and he decided to go for broke. Pressured by the media, the adulation for Gregg, the funds flowing into the ACP and also, it must be admitted, the jealousy of his former friends at the Coral Gables Church of Christ, Myron decided to go for Dolphin Stadium.

Gregg was building in confidence and instead of worrying whether he would be able to use what he (heretically) thought of as his powers, he was thinking even more intensely about the American Church of Perpetua. He didn't want the money which he knew was Myron's priority, but he did want profile and power. Being a nominal "Patriarch" wasn't good enough and so when Myron proposed Dolphin Stadium it fired Gregg's imagination. Their respective need for money and power had found a perfect fit.

It was the last week in May and the media was suffering from a period of calm. With space to fill, expectation of the Miami event grew to hysterical levels. Not even Myron had the gall to sell tickets, which would have been one method of arriving at the audience. Instead he pulled together a small team of investors to put up the funding for the hire cost, the indemnity insurance, stewarding and the list brokering company that selected invitees, integrating income and wealth data with age, faith and frailty. What Myron was afraid of was a riot of the unhealed. He took out private insurance against a healing rate of lower than 25%.

As it turned out, the healing rate was 20% so Myron collected on his insurance, but the exit donation level was startling. 20% looked low, but it meant that nobody was more than a few yards from somebody who had been cured. Myron paid off the real estate obligation of the Coral Gables Church of Christ and made himself the President of the American Church of Perpetua. Gregg was recovering from his exertions on the quay.

◆   ◆   ◆

"He never mentioned God," said Trina.

"He never mentioned Perpetua," said Max

"He didn't say anything," said Stacey.

"Only that sleek Myron said a strange prayer that made Perpetua sound as if she was some kind of disembodied Greek Goddess in a pantheon," said Wayne.

"It was like poor Fidel's unfaithfulness," said Cara, "except that it worked.

That's our problem."

"There is consolation in everything," said Trina. "Setting up the American Church of Perpetua, which Myron has done, might be our problem, but the actual event was helpful because it carried the reality of Gregg's activities further away from us. Now we are ready to take to the road."

◆　◆　◆

The body of a female dressed only in bikini pants was washed up on a Miami beach, such a regular event that nobody noticed except Myron, a man at Langley and Sir Pluto Millman. It was the supply girl for the quay where Gregg was staying.

◆　◆　◆

Trina worked hard to revive the spirit of Perpetua without attempting to imitate her. Although she never refused an invitation to speak in a Christian church she concentrated on deprived areas where just about nobody even thought about church. She knew that God was not a broker who rewarded those who tried, but she was sure there was a link between hopelessness and Godlessness. She was asked why, if God was so benevolent, "he" was not compassionate towards the hopeless. Her response was that it was up to God's people to bring hope on God's behalf. Christianity had failed to bring hope to the poorest. It was well and good for Christians to be taking Jesus into the jungles and into the favellas, but he should also have been taken into the British slums and tower blocks.

Her progress was relaxed and without ego. She talked to mothers struggling alone with young children. She went to pubs and betting shops. She said short quiet, prayers, and told everyone that God loved them. They could understand God best of all through understanding one of their own, an ethnic minority female Hypo shelf stacker. Occasionally she found that she had done something wonderful in the power of the Spirit, but she asked people not to make a fuss, and to steer clear of complexities with the Government and its funding mechanisms, they happily agreed. In every place she visited she worked to set up house groups of mixed background, ability, and race and pointed them towards a Guide. She brought Guides together to arrange for Sacraments to be brought to the people. She was frequently asked to preside at big Sacramental events, but she preferred to work with house groups and leave Guides to preside. Occasionally she was asked by a professional type what Perpetuanism stood for, but most people wanted to know what she stood for. They had tried everything within their grasp, but nothing had changed. She had thought that their key problem was physical poverty, and she saw plenty of that, but what these people had in common was a poverty of hope. Whenever they agreed to do something to effect a modest change, they somehow found the money. She occasionally met rivalry from Christian "fresh expressions", but the major hostility she encountered was from Government officials who wanted her good offices without her religion. Even the kindest hearted seemed to believe that religion was dangerous. They were liberal, but their liberalism did not extend to religion. It was precisely these people—not so much hostile as indifferent—whom she wanted to influence because they provided local leadership. Their outlook was critical to the generation of hope.

Most of the time what she said and did was hardly noticed. She steadily picked up adherents, but because these were not former Christians there was no reaction from the establishment. As she gently transformed some of the worst places, the middle classes went on living their unchanged lives. When she was just occasionally noticed, she repeated her message of hope, studiously avoiding any reference to miracles and refusing to comment on reports of Gregg, simply saying that he must be responsible for what he did, just as she was. As May turned into June, she felt intensifying hostility.

Horace Strider had hoped to plan his campaign carefully but, as usual, his initiative was scrambled out so that he could be seen to be doing something. The immediate issue was a trade union complaint to the Secretary of State that the Hypo experiment in encouraging voluntary reductions in personal consumption might begin to have an effect on the size of the labour force. This might not have mattered, but negotiations between the Party and its largest funder, Protect, had reached a critical point. The union had discovered, to its extreme chagrin and annoyance, that the Prime Minister was turning out not to be as radical as it had hoped, and it wondered whether it was worth investing in a Party whose leader seemed determined to lose the General Election no matter how much money it had. Horace was "tasked" with making a splash and thought his best line was to attack Hypo on the basis that people might enjoy patronising supermarkets, but they also enjoyed complaining about them. Horace still liked and respected Sir Pluto, but he was, not for the first time, collateral damage. Strider made a direct attack on Perpetuanism saying that it was an insidious sect with primitivist economic instincts that would pull the country down. It was well known, he said, that it was the job of Hypo to serve its shareholders and customers and it would damage both if it pursued this irresponsible notion of economic contraction. Where would the economy be if only a handful of large enterprises followed Hypo? Jambo and Lakshmo were not slow to pick up the message and as one or other of them had a branch in every major town, and as they supplied local newspapers and commercial radio stations with the bulk of their advertising revenue, they became increasingly shrill in their condemnation of Perpetuanism. The knots of protesters that turned up with placards when she arrived in a new town soon grew into vocal crowds requiring police intervention. Trina had to decide whether to face or avoid controversy. She had settled on her quiet mission so she did not want confrontation, but she did not want to run away and abandon her mission as she had at London Minster. Out of courtesy she consulted Sir Pluto who said that he could withstand anything that came his way and that she must follow the Spirit. She asked Max and he said that she must do what was right regardless of how people reacted. One of the great errors of society was that it adjusted behaviour to take account of reaction, resulting in stifling self-censorship.

She laboured on through June, steadily building new house groups, but having to take more time for each, until the final days when the impact of Strider's initiative wore off.

"People so often think that what they are doing is important," said Max, "and they are easily blown off course. It is better to keep it straight and simple, as we have. Even if your policy is to stave off criticism by tailoring what you say, you can only meet a small number of objections because in most circumstances their is a heterogeneous majority against anything."

By the end of June the Perpetuans were quietly satisfied. Their numbers were growing, house groups were consolidating, and although they were aware of future challenges, they felt they had got over the worst.

◆　◆　◆

Sir Pluto found himself taking an inordinate interest in Gregg's affairs. It had not been difficult for him to make an arrangement with Langley to deposit him in Miami and he had been able to monitor events. He had noted the "miracles", investigated Myron's money and marriage, and received reports on the finances of the Coral Gables Church of Christ, the American Church of Perpetua, and the Obadiah J. Skraun Memorial Hospital. He had also received the transcript of an interview with Myron's supply girl whose death he had noted without surprise. Just in case he needed to act unilaterally outside the Perpetuan movement, he decided to keep his counsel so that his friends only knew about Gregg from occasional feature pieces from America.

Myron was petrified. He did not want to be implicated and he certainly did not want his miracle man to be suspected of homicide, but neither did he want to spend all his new wealth to avoid being implicated. He took the unusual and risky step of being taken over to the quay to have a private interview with Gregg.

"I suppose you have noticed," said Myron, "that you have a new supplier."

"Yes."

"Did you like the girl?"

"Not particularly. Well, that is to say, I didn't notice her on the few occasions when I saw her at a distance. Most of the time I was asleep, recovering."

"Solid, black, sleep?"

"Well, actually I had a nightmare about a porn queen?"

"Very strange. Like this?"

He produced a photograph. Gregg went pale.

"Yes, like that," Myron answered himself.

Myron knew and Gregg knew and each knew that the other knew.

"You better stay here," said Myron, "for your good and mine."

He was paralysed with fear. In the end he had to tell Dolorez.

"I know," she said. "I knew all about him when you took me to see him in the clinic. There was something horrible about him."

"But he's paid off all our real estate debts and left us with enough to live on."

"Myron, we should quit while we're ahead and get right away from Gregg."

"We can't do that. God is calling us to spread his word to all people."

"He isn't, Myron. Look, I have lived with you quietly, barely saying a word and I am grateful for the way you have conducted yourself with me. We cannot hide from ourselves the fact that God—religion—is as much your career as selling things is a career. You don't believe in God, but you do believe that God is a good commodity to sell. Myron, Gregg isn't a good commodity to sell. He's risky. Even if you keep this incident quiet, you can't keep him under guard forever. I know you are planing to take him to New York. Be careful Myron. I will not leave you, but I feel that I have to say something to protect us. I expect that the police will find that the woman was raped and beaten to death, that she was one of your employees, and that she regularly went to the quay alone to take supplies to Gregg. I have looked up the 'favourites' list on your computer and have read the reports from the Caribbean."

"So what do we do?"

"We can only wait or run. I think, on balance, running will be more dangerous because it will be difficult for us to disappear and the flight will draw attention to us. I advise that we sit tight and wait for a few days. Something may turn up but, if it doesn't, we need to detach ourselves from him. Or him from us."

The climax was reached just before midnight in the arrival of Police Lieutenant Willow. Myron wanted to pretend that he wasn't at home by sending Dolorez to the door to lie, but she judged it better to let him in.

"I am sorry I am calling so late," said the Lieutenant, "but I have to be careful."

Dolorez breathed easier and escorted him to Myron.

"Our prayers have been answered," she said, using their customary pious code.

"I am sorry to disturb you so late at night," said Willow, "but it is not usual for the Department to send single officers to suspects of serious crimes. This is strictly unofficial. You had a girl working for you who used to take supplies to one of the quays and there was a man there—Gregg—who is a prime suspect in our enquiry into her rape and murder. The autopsy shows easily enough what happened and we would not need anything so fancy as DNA to prove whether Gregg was, er, involved."

"I see", said Myron, cautiously.

"I doubt it. Gregg cured my wife of a cancer that was about to strike her down. I can't thank him enough. Whatever I think he might have done, I can't deny his powers to others who find themselves in a similar situation. The girl's body has gone missing. It won't be found. It will mean a few more felons on the streets for a few more months, but that's a small price to pay for more miracles.

"All the same, Mr Skraun, you will need to be careful. The rape is beyond doubt and the attack was much more extended than was strictly necessary to kill the poor girl. I would characterise it as frenzied."

◆   ◆   ◆

On the last evening of her tour, flanked by Wayne, Father Joe and Pastor Drone, Trina talked to a large crowd. "I don't like to say unkind things about other beliefs and I have tried very hard not to, but so often on this tour I have come across people who seem totally to misunderstand Christianity and Perpetuanism that I feel I must say something.

"Most people I have met who object to religion do so on two grounds: that it is superstitious and that it is moralising. I don't think on the first count they equate it with black cats and broken mirrors, but they seem to give very little credit to the idea that millions of rational—even very clever—people have ascribed to religious beliefs. However, that is not my main concern. What interests me, because it is what interests all of us, is the second charge. It was the habit in the Old Testament to divide society between the conforming and the non-conforming, to put the conforming inside the city walls and the non-conforming outside. Jesus turned the process inside out. He died outside the city walls, the place of the beggar, the leper, the prostitute, the exploiter, and the rough soldier. We, God's people, are outside the city wall. I am sorry to say that many Christians—and, increasingly, Perpetuans—are reverting to the Old Testament and forgetting the revolutionary Jesus—literally the revolutionary, who turned the wheel through 180 degrees—by excluding the people they term "sinners" such as gay people, partners living together, and addicts and their dealers. Indeed, many people, because of the way that society is demographically organised, avoid any contact with what they think of as evil. Not only do they resent the violent man, they avoid the battered woman. They resent the drug dealer and avoid the addict. When they see and avoid the beggar I am not even sure that they resent the economic arrangements which have put him there.

"There has naturally been a good deal of intellectual discussion about the relevance of Perpetua but, put simply, it is this; she came to remind us, in her manifestation as his sister, of what Jesus said. What he said is not less relevant, but it grew pallid in our Western culture. She came to revive the message. Jesus and Perpetua belong to us just as we belong to God our Parent. "Whatever else you remember, just remember this: that we are all God's children who can learn how to be as we should be through the lives of Jesus and, more recently, Perpetua."

It took a bit of swallowing for Pastor Drone, but he was very good about it when Trina brought out some pictures of the Sacrament of Commitment for Wayne and Father Joe.

"Come on, Pastor," she said, "you can't nod at my sermon and not enacted it."

Before the Summer break, Trina gathered the core group together. "So far we have prospered and have avoided becoming too structured. We have Kylie, Wayne, Brian, Cara, Stacey, and Max as the core group and Father Bill, Father Joe, Quintus, Chris, and Clement working with us. We have more than 3,000 Guides and more than 3,000 house groups. We have the support of Sir Pluto Millman and the benevolent wishes of Archbishop Hawthorne and Sir Granville Brompton. We face yet more difficulties, but we will be strong in the Spirit and soft in what we say. We must remember that people who are aggressive need our pastoral care."

Archbishop Hall was gloomy. He had lost Clement and only had the gloomy Crozier and Janet Burns as a stand-ins until they yet again went through the recruitment processes. Crozier only cared about money and the dignity of the Archbishops Council and if there was a choice between saying something and nothing he usually opted for nothing. Janet was a nice enough woman when you got to know her, but her media training had made her aggressively sharp and fond of her own sharpness. She habitually formulated unpleasant aphorisms which were not quite apt and she never saw good in anyone. James wondered whether her temperament had led her into attack journalism or whether she had gone in that direction out of insecurity. He supposed that the only thing worse than being an attack journalist was being a failed attack journalist. He was comfortably pastoral with her, which she found difficult at first but grew into appreciating. This was all very well, thought James, as far as it went, but the relationships were both one way. He was helping Crozier to articulate and helping Janet to become less sharp, but they was hardly helping him at all.

There were times when he wished that Archbishops were not be above the fray, but allowed to be in it. The problem with the defection of so many bishops to the Perpetuans, all from the liberal tendency, was that he was left with Torans, Petrans, and BCP Medians. At the meeting of bishops to discuss the major items on the Grand Synod agenda, Dean Crowther had secured the services of his successor, Bishop Rodley, to organise the anti-Perpetuan forces. In a cursory discussion, the bishops agreed by a substantial majority to condemn the Perpetuans as a "parasitic sect" and blocked the notion of any dialogue with it before going on to a tortuous debate on women bishops.

There was no problem getting the major motions through the Grand Synod which was consolidating after its losses. Archbishop Mwanga did not mention the Perpetuan issue in his Presidential Address and James spent as much time as he decently could praying. Pensions and women bishops rumbled on and the

Perpetuan item was hardly a debate. Nobody noticed. The Church of England, though yet a little more curtailed, was back to normal.

Reviewing their progress, Lord Warpley, Sir Horace, and Dean Crowther were not best pleased. They had achieved two of their aims in mounting a campaign against reduced consumption and a motion at Grand Synod, but it didn't seem to make any difference. The publicity flared and died and Perpetuanism went on growing steadily. There were still the education and terrorism options, but there was little enthusiasm for them.

In Sir Granville's nearby Georgian house, Sir Pluto summarised, "we are growing; they are stuck. We have made a little headway in Africa. We are worried about a maverick called Gregg in North America, but he has bad form and we're keeping our options open. We shouldn't be behaving like this, but we're friends of rather than strict Perpetuans. What next, Granville?"

"Well, the cult of the bullets which killed Dexter, Miles, and Will seems to have died down, and you don't see many of those luminous statues of Perpetua these days, do you? Trina had a very good, low-key tour just as Perpetua used to travel around. It seems to me, counter intuitively, perhaps, that it's a time to do nothing out of the ordinary. The trouble with humans is that we over estimate the impact of what we say and do. Look at how much heavy lifting old Reggie, Griswald and Horace have been doing, and for what? What's strategy against the power of the Spirit?"

◆　◆　◆

The relationship between Myron and Gregg had shifted radically, for although they each knew what they knew, instead of giving Myron the upper hand because of his potential power of blackmail, Gregg had attained superiority because Myron was frightened of him. No matter how formal he tried to be, no matter how decorous and consultative, he could not hide his fear.

"New York," said Gregg. "Madison Square Gardens."

"We haven't got the funds."

"After last time you've got as much credit as you want. How can I be a real leader if I'm stuck down here in this swamp? You can keep your filthy money, but I want leadership. I've waited long enough. I'm thinking some big new thoughts for New York—Perpetuan thoughts—but big and new."

"I just wish you could lend some credibility by mentioning Jesus and Perpetua now and again. I wish you could learn how to pretend to pray. It's not difficult, really. If you can learn to act you can learn to pray. You need to say something while you're exercising your powers, like, 'God give you strength that you may be healed in mind and body'. It covers all angles, you see. Even if they're not healed in body, which is the only thing most of them care about, they might be healed in mind, and we get the credit."

"No, you get the cash, I get the credit. Don't look like that, it's a joke!"

It might have been, thought Myron, but he looked pretty murderous.

His fear and his greed overcame his natural caution and he booked Madison Square Garden for the last weekend in June. There should have been a world boxing title bout, but it had been called off because the challenger had been arrested for murdering his girl friend. Myron wondered gloomily whether Gregg would not have been better off taking up the challenge rather than healing the sick.

Meanwhile, the affair of the girl's body had died away. There had been an enquiry and it had been found, to nobody's particular surprise, that three in every hundred bodies referred to the police disappeared without explanation. Nobody seemed interested in doing anything about it. They were, everybody assumed, the bodies of the poor and benighted, addicts, prostitutes, and hobos. With each day that went by, Myron became less frightened of anything turning up, but that had the unfortunate effect of increasing Gregg's self-confidence. As the two trends ran in parallel, Myron gained nothing, another case of his inability to experience unalloyed peace.

In the middle of June he also began to suspect that Gregg was looking darkly at Dolorez, with that look he interpreted as predatory and murderous. It wasn't that he needed Dolorez so much as he needed to avoid any more scandal. A supply girl was one thing, a supply girl and a wife quite another. He wondered whether to warn her or whether he should just leave it, but when he tentatively mentioned that Gregg was looking a little strangely at her, she said she already knew what he was up to and was watching carefully. More carefully than Myron could have imagined. After her husband's somewhat tepid love making she enjoyed Gregg's more definite style, laced with danger. On the first occasion that they availed themselves of intimate relations—it could not have been characterised as love on either side—she was ready when his hands went towards her neck. "You forget the street brawling," she said, as she kicked him strategically and tied him up. "It would be a pity if you lost your means of giving pleasure, but I prefer doing without you to dying."

Dolorez expected much of the New York adventure from both of her men who expected much from each other, but little from her.

◆   ◆   ◆

The Summer of 2008 was to banking and finance what the Summer of 1914 was to diplomacy and warfare. There were a few—a very few—who were seen afterwards to have "called it right", but they were ignored on the quite proper basis that where you have a consensus there is always a little money or reputation to be made at the margin by refusing to go along with it. To some extent the mood was sustained by a herd instinct that as long as the big beasts all stuck together the party would continue, but there was also a more sinister, restless undertone as brokers passed potentially explosive, mystery parcels of supposed assets. Nobody refused them because there was a good premium to be made very quickly by acquiring these and passing them on without opening them. It became such a desperately enjoyable game that different units of the same corporations were hoodwinking each other. Indeed, it was a high summer for financial fun and games, and while these went on, the referees ticked their boxes and filed their statistics and sat in their board rooms, unworried by the mounting evidence of turbulence just below the surface. Nor were the great protectors of our freedom, the fearless investigators of scandal and the tireless watchers at the gates, aware that anything was amiss. The silly season was sillier than ever. For years some grave heads had said that there was an underlying weakness in the pensions market, that the good times could not last, that a gentle falling-off in the property market might be the precursors of something worse. It was a well known fact that readers, whose largest two lifetime items of expenditure, after taxes, were housing and pensions, found the technicalities boring. All they wanted to know was how the markets were doing and how much "windfall" profit they had made on their houses.

There was, then, a terrible collusion, not so much of silence in the face of the facts, but of indifference to duty. The financial, regulatory and journalistic establishment were so busy telling others how to behave while indulging themselves, they had lost the capacity for reflection. A general belief had arisen that to log something was to deal with it, and so everything that could be logged had been logged. Never had the risk register been so prominent and comprehensive. The politicians, who had instituted the logging culture as a way of distributing responsibility, such that because everybody was responsible, nobody was, went to their holiday homes. In America they could only snatch a few days as the Presidential campaigns were in full swing, but the British elections were still almost two years away and there seemed no good reason to worry as they sat on the patios of their Tuscan villas.

It was strange that two so different men should have been so complacent. President Bush, cleverer than he allowed most people to know, was, nonetheless, less clever than an American President ever should be and was borne along upon a tide of reckless, selfish optimism, whereas Gordon Brown, perhaps a little more clever than a British Prime Minister ought to be, trusted the markets in spite of his socialist upbringing. They were so enchanted by the mood of the times, the taxes that flowed into their treasuries and the general sense of well-being, that they lost the capacity to wonder.

All over the capitalist world, the holiday flights flew, and the tills whirred and the funds travelled up and down the wires and bounced off satellites. In faceless, windowless repositories, strangely old fashioned bundles of documents were heaped high, the physical manifestations of the agreements executed in the dealing rooms. Nobody had yet noticed the trickle of defaults as main street began to realise that it had been duped by Wall Street.

◆ ◆ ◆

GREGG TO NEW YORK CITY AND THE WORLD—BLOG 4

Fellow Perpetuans,

1. You will recall that since we began to bear witness to the life and teaching of Perpetua, we have always been keen to emphasise the importance of free choice, of our fundamental aptitude as children of God to exercise our own consciences in the face of a hostile world so that we may be held accountable to God our Parent. I have also emphasised continually that in order for our free choice to be properly made we must live our lives within a moral framework.

2. Now some of you have asked how this framework can continue to contain our lives when God has chosen to free us from it by the exercise of my mighty powers. We have indeed, through the Grace of God, given new life and hope to thousands of people. Some people have found these two states to be incompatible.

3. I therefore say to you that we are living in an extraordinary time where the usual rules no longer apply. We must all, naturally, continue to exercise our freedom within the moral law when we know ourselves to be living in an ordinary way, but when we feel the power of God exercised through me, then we know that it is time to suspend the usual rules of living. Just as a person who pays medical fees to be cured of a serious illness finds that I have cured it, so anybody who comes into contact with me will know that they no longer need to worry about the tedious details of prudential financing.

4. For I say to you, solemnly, that I bring with me the power to make all things well, to bring God's prosperity to the American people. I can go further because it has become clear to me through my work as a servant of Perpetua that we can see how powerfully her witness works in us according to how much faith we have placed in her power, which I now exercise on her behalf.

5. So, Perpetuans, do not be afraid, put the power of your money behind the power of Perpetua and you will be amply rewarded because those who trust in God will always enjoy the fruits of creation as a sign of the enjoyment to come in the life everlasting.

6. What was not clear when Perpetua left our earth is abundantly clear now: that we are living in a new age of prosperity which matches the new age of health. The miracles of healing will be matched by the miracles of prosperity, but to enjoy the prosperity you need to demonstrate the same faith you have shown in healing. This is not a passive faith but is active in the eagerness with which you approach the throne of God through your investment in Perpetua and Christ.

7. I urge you, therefore, the people of New York and the wider world , to invest in faith. Whatever you give to the promotion of Perpetua you will more than regain in her gifts to you. This is not a pyramid scheme in which you give and we pay an unrealistic return from the invested funds— although that is what we have been accused of—no, our proposal to you is a simple act of faith. You give to us and, through God's power in us you will be rewarded abundantly. If you doubt, consult our web site. There you will see how faith has been repaid in thousands of cases.

8. I understand that some of you may be reluctant to invest because of some previously doubtful religious enterprises, but you should know the difference. No Christian enterprise since the beginning of television has such a track record of healing to offer. You can believe us because we have so far been true to our promises.

9. I am writing this brief blog to you because we will soon be arriving in New York City and we wish to meet as many of you as we can, to bring the good news of God, in the reality of the life of Perpetua, so that you may prosper in the Spirit, in truth and your own lives and fortunes.

10. For too long, Christianity wanted to persuade you that there was an opposition between being a true child of God and being prosperous. Some orthodox Christians refused to give way and continued to believe that God's love shines through a prosperous life, but now we are restoring the true link.

◆ ◆ ◆

Myron was astounded by Gregg's audacity. "I can see that millions will flow in to the Church and it will make people feel good to give, but how does that make them better off?"

"We won't be attracting the widow's mite," said Gregg. "If they're investing in us they will be investing in far bigger things. That being so, they would have prospered without investing in us, but a certain kind of person likes this kind of giving."

"So what do you get out of it?"

"I have decided that it would be wonderful to run a church and to exercise strong moral leadership over weak people. You may have gathered that my past has been quite difficult, full of difficult people, and full of personal difficulty. I want to be above it. I want to be able to escape from all the entanglements."

"But what about the incident on the quay?"

"Myron, how can I be plainer. When you're at a certain level in society you can do anything. Celebrity is my protection."

New York went wild when Gregg and Myron came into town. They were invited onto all the local television channels and divided their efforts between

Myron's "soft" and Gregg's "prophetic" approach. For a city so often accused of being the hedonistic capital of the world—the new Babylon rather than the new Rome—it was, it might be thought, surprisingly receptive to a religious "happening", but the truth was that it had been promised sensation.

Donations flooded in to the American Church of Perpetua which Myron syphoned judiciously into a variety of gold and gem enterprises. He had heard the word on the street which so many others had ignored. He was the perfect specimen of the being torn between greed and fear in which fear marginally predominates and so the bulk of the funds were turned into small, portable, eminently liquid assets and the remainder was kept personally by Myron in cash.

Sir Pluto sat in a private lounge of an exclusive hotel overlooking Central Park, so exclusive that there was no name plate on the buzzer panel. One press of button 30 would draw the attention of the staff to the CCTV screen and would then bring a security guard, a porter, and a butler. It was not a place where Sir Pluto had stayed before as he was fond of bustling hotels with piano bars, but he had been steered there by his friends who had been keeping an eye on Gregg who was sitting in an identical lounge one floor below. Myron had not known what to do, but it was not difficult to route advice to him once his plans were known. Pluto wanted to keep an eye on Gregg, as did his friends from Langley, part out of curiosity, part out of a code of honour which expected old comrades to look after each other. Those who had tortured and been tortured were particularly liable to strange turns and needed special protection. The very worst were dead or serving life sentences, but the next cardre up was too big and varied to be disposed of in either of these ways. Most of them got by without disgracing themselves until the bottle's grip was unbreakable, but there were some, like Gregg, who had very active tendencies which might break out at any time.

Once he had arrived, Gregg began to behave like a rock star. He demanded the strangest and most expensive food, he insisted on a daily visit from a coiffeur to tend hair that he had grown for the past two months, he wore golden robes specially commissioned from a fashion house, and he demanded a steady supply of women all of whom had to be trained in advance of their visits to deal with his particular proclivities.

Sir Pluto was unusually gloomy. Being a man of the world he was under no illusion about the comparative prospects for Gregg's Church and Trina's movement. Gregg and Myron had worked up an enormous head of steam while Trina and her group were just working steadily away. He consoled himself with the story of the tortoise and the hare, and then he reminded himself that, with the Spirit, these comparisons were useless. Yet he vowed to keep watch.

At a welcoming party Gregg was forced by his hosts to make a speech.

◆ ◆ ◆

GREGG TO NEW YORK CITY AND THE WORLD—BLOG 5

Fellow Perpetuans,

1. I grieve that I worry that that I might not be able to call you so—and that is the clue—for we need to be united. Since I came here I have discovered various factions among you which, I suppose is predictable in such a global trading city, but we must come together. Now I have heard that there are among you those who follow Trina and her self-styled leadership group, and those who follow a strange sect started by Bob and Andy to cash in on the Perpetua name, and those who, God help me, claim to follow me. When you say you follow these people—even when you say you follow me—you are wrong, for we are all citizens in Perpetua.

2. I know that some people will say that the majority can be wrong, that there are courageous minorities who stand out against the tyranny of the majority, but such are exceptions to the general rule. That rule is made more sure if it is in the pattern of the Spirit. I want you to know, and to be in no doubt, that I have suffered in bearing witness to Perpetua. I have been pursued from place to place, I have been confined, and my sanity has been called into question. Yet I stand here before you now as the living witness of the Spirit's grace working in me to proclaim the true Perpetuan gospel. I need say little about the core group in London led by Trina. They are good people by their own, limited lights, but they do not carry the full mark of the succession. I alone bear that mark and so I ask you to unite behind me in the name of Perpetua. I can dismiss the tiny sect of Bob and Andy, but I have to spend just a little more time on the sect which claims to have been founded and confirmed by Max, that arch schemer, discredited banker, alcoholic, and impostor. He claims to have founded a church with a certain Thomas of Boston, but our investigations show that this Thomas, like many of his episcopal fellow travellers, can easily be shown to be another impostor.

3. Now these may sound like harsh words, but there is nothing more important than the Gospel which it is my mission to carry to the world. Trina and other such primitivists who claim to be closest to Perpetua have missed the point revealed to me, as a true follower, by Perpetua herself. The primitivists have adopted a corrosive fatalism, claiming that Perpetua wanted them simply to be passive in the face of the world, its good and its bad, defining faithfulness as submission. Let me tell you what the true Gospel means for the people of the world:

4. Firstly, Perpetua believed, above all else, in individual and community self-determination. From her own humble background, struggling to be faithful and moral, she saw that the state crippled responsibility. She saw so many well intentioned initiatives end in failure and waste. She saw well intentioned officials spending public money to try to lever apathetic people out of their degradation, but she knew from her own experience that the only way out of degradation is affirmation. She saw that the true fail-

ure of the Christian churches was their alliance with the state. In spite of their anti-socialist rhetoric they bought the dirigiste agenda. They might have kept their structural distance, but they still colluded with the state. This is why Obamans for Perpetua is a nonsense, it is a denial of all that is true. Some of you will have heard the old English expression that we must keep religion and politics apart. So we should, in practical terms, but we are duty bound, by the terrible death of Perpetua, to proclaim to you that not all expressions of political and religious organisation are compatible with Perpetuanism. Individuals and communities must be left to affirm their faith from their own resources.

5. Now it follows from that, secondly, that the resources we have directly relate to our faith in what is right. There is a sentimental tradition in Christianity, taken over by Trina and her defeatists, which says that it is the obligation of the well off to assist the poor. Now we who are faithful understand that there is a certain degree of pragmatism in ensuring that the idle poor do not resort to violence instead of work, but we know that the poor are in their abject state because they will not put their trust in the Godhead. Is it a coincidence that Churches are full of prosperous people while the unchurched, those who wear the badge of victimhood, are poor and degraded? There are still strong elements of moral force in the United States which follow this analysis and we must unite with them.

6. Let me turn now to how this view of the true Perpetuan life should be lived by us all. The Perpetuan movement must spread throughout all the world and make itself felt wherever there is a need for moral responsibility and free trade to replace statism and protectionism. I can think of nowhere more suitable than New York City to launch a global campaign for Perpetuan purity. Yes, there are those who tell me how excess wealth might lead to moral decadence, but that is our temptation which we are worthy to confront. It is our responsibility to understand evil for only by doing so can we preach with conviction against it! Is Gregg a sinner? Of course he is. Are followers of Trina sinners? Of course they are but, they will not admit it, hiding under a cloak of fatalism. Are we all sinners? Of course we are. We will all fall short and, in doing so, will be hardened to the moral imperative of struggling against evil.

7. The next thing that follows is that we must build a worship life which reflects our moral life. Perpetua occasionally held uplifting, even picturesque, little rituals to give encouragement to the faithful and we must continue this tradition. Yet we must renounce the Papist Sacramentality which Trina and her people have sought to impose on Perpetuans. We are Perpetua's faithful community, but we want to have nothing to do with the idea of a church or a hierarchy. Anybody can find symbols to reflect the spiritual dimension.

8. Before I close, I want to say a few words to you about moral issues which are constantly being raised with me as your spiritual leader. On the mat-

ter of money, I have already spoken, but I want us all to beware of the sin of envy. There is enough wealth in God's wonderful world to furnish us all with the riches we need. Those who will not strive and will not work envy us and we must counter their envy by our good example of finding joy in the good fortune of others and sharing that good fortune, not to undermine self-determination and to increase dependency, but to show the world how we are blessed.

9. The other matter which I must raise relates to sexual morality for there is nothing which rouses such confused and ill-informed debate. The Christian doctrine of monogamy is property-based. It was an attempt to impose artificial limitations on the way we live, just as, in an extreme form, clerical celibacy was an imposition of an economic kind. The way we enjoy intimate relations should mirror our understanding of the economy. Men must have the responsibility for self-expression. for some, the limited self-expression of monogamous marriage will be enough, but for those with large fortunes there is the responsible option of caring for more than one woman. Some may wish such women to be contracted to them as wives, but we would argue that the woman must also have the option, as an independent person, to live in an uncontracted relationship. Now whether this should apply to a woman having a relationship with more than one man is quite another matter, for although women may prosper, we uphold the ancient traditions.

10. And so, in the name of Perpetua, make your wealth and your fruitfulness known throughout all the world. Keep on dealing and I will keep on healing

◆　　◆　　◆

Sir Pluto was incensed and wrote a hurried rejoinder to Trina and Max. "If we do not stop this immediately, Perpetuanism as we know and love it will be overwhelmed by this shallow materialism and sexual self-indulgence. There is nothing more dangerous than a religion which embraces greed and lust. I understand the Perpetuan ethic of love—I really do—but if you do not make some kind of compromise which protects you when giving your unconditional love from organised rape, you will be lost—Pluto."

Trina and Max did not want to give in to Pluto but they thought that it was proper to hold a discussion and emailed back. "We will hold a discussion between our kind of Perpetuanism and any others who claim adherence."

Sir Pluto deliberately misunderstood this message. He had a word with his friends, agreed to take total responsibility for ensuring Gregg's safety and others' safety from him, compelled him to get into the back of a large, black car, forcibly put him onto a private jet and accompanied him to London.

Myron was bewildered and angry when he received a note from Sir Pluto. "Gregg gone to London for assessment of Perpetuan credentials; leaves you in charge. Careful what you do; many closely interested in your conduct."

When Pluto was forced to tell Trina and Max most of the truth they were deeply distressed, but they recognised that some dialogue might be possible. They did not want a confrontation so it was agreed that only Trina and Max should represent the Perpetuans.

The meeting took place in Perpetua's chapel. When they met Gregg, who was being watched by veteran Adam and two other of Sir Pluto's assistants, he frightened them. Since he had left their offices, he had become bigger, stronger, and more aggressive. Pluto had ensured that he came in conventional clothes, but these, expensive and a little shiny, made his body and limbs look even bigger.

"Welcome back," said Trina.

Gregg remained grimly silent.

"Gregg, I said "welcome back' and I meant it. I realise that you have not come here under ideal circumstances, but you must recognise, surely, how we have not curtailed your freedom even though most people might think we have a cause."

"Thanks."

They had agreed that Trina should take the lead. "So now you are here we would like a dialogue. We would genuinely like to know how what we say and what you say might have things in common. We can't own the name of Perpetua and we are not interested in the Christian idea of orthodoxy. We offer Sacramental celebration, Guides, and house groups which all serve to promote what Perpetua taught about love, but we are not going to develop a kind of creed that keeps people out."

"Thanks."

"We hoped that when you were with us you would have learned something about us, but it seems, from what we can gather, to have come out strangely."

"It's strange to me too. Nobody seems to realise how alone I am."

"You can talk to us."

"Nobody seems to know how much I've suffered, how much I've had to undergo for Perpetua."

"You can talk to us."

"Nobody understands how hard it is."

"I am sure we don't, but you can talk to us."

"I've got this compulsion. I'm drawn to Perpetua, but at the same time I feel alienated from her."

"I suppose that some people would call that psychological, Gregg, but I'm inclined to call it a quite common attitude to the good we know and the falling short of good that we are. It's so hard to be as receptive as Perpetua would like."

Max, who had heard an outline of Gregg's history from Pluto, watched as Gregg presented the duality of his physical approach to Trina in lust and revulsion. Trina, who did not know the history, noticed it too, but saw it as a test of her openness as the beloved to the lover.

"As I said," continued Gregg, relaxing just a little, "I didn't ask to come into this and it's wrecked my life ever since. You don't suppose I wanted to do miracles, do you? It's turned me into Myron's circus animal."

"You could come back to us."

"I wouldn't survive. That's the trouble. I'm too torn, but I tell you this—I am one of the true followers of Perpetua. I've said it in my blogs because I believe it."

"You've also said," interjected Max, gently, "that we are impostors."

Gregg shifted, torn between dejection and aggression. "Well I'm sorry. I suppose that was going a bit far, but it's difficult when you're all alone on the road proclaiming the truth."

"What truth is that?" asked Trina.

"The truth that Perpetua taught individual responsibility."

"True, Gregg, but she also taught solidarity and self-restraint. I say this gently but firmly, she did not teach that faith in God was translated into worldly wealth."

"Perhaps not," said Gregg, obviously suffering some internal struggle, "but the main thing is choice."

"Oh Gregg, the main thing is choice for the other, for the lover if one is marked out as the beloved."

"Freudian socialist crap!" flared Gregg.

Max looked as if he would interject, but Trina walked half a step forward to up-stage him.

"Gregg, there's no need to be so tormented. You and I have different views of what Perpetua said and meant, but this is an exploration not a competitive argument. We want to hear you, but we don't want to change you. You say her core idea was choice, we say her core idea was facilitating the choice of the other. You seem to think that this can be settled by argument, we think it will be settled by Our Sister the Spirit in each and every human heart. Although we have little time for the old ideas of doctrine and theology, we think that spiritual enquiry should clear away mines. We don't think that theology should be used as ammunition."

"So what are you going to do to stop me?"

"Nothing. Does the Christian church, or churches, as currently constituted, own Christ? No, inasmuch as Christ owns anything he 'owns' the churches he founded. We do not own Perpetua or even the name of Perpetua. We urge you to study with us and to go on talking with us through which you might have a closer knowledge of why we believe what we believe, but we can compel you to do nothing."

"She appeared to me. I'm as much of a follower as you. I don't need to be with you to learn anything."

"There are some people, and you may be one of them, although I doubt it from your demeanour, who can learn deep truths by being alone, but most of us learn by being with each other, in silence created by dialogue."

"Is that Wittgenstein or some other brand of socialist crap?"

"I don't know. Max tells me it's Bruckner, but that's beside the point, Gregg. We don't want you to be with us so that we can make you like us. We want you to be with us so that we can help each other to be faithful to Perpetua."

"But I do more miracles than you."

"Ah," said Max, "I wondered when you would get round to that."

"So?"

"As far as we can tell," said Max, "Perpetua performed mighty acts through the power of God our Parent very sparingly and for highly specific reasons, giving people a new start. You seem to have the power, from somewhere, to perform mass healings. This is very impressive, but we are in no position to confirm or deny—sorry about the diplomatic sounding language—whether this has anything to do with Perpetua. We just don't know. On occasion Trina and other followers have undertaken mighty acts, but they have always invoked the help of God our Parent through Perpetua. Maybe you did that under your breath, but none of the records show it."

Gregg again looked torn. "I know. I become engulfed. I don't know what, and then the healings take place. Then I go into something like a coma."

"We can say nothing," said Trina, "except for this which we will write down. I hate writing things down as Perpetua seems to want us to operate entirely by human contact with nothing written down, but perhaps she will allow our writing to last for a few days, if it helps. Thank you for coming Gregg and, again, I am sorry you came under such circumstances. Sir Pluto was just a little beyond his remit, but we know he is sorry already."

As he accompanied Gregg from the room, Sir Pluto showed no sign of contrition, but it was in Trina's nature to be generous.

◆　◆　◆

TRINA TO THE WORLD—BLOG ONE

Beloved children of God in the power of Our Sister the Spirit and in communion with Jesus and Perpetua.

I wish to reaffirm on behalf of the followers of Perpetua who walked with her in her life and those who have directly received from them full membership as followers in the movement, that Perpetua's core belief was in the provision by the beloved of unconditional space for the lover. It follows from this that the lover acts in freedom and that the two orientations are symbiotic, although not reciprocal, for they are not equal. The exercise of choice by the lover is a necessary precondition for the higher calling of unconditionally making space for the lover who, in being received, is the beloved. This may sound unduly metaphorical and tautological, but it is not. The teaching is clear. The exercise of freedom is necessary, but inferior to the exercise of reception. The culmination of the exercise of freedom is not to do, but to be done to.

We must also choose to care for people as sisters and brothers of Jesus and Perpetua as we are all children of God our Parent, but caring for people and taking responsibility for our own choices are "lower" virtues than offering to receive the love of the other without condition.

◆　◆　◆

Myron's resentment at Gregg's sudden absence was overcome by his relief. Gregg had 36 hours to get ready for his big gig at Madison Square Garden. It was a sell-out in spite of Gregg's media absence because Myron had turned this into a feature of Gregg's mysteriousness.

The first part of the evening was almost staid. Gregg went through his well rehearsed speech to the assembled magnates on the connection between faith in Perpetua, moral living, and prosperity and blessed the crowd with his newly composed blessing while the pledge cards were completed. Those with a loved one in need of a cure were assigned prime seats for the second half which began, incongruously, in Perpetuan terms, with a hell fire preacher to warm up the crowd so that when Gregg appeared at the top of the bill the crowd was in a state of near hysteria. Gregg said a cursory sort of prayer—but better than any previous attempt—and then asked the stewards to organise the people for the healing. There was chaos as they refused to obey orders to wait and some, New York style, were knocked to the floor. Gregg called the place to order and said he would withhold his mighty powers unless there was order. For more than an hour and a half he laid hands on people as they came past, escorted by helpers. When the ceremony was complete, Myron asked for testimonies. There were plenty. People were given a roving microphone to proclaim how they had been healed, but the more people who rose to speak, the louder were the shouts of those who had been disappointed. Coincidence or not, there had been no cures on the North side and its occupants began barracking and threatening. Had the conditions not been so cramped, they might have stormed the dais. As it was, by the time that the trickle of protesters had reached the front the stewards were alive to the threat. Four security guards almost physically picked Gregg up and carried him back stage. That wasn't how Myron had wanted it to end, with chanting, counter chanting, and Gregg whisked away, but the donations at the exits were more than handsome. It was only when Myron had arrived at a satisfactory estimate that he thought about Gregg. He went to his dressing room, expecting him to be in his coma, but the room was empty. He ordered a full search by the security guards, but they did not find him.

Distracted, Myron wanted to contact the police, but one of his minders advised him to wait. A few minutes later a motor cycle courier rode by and tossed a canvas bag at Myron's feet. Inside there was a note.

"We have some of our own in need of help not received at the ceremony. You will get him back once he has done what we want. Do not contact the NYPD."

All the next day Myron waited at the hotel, unaware of Gregg's old comrades who had easily located him. He was returned that evening. There were rumours that his kidnappers had been killed, but no charges were ever brought.

Then Gregg went on a tour of the major cities, holding two part services like that in New York with a remarkably constant healing rate of 10%, followed by days of coma. Myron was disappointed, but the success rate was just enough to maintain his credibility. In San Francisco Gregg was surrounded by a crowd of robed adherents who proclaimed him to be the Fifth Person of the Godhead and Gregg was tempted to allow them to become his personal guard, but Myron hired private security guards to keep him on a leash. Soon after this alarming incident he was flown back to Miami to recuperate.

◆　◆　◆

On Friday 12th September, Fagen Broom sat at his desk yet again conning his accounts. He had not slept and there was an empty bourbon bottle anchoring a pile of bank statements. His wife came in, saw the bottle, and rushed over to him.

"You'll kill yourself if you go on like this. You haven't slept this week."

"I might as well kill myself, Suzie, for there's nothing to be done. I will have to default on our payment and we will be turned out."

"Don't despair, Fagen, we can go back to mother until things straighten out."

"We will never go to your mother and they will never straighten out. I've failed you, Suzie. I believed what they said about the payments, but I was duped."

At 3pm Grant Crumm noted Fagen's failure to pay. This tipped his debt indicator from amber to red. It had been amber for weeks, but he had promised head office an upturn and prayed for a miracle. Grant's red tipped Ohio's cumulative indicator from amber to red and Ohio's red tipped the federal indicator from amber to red. Over the weekend finance managers were tied to their desks trying to shore up their banks and finance houses, but by Sunday afternoon there was panic in what should have been a deserted Wall Street. The President was asked for Federal assistance but, just before midnight, when he refused, the great bank of Silberman Brothers crashed. Through the night the tsunami of failure washed through the skyscrapers of New York and across the Atlantic to a waking London. Fagen never came home.

Myron's timing could not have been worse. On the Monday evening Gregg was scheduled for his New York comeback. Myron wanted to cancel the event, but Gregg, fired up by his rest, was insistent. When he appeared in his golden robes and began to speak about faith and prosperity he was jeered and people began to throw coins and tear up seat cushions. A shot was fired and Gregg fell to the ground, but it hit a security guard in the arm. Gregg was bundled off the dais and his guards tried to sneak him out of a side door, but the crowds were too wise for that device and, in the end, he was brought out through a redundant sewer.

Back in Miami, Myron thanked God that he had not bought securities with his earnings.

◆　◆　◆

In London, Max was one of the first to establish an advice centre to deal with City panic. He told people that he had been left with nothing after a bank merger and that, with the strength of Perpetua, he had taken control of his life, but he also immediately recognised that it would be the low paid workers who would suffer. The bankers would soon be back in the harness, but lowlier workers would be on the scrap heap. While the Government and the media thrashed about Max and his fellow workers went calmly about their business, quoting their golden rules:

» It was never as good as they say it was
» It will never be as bad as they say it will
» With the strength of Perpetua you can keep control of your life.

After two weeks of hard work, there was a steadying of temperament and Max and Trina decided that they must go to New York. Accordingly, they held a meeting of the core group and laid hands on Clement.

◆　◆　◆

Gregg was restless almost to the point of going out of control. He had grown tired of his seclusion, he had grown bored with the women and he felt the call of the public platform. He wanted to follow up on his latest message

GREGG TO NEW YORK CITY AND THE WORLD—BLOG SIX

Fellow Perpetuans and those who have despaired,

1. We have recently experienced a tidal wave of catastrophe sweeping across the world, but this is no time to despair. We need to listen to what God is saying to us through the life and teaching of His Special Daughter Perpetua. In times of plenty we tend not to focus on the meaning of suffering in our lives—and that is a pity because contemplation is better in a period

of calm than a period of crisis—but now we have been brought to a critical hour. Now is the time for us to take stock of what it is to be human, to live in times of famine as well as feast, to remember the story of Egypt and the Lord's mission through Joseph.

2. Some of you will quite properly point out that I have tried to relate faithfulness and prosperity and have drawn the quite false conclusion that a reduction in prosperity means a waning of faithfulness. Nothing of the sort. The true meaning of self-determination, as preached by Perpetua, is that you have the inner strength to persevere and become yet more favoured in God's sight. It is those who give up the struggle who show the want of faithfulness.

3. So in these more difficult times it is important that you grasp every opportunity. Many of you will have suffered a loss of assets, but you still have your skill and your bravery born of faith. Every sacrifice of instant gratification you make now will be rewarded a hundredfold in the future. It has also been pointed out to me that some people are saying that we think that the poor are damned because their poverty shows a want of faith—and it is certainly true that many poor people are scandalously Godless—but everybody has the chance to share in the Perpetuan dream. It is open to all. If a person of modest means works hard and contributes generously to the cause then he will be as safe in God's love as the richest man. Nobody is shut out. That is why during these times of trial that we have to do our utmost to bring more people to the true faith.

4. When Perpetua appeared to me she made it clear to me that I was her true follower, sent to save all people, but, as you all know, the truth is that only you can save yourselves. Perpetua was murdered by a gang of feckless teenagers who were not without means, who represented the absolute betrayal of all she stood for. When people say that we are unsympathetic to the poor, they miss the point. The people we really are concerned about are the children of the prosperous who have turned away from God and only care for material things. They, who squander their wealth, will be the true losers if they do not turn back to us.

5. I want you to know that this is a special time for the Spirit who will be amongst us, urging us on to heightened efforts, to deeper sacrifice.

6. But the most serious charge laid against us is that the very self-determination which Perpetua died for is the cause of our current catastrophes. There are dangerous fanatics closing in, saying that everything would have been fine if there had been a more powerful government and more rigourous regulators, but they entirely miss the Perpetuan point. How can somebody act well of his own accord if he is regulated to act in a certain way? Regulation robs us of our freedom to act properly. It is similar to the situation of two people who wonder if they are falling in love. If one keeps asking, "do you love me?" and the other keeps replying, "yes I do", then the person being pestered is robbed of the opportunity to volunteer, "I love

you." Perpetua was crystal clear about this. The essence of the holy life is the ability to love freely. Our whole religious way of life is being threatened by socialists who are planning a persecution of honest, voluntarist people.

7. So beware the temptations of using the public's money to crack down on right living. President Bush has already shown himself to be a traitor to the cause of true religion by using public funds—our money—to bail out the banking system when we all know that, given backbone, the banking system could sort itself out. People who want to do the right thing for themselves do not want to be deprived of their liberty at a time when they need it most through being forced to give up hard earned money to a pitiless state. In spite of the pieties of the President and his people, it is beyond doubt that all states are necessarily anti-religious because they all curtail God-given freedom.

8. Obama will be worse. True religion has only survived in America because there have been enough brave people to stand up against Washington.

9. Nobody knows more than me the value of freedom. After my recent exertions on behalf of Perpetua I am a prisoner of my own weak body, I must take rest before I come to you again.

10. I keep you all in my prayers as I suffer for Perpetua. I will come to you soon.

◆   ◆   ◆

Myron was a little doubtful about some of the language and he was a little sensitive to the charge that he was, in effect, keeping Gregg confined but, on balance, he liked the letter.

Gregg was becoming ferociously restless and the only thing that kept him under control was Dolorez' erotic inventiveness. She was in such great demand that it became impossible to conceal her vital role from Myron who accepted the situation with good grace as he continued to prosper against the national trend.

Trina and Max arrived in New York city just at the point when Gregg's latest blog was making headlines. The problem was not how to rebut what he said, but to build enough trust in those who really needed help. The immediate criticism they faced was that they were proselytising the vulnerable, but their reply was that, as Perpetuans, their only role was to offer unconditional love, and that meant listening. However, they found something profoundly illogical in the Christian position that you could not bring Jesus to the vulnerable, but had to wait until they were robust. It seemed like a sell-out to the secular. As Perpetua had wanted, above all, like Jesus, to strengthen the vulnerable, it was logical to cite her example.

They would not confront Gregg with argument, but with the example of what they did.

While Max worked in Manhattan, primarily with desperate bankers and financiers, Trina sought out the poor who had been hit by the collapse of great institutions, but also by the collapse of their hopes as their homes were re-possessed.

Max opened up a centre where people could come and talk about what they had done and not done. Some bankers were desperately sorry, others were angry as if they had been singled out for bad treatment, but most were bewildered. They had gone into ever more complex deals, one tiny step at a time, and by the time they could no longer understand what they were doing, there was no exit. The ride became ever more exhilarating and dangerous. They knew that it would end in a crash, but they just had to enjoy it while it lasted. In some ways, the crash had been a relief.

"But do you think that this Gregg is right when he says that faithfulness is demonstrated in prosperity?" asked one.

"Gregg is right to say that the true Perpetuan stands for self-determination, but solidarity means that we must enable it. Anyway, you know yourself there are plenty of faithful poor people and idolatrous rich people. But you can spend too much time on that," said Max. "What counts is caring and, above all, loving. Our form of loving at the moment is simply to be here. We don't have the means to erect a caring structure—other people can do that—but there's so much talking in New York City at the moment and it seems that very few people are listening. People are talking at or even past each other. To listen to them, you would think that all the pundits got it right. I don't say this as a Perpetuan, but simply as an observer of human nature. I don't see how most of these people can dare to go on speaking and being paid for it when only a couple of weeks ago they were on the gravy train talking about a boom that would, apparently, never end. It's the illusion of pride, but also a failure to recognise helplessness. If I can, I want to be an ear for these people when they see how deluded they have been. In the meantime, we will do our best."

Max had found it hard to gather round him a group of like minded people. There were a few "native" Perpetuans, but in spite of their faithfulness they found it difficult to sympathise with the Wall Street community. Trina, on the other hand, found it easy to gather together scores of willing helpers and she was soon establishing her classic house groups. Frequently the better off people helped the poorest, but Trina always urged them to think of this as the second stage as it was important not to bypass the first stage of all members being open to each other. If there was to be giving, then the giver and the taker needed to understand and respect each other so that there was no victimhood on the one side nor power on the other. They had to work hard to overcome old prejudices about charity and welfare, comfort and envy.

"Look," said Max to a redundant banker, "it's easier for the poor man to reach you if you live at ground level than if you're at the top of a tower with security guards and teams of intermediaries. Life isn't about protecting yourself, but about opening yourself to the other. When you worked at Silberman you preached a gospel of freedom, of free markets, and free choices, but you were hidden behind jargon and glass; it never was true freedom."

"It's like this," said Trina. "It's plausible to think of poverty as a prison but you can get out by being open to the possibility. That includes the possibility that you are open for others, not just making an opening for yourself."

By the end of October the worst of the hysteria was over. There were still millions of desperate, bewildered people, but a kind of re-building had begun, not the rebuilding of what had been Babel, but something more humbly provisional. People would, as Max knew, make all the same mistakes again as many wounds had not become scars. They laid hands on Sarah as a member of the core group, affirmed more than fifty Guides, gave strength to Thomas in Boston, and were about to return to England when the news broke that Gregg was about to descend on New York City for his third visit.

◆   ◆   ◆

"Oh no!" said Bishop Ignatius quietly to himself when he saw the email. "How could they have done that to themselves and me?" He was sitting in the internet centre in the Stanley Hotel in Nairobi when the message came. After printing it, he deleted the file and hoped that the police would be their usual inefficient selves and not check the international traffic. "Of all the people they could have sent in response to my request for help, why are they sending Wayne and Father Joe?" Their plane had already taken off. There was nothing for it. He would have to go to the airport.

He engaged two taxis and when the men came into the arrivals hall he deftly signalled one into each taxi. They drove to a modest guest house near the Blue Posts Hotel and then took stock.

"I thought I emailed", said Ignatius, "for an urgent supply of educational materials."

"There must have been a mix-up," said Wayne, and then stopped. "No, Ignatius. It wasn't really a mix-up. I was impetuous. I wanted to get out of Stumpy Knoll, out of England, to do some real good. Joe tried to dissuade me, but when I was determined to go he said he wouldn't abandon me. We didn't tell London. I suppose we better tell Clement."

"This could be very serious for both of you," said Ignatius, courteously failing to mention how much danger they had put him into.

"We promise to be very careful," said Wayne, almost in tears.

"There's no help for it," said Ignatius. "We must do what we must do quickly. We can't get you on a flight until tomorrow night. It will be dangerous for our sisters and brothers to meet, but you must lay hands on Simon and we can then confirm our first Guides."

They spent all day in prayer. In the early evening Simon came and Wayne hurriedly laid hands on him and then they resumed their prayer.

Steve, who had never shaken off his resentment at being rejected by Dexter, was now part of a cosmic Evangelical cell. He had picked up the news about Wayne and Father Joe and contacted a cell in Nairobi. Just after midnight five men armed with machetes came to the door. They would have broken in, but Ignatius begged them not to disturb the neighbourhood. He opened the door and the five men rushed in and killed the three Perpetuans in less than a minute and drove away.

Clement read the note which Ignatius had written. "We thank God for those brave Perpetuans who came to help us. If you receive this note, they will have died true martyrs—Ignatius."

"One truer than him," said Clement, failing to hold back the tears. "It was a foolish act, but I don't suppose they are any less martyrs for that. Martyrs, in the end, die for who they are. It doesn't have to be heroic, it just has to be a statement of being."

He emailed Trina and Max saying that they should stay where they were. There was nothing they could do.

The Kenyan police went through the motions to satisfy the British High Commission as delicate development assistance negotiations were in progress, but everybody knew that Kenya classified Wayne and Father Joe as criminals and the Kenyan hierarchy let it be known that Ignatius was an accomplice. Simon was temporarily in danger, but when the Chief of Police was told that he was a distant relative of the President, he was safe as long as he kept a low profile.

◆   ◆   ◆

The core group was breaking up. Forces were pulling them apart. Whether it was the Spirit or a series of coincidences Clement did not quite know. Stacey, Brian, and Kylie laid hands on Philip, who was sent to Stumpy Knoll, John who was sent to Silicon Ridge and Bronwen who was to stay in London with Clement while Kylie went back to Alchester. Brian would continue to look after the god4u Network and Stacey would soon depart for the European mainland.

◆   ◆   ◆

It was the Spirit. As the world continued to reel under the blows of successive financial failures, the Perpetuan movement grew in scope and strength. As people watched their houses re-possessed, their pensions shrink, and their jobs disappear, the engaged gentleness of Perpetua's example reached them. Brian took on Wayne's responsibility for education and new materials populated the Network. With leaders in different places, they soon learned the value of broadcasting a series of Sacramental events from different locations on the same day, bringing a sense of the special occasion to viewers.

The one great danger which threatened the whole movement was the charge that Perpetua's promotion of individualism was inseparable from the reckless behaviour of financial institutions and that Perpetuanism would resist regulation. This charge was given much greater credibility through the blogs of Gregg. Given the reluctance of the original leaders to confront Gregg head-on, it was a while before the original message and Gregg's corruption of it could be properly separated. The key player in putting the record straight was Max, who spent most of his time in the City of London and then in New York, listening to the bewildered and broken, and leading seminars on the difference between Perpetuan love practised in imperfection and the secular responsibility for handling that imperfection. Perpetuans were not against secular law, they just refused to confuse its necessity with the higher laws of care and love. They recognised that failures of care by individuals and communities required collective care, and they recognised that individual and community criminality required restraint. However, they insisted that God did not behave like a secular judge and that Perpetuan love had to be radically separated from utilitarian morality.

Max was careful to separate fatalism from the capacity to be content with one's lot. He emphasised the Perpetuan virtue of exercising whatever control one could over individual and community matters. To accept the hand dealt was quite different from refusing to play. Poor people tried to play poor hands well, while many rich people had played good hands badly. The most important immediate tasks for Perpetuanism were those which society in its post-financial shock phase should welcome: the effort to prevent the suffering from sinking into victimhood, and the effort to prevent the powerful and the rich from falling into a new cycle of recklessness and greed. Perpetuans, contrary to what Gregg said, were in favour of regulation because it transmitted a sense of fairness which prevented victimhood and recklessness. It was a proper secular response to a secular crisis. The more hysterical Gregg became, the more important it was for mainstream Perpetuanism to stay calm. From whatever source it came—and Max and his friends did not know—Gregg's capacity to perform acts of healing did not necessarily make a person a good Perpetuan nor a good social analyst but, still, Max continually had to reject the charge that Gregg was a more effective Perpetuan because he performed healings. The media wanted hierarchy and conflict, but Max steadily refused to comply and although he made little headway in the media which thrived on the generation of discontent, Sneer's analysis, that he would be effective over the long term if he kept to his own story, was correct. The Perpetuan movement grew steadily and, although it was not its objective, the influence of Gregg began to decline.

In trying to come to terms with Perpetuans, the established religions faced the same problem as Archbishop James of not knowing whether to treat them as a Christian sect or a completely different religion. The Roman Catholics, who are always more comfortable with non-Christians than different Christians, chose to designate them as a completely different religion on Trinitarian grounds, arguing that the inclusion of Christ in their worship was not materially different from the Islamic view of him. The Evangelicals, likewise, excluded Perpetuans on the ground that they had enough of a struggle on their hands with "liberals". It was only those liberals who had to struggle with the problem, with their customary mode of dialogue, who could not decide whether Perpetuanism was a different, but potentially helpful, ally. Needless to say, Perpetuanism was never allowed to speak for itself through the mass media which had its own agendas.

For their part, the Perpetuans had to face the question of their own identity. Trina decided that they needed a global meeting to resolve the key issues and initially proposed that this should be in England where they had most adherents, but Max argued that out of solidarity they should meet in the United States where their influence was most needed. It would not be, he argued, a meeting of Guides to settle matters democratically, but a meeting of the core leadership to discern the proper direction.

Accordingly, at the beginning of November 2008, the whole of the core group met in a country mansion just outside New York city: Trina, Max, Brian, Kylie, Cara, Clement, Philip, Bronwen, and John (with Father Bill) from England; Stacey from mainland Europe; Simon from Kenya; and Thomas and Sarah from the United States. The main decisions they needed to take included whether rules were required for the laying on of hands to perpetuate the core group and Guides, and whether rules were required to guarantee a certain uniformity in the Sacraments.

Some of the group asked whether there needed to be a doctrinal discussion but Trina said that they were settled on three issues. Firstly, the nature of the Godhead consisting, up until the present, of four "persons". Secondly, the nature of Perpetuan love exercised within the necessity of human imperfection. Finally, the universality of salvation

Although there was no structure or timetable, the meeting fell into a natural rhythm. Each day began with the Sacrament of Union followed by prayer until the late afternoon. As Trina had anticipated, there was no tension and there were no votes. The group agreed that they should continue to operate entirely on the basis of trust: except in exceptional circumstances like those applying in Africa, there should be two members of the core group to confirm a new member, and a member of the core group plus sponsoring Guides should confirm new Guides. Guides should perform Sacramental acts as they had been taught and make reverent and appropriate changes, but these must remain within the spirit of the initial purpose of the Sacrament. Core group members should only intervene if asked or if they saw for themselves that the spirit of the Sacrament was being compromised.

The reaction to this consensus was greeted with cynicism by the religious media which chose to comment. They did not believe that religion could be properly regulated through trust. They pointed to the basic imperfection of humanity and did not accept that this could be self-regulated through goodwill. They found a Guide in Ipswich, England, who had introduced the drinking of considerable quantities of alcohol into the Sacrament of Union and implied that there had been drunken brawls, and worse. Cynicism soon gave way to indifference and Perpetuanism was left to make its quiet and steady way.

◆　◆　◆

Gregg finally persuaded Myron, near the end of October, that it was the right time for a wealth and health revival. So, after weeks of being confined in his exclusive hotel he, no longer being a mystery, was loosed on the media. In spite of past doubts about his links with the financially irresponsible and his outright opposition to Presidential Candidate Obama, he was lauded in New York as if he were a saviour. Interviewers liked his forthright style. Producers loved the golden robes. Whenever a whiff of his exotic private life reached the tabloid press and most popular radio and television channels, it heightened his popularity. It was rumoured that he only maintained his healing powers by keeping himself at the peak of sexual fitness and there was a good deal of speculation about what he wore—or not—beneath his robes.

The major scoop was gained by the New York Mercury.

HOLY MAN GREGG—SEX TIGER

In an exclusive to the Mercury sassy escort girl Nina has revealed that holy man Gregg is an extraordinary lover.

"I've never had such outright violent sex in my life. Love tiger Gregg almost blew me away."

Nina said that she had been specially trained to pleasure the most vigourous and violent male customers but that "Gregg really pushed the limits. If he heals as powerfully as he makes love, nothing can stop him."

Sir Pluto, who was apparently living quietly in the exclusive hotel occupied by Gregg, Myron, and his burgeoning team of minders, not to mention "friends" from Langley, put through a call to his Mercury Editor. "Good morning Randall."

"Line's clear. Where are you Pluto?"

"I'm in your highly excitable city, phoning to ask about the Gregg and Nina story."

"It's great, isn't it?" said Randall, a little disappointed at Sir Pluto's reticence.

"What I was curious to ascertain, Randall," said Sir Pluto, deliberately bringing his speech to a decorous crawl, "is whether you actually approve of Nina and her activities."

"Well, Pluto, I've heard some strange questions—forgive me—before now but never one quite so strange as this. We at the Mercury neither approve nor disapprove of anything except for approving the free market. We simply report the news."

"There's no need to get defensive, I simply want to know whether the text you used in the Nina story was supposed to prompt admiration or disgust."

"There you've got me, Pluto. She's certainly a sassy lady, though."

"And she's certainly a prostitute."

"So what's wrong with that?"

"Randall, you know that I'm not one to quibble and I'm not moralising, but isn't prostitution illegal?"

"Well, sort of, Pluto, but nobody cares about that any more."

"So which law breaking do we care about, Randall? I mean, if 'sassy Nina' had miscalculated a move and Gregg had killed her, would we have bothered or would we have said she was taking a calculated risk as a highly specialist sex worker? No, Randall, please don't reply now. Just think about it and, while you're about it, while I respect your absolute independence as my—er the—Editor of the Mercury, I don't think you've been quite thorough enough in exploring Gregg's claims."

"Well, his healing track record here in New York is impressive."

"Very true, but is that all there is to it? I mean, Randall, what kind of man is it who uses extreme violence as part of his sexual repertoire? How would you like your daughter to be Nina or your son to be Gregg?"

"That's the oldest trick in the book, Pluto, personalising it like that."

"I know, Randall, it's called the exercise of conscience. Think about it, and see if we can be the leading paper on the Gregg story."

It was the kind of reception which only goes to show that there is no logic in celebrity. He was a moralist libertine, a total free marketeer in a Democrat city, a healer in a deeply sceptical society, and a person who clearly broke conventional religious archetypes and yet he was promoted uncritically by the whole media circus.

Matters became even more colourful when some of the slightly more assiduous journalists managed to link the close of the Perpetuan core group meeting and Gregg's presence in town. In spite of Trina's refusal to be confrontational, much could be made of alleged bad blood if Gregg could be roused. To give him his due, he was not inclined at first to tangle with people who had tried their best for him, but the temptation became too great as the day of his major event came closer with places still to be filled.

In the event, Carnegie Hall was full to capacity. Myron had chosen the venue because he had found the boxing overtones of the Garden distasteful. He knew that he could not tame Gregg's wild showmanship, but at least he could soften it just a little. At the last minute, after much indecision, Max had persuaded Trina to attend the event and Sir Pluto had arranged for tickets.

Gregg came onto the stage in a sober suit, white shirt, and striped red and blue tie and proceeded to make a calm speech based on his most recent blog entry. He emphasised faithfulness to Perpetua and how it would ultimately result in great rewards. As he and Myron had calculated, those in attendance had hung onto a great deal of what they had always had. Perpetuanism was just their little indulgence. They did not blame Gregg or financial irresponsibility for anything because they had not been hurt but, still, they did like to hear that religion was on the side of ultra free market capitalism. If Gregg could make his contribution while appearing not to be too closely aligned with a Republican Party about to lose at the Presidential polls, then that was all to the good. This audience, too, had the curious, impartial characteristic of not being deeply partisan on religious grounds. There were Roman Catholics and Protestants there, but the majority were Jews, observant or indifferent. They were socially and ethically liberal and quietly, economically liberal. They would not mind a cure if it was going. The logistics of the second half were difficult because of the rigidities of the Hall, but Gregg, in a burst of self-confidence, had said that he only needed to lay hands on a select group to symbolise laying hands on everyone. At the end of the wealth part of the proceedings, the pledge cards were passed back down the rows and collected by Stewards. Myron, taking a random sample, was pleased to see that the great dive in September had not produced any permanent damage. They might be floundering in Washington, but these people were solid.

For the second half, Gregg strode onto the platform in his golden robes. As usual, preparations were peremptory with a single reference to Perpetua. Max saw Trina rise from her aisle seat and walk steadily towards the platform. She might have been the carer of one of the representative wheelchair users parked where the first rows of seats had been removed, but on she went, past the chairs and up the temporary ramp. All eyes were still on Gregg, about to raise his hands in a gesture of healing. She might have been a personal assistant with a message as she came up, quietly, beside him and said, "impotent. Go while you can."

He looked at her, at first without recognition, but when he saw whom she was he twitched only sightly before raising his hands and declaring, "in the name of God, manifested in Jesus and Perpetua, who have entrusted me as the agent of their sacred powers, may you be healed in body and in mind. Amen."

He lowered his hands and waited in the complete silence for the first manifestation from one of the wheelchairs. He had never scored lower than 10% and there were more than 50 chairs.

Silence. Nothing happened.

Trina moved silently to his side again and said, "Gregg, go while there's still time. Your healing powers have gone. I knew it when I saw you emerge for the second part of the evening. Just go. Just go."

Silence.

Then a lone voice from the back of the balcony shouted, "cheat!" Another shouted, "I want my pledge card back!"

Gregg, absolutely still for almost a minute, suddenly threw off his golden robes and, clad only in golden boxer shorts, sprang towards Trina, fists flailing.

Quietly she said, "impotent", and fell to the floor, speechless.

Immediately Myron's hired bodyguards picked him up and disappeared back stage. Myron, swiftly, but without appearing to hurry, picked up the bundles of pledge cards and walked out of the main entrance hoping to haul in some profit before pledges were revoked.

Once they had dumped him in his celebrity dressing room, the security guards withdrew to keep some measure of control of a hall on the verge of riot. When Gregg came round he was alone except for Sir Pluto. "Take those ridiculous shorts off and put on your sober clothes as quickly as you can," he said. As the noise of people rushing down the corridor, throwing doors open and slamming them came towards him, Gregg needed no further encouragement. Another set of guards appeared through a door so closely set into the wall that he had not noticed it. They pushed him through it, followed by Sir Pluto, and got him into a waiting car seconds before the crowd poured out. A few coins hit the departing car, but it was soon out of danger, heading towards Central Park.

When the car arrived at Gregg's exclusive hotel he was surprised to be taken to a floor different from but almost identical to his own.

"If I were you," said Sir Pluto, to Max and Trina, "I would keep the guards."

"But you're not us," said Trina, "so we'll dispense with them, thank you. I'm sorry to sound a little sharp, Pluto, but you've been playing a strange game."

"Yes, indeed."

"I'm not sure what you have been doing, but you have been extremely secretive."

"Yes, indeed."

"I would hazard a guess that you have not acted properly on my behalf."

"No, indeed not, on two counts: firstly, I think that I have not behaved entirely properly, though prudently, and secondly, I have certainly not acted on your behalf. Oh no! I would not have asked, and you would not have thanked me for it. My friends from a variety of places and Gregg's old friends are mutual friends."

Gregg looked at Sir Pluto. "Yes, Gregg. Your guardian angels from Langley and some of my—er, roving assistants—have ensured that you have not entirely disgraced yourself."

Gregg, now fully recovered from his temporary shock, looked straight at Sir Pluto who was sitting between Max and Trina, apparently relaxed but, as Gregg could see, and was meant to see, obstructing his line to the door. Desperate, his long years of hard training kicked in as he reached inside his jacket and pointed a gun at Sir Pluto before he could react.

"I've killed before and I'll kill again," he said.

"'we know," said Max.

"I've killed your people before and I'll kill them again."

"We know."

"What do you mean, 'we know?'"

"This is silly," said Max, "Like one of those lengthy scenes in a who-dunnit or an opera where the explanation goes on for hours when you just want the final act to take place. I'll keep it brief as your hand might get tired holding the gun. Yes, that's better, just put it down. Anyway, if Trina can make you impotent—sorry for the use of that word in view of your raunchy reputation—in matters of healing, I am sure she could disable your firearm or your firing arm, or both."

In spite of his renunciation of the clichés of thriller and opera Max behaved like a character in the library scene in an Agatha Christie novel, pouring four substantial brandies and handing three to the others.

"You will remember, Gregg, how I was frequently worried that I had seen you before, but I could not work out where or when. I first saw this enigmatic profile—or, rather, as it will turn out, I saw it for the second time—in the American Embassy. I saw it again on the aeroplane home from Washington DC when you sat next to me and deliberately ignored me so that I had plenty of time to look at it. I had even more time when you worked in our office. Then—this is silly as I'm telling you things that we all know—you were accused by the dying Jim of being evil and, as if to confirm this, you tried to run away with some of our valuable data. Sir Pluto showed me a picture of you taken in the Caribbean, dressed—I am sorry to say—rather scruffily and with some days of stubble. That is when I knew. All the times I had seen you since the first time you were dressed in a suit and were meticulously clean shaven. But your uncharacteristic, but very memorable, scruffiness in the caribbean picture took me back to the night when Dexter, Miles, and Will Dignot were shot. Yes, you could have been one of the hundreds of the faithful or you could have been one of the twenty or so ruffians who came along with Olly and Rory. But you didn't leave when they left and you didn't pray when we prayed. I can still see you now, as we prayed for the dead Dexter and Miles, walking, like a sleep walker, gliding almost, on the fringe of the crowd. I saw your profile, and then I saw you, from side on, shoot Will. Before I could do anything, so skillfully had you chosen the optimal point for firing and escaping, you disappeared into the shadows and were gone. It was that exquisite positioning, shooting, and flight that persuaded me that you were a trained killer. The only thing we knew about the murders was that the bullets were rather special and were used in a highly specialised gun. That, too, reinforced what I suspected."

"But if you suspected all that, why did you hire me? To nail the accusation, I suppose, hoping that I would slip up."

"Just the opposite. We wanted to learn from your behaviour, as we trusted you, that we were wrong. I have to admit that Jim's prophesy gave us a terrible jolt, as did your flight. We continued to try to have faith in you right up to the Caribbean picture."

"So what are you going to do now?"

"Oh, Gregg," said Trina. "what are you going to do now?"

Gregg looked at the gun.

"I wouldn't bother," said Sir Pluto, picking up the gun. "Oh, very poor form for someone so well trained, Gregg. It's your old Eastern European favourite, I see. I used to be very interested in rare hand guns at one time. I could say that even if you shot all three of us you couldn't escape because there are guards outside—I do find this rather literary set piece a little embarrassing—but it might help you answer Trina's question if you told us how you became so hopelessly muddled about Perpetuanism. After all, you killed my wife's—er—partner, Perpetua's successor, and Trina's husband."

"People always want simple stories, lines of causality which supposedly explain behaviour. It's taking Freud to absurd limits, and it's profoundly anti-Perpetuan because she said—I don't have to tell you—that we should make our own decisions. I started making my own decisions very young, almost before I went to school. My parents were 'white trash', hard drinking, hard hitting, hard done by, with big ugly Christianity and big chips on their shoulders enlarged by black progress. If my father hadn't drunk himself to death he would have murdered me; but I'm not blaming him for my violent nature; I neither think it was inherited nor beaten into me. I was an only child, probably begotten in an accidental, never to be repeated, sober moment. My mother died within a year of my father and I was taken on by her much elder sister who was like a non-person, vaguely kind, tentative, ineffectual. She had never wanted nor expected to care for a boy. She did the minimum for me and I did the minimum for her. We were both solitary. I say this to show that there was a very long placid period in my childhood but it didn't make me placid. I'm going to make no excuses. I was average at school, averagely liked and disliked, averagely respected and mistrusted, averagely clever, but I learned about the wafer thin marginality of advantage and disadvantage in relationships and calculating these became my main interest. I suppose now it would be called an obsession. Whatever you call it, I watched people minutely and watched how they watched or didn't watch me. I thought when I was fourteen that I would be a policeman and earn my living watching people. I had a fantasy about being a novelist, but was only average in creative writing. Then quite by chance—and that's important, again rejecting the causality chain—a mobile army recruitment truck came into town. It was the mid-1980s. We were fighting no serious wars anywhere and I thought I might enjoy the army life without running any unnecessary risks. I passed all the tests and thought I would be sent for basic training, but one test picked up on my observational skills and I was sent for special training which turned out to be the basic course for the Intelligence Service. I found the work fascinating. I don't want you to think that I was patriotic—I wasn't—but I did like to compete intensely. By 1987 I had killed a Czech agent in self-defence and by the turn of the century I had tortured captured guerrillas in Columbia and been tortured in a dirty little proxy war in Angola which nobody bothered to report. I discovered that I enjoyed inflicting violence and, to a certain extent, having it inflicted on me. I didn't know how bad this was until my first serious sexual encounters when I introduced violence into the mix. The Service was neither surprised nor censorious, but made sure I knew that it knew and that my behaviour, and the amount of mess I left behind, would be part of my performance record. I became more careful and more violent. Again, I have to say that I don't blame my training for this, or my upbringing, or my genes. I made my way through the ranks to a point where I knew too much ever to be allowed to leave. Just as you knew how to win by minutely observing the behaviour of the other side, you could only survive if you knew about more skeletons than your colleagues. Just as a footnote, I have known for years that I am being tracked by US intelligence which is profoundly schizophrenic about people like me, both loving me and frightened that I might talk. If it were a more ruthless service it would cut the love and kill me because I do know too much, but human institutions aren't that simple.

"On an assignment in the UK in early 2007 to check on the efficiency of its intelligence services—they were found to be, incidentally, Sir Pluto, pretty damn poor—I came across the Perpetua thing. As soon as I saw her I suffered from terrible convulsions. I loved her—or, rather, it's fairer to say that I became sexually obsessed with her—and, of course, violence was part of that package. Although I wanted her, I also hated her blackness, but the clinching factor was that I really understood her doctrine, I suppose you would call it, of liberty. I was so used to boring white guys talking about true Christian liberty, wanting to cut the Federal Government down to size, fulminating about those 'traitors back East'. Here was a black woman denying victimhood, asking for nothing. Then I was posted briefly to Pakistan on some pretty nasty extraordinary rendition cases—no, in case you're wondering, it wasn't my conduct that was nasty, but what these people were planning—and by the time I got back to England she was dead and I was heartbroken. Then her role was taken over by—excuse my frankness, a black thug, gays and trash, excluding you two—and I wanted to hit back. I wanted to dedicate my life to her, knowing that I'd never be able to physically harm her, hoping—and this is a bit of psychobabble I can't help—to sublimate the violence by giving my life to her. It should be falling into place by now. That weirdo Sir Rufus Tartan raised the flag of liberty, as he supposed, though it seemed to me more like the Christianity of my childhood under a not very different name. So I couldn't stand him, but I thought he had given me the chance I needed to eliminate Dexter. Miles was really a bit of enjoyable target practice. I was so into what I was doing that my professionalism left me. I should never have killed Will because if I'd been thinking straight I would have known that his pictures were being sent back to the studio and that grabbing his camera would do nothing.

"Still, I couldn't keep away, and after seeing Max a couple of times, as he's mentioned, I thought it would be dangerous fun to try to join the movement. I was absolutely convinced that I would fail, that your supposed open-mindedness was a front. I soon found out that Perpetuanism was what it said it was and I was actually moving towards trying to control my love of—I refuse to medicalise it and call it an addiction—to violence when Jim saw right through me. To be fair, a couple of days before he died he had told me straight when I was standing near him in a shopping mall in a break in his flute playing, that he thought I should leave as he saw a threatening aura around me. I don't go in for all that coloured auras stuff, but I give him credit for saying what you probably thought. So when he actually prophesied, or whatever you call it, I thought it was time to leave. I genuinely wanted to go on understanding Perpetuanism and spreading the word while learning to curb my own violence which is why I wanted the documents.

"Then—and this is really important—Perpetua did appear to me while I was driving North, but I've re-written this piece of history so often that I've almost forgotten what she did say. But she told me off for being opposed to her and offered help. The first part was strange because she said that my head was against her although my heart was for her, or perhaps I thought that my head was against her. I only realised much later—and you've been kind enough not to point this out—that I had been pretty selective in filtering what she had said. That's the real trouble with neat and tidy theories of life. The story of my love/hate affair with Perpetua is based on a post-hoc narrative that adjusts as it needs to. I'm neither intellectually consistent nor coherent."

Max shifted as if he was about to say something, so Gregg pushed on, not wanting to be interrupted.

"You know all about Father Joe and the empty memory stick and Christmas. I really wanted to stay with the movement and I suppose you are thinking that what really turned me off was the fact that they were gay and falling in love. well, that might have been part of it—I think at the time that was most of it—and they didn't have much space for me and what I might have contributed. The clincher was the fact that I couldn't see Perpetuanism in them. Wayne had quite a lot of the victim about him and Father Joe was still very old Roman Catholic in spite of his best efforts."

Trina nodded slightly. "We all take time to change," she said, "and it's never completed."

"Yes," said Gregg, "but I can only tell you what it was like at the time. Then I decided to start my own kind of Perpetuanism, but I made the stupid mistake of going to the Caribbean. I thought that it was a good place to start for a variety of reasons, but the stupidity was in overlooking—or something worse, denying—the effect that near naked women have on me. I should have started in a deeply conservative place with no tourists. Anyway, you at least, Pluto, know most of the rest. What I can't explain is the healing."

"Nor can we," said Trina. "People from the core group have performed some healing acts, but it's been selective, I hope along the lines that Perpetua would have undertaken, healing to give some specific person a new start. She undertook some mass healing on the Sunday before she died, and we just can't understand that in the context of the rest of her theology and behaviour. We put it down to God our Parent but we expect it to be a mystery instead of expecting to find a solution within an intellectually consistent framework. We are not—if you'll excuse the lapse—going to get Christian about it. The reason why we have been so concerned about you, Gregg, is that we recognise that you are gifted with special healing powers that can only be operating through you from the Godhead. We never wanted to own or control you, but just to be alongside you. You never believed that. Anyway, you know your own mistake, of attributing the powers to yourself, so we don't need to go on about that."

"But we do need to 'go on' about what happens next," said Sir Pluto.

"I think," said Trina, as kindly as she could, "that Gregg needs time to think. Can that be allowed?"

"I suppose so," said Sir Pluto. "There's nothing that can't wait. I'm sure I don't need to tell you that this place is secure, so no silly tricks, Gregg."

◆   ◆   ◆

Myron was pleasantly surprised at the small number of people who stopped their pledges, supposing that in their own terms the contributions were slight.

When he arrived back in Miami he put enough funding by for the rest of his life and still had a handsome enough residue to be able to buy his way back into the Coral Gables Church of Christ. His life returned to what it had been except that Dolorez, having tasted the pleasures of Gregg, drove him into sexual frenzies for her own gratification and when he protested she simply said that what she could not get from him she would get from someone else. After a vain effort to satisfy and then pacify her, that is precisely what she did.

The only legacy of the Gregg story was that he thought he saw the supply girl going towards his quay in his motor boat. He was so terrified that he did not dare to wait and confront her when she returned. After a while that memory faded.

◆   ◆   ◆

His own narrative had helped Gregg to sort himself out. He recognised that he would have to turn himself in—Sir Pluto gave him no alternative—and that in doing so he could not nearly calculate what would happen to him. He was not sure how many rapes, assaults, and murders he had committed, where they had taken place and what the state of political relations was between the Federal Government and various Caribbean islands or between the diplomatic and intelligence services and other places he had been in the service of his country. He knew that Myron would not hang around and that he could only blackmail him for a very limited period until Myron figured out how to put a stop to it. From a practical point of view and because he was still obsessed with Perpetuanism, his best plan would be to stay loyal to Trina and her followers who had never unduly interfered. He might even learn to moderate his violence.

He sat on his bed, calculating, when the room was filled with a not entirely unexpected golden light.

"Oh it's you, is it? I wondered if you would come."

"Very reluctantly, Gregg. I hoped once would be enough."

"But aren't you supposed to be omniscient? To know what's going to happen in the future?"

"In terms of human understanding of what Godhead means it's entirely logical to think that any phenomenon with the term God must be all everything, but in human terms God is all nothing. As God does not live in time, except in incarnational manifestations, God neither knows the past nor the future, but lives in the eternal present. I am talking to you in your time, not mine. Anyway, you have never been really interested in theology before, so shall we get on?"

"What do you want?"

"There you go again, Gregg. So many religious people think that God—or gods—want something. If I want anything of humanity it is that it should freely love me, but it is not a 'want' in the ordinary way, it is a desire that humanity should act in its created nature rather than against it. The Godhead does not 'want' anything specific from individuals so I do not 'want' anything from you. You being human and me being God, however, it might be supposed that you might want something from me, rather than the other way round."

"I might, if only I could figure out what. I suppose I should want to be cleansed of my violence, but your line always was that I should cleanse myself rather than calling on you."

"Very good, Gregg. Very good. We need to go a little further back to what I said about your heart and your head. Your heart has always been with me, but your head is full of calculation which is a nice word for pride. You would never go with my flow, you needed to work out how you would manipulate the world on my behalf when I never wanted it manipulated. You received immense powers from the Godhead to use sparingly the way I used them, but you kept turning on the tap to enhance your own reputation and self-love."

"So why didn't you stop me?"

"Because the use of power is the ultimate kind of choice. You preached about liberty, but you steered clear of the real issue which is the use and misuse of power. Secular society has built a massive edifice of control against a world it thinks is going out of control when, in fact, it was never in control. Churches have, scandalously, followed suit. It is for the Godhead and churches which claim to follow God to serve and to trust rather than to rule and control. The Godhead entrusted you with powers which you abused."

"So how did Trina take my powers away?"

"You were given powers and she was given powers. For all her good intentions, she misused her powers to abridge your powers. Do not look smug, there is quite enough against you! Put yourself in her position. She knows you have used your powers to aggrandise your reputation rather than mine. She was sorely tempted. She also knew by the time she reached New York that you had killed her husband, her leader, and Will, and that you had probably killed other people as well."

"Who have I killed or harmed?"

"It is not for you to know. I have put right everything except the deaths of Dexter, Miles and Will."

"Why?"

"Because I am God. The earth language would add, 'I have my reasons', but it is much simpler than that. My personhood in the Godhead being incarnational, there are uses of power which enhance that purpose and uses which detract, and, necessarily, uses that do neither. Usually the Godhead 'allows' people to choose freely and such choices include the infliction of suffering which, in turn, engenders other choices on the part of others. This might be supposed to be God being cruel. The Godhead's incarnational purpose through me is not served by your wanton, pride driven, acts of violence and so they have all been reversed without the victims suffering from the psychological consequences of your cruelty. Incidentally, if I were you, I would sort out your attitude to women as the starting point for curbing your pride. Calculation is a useless prologue to real pleasure."

"But that is all theoretical as I am about to go to prison for a very long time."

"I suppose by secular standards, you should. I do not, as you have surely guessed by now, operate subject to humanity but, rather, hope that humanity will operate, not subject to me, but in observance of its created purpose.

"You are no longer Gregg. I name you as my faithful Guide Gregory who is to encourage my people in Vermont."

"And how is that to happen?"

"There is no need to imitate Zachariah and Mary in Luke. Just get dressed, in your nice suit, not those silly golden shorts and robes, and go."

As if he were in a dream, Gregg dressed, gathered his few goods, noticed that he had some unfamiliar papers and a wad of Dollars in his inside jacket pocket and walked out of his room to the elevator which he took to the ground floor. The atrium was empty and he went unimpeded through the security door out into East 59th Street, took a cab to La Guardia and caught the first flight.

Trina and Max smiled as Sir Pluto fumed over his breakfast.

"You really must stop exempting yourself from full commitment to the Perpetuan movement," said Trina. "It prevents you from seeing things straight. You organise the earth in ways which you see fit, but now and again the Godhead organises the earth for quite different purposes or, to put it the other way round, reminds us that we can't organise it. My guess is that Gregg's departure is one up to Perpetua over you, Sir Pluto. Never mind."

The comet that was Gregg soon disappeared without trace. Nina sued the Mercury and Randall, under pressure from Sir Pluto who was in the process of selling all his North American interests, settled. The men from Langley faithfully pursued all possible leads, but ultimately gave up their love and fear of their erstwhile colleague. The healed soon took their good fortune for granted and the unhealed soon forgot their false hopes. Not unusually when a bright new President is elected, the citizenry harboured unreasonable hopes of what he could do for them, rather than what they must do for themselves. Another new dawn broke.

◆　◆　◆

As the last leaves and the first snow flakes fell, Gregory drove into Morrisville, Vermont. He had been Affirmed as a Guide by Thomas in Boston in a simple ceremony after the minimum of fuss. He was astonished at the degree of trust which was extended to him. He was worried that the truth would disqualify him—whether it was the details of his career or the "appearance" of Perpetua— but he was simply asked whether he believed and would teach the core values of the movement. He was guaranteed a basic but perfectly respectable salary for two years to meet his needs and was urged to raise the funding to create a foundation to meet his costs after that so that, after an initial burst of activity, he would not be saddled with interminable fund raising for the same purpose. Other religions, he was told, spent far too much time on fund raising for themselves and this left less room for good causes. After a week-long induction with other Guides, he was sent out.

His activity centre was a neat little open-plan house of worship acquired cheaply by the movement from a strict Presbyterian sect that had been forced through dwindling numbers to rationalise. After two nights in a chintzy bed and breakfast he found an apartment and furnished it simply. He made himself known to the local house group leaders and asked that he be given two weeks to get himself ready. His main priority was to form a habit of prayer. He remembered well the formal ritual of his childhood, but except for cursory prayers with his aunt before he went to bed, he knew nothing of private prayer.

He knew that Perpetua could have cured him of his weakness, but had not done so for a purpose. It was for him to overcome, and he trusted that prayer would give him the resources to do so. In a gentle note from Max, who had somehow learned what had happened and where he was, he was urged to concentrate on the Gospel of Luke and on Perpetua's basic teaching. He resolved to adapt the basics of his training methodically to cultivate virtue. He was not at peace, but he almost immediately recognised what such a state might mean. Soon he began to notice details that had previously been outside his observation. Instead of looking for weaknesses in people which he might exploit and seeking grounds for suspicion, he noticed kindness and how he was trusted by strangers. He even began to notice the rhythms and details of the natural world to which, in spite of his country upbringing, he had previously been indifferent.

When he took up his official duties he found that there were six house groups scattered across the small farming towns with a good balance between the financially and intellectually well off and their poorer brethren. The disparities were not so extreme as those in bigger cities and he felt he had been given a comfortable berth where he could make a positive start. His first Sacrament of Union was simple and moving and he was surprised to feel that he was in the right place and even more surprised that those present seemed to feel the same.

After a few weeks he began to feel lonely in spite of the support that he received and he felt the stirring of his old cravings. He was tempted to run away to a deserted place until it passed even though this would only increase his loneliness, but after the most intensive and lengthy prayer session that he had ever undertaken he decided to stay. He had to trust in God that he would be given the means to survive.

The next day, while he was shopping, a neat, pleasant looking woman in her early 30s approached him with a modest, but definite, step. "You look puzzled," she said. "I suppose you are finding it difficult to decide what to buy. Single men are either very good or very bad at taking care of themselves and you look like the second sort."

"True. I seem to buy too much and then over react and buy too little."

"You are Gregory, the Perpetuan Guide, aren't you? I have just joined a house group. Can I call you Gregg?"

He controlled himself. "Please, I would rather be called by my full name. I don't think the short form suits me, although that isn't because I want to be aloof in any way. We can be as informal calling me Gregory as we could calling me Gregg."

"That's lovely, Gregory, I like a man who can say what he thinks without causing discomfort. I was baptised Catherine, but the whole place calls me Kitty, so that's who I am."

They both faltered as they approached the check-out. Gregory, who had never been good at small talk, rummaged around furiously for something to say.

"It doesn't matter," she said. "Silence will do as well as talk unless there's something one of us needs to say."

"Coffee?" he said.

"OK, fine," she said.

It was, he thought, as they walked towards the diner, predictable that he should find her attractive even though she was properly dressed for the season, but he was surprised that his old cravings were quiescent. When they got their coffee, she said, "it is, I suppose, a little forward of me, but when I saw you in the grocery store I immediately liked the look of you. I like strong men. My husband was a strong man, built like you, physically strong and mentally tough. he was killed in a freak storm in his lovely little boat."

Gregg thought he needed to say something pastoral like, "I'm terribly sorry" but instead he said, "I am sure he admired and loved you as much as you admired and loved him."

He thought she was going to cry and he would not have known how to deal with that—they hadn't gone into crying during his induction—but instead she said: "Yes, we both loved and admired each other, but I have learned to suffer but not to grieve. Suffering is surely part of who we are, but after a proper time of grieving we must be cheerful on God's earth. The important thing is both to suffer and to smile at the same time."

He was still struggling for something to say.

"Don't look so sad, Gregory, you know better than me how wonderful are the gifts of God."

He wondered whether he did. They finished their coffee in companionable silence. He felt that he had failed her, but as they parted she said, "prudent silence is better than the wrong words, Gregory. I hope we will meet again soon, and not only at the house group."

He knew he was in love, but he did not know what to do about it. He thought it unbecoming to send flowers or write a letter. He felt it inappropriate to engineer an encounter, for he knew that if he did he would not know what to say. He had never prayed about love, but now he did and what came back in the few occasionally intense moments of flowering which came during days of laboured ploughing of barren soil was that he must trust in God, leave himself open and do nothing. Kitty was a gift or she was nothing.

She came to invite him to the family Thanksgiving party and he offered her coffee.

"You would think, from your behaviour, Gregory, that you are trying to avoid me."

"I think I am."

"Don't say any more. I know why. I should not have started our conversation that way. You think that you don't know what to say."

"True."

"Say nothing. You are a pure gift."

They sat in silence, their coffee growing cold.

"It's so difficult in our culture for a single woman to talk about giving herself without its seeming indecent. I never expected to receive such a gift as you. I never pray for anything for myself—that might sound pompous or over exacting, but we pray for others and trust that they pray for us and we all live in the trust of God—but if I had done so it would have been for someone like you. I want to be yours in whatever way you want to be mine."

"Kitty, I would like to say exactly the same thing, but I don't know how to be anybody's. Until I was made a Guide I only knew how to exploit people for my own needs."

"It's honest of you to admit it, but hardly necessary. That's how most people are, including me, but it's only through the practice of giving and, even more importantly, receiving what the other has to offer that we learn by degrees to turn our selfishness into generosity, to turn our self-expression into tutored listening. This cannot be done in the abstract, by making a resolution. If you try to give me space to love you in the way I can at this moment I will try to give you space to love me the way you can at this moment. Tomorrow it will be different and better, and so it will grow. Today all we can do is what we can do today."

He thought that the one thing in the world that he really wanted to do was to make love to her, but found out that in spite of her encouragement he could not. Reverting to his past life he thought himself a failure, but she said, "strong men take a while to learn the love that is no conquest. I've been through this before. This is a blessed sign of our future."

As the weeks and months passed, his cravings subsided and he learned to live the openness he taught.

◆　◆　◆

The Perpetuan movement in America grew calmly and gently alongside the torment of the Episcopal Church which grew so acute that Thomas was asked to offer some help.

"It's difficult to know how to help you unravel your problem," he said, "but let us start with something relatively simple, not easy, but simple. When Europeans first came to the Americas they were divided about the status of the natives they found. Some said that they were biologically inferior, that is their inferiority was genetic, while others said that they were biologically equal, but intellectually inferior. Some Christians respectively concluded that natives were sub-human and could be slaughtered with impunity while others thought that they were entitled to the same concern and respect as Christians. The point is, whether you accept the position of one side or the other, that neither side could call on biology to settle the issue, but the tolerators could show, through education, that the natives were capable of massive intellectual improvement.

"Now what light does that cast on today's issue? In this case it is what we call the conservatives who point to the possibility that sexual orientation is within the intellectual control of individuals whereas liberals appeal to biology. Again, no matter what your point of view—and this is where you need to be recipro-cally humble—biology, genetics, has not yet settled the issue.

"Now let us go one layer deeper still. One of the pragmatic, as opposed to moral/theological reasons why Perpetuans refuse to judge behaviour—although we accept the secular necessity of exercising sanction and control over conduct resulting from necessary human imperfection—is that we cannot make any kind of clear distinction between sin and sickness. Our starting point is that all God's children were created to do their best and then to be enfolded back into God's perfect love. We cannot conceive of a God who would create any child knowing that it would somehow fail, be punished for its created imperfection, and so we are disposed, as a starting point, to question the concept of sin, that is, the deliberate act which denies God's love. On the other hand, you might object quite properly, that the imperfection of which I speak necessitates wrong choices which could be called sin. Well and good, but that is about as far as we can go. What we cannot know is the extent to which behaviour is conditioned and the extent to which we possess the resources to counter that conditioning. Take the recent example of that wild miracle worker, Gregg. It is said that he had serious sexual/sadistic tendencies and that these were trained into him while he was learning to be an intelligence officer. We don't know whether the tendency pre-dated the training and prompted him to seek that kind of training or whether he was a moral blank surface into which sadism was branded. Or, to put it another way, if he was a more or less blank surface—and I am not sure whether anybody can be wholly blank—we do not know what resources he was given from God or his upbringing to resist the sadism. Equally, looking at the other side of him, you would at least want to ask whether his mighty acts came from God or an evil source. My answer is that we cannot know.

"In short, we all need to be much less definite in what we say about the behaviour of others. Secular society must deal with outcomes and, to give it credit, it does take motivation into account, but as religious leaders it is even difficult for us to untangle the roots of motivation. We know enough about people's power of self-delusion to know that they can persuade themselves that they are 'pleasing' God when they are hurting others. So if the self-delusion is itself unconscious, where does that leave the nature of the motivation?

"In conclusion, my friends, you might think that this analysis is purely liberal, that I have not been even-handed, but this is not so. Liberals tend to exaggerate what they know about the relationship between genetics and human behaviour on the one hand and social engineering on the other, but they always tend towards explanations which emphasise nurture rather than nature. For example, on the issue of behaviour which society condemns, they appeal to nature, assigning a role to illness as an explanation for bizarre behaviour, and over the issue which most concerns you, they assign a biological role to homosexuality. They may be right, but both 'sides' should be much more open to argument and much more humble. Now by this I do not mean that each 'side' must be more open to the prejudices of the other. There is quite enough uncertain ground 'between' you that should allow you to work together to understand the relationship between God, biology, and intellect."

"There is one more thing which I think I ought to say. There is a difficult tension for many Christians between what they see as the rather severe God the Father in the Old Testament and the gentle Jesus in the New. Puzzling this, as God the Father hardly appears in the Old Testament at all. Putting that to one side, the tension arises because many Christians on the one hand have taken on so much enlightenment baggage that they treat the Bible either as a moral and intellectual arsenal or as a text requiring minute critical analysis and on the other, have given themselves freedom—or should I say licence?—to please themselves as to what Scripture signifies. The main point however—forgive me for saying this, but I am trying to undertake the task you set me—is that the Bible is a spiritual phenomenon that speaks to us in many different ways at many different times. If it stops being spiritual it effectively stops being the Bible at all."

His listeners thanked him and left, still not talking to each other. Thomas was sad, but unsurprised, as he returned to the visiting Sarah. "Christianity has gotten itself into a terrible cul-de-sac over morality," he said. "I just wish they would spend more time praying and less time arguing."

"Yes," said Sarah. "It's a power problem. One of my great hopes for admitting women into the Christian church was that it would reduce the power dynamic."

"You might be right, but let us not get sentimental about the moral superiority of women or we will simply be in a different kind of power game."

"True. Thank you Thomas. I needed to be warned. The greatest danger facing Perpetuanism is moral smugness. Our own suspicion of conventional morality is a kind of morality that claims to be superior. The most difficult thing of all is saying and doing nothing as humble service to God our Parent and all of God's children. Most religions seem to have asked humanity to go against its grain—against aggression and competition, against territory and power—but we seem to be asking humanity to be against power, which is fair enough, but also against articulation."

"Not against articulation in itself, Sarah, but against the use of articulation to usurp God's 'power', if you could describe the exercise of loving parenthood as power in any way. We've still not found the language. For instance, I keep wondering what to call our practice of virtue. It isn't fatalism or passivity, it isn't facilitation or even tolerance. It is the provision of our own space for others, but I can't find a word for it yet."

"That is, I think, as it should be," said Sarah. "Naming is power. Talking of which, Thomas, there is a very wonderful new Guide at Morrisville, Gregory. I've never known anyone like him. He's got the bloom of a convert. I presided at a Sacrament of Affirmation for him and his partner, Kitty. It was the most amazing thing that I have experienced, probably the first time I have seen Perpetuanism actually being lived."

"I'm pleased to hear it because I had little to go on, so I prayed and trusted in God."

"I only mention it because of this problem of power. I have never seen such a conscious absence of power in any relationship as I saw then. Yes, they surely love each other, but there was a sense of—I know we can't name it, but I will try—a sense of temperance, that everybody deeply admired. Watch Gregory, Thomas, he will be a very great resource for us, when God wills."

"It's a good name. I always liked Gregory of Nyssa's *epektasis*."

"You might be on the verge of showing off, Thomas."

"Perhaps Sarah, but it's much more a case of enjoying myself. One of the things we will have to work out is how to be Perpetuan and teachers. We might want to leave ourselves unconditionally open to the other, but that does not mean to say that everything that is said to us is of equal value. I suppose we have to distinguish between opinions on the basis of what is rational—which we hold in common—and what most informs us as spiritual creatures. After all, being a

Perpetuan is a choice we have made to elevate it—I don't like the word, but let us use it provisionally—above Christianity."

"I think it's better, Thomas, to think of Perpetua, as she said herself, reviving the testimony of Jesus Her Brother. We are not superior to Christians we are simply appealing to a fresher, not superior, testimony."

"That is very helpful. We must be careful not to take any kind of moral or spiritual high ground. We will almost certainly not do this on purpose, but the great danger is that we might do it by accident."

Fortified by this discussion, they went their separate ways, determined to bear undramatic witness to God's fresh incarnational gift in the life and teaching of Perpetua. Snow fell thickly on Morrisville and all was calm.

◆　　◆　　◆

Clement was glad to see Trina and Max returned. During their absence there had been a sense of hopes frustrated. Nothing serious had happened, but it was like being at a party where minor problem kept cropping up. John had encountered serious problems with a would-be Guide called Monica at Silicon Ridge because he did not know how to refuse her. As he said to Clement, "I know we have to trust the calling of those who come to us, but we cannot always entrust them to the people. I don't know how we are going to face the problem of unsuitability, but we must try. I love my neighbour, Clement, but I would not equally trust every person to look after my garden or my pension fund."

"There's a difference," said Clement, "between trusting a person's sincerity and trusting her competence. We still have to find a way of accepting Monica that does not involve her pastorally."

"What's worse," said John, "is that she's accusing us of wanting to exclude her because she's a lesbian."

"I don't feel qualified to go any further with this," said Clement. "I've never understood whether there's a difference between gay and straight love. We use the same word "love" and, more confusingly, novelists who ought to be the most careful people with words, use the same word, too. I mean, without going into too much detail, the notion of 'making love' is concrete, not abstract, and the reality of the concrete is different between gay and straight transactions. I mean, I can't really get my head round gay love and I suppose many gay people can't get their head round straight love. I get it in the abstract, but I have imaginative, and therefore, empathetic limitations. I can understand from the standpoint of the oppressed why an issue is an issue, but I wonder whether the gay issue has become disproportionately salient. Monica is definitely one for the Trina in-tray."

Then there was the case of Stella and Lucie in Stumpy Knoll who wanted to be Guides. "Pastor Drone—I mean Philip," said Clement, "just because they are reformed sex workers, or perhaps particularly because they are reformed sex workers, you can't deny their calling if they solemnly declare it to you."

"I know the theory, Clement, but you try persuading your local congregation—er, house groups—that former prostitutes are fitting spiritual and ethical leaders."

"Philip, I can't make you do anything. I could refer it to Trina, but she won't make you do anything. In turn you can't make people do things to suit you, for instance you can't actually, in Perpetuanism, exercise 'ethical leadership' and I'm not really sure if you can even exercise 'spiritual leadership'. You have to come to terms with the idea, contrary to much of contemporary Christian practice, that people must have control over some aspects of their lives, but there are other things they can't control at all. We've become too obsessed with control; the power thing. As far as I can remember, Dexter healed these ladies of addiction and they've stayed clean ever since, so they combine God's grace of healing with subsequent self-control. I would have thought that was a pretty good start."

"But people have long memories."

"Not as long as God's if you frustrate the love of children like Stella and Lucie. I'm not threatening retribution by saying that, Philip, I'm just reminding you that we are there to bring all God's children closer to their Parent, and we must not make the mistake of equating being a Guide with some ethical purity standard measured externally by somebody who, implicitly, thinks she is nearer to it than the person being measured. I won't anthropomorphise God, but there has to be some sadness in the whole framework of existence if love is denied. There's a bit of a problem here that we haven't worked out. Theoretically house groups elect leaders many of whom become Guides, but in practice many people come to us saying they have a calling to be a Guide quite independent of the house group route. We will have to work something out. In the meantime, Philip, please seriously consider the idea that the two ladies have a much clearer idea of whether they are called than you have. You just have to trust them."

Kylie had the opposite problem. She had many more house groups than Guides. Initially many Church of England clergy had signed up to be affirmed as Guides but they kept havering. Bishop Hall had not yet been replaced, so there was not a focal point of dialogue between the Perpetuans and the Church, and his two Assistants, although quite friendly on the surface, just couldn't commit themselves or speak on behalf of their clergy. The house groups, which were largely formed from Church of England liberals, were not inclined to elect their own Guides as they were still in the shadow of the Christian clerical tradition and felt uncomfortable with the election of what they saw as parallel jurisdiction.

"I sympathise," said Clement, "as I come from there or, rather, have lived there for over twenty years. You will have to ask the Dean's advice and be patient. Nothing comes easy in Alchester."

Trina brought a sense of calm and Max brought a sense of purpose to the leadership and morale improved. They agreed that the biggest problem facing them now was a lack of momentum. There seemed to be no crisis on the horizon. Trina had settled the minor disputes in her in-tray and the various schemes of Lord Warpley, Horace Strider and Dean crowther had been buried by the financial crisis and Sir Granville Brompton was keeping a close eye on events.

◆　◆　◆

Dear world,

I hereby wish it to be known that the person named Perpetua, of rather doubtful background, was not, as some claim, even a paragon of virtue, let alone a "person of the Godhead".

I know to my own personal cost that she was a woman of loose morals, a promise maker and a promise breaker.

What is worse, while preaching moral purity she was a lesbian.

When Perpetua visited Silicon Ridge during her supposed "mission" she told me that she loved me. I took this to be the general sort of love that Christians, and Perpetuans, generally bandy about but when I reflected on precisely what she said, I realised that she was making sexual advances to me. I had only just come to terms with this situation when I saw her making a similar approach to another woman, and a couple of days later she left me without saying anything more.

How can anybody trust such a woman as a woman, let alone someone who made such outrageous claims?

Monica

◆　◆　◆

In mid-January, Dean Crowther finally achieved his ambition of returning to the episcopate. Admittedly, a close was not Canterbury but it was one up from South Yorkshire. The position of Dean of London Minister had been superficially attractive, but it had come to nothing much. London had been limiting rather than liberating and his restless spirit craved new challenges. He liked the Palace and he was determined to get on with his two Assistant Bishops.

"It is my intention," he said at his first meeting, to lead the orthodox response both within the Church and to the Perpetuans."

"We have tried orthodoxy," said Hilary, somewhat primly, "and look where it got us."

"And anyway," said Bruce, tartly, "it requires an example of holy living which is not always easy to maintain."

Reggie wondered what he knew, but decided to go on as if nothing had been said. "What is the state of affairs?"

"The Diocese is in a state of turmoil," said Hilary. "The Petrans are losing heart, the Torans—I am sure Bruce will agree—are more interested in fighting the liberals than the Perpetuans, and the Median BCP people are just going on as they always have. The Petrans and Torans sorely miss the goad of the liberals who have largely gone over to Perpetua."

Bruce stayed silent.

"And where do you two stand?" asked Reggie.

"Well," said Bruce, "we were, as you know, pretty clear where we stood as Torans and Petrans, in tension over Scripture and Sacramentality, but together on the gay and women issues. We were shaken by the rise of Perpetuanism, particularly since the events of Pentecost, and have been trying to get along with The Dean, ..."

"... Ah! The Dean! ..."

"... you see his unfaltering niceness rather puts people off their aggressive stride. He knows that you might be embarrassed to be consecrated in the Cathedral, but he offers it nonetheless."

"I will take up his offer and make my point."

"Not too strongly, I hope," said Hilary.

"There you are wrong, Aleford," said Crowther, somewhat severely. "Now is precisely the time to make my point."

"There are many of our clergy who are treading a delicate balance as loyal to us but sympathetic to Perpetuanism."

"Well, they are going to have to make up their minds."

"But the practicalities," warned Hilary. "There is money to think of, and stability and, of course, pastoral and spiritual care."

"We are going to have to get it straight."

"Bishop James thought about some kind of oath of allegiance," said Hilary, "and it came to nothing. It just caused problems. There was nobody more faithful than the two of us in our different ways, but we had to admit that it was a disaster. Now is the time to watch and wait—I mean watch and pray—and see how things bed down," said Bruce, trying to be conciliatory.

"That's the trouble," said Reggie, trying to control his irritation. "You can't get anybody in this Church to stand up for anything."

"So what," asked Bruce, with a hint of steel in his voice, "do you stand for?"

"You mean you don't understand plain orthodoxy?"

"Well, the trouble is, it's a nice word, but it's not plain at all, as Hilary and I have found to our cost."

"Plain orthodoxy means the Queen, the 39 Articles of Religion, the BCP, the Authorised Version, Sunday schools, Harvest Lunches, the Mothers Union, that sort of thing."

"But isn't that tradition rather than orthodoxy?" asked Bruce. "I mean, if we had stuck to tradition like that, we wouldn't have had the Reformation. It's not what I usually say—in fact I find it hard to articulate—but that isn't good enough any more. The Torans who look to me for leadership want to shift the idea of orthodoxy towards vigourous evangelism."

Reggie was tempted to show his contempt, but controlled himself.

"We are faced with paganism and Perpetuanism and of the two I'd prefer Perpetuanism," said Hilary. "I mean, on the whole I would have liked to have kept things as they were about 1975 when I was ordained, but it's not possible. We don't have the commitment, the clergy or the money. We keep trying revivals and although Bruce seems to have the knack of getting this to work, most of the Church, particularly my Petran bit, is literally dying of old age."

"But I ask you again," said Bruce, "are you saying that you just want to keep the traditions and not change the inner spiritual dynamic?"

"The what?" Reggie blurted, unable to stop himself.

Castlegate looked contemptuous. "If we don't get right down to Scriptural and spiritual fundamentals ..."

"... and Catholic Sacramentality ..."

"... we will get nowhere."

Crowther went to see the Dean and it was immediately obvious that he neither liked nor was taken in by the charm of his new Bishop.

"Mr Dean. What a very interesting variety of displays you have here. Quite eccentric."

"Eclectic."

"Yes, quite eclectic, colourful, rich."

"For the poor."

"For the poor, indeed. I see your liturgy is quite as eclectic as your displays. I am not sure it is as it should be."

"I am sure, Bishop, that nothing is really as it should be, no mater how hard we try."

"Very true, Dean, very true. Might that liturgy, do you think, embrace my ceremony—er service—of Consecration?"

"Certainly, Bishop. This house of God is available to all who count themselves as creatures of the Creator."

"Quite, and brothers and sisters in Christ."

"Quite so."

"And living in the power of the Spirit?"

"Naturally."

"But you include those who count Perpetua to be an Incarnational manifestation of the Godhead on a par with Christ."

"Yes, but I do not insist on it. The Apostles continued after the death of Jesus to worship in the temple and, had things worked out differently, we might still be sharing spiritual space with Jews."

"Yes, Mr Dean, but we aren't."

"More's the pity, Bishop, but to come to the point you so delicately raise, those aspects of our liturgy and symbolism which refer to Perpetua are confined in time and space to modest proportions. You are always welcome here. Indeed, Archbishop James has told me informally that he would very much like to come back to his old stamping ground to Consecrate you."

"Very well, Mr Dean, but you must expect me to be unequivocal."

"I am told by those who know you that you are unequivocal in all you say, and do, Bishop," said the Dean, not quite as sad as he should have been when he had said it.

◆   ◆   ◆

Bishop Crowther, for all his evangelical trappings, had never been much of a preacher, but at least he had enough good sense to realise this and therefore eschewed subtlety and relied upon what he called common sense. He did not expect what he said to be treasured, but he did expect that those for whom he was responsible would take notice, and so he began.

"On this most personally auspicious day when by God's grace I have been returned to the episcopacy, I wish to lay down the fundamental tenets of the Church of England which, I believe, all of us should take account of as default positions not to be departed from without great thought. My justification for speaking thus rests on the premise that without bishops the Church of England is nothing. In the seventeenth century the cry went up, 'no bishops, no king'. I would amend that cry for the twenty-first century and say, 'no bishops, no safety' for it is my thesis that the central purpose of the Church of England is to provide the people of England with a place that is spiritually safe. Now what do I mean by that?

"I will start with structure. Today there is a widespread management theory that structure should organically develop out of vision and mission. I deny this. It is only within safe structures that people can work out their vision and their mission. It might be the case that there are some very brave and very clever people who can work out their vision and their mission while subjected to the rough storms of this wicked world, but I do not count myself among these and I do not suppose that most of you do either. We like to have familiar structures, whether it be bishops or churches, in which to work out what we want to do with our lives, with our opportunities and our challenges. That is why heritage is so important. That is why old churches are so highly valued. Now some people might think I'm being rather mundane, but one of the problems of the contemporary Christian churches is that they're in the thrall of two kinds of people, fanatics and intellectuals, and most of us want none of it. We want old churches and comfortable bishops. We don't want sharp controversy and mystifying subtlety. Some people say, for example, that Archbishop Hawthorne was a great theologian, and so he may have been, but most of us didn't understand a word he said. Others claim that various figureheads in the Toran and Petran factions are holy men—they are, as you will note, all men—because they are said to stand up for their principles. Well, that is supposed to be a cause for admiration, but the act of standing up for something isn't virtuous in itself—well, not according to my kind of common sense—because it matters what you're standing up for.

Standing up for fanatical positions is not a proper religious stance because we exist as clergy to provide ordinary people with the stability and comfort they need. When I was in my previous Diocese of South Yorkshire, I was frequently accused of being 'middle brow' and 'theologically illiterate', but my hard-working people wanted religion which went with the grain of their simple faith. They did not want religion to keep poking them in the ribs or in the eye.

"I therefore undertake that I will do my best to enable all of the people in my care to be tranquil with their God Now I say I will do my best because that is all I can do. One of the more distressing aspects of the Church of England is its peculiar lack of line management from the Bishop to the minister. I will do my best, particularly during the discernment and recruitment phases, to see that people receive humble and faithful ministers. I mean much the same thing by these two terms: humble in their attitude to what is given and faithful to what is given. Which begs the question of what is given. I may be being just a little controversial here, but it is as well to be clear. The Thirty-Nine Articles of Religion are venerable and to be respected, a default, as I said, but very few people undergoing ordination or consecration—forgive me, Archbishop James—take them to be either the literal truth in themselves or the sum total of Christian doctrine. Having said that, excessive attention to the details of doctrine is dangerous, for, although I think that clerical hierarchy is important for stability, I also believe that the Holy Spirit works through God's people to develop doctrine. The idea of 'reception' is not, as many think, that the clergy think something up which it takes the laity a while to come to terms with. Reception means that a doctrinal idea percolates up from the faithful people until it cannot be gainsaid by authority. That way we avoid controversy and nit-picking. Too much emphasis on doctrine is the ruin of good, Christian, order. We need to be much more relaxed, letting the Holy Spirit work through the people, being very careful not to spend all our time legislating. That's the problem with the Grand Synod. Like Parliament, because it exists to pass laws, it can't help itself. Just to take the two big issues of the moment, gays and women. Nobody denies there are gay people, nor that there are gay clergy at the moment. Let us just leave them be. I do not mean by this that people must be furtive, nor do I support a policy of 'don't ask'. I simply mean that to turn this into a doctrinal dispute is, to be blunt, fatuous. The same applies in a different way to to those who oppose women as priests or bishops on what they call doctrinal grounds. I have never been sure of what this means—it looks like a fancy name for misogyny—but their quibble about 'sacramental assurance' was settled, so I'm told, in fifth century North Africa when Saint Augustine triumphed over the Donatists. I think part of the problem is that everything about the Church is called 'theological' when much of it is nothing of the sort.

"It is my experience that people are pretty well capable of sorting out ethics for themselves. They don't accept silly strictures about women not being legitimate priests or gays not being proper Christians. These are ethical matters, not doctrinal. It is rather ridiculous when clergy end up making gays or women inferior to the rest of us when most of the people in the pews wouldn't dream of it. I have my quarrels with Perpetuanism, as you all know, but one thing that it has got right is that Christianity has become too ethically aggressive and has cut itself off from the people. I want us to get back to giving our people comfort, not attacking them for their supposed moral infractions. Equally, we need to be much more humble in the face of the mystery of God. Both Torans and Petrans in this Diocese will need to back off. I won't stand for any nonsense."

"Well, that puts God in her place," muttered the Dean.

"Very convenient to relegate morals," muttered Castlegate, "considering his track, field, and bed record."

"I'm not sure how he expects us to do religion without Sacramentality," mused Aleford.

However, on the whole the new Bishop's sermon went down very well. Most people were heartily fed up of their Church being a source of controversy rather than comfort. Brian Sedge had his private doubts about what had been said, but in his public capacity he knew that if people went along with Bishop Crowther, life would be a great deal easier. There were activists who would not give way but, on the whole, he thought the Bishop would be a settling force. "Better," he thought, "to have a practical man than an holy."

That was the essential advantage of Bishop Crowther. When he had pretended to be holy he had been a laughing stock, but now that he was being who he was he gained respect. "Better to be the Richard Nixon of the Church than the Bill Clinton," quipped Mark Price who was now watching events from the sidelines as a Perpetuan Guide. "There must be some kind of holiness we haven't yet given a name to in people just being who they are and getting on with it."

Archbishop Hall, looking round affectionately at old friends and old surroundings found himself surprisingly sympathetic to this most venal of prelates. He longed for peace and quiet, not to make his own life easy, but to restore tranquility to God's faithful people. He did not think that they got what they deserved. There were some who blamed the turmoil on Perpetuanism, but it had begun a long time before that or, rather, without the massive self-restraint and minimalism which the Church had developed since the Civil War, it would always be in danger of injuring itself by falling into the cracks it could not paper over. His way of trying to resolve the problem had been to lean towards Rome, but his few months as Archbishop had taught him that what the Church needed was peace and quiet. Some might call this mediocrity; well, so be it. God worked in mysterious ways, none more so than in the flamboyant person of Bishop Crowther. If it could only settle down it might find a gentle accommodation with the Perpetuans. It should not make the mistake it had made with Wesley. Trina and Max were reasonable people. Rome would object, of course, but he was coming round to the view that what was needed was an English settlement for an English Church. There was no point in talking to Benedict. He was busy taking the Roman Church back to the First and away from the Second Vatican Council. as he stood at the door, saying farewells, he saw Schuhorn trying to slip past. "Mr Secretary," he said, with a low but carrying voice. "I don't know why you were slipping away."

"Well, to be honest, Archbishop, ..."

"... an unnecessary qualification ..."

"... Thank you, Archbishop. Well, I thought you might not approve of the choice of the Nominations Committee."

"I could have vetoed it."

"Well, I know, technically, yes."

"But I didn't. I approve."

"That is gratifying. I thought that you might find Bishop Crowther a little—er—worldly."

"Worldly he is—and not just a little either—but that is just what we need at the moment. By the way, where are we with the move to hand over episcopal appointments entirely to the Church."

'We would be there if it were not, I am afraid to say, Archbishop, for some of your own people who would be much more content to leave things as they are, reserving the capacity to complain—or at least grumble—rather than taking on the full responsibility. Some of them actually think that they need the Prime Minister's protection against their own partisanship. They think that, left to itself, the appointments process will become factional."

"They may be right, Mr Secretary. I am relaxed either way. Once again, well done over the Reggie appointment. I hope you can find others like him. I'm not saying I want headlines about bawdy bishops, but that's better than headlines about silly bishops of whom we have far too many. Sorry, that wasn't supposed to be a rebuke but I suspect that we have all been victims of changing fashion. In the 1960s it was trendy, in the 1980s it was missionary, and more recently it's been holy or, at least—and often mistaken for it—unworldly."

Schuhorn was relieved to get away without having to commit himself. At Alchester Crowther solved a number of intricate problems which had nothing to do with the tone of the episcopacy. It was one of those inconsistencies which Schuhorn deplored that Hall's poor performance in Alchester had given him Canterbury, so poor that it needed a practical man like Crowther whom he had quite properly turned down for Canterbury in favour of Hall. Left to himself, and he largely was if he ignored his Synod and Council—and most did—a diocesan could wreak havoc whereas a Primate might be pilloried in the media for all kinds of supposed faults, but was unable to do much harm. Then there was the little matter of London Minster whose Dean was expected to play a pivotal role in discussions between Church and state in matters best not brought to the notice of Lambeth. Crowther had been put there primarily to reward him for the loss of Canterbury, but it had also been hoped that his worldliness would enable him to execute the political brief. In the paranoid days of Prime Minister Brown he had hopelessly compromised himself by getting mixed up with Lord Warpley—one of the chief financial backers of the Tories—and, even worse, with Horace Strider who had been a firm Blairite and he had snubbed the Church Commissioners' House of Commons trusty, Sir Justin Peal, as a pedant. Business was being delayed and there was no point having patronage if you couldn't exercise it.

Schuhorn's eye was caught by the Dean. "Now then, Mr Secretary, we have to hold you accountable for the appointment of this godless man."

"I thought you were the sort of person, Mr Dean, who put himself above judging others."

"One to you, Mr Secretary. Perhaps I should have said that our new bishop is, on the surface at least, not much interested in the instruction of his flock which is what a bishop is supposed to interest himself in."

"Praxis, Mr Dean, praxis. Admittedly, he does not have a taste for the 'high' level of debate in which you revel, but he may yet turn out to be a practical boon to his flock."

The Dean, who saw that his irony was getting him nowhere, became serious. "I am worried, from my personal perspective, that Bishop Crowther will not appreciate the subtleties of our current cathedral accommodation between Anglicans and Perpetuans."

Schuhorn, who would never allow personal feelings, such as his resentment of Simon Prior's ironic pugnacity, to get in the way of scrupulous attention to the matter in hand, said, "your current practice could be a template, an exemplar, for good practice going forward. If Reggie can't grasp the subtleties, perhaps the best solution is to make your arrangements less subtle. You didn't have to rite a detailed agrement for dear old James as he was instinctively good at seeing where the lines were that he would only cross after a great deal of thought, but Reggie needs something a little more stark and—forgive the ugliness of the phrase, only excused by its peculiar accuracy—in your face. After all, Simon, his sermon wasn't a bad as we feared."

The Dean acknowledged the truth of this and the two men bade each other affectionately cool farewells in recognition of their inter dependence. The Dean kept Schuhorn in touch with Perpetuanism from a Church of England perspective that Max, were he ever so honest, could not supply, and Schuhorn made sure that there were no sudden, irrational anti-Perpetuan outbursts. What he had not told the Dean—his customary discretion overcoming the temptation—was that the precariousness of his current position as the result of the inevitability of the abolition of his position—timing being the only uncertainty—meant that he had agreed to succeed Clement Sutcliffe as the Archbishop's principal adviser. There would then be a great deal more that the two men could do for each other.

Clement had come down to Alchester not just for old times' sake, but also to commune with the Dean. He had enjoyed seeing Archbishop James and he found himself engaged by Reggie's sermon. It went against everything he thought or stood for, but it had a demotic sharpness which he could not help but admire and, on the whole, he thought he would prefer to deal with a pragmatic rather than a doctrinal Church of England. When it came to it, the Perpetuans were no more keen on doctrine than Reggie. He could not help thinking about the tortuosities of ecumenical commissions.

Settled in a snug corner of the cavernous Deanery, Simon said, "I suppose I must congratulate you, Clement, on becoming the nearest thing we have to a bishop."

"I hope I wear it lightly, Mr Dean.."

"I wish you would call me Simon."

"No. I love the deep, slightly awed overtones of fear and suspicion which the title suggests, in your case at least. There's something sardonic, too. It's the kind of fear people enjoy, the self-created sort which appeals to children in bed-time stories. It was the 'Red Dean' once but now it's just 'Mr Dean'. There is a deeper purpose in thinking about titles now that we are settling down. We will soon have to consider precisely what we want to do about succession, hierarchy, heresy and, by extension, membership."

"Ever the tidy mind, Clement. We might be better off leaving it to the Holy Spirit."

Their dialogue was disturbed by James who had let himself in through a familiar side door.

"Perpetuan plots?"

"Clement was worrying about the form and structure of Perpetuanism and I was suggesting that we leave it all to the Holy Spirit."

"Very wise," said James, "although, to be honest, I've never been able to manage it myself. There's a world of difference between being a bishop and a dean you know. Anyway, that's not what I came to discuss. It's Bishop Reginald."

Clement kept his face impassive. The Dean barely moved a muscle. James smiled, not displeased with the dead pan reaction. "I sometimes wonder how Schuhorn's mind works. It's certainly more tortuous than anything I can unravel. How can he put an old bumbler like me into Canterbury and a—er, libertine— like Reggie into a quiet back-water like this. I told Schuhorn it would have been infinitely better if he'd left me and Reggie where we were, but he said he had his reasons. Now I gather, without any reference to me, he's going to be appointed my chief adviser. Anyway, Mr Dean—though I suppose I can call you Simon now, and I don't mind Clement knowing this as he's a clam of a Clem—I would like you to keep an eye on him.

"A couple of Perpetuan renegades spying on a C of E Bishop!" said the Dean. "What next?"

"Well, what else can I do? Crozier isn't much good and I do find that lawyers get a bit precious about this sort of thing, particularly the human rights sort. Hilary and Bruce are so self-preoccupied and, anyway, they wouldn't know how to do it."

"But what do you want? And what do you want it for, James?"

"I suppose I want to know if he's a potential source of scandal before the news breaks. Janet Burns is getting very fierce. She says we are entering a new age of austerity; she calls it the age of the 'New Puritanism'. She says that now that bankers have been hauled over the coals, everybody will have to take their turn in the public stocks, being pilloried by journalists with the enthusiasm of the convert to sparkling water."

"I was teasing you, James. I would like to discuss the last point in a minute so let's get the first bit out of the way. Reggie is about to have a fling with Lady Gowers."

"What! How do you know?"

"I saw their extremely unpuritanical exchange of glances as he found an opportunity to halt his procession not two yards from her. Whatever she was consecrating, James, it wasn't her virgin soul to Christ. She plays a very stiff lip and a very big hat, but she's no better, as they say, than she ought to be. It's not commonly known in these parts that she has re-made herself in a manner not dissimilar to that in which Bishop Reggie re-made himself before he wisely decided to revert to type. If I remember correctly, she had two younger sisters up North who were—er—ladies of the night."

"How would you know such a thing, Mr Dean?"

"Well, it just happens that these ladies—Stella and Lucie—were 'cured' by Dexter on one of his visits and they now grace the activity centre of the erstwhile Pastor Drone who has so reformed himself, alongside the ladies, that he's Clement's equivalent in the North of England working under his Christian name, Philip. I suppose, James, that it takes one to know one. Old Gowers married when his sap rose because he couldn't imagine, respectable old buffer, just living with her or, better, paying her a visit when the sap required. Since he died she's been something of a merry widow, James. For a while she was in pursuit of poor, bachelor Brian Sedge, but his utter blankness wore her down. I imagine Reggie is a much more attractive prospect. There's plenty of contemporary instances of the clergy—er—having improper sexual relations, but I suppose it's quite rare among bishops."

"Let us hope so, and among Deans. Anyway, Simon, what news from the political front? I'm geographically nearer than you, of course, but none of my supposed advisers have a clue. People are only in Church House a few months before they forget everything they've learned about the world and begin to believe their own—sorry Jesus'—good news."

"There is nothing very striking going on in the Government that directly affects us. The Prime Minister is pleased to take credit for saving the country if not the world and, to be fair, he's much better liked in the world than he is here. Underlying this there is a much graver situation. The deficit was bad before the crash and it will get a lot worse. The Government is hiding the extent of the problem and is spending much more than it ought in expectation of losing the Election and making it as terrible as it possibly can be for Cameron. If they have to lose they want to make it as good an election to lose as they can. From our point of view, the austerity cuts both ways. It might introduce some morally bracing rhetoric, but we ought to be suspicious of that. At the same time, there will probably be deep and permanent damage inflicted on the poor in the way that Mrs Thatcher inflicted it. Your problem, if you will forgive me, is that the Church has almost completely lost public credibility, I suppose we are in better standing, but we are rather obscure. The reason I am really pleased to see you, James, is that we ought to form a common front. I was going to discuss this with Clement, but you've pre-empted us. There may be all kinds of doctrinal nonsense—I mean nuance—which might make things difficult at an official-to-official level, but there surely isn't any reason why we can't take joint practical measures. Why, even the Romans go in for that sort of thing."

James looked embarrassed. "I think the Grand Synod has probably clipped my wings just a little too severely, but we can try. Lady Gowers, eh?"

When James had gone, Clement relaxed and looked straight at the Dean. "Why did you tell him that?"

"Sometimes, Clement, your ethical purity is disproportionate to your judgment. James is going to hear sooner or later anyway in some sort of distorted way, so he is better off learning it directly from me and I am better off if he does. You know Mark Price much better than I do. He's a lovely man, but he can't resist a nice piece of gossip. Neither His Grace visiting the Grange nor her ladyship visiting the Palace will escape notice. We had better leave that and turn to the lady we met to discuss."

"Oh Monica!" said Clement, exasperated.

"Why so worked up Clement? You are usually so calm."

"It's not the run-of-the-mill sort of exasperation. Thankfully, if there is any such thing as discipline in our movement, I'm not responsible for it. No, the reason I wanted to talk to you about Monica's letter is that it raises some really fundamental questions. Namely, in what way does it matter whether Perpetua was God or not and, therefore, what does it mean to be God and what does it mean to be human? Secondly, if we work out something general about what it means to be human, what does it mean to be male or female, lesbian or 'straight' and, by extension, what does it mean to be sick or a sinner?"

"You do have a habit of going deep, don't you Clement? We all have to face these kinds of questions sooner or later, so I will try to make a start.

"What does it mean to be God? Let me start this precisely the wrong way round. My starting point is catastrophic apophaticism which has crashed. It was doomed, I suppose, from the Lisbon earthquake of 1755 which gave the 'Enlightenment' its first real breakthrough on the God front. Having lost the sense of God and human integration and relaxation in the Middle Ages (I owe this to Charles Taylor), God simply became the watch-maker and then people found out, in the earthquake, that it was a faulty watch. Then, when God was reduced to being an ethical referee people found that there were other referees. End of story. So my genuine starting point is that we have to stop anthropomorphising God. We can't judge God, but must be content for God to judge us. People keep shouting 'why'?" but it's a silly question to ask of God. Anyway, most people only ask it when something goes wrong. They don't often scream 'why me?' when they gain something by chance, like winning the lottery. So let us say that, put simply, God is Creator, love and Spirit, incommensurably different from us, but facilitating two-way communication. I accept that communication is central and that Christians have, by and large, not been as adventurous as their Jewish forebears, but our intellectual frame of reference is all about ascertaining, about what we call fact and truth, That means that we are not very good at trust. I suppose if I have to think of words appropriate for creatures I have mentioned love as our purpose, but I would add worship as our thanks for being here and trust because if we have to accept anything about incommensurability it is that, all things being equal, God ought to 'know' more than us about ourselves.

"That is difficult enough in itself, but let me leave it there for the moment because the missing piece is incarnation. That idea was well settled by Christians after half a millennium and we can use much of that discerning to tackle your important question. How does it matter whether Perpetua was God incarnate?

"The incarnation was a promise. We might say that God only needs to promise once and that promise was constituted in Jesus, but we know from the Old Testament that YHWH needed to make covenants more than once because of who we are. So the real question about Perpetua isn't so much whether God could be incarnated more than once—clearly the Christian idea that it's a once in the universe event is not only presumptuous, but highly unlikely—but whether humanity had reached the state where it needed to experience, to live through, the repetition of the promise. If Perpetua was simply a good human being we can learn from her teaching and try to hold onto the reality of incarnation in Jesus, but if she, too was God incarnate, we are given new life and new hope. It's no denial of Jesus, but is, rather, confirmation of God's love for our imperfection. We need to be sensible about this as the issue of whether Perpetua is incarnational is far less critical than was the question of whether Jesus was incarnational because once you have established the divine communications vehicle, so to speak, how often it is used is, I think, a secondary issue.

"What we need to think more about is the symbiotic relationship between human imperfection and the necessity of divine incarnation. Surely the first requires the second, for without it humanity would struggle and, ultimately lose contact with God and lose created purpose. It is not that, theologically or philosophically, incarnation is a logical consequence of human imperfection, rather, it seems to me to be, as I have said, symbiotic. If you understand us as creatures the symbiosis is easy enough to grasp."

"You have put that very well, Simon. As well as I've ever heard it put. What it suggests, then, is that, given the level and degree of human imperfection, one incarnational manifestation for all time in Jesus hardly seems adequate. Yet, as you classify the incarnation of Perpetua as less radical because it is a repeat event, you call into question the importance of the distinction between th incarnate Perpetua and a Saint Perpetua."

"I see what you mean, Clement but, still, I think the difference between the two Perpetuas you describe is incommensurable. Perpetua is not less important than Jesus, it's just that the theological issues her incarnation raises are, because of Jesus, less pressing that's all."

"Which naturally leads to the question, with imperfection as a given, of what it means to be human."

"Let us grant between ourselves that imperfection is a given, but let us not duck a brief exploration of the meaning. The chief heresy of Christianity is to believe that we are imperfect gods, to assert that we do not 'live up to' the expectations of the Creator or the example of Jesus. Well, I firmly believe that, simply because we were created imperfect that we live up precisely to the expectations of the Creator and never can equal the example of Jesus. That's the point."

"Doesn't that lead to the conclusion that because we are created imperfect we can't be held responsible for conduct arising out of imperfection?"

"Quite the opposite. Because we are imperfect we are absolutely responsible for our own decisions insofar as we have control over them."

"That's a rather big get-out clause, isn't it?"

"No. The necessity of imperfection arises because we were created to make decisions, primarily about whether or not to love God and, consequentially, whether to love our neighbour."

"So to be a creature is to be created to make decisions in the context of imperfection?"

"Yes, but within the context, too, of who we are."

"Who we are?"

"The genes we have inherited and the cards we have been dealt. We are imperfect creatures both in nature and nurture. Imperfect in nature because we are not all equally robust, athletic, clever, and so on. Imperfect in nurture because of the aggregate of wrong choices we make about God and each other."

"What do you mean by 'the hand we're dealt'?"

"Well, in one way it is obvious and simple, but in another way it is mysterious and complex. Take the issue of gender. We know the difference between men and women in respect of reproductive functions, but not really in terms of emotional response. We think we know that women are more emotional than men but we also know from experience that men are more violent than women. Might that not make men more emotional than women because their emotions drive them to extreme actions? We know quite a lot now about the bonding between women and their offspring, and we know something about the necessity of women bonding with the fathers of their offspring, but we know nothing about the real difference between men and women that are either independent of, or in some ways flow from, the reproductive process. We suspect, for example, that for women to live with the biological father of their offspring is better than not doing so, and most of us assume without going into it, that heterosexual love is 'superior' to—deeper, more satisfactory and, yes, more natural—than lesbianism. So, setting aside Monica's deep ambivalence about lesbianism, we need to ask what the accusation of lesbianism means. Is it, at one end of the spectrum, sinful or, at the other, merely pointless. Of course I can't say, but the ideology of individual self-assertion and the danger of causing offence have taken large chunks of discourse off limits."

"Gregg used to make a lot of the idea of individualism whereas you seem to suspect it."

"I am totally in favour of individualism, but part of exercising individual choice—and this is not a clever paradox—is the choice to be communal and act in solidarity. It's the difference between being an individual and being a person. The problem with the contemporary idea of choice is that it refers to individual, autonomous, discrete, immediate self-gratification. We are getting away from where I wanted to be. It is so easy to slip into regret at our imperfection instead of accepting it. I am making the mistake of which I accuse others."

"Well, if you want to get back, Simon, how about this? We don't know very much, really, about gender. There's all that stuff about right brain and left brain, but it's scarcely better than astrology. If that is really difficult for us—and I suppose I'm saying that we are arrogant, assuming that we know much more than we really know. Maybe arrogance is a synonym for platitude—how do we distinguish between sickness and what's loosely called evil or sin?"

"We are back with the nature of nature and nurture. We think about genes and the environment in which people grow up, so we have this very neat dichotomy between genetics, which are supposed to be the hard wired, and the sum total of people and things we experience which are supposed not to be hard wired. I am not sure whether we think this purely because of our determination to keep God out of it or because we are in thrall to dichotomy, but we don't have a third idea that God determined the genes and the environment and that there is not such a sharp distinction. You know how something quite often starts out as hardware and becomes software or how something starts out as relying on a human being, a kind of software, and becomes automated.

"The problem most often arises in the case of people like Hitler. Was he evil or sick? Before I answer that we need to consider whether that is a dichotomy to start with. Evil isn't a big heap of something you have in a sack that you throw around, its's an absence of something. So in a way, is illness, it's an absence of normative functionality just as evil is an absence of, not normative, but perfect, spirituality. So they are not so different after all. We might, then, better put this question: is what we call evil a necessary consequence of imperfection? If so, does this leave our attitude to evil in the same category as our attitude to Judas Iscariot who betrayed Jesus in order to 'fulfill the Scriptures'?

"My starting point is that we don't know enough about how we work and we certainly don't know enough about the effect of our genes and our ecology on what we do. We don't know how determinist either of these things are and how much room we have for real choice. I would take a second step and say that if the essence of humanity is making choice we will have people who make more bad choices than others, but we still don't know. About every decade there is a mass murder by somebody who then kills himself. We don't know what 'flips the switch' although instead of wondering we might better wonder why he went that far and didn't feel able to talk to anybody about his anxieties or neuroses. We might ask whether we created an unhelpful ecology in which he then suffered, tortured himself, and took on guilt. I don't deny the role of the civil power in trying to regulate the results of human imperfection, but theologians ought to be wary. We know far too little, particularly about biology. Until I know more, I am inclined to say that evil and sickness are simply different consequences of imperfection for which God is not to be held accountable because we have no way of knowing why anything is the way it is."

"So, to get back to roughly where we started, we should do nothing about Monica's letter because there's nothing to do?"

"Only one thing. See how we can make her happier with herself so that she makes better choices. There's a relationship between happiness and making the right choices. I don't know how it works, but I am sure of that."

"John will give her as much room as anybody could," said Clement. "Thank you for your help. I sometimes wonder whether we are going to be scandalously unfaithful scandalously soon, as if She had never come, but you give me hope, Simon. You give me hope."

♦　♦　♦

John, having been a Professor of History before he became a Guide and then a member of the core leadership of the Perpetuans, knew more than most people about the ways of humanity as a species and a good deal about its more egregious members who fought, legislated, agitated, demolished, constructed, explored, conserved, recorded, and distorted, but none of this prepared him for handling an interview which, he knew, would be awkward. Monica had formally applied to be a Perpetuan Guide, duly selected by a house group she had formed for the purpose. Indeed, to John's considerable regret—for although as a Perpetuan he knew he should not stoop to technicalities—she had not put a foot, nor even a finger, wrong except, of course, for that letter. Her grasp of Perpetuanism was firm, but flexible, her experience in left-wing movements had, unusually, equipped her for dealing in a competent, if slightly prickly, but constructive, way with all manner of people and somehow she had managed to gloss over the plain meaning of what she had written.

"You can't hold me back just because I'm a lesbian," she said, as soon as they sat down.

"I had no intention of doing so. In fact, I had no intention of even raising the matter of your—er—sexuality."

"I should think not, or I would have to lodge a protest."

"You will not need to do that although, as you probably know, we don't have mechanisms for protest, we are inclined to believe what people say. I do need to mention, however, that it was you, in your letter, who implied at least that there is something wrong with being a lesbian."

"No. I just wanted to point out the hypocrisy—sorry, the inconsistency—of those who attack lesbianism when they are lesbians."

"I am not sure I see what you are driving at, but the second part of the proposition is much more serious. You implied, you see, that lesbianism was a sin of some sort and then implied that Perpetua committed such a sin. As you know, a member of the Godhead can't commit a sin. Which leads to the bigger problem."

"What problem? I haven't got a problem. I just don't want you to be judgmental."

"I think you need to be careful, Monica, that you don't allow your anxiety to lead you into denying Perpetuan principles. We, as you know, reject the notion of approval—or, for that matter disapproval—of individual actions."

"Yes, of course. What I meant to say was ..."

"... I'm sorry to cut across you," said John, seeing that she was digging herself into a hole, "but we need only attend to one matter and that is whether you accept the central tenets of Perpetuanism so that you can be counted a reliable Guide. Your letter to the world suggests that you don't accept that Perpetua was an incarnational manifestation of the divine."

"Well, I was a bit upset at the time."

"So you made a public denial because you were 'a bit upset'?"

"We all get upset."

"But we're not all called upon to be Guides."

"Are you saying that I'm not called?"

"I am saying that I accept that you are called, but that such a calling needs to be moulded by you to fit the place in which you find yourself. You might have a calling to be a systematic theologian, but it wouldn't be of much use if we needed a community Guide in a highly deprived area. In your case I am sure you do have a calling to work with people to help them establish closer relationships with the Godhead, but it may be a Christian rather than a Perpetuan calling."

"I've had enough of them."

"Which isn't, in itself, a good enough reason to be a Perpetuan. I know that some Anglicans have gone to Rome because they're against women clergy but it wasn't a good enough reason, you know. Being against something doesn't automatically make you in favour of something else."

"I'm glad they went. They caused people like me so much grief."

"I am not saying that people who are grieved, or even highly emotional, are not fit to be Guides in certain circumstances, but where we are now, we need a listening Guide, somebody who can, in the Perpetuan way, absorb a good deal of the trauma and guilt of other people. You seem to me to be in need of somebody to take on that role for you."

"I don't need therapy."

"Therapy, Monica, is a poor substitute for good neighbourliness in most cases. Society has simply medicalised anti-social behaviour, by which I do not mean the minor infractions of youth, but the steady, callous indifference of largely well educated adults towards each other."

"People always think that lesbians need therapy."

John wondered whether to go on with the discussion or whether it would be better for her if he came to the point. "But, Monica, perhaps I shouldn't say this—and it's taking a risk—but I don't think you are a lesbian. There would be nothing wrong if you were, but I don't think you are."

"I'll report you for being outrageously anti-lesbian."

"I have just said that I am not; and as I trust you, you have to trust me."

They sat in silence for more than a minute.

"I'm not a psychologist, Monica. I just think you have problems with equal relationships and think that these would be easier with women than with men which might be the same as lesbianism, for all I know, but the important point for us is not the kind of relationships you want with equals, but your capacity to form relationships with equals. Only then, I think, can you become accustomed to listening and, after that, to adopting a Perpetuan stance towards love."

She was about to protest when she crumpled. "I could give you a load of Freudian drivel," she said, "but I'll spare you. I do have problems. I frighten people, particularly men. I thought women would not mind if I was a bit assertive. But I don't know when to shut up. I've become a serial protester."

"That's a good start, Monica. If I were you I would ask your house group to be your collective mentor for a while, and then come and see me again. Remember, I don't doubt that you are being called by the Godhead to do something. We just have to spend more time listening to find out what."

◆   ◆   ◆

Philip, having been a career Pastor in a run-down industrial town, knew both about moral authority and community projects and so he should have been well equipped to accommodate the callings of Stella and Lucie, but their moral assertiveness, threatened the Perpetuan outlook he had tried so hard to cultivate as the result of his admiration for Perpetua and then Dexter. He found, as he came to embrace what they said, that his own moral training had given him a radically divided persona as his moralising had been incompatible with his mission. Perpetuanism, though strange at first, was liberating and now Stella and Lucie were threatening to tie him up in old knots.

"We need to get the women off the streets," said Stella.

"And into respectable work," said Lucie.

"So we need a rehab centre for addicts," said Stella.

"And a needle exchange," said Lucie.

"Worthy though all this caring is, it misses the point," said Philip. "What we need as Perpetuans is to be open to the love of the other, accepting how they offer their love."

"We've been there," said Lucie. "Except for their evil desires, they've got nothing to offer."

"We've had enough of that," said Stella.

"What these people need is some tough love," said Lucie.

"Perhaps," said Philip, "but that's not what Perpetuans dispense."

"Well, we knew her and we're not abandoning her just because what she asked was difficult, particularly for us who've been sex workers."

Philip looked at the paradox of accepting what was unacceptable and decided to accept it. The women loved the memory of Perpetua, had been cured by her, and had vowed to dedicate their lives to honouring her memory, as they put it. For three decades Philip had preached sermon after sermon about trusting God, abandoning calculation, and Perpetua was summoning him to do this in his ministry. He would accept Stella and Lucie as Guides, resigning himself to constant vigilance.

◆   ◆   ◆

Keith wasn't really sure why he continued to go to the house group. It took place on Wednesdays which was always the night of his favourite soap opera and often the night of big football matches. He could record the stuff, but it wasn't the same. People like Ronald from the church did their best to simplify their language but it wasn't that. Keith and his friends were simply not used to having discussions. It wasn't that they couldn't talk but they didn't use talk for pleasure or stimulation. He could have just stayed away but that would have been cowardly. Instead he just kept on coming, hoping that something useful or interesting would happen.

It did, but Keith was the last to recognise it. He had always been accustomed to think that everything was somebody else's fault, usually an undefined entity called "them". "They" always seemed to be after him in particular. "They made it difficult for him to claim benefits, stopped him enjoying his car, didn't look after the park properly, made silly rules about dogs, and, in short, saw to it that he never got what he deserved. Because of these irritations, his life was in an almost permanent state of "chaos", "disaster," "shambles", and "nightmare". The harm wasn't in anybody taking notice of what he said because most of his neighbours said precisely the same things of themselves, the harm was in his inability to take control over his own life. In the house group, all kinds of issues were discussed, but the question always came down to "what will you do about it?" He was irritated at first, but after a while yesterday's radicalism became today's conservatism and he began to adopt the habits of mind applied in the group. Neighbours who didn't attend the group noticed that he moaned less and did more. He accepted help to learn how to fill in forms. He put himself on the park well being rota. He even went to a "You and Your Dog" evening class. He still moaned about all things automotive but, on the whole, he was a different person. Then he discovered that the lady who had taught him to fill in forms was hopeless with cars and he gained a certain status in the group.

Observing this, Kylie suggested to Trina that the emphasis in house groups should be less verbal and more practical, that they should act as mutual help groups that transcended geography and class. Perpetuans weren't interested in interminable doctrinal debates and most people weren't either. They needed practical activity. There should be discussion about Scripture, Sacrament, love, care, and self-restraint, but in a lively, down-to-earth context.

There might be controversy between the Church of England and the Perpetuan movement in London, but church life in Walmbury went on as before. With guidance from Trina, Father Mark had made some minor adjustments to the Creed and the Eucharistic prayer, but everything else remained the same. No Perpetuan Hymns or special prayers had yet been written, the fragments of what Perpetua had said seemed to have disappeared and the only matter that really exercised his neat mind was the name of his church. Part of him wanted to keep Holy Trinity for historical reasons on the grounds that, for example, there were many churches dedicated to fictional saints, but part of him wanted to recognise the new settlement in the name. He couldn't stand the Holy Quartet, so he had decided to go the whole way and call it Church of The Sacred Vessel. Ronald and Violet, recalling an earlier conversation, persuaded him to stick to his plan of naming it after the old church and the current school, Saint Damian.

"The trouble with change," said Ronald to Mark, "is that it's rarely clear cut. You decide something quite small, like this name change, then something else happens, and something else. Saint Damian isn't Perptuan but it avoids the doctrinal problem and that's good enough for now." Mark agreed.

People protested, as they always do, at a name change—much more so than at the changes of doctrine and liturgy—but it soon stuck. The Mothers Union was still the Mothers Union, subtly adjusting its house prayer. After a slight feeling of discomfort over Christmas, Trina had announced that it should be celebrated as usual, although it would be nice if there was a Perpetua figure at the crib. Perpetua's own life and death would be remembered as an integral part of Holy Week and the Triduum, but this would need some sensitive working out. The Christians would be offended, but she saw no other option. She did not want to impose, but you could not claim the importance of Perpetua and then demote her to the status of a minor saint celebrated on a Wednesday in February. A local musician offered to write a couple of Perpetua songs for the family service because she was so popular there—much more popular than Jesus—and Mark had no objections. The choir were tranquil, the PCC had re-constituted itself under the Charity directorate as the Council of Perpetua the Sustainer. There had been fearsome legislative wrangling at Westminster over the power of Christian churches to transform themselves into Perpetuan entities. The problems were not in the least doctrinal, but turned on probate, assets, and thickets of precedents. Strider did his best in the Commons with Warpley in the Lords to

be obstructive but a harassed Government was in no mood for pointless joust-
ing and whipped through the changes. The new body was soon referred to affectionately as the CPS. Lady Gowers, who might have been a nuisance, had
other things to do and a spring in her step. The long looked for re-ordering
went ahead with the blessing of Violet and Ronald. Mark knew that the Perpetuan emphasis was on house groups with corporate worship reserved for big
occasions, but he could not go that far. He and Clement discussed the form of
the Perpetuan Sacraments and how they might be slowly introduced, but what
counted, they agreed, was changing the fundamental theology of the people so
that they understood, even if they could not practice, the Perpetuan concept of
love. Mark might be a Guide, but he still insisted on being called Father and he
still needed his weekly Sacrament of Union.

Down at the Oak, Nigel Bourne held his customary court. "It's as I said," he
said, comfortably, to no-one in particular. "We're more or less back where we
were. We always are. People make changes, it seems to me, to pass the time or to
justify their rank. But it always goes back to where it was before."

"That's not quite true," said a man he had never seen before. "Perpetua has
given us hope. She's closer to us than the Jesus we struggled to understand."

"Is that so?"

"There's no need to be aggressive," said the man. "I'm really happy for those
who can find God through Jesus. So be happy for me that I can find God through
Perpetua. Have a drink."

Nigel had never been known to refuse. "I didn't mean it to come out so harsh.
I'm sorry—er ..."

"... Keith ..."

"... I'm sorry, Keith. The Perpetuan thing must be catching."

◆　◆　◆

Kylie and Clement had a glass of wine after a house group. "To be honest,"
said Clement, "I still miss Living Water where we were all so close and comfortable, but after a while you knew what people were going to say and because it
was comfortable it stopped being challenging. The new dynamic is good for
people, particularly those who came from the old group. They are ever so nice
but, kind though they were, they fell into an easy assumption of superiority."

"Talking of which, Clement, what are we going to do about the work? I'm
here full time, you're here when you're not in London, and the Dean is just down
the road."

"I think, in reverse order, that the Dean is conducting a vital piece of research
in action trying to share his cathedral with Bishop Crowther. I will only undertake very local duties under Mark's direction as he's the local Guide. I don't mind
being in the core group in London and putting myself under Mark, and you will

have the run of the country."

"What should we do for people when the economic downturn really hits?"

"We should," said Clement, "teach people not to be sorry for themselves, to moderate their habits with good grace, and to recognise that this is a time for giving."

◆　◆　◆

This was a message which Max was not finding easy to promote in the City. There was a surge of self-pity, almost amounting to victimhood and, at a paradoxical right-angle, a deep sense of denial that anything was its fault. The bankers and financial services organisations that had nearly brought the country to ruin found an escape route by calling for savage cuts in public expenditure. Otherwise, they said, the country's credit rating would plummet. Max wondered, under these conditions, whether there was a country where the credit rating would not plummet and, on the grounds that everything is relative, thought that if they all plummeted together, investors would still want to put their money somewhere. If you had to cut savagely to save your credit rating you might damage your growth and end up worse off. He didn't mind the economic dispute—he could see both sides of the argument about cuts and growth—but his sadness was the motivation for the advocacy. The people who advocated the savage cuts did not do so because they would benefit the country, but because their long term agenda was to shrink the state and reduce taxation on the rich which paid for welfare benefits. Those who resisted cuts did not do so because it would protect growth, but because they wanted more time to live as they had lived, denying that borrowing is deferred taxation.

Max called round to see Sir Pluto. "I hoped to see Annie."

"So did I, but there are difficulties. The economic down-turn is beginning to affect our experiment in lower consumption, or, rather, in the consequent redistribution we called for. People are cutting their consumption, right enough, but they are not volunteering part of their savings to help poor people here and abroad. I suspect the problem is that they're cutting because they feel they want to save rather than because they have less disposable income. Our weakness is that it's most difficult to get money off people when we need it most. Now that the world is going through a down-turn it's difficult to persuade people to make even bigger sacrifices than they were prepared to make in the good times. We need a new approach or we shall fail."

"What about persuading people to put their savings into good causes. People in the UK seem only to want to give; they rarely loan. As interest rates are near zero, why not set up a philanthropic bank, all digital, no paper, where people deposit money when they've finished shopping and it's shown on their account in the way that their loyalty points are shown. They can only get a fragment of interest at the banks, so don't offer any for the time being. Get the administration costs by lending the money to good causes at, say 3%. There will be defaults in such a crisis as we are going through now, but you should be able to persuade your friends that in a time of crisis we need more capital in the charity sector and that such a scheme is cheaper in the long run than outright grants."

"We can do that," said Sir pluto, looking pleased. "It's not that difficult. We've been looking at the logistics of setting up a Hypo Bank for ages, but this would be different. That's not what you came to see me about, is it?"

"Partly. I get worried when we veer towards the doctrinal and away from the practical. At this time of great distress for some people and more distress on the way, we ought to be doing something."

"Caution Max. Caution. In the first place, I accept that we should all be practical and all love our neighbour. So we must encourage people to be generous with their resources—time, money, patience—but Perpetuanism isn't primarily a philanthropic enterprise. Forgive me for saying this, Max, but your unique selling point is the Godhead in general and Perpetua in particular. What you have to sell is the Perpetuan slant on the general need for philanthropy and that is, primarily, listening. I know that you started out by being very interested in lowering consumption as a Perpetuan virtue, and I still think this is important, but it's the wrong message at the moment. I can do what I'm doing because I'm only a semi-detached Perpetuan. In this era of screaming and shouting and arms in the air, Perpetuans need to be emotionally absorbant. I've always liked the image of Perpetua as the Sacred Vessel although it leaves itself open to bawdy caricature."

"Yes, Pluto. Of course you're right. I suppose I'm straining to be relevant."

"What you need to do, Max, is to empty your head of what's happened since Perpetua's death and go back there. It will be painful for you, I know, but the danger is that we're all losing the vision and suffering from the hotel effect whereby different organisations doing broadly the same thing all end up in the same place. Be brave. Stick with the brand. You might have to play a long hand, but the age of the Enlightenment is over. Dawkins and his kind are the last gasp. Anybody who thinks about it knows that intelligence isn't enough for human beings. Science didn't save Jews from the Shoah, and we still need to solve the problem of how death camp staff could go home and listen to Schubert or, rather, how they could listen to Schubert and then go back to the death camps. Whether you think that the Nazis tossing babies into fires were evil, sinful, sick, lacking in religion, scientifically driven, or simply misled, you have to admit that the twentieth century was a moral failure ... I know, I know ... Perpetuanism isn't primarily moral, but I need to make this point; morality points towards the non-materialist dimension of human beings. Religion, even in its crude moral form, keeps culture honest. It had a hard fight in the last century, but I think the reaction is coming. This isn't speculative optimism, it's the kind of judgment I'd make about a new product at Hypo. The grim times will cause resentment in some places, but deep thought in others. People know that wealth hasn't made them any happier than they used to be, and they know that vague, consumerist, selfish spiritualism hasn't made any difference to them or anybody else. The reason we don't see these changes is that we keep looking for them in church attendance. We think that there is a revival of godliness when church attendances begin to rise. That is not the right place to look. If you ask me, the place to look is in what I call the emotional temperature of society which, I believe, will be lowered by temperance, proportionality, and prudence, all Perpetuan virtues. The lower the temperature, the more space and time there is for people to be absorptive of otherness and also in listening mode for God."

"Pluto, you're turning into a theologian."

"No, just watching and thinking. Since I divested myself of many of my extraneous interests I've had more time, and falling in love has made an enormous difference."

"So how do we lower the social temperature when we've got such screaming media?"

"Frankly, my dear Max, that is a rather silly question. It requires self-control. Don't buy a newspaper, and don't turn on the television. For some people it's an addiction that needs drastic action. When people tell me they don't have time to do this or that I usually ask them how much television they watch, or how many hours they spend on the internet. I'm sorry for characterising your question as silly—I was getting excitable while simultaneously deploring it—but if people don't consume something the makers will go bust or make something different."

"No offence taken, Pluto. I rather walked into that. So, at the risk of being called 'silly' again, should we campaign against the media?"

"I think Quintus and Chris will both tell you that it's useless because your campaign against the media at best will be carried by the occasional media maverick. The rest will pillory you. Quintus will tell you to keep control of your own story and tell it, not a a campaign, but simply as a series of statements which accord with Perpetua's message."

"Finally, Pluto, what about our general media strategy. The god4u project seems to be losing support even though the number of Perpetuans is steadily rising. We have enough money to put more in, if that's needed."

"Talking to people via media is a necessity when you've got a mass audience that wants to know about you, but you don't have enough human power to listen and talk. I suspect that the Perpetuan culture will be, as they say, viral. You will need to reach outside the core Perpetuan centres of activity, but don't worry about audience figures, they're like Christian pew figures. Watch the real growth in numbers and the cooling of the social temperature." Sir Pluto handed him a list.

» More self-help and learning and less protest and complaint
» More saving and giving and less consumption
» More community service and mentoring and fewer criminal charges
» More trust and less surveillance

» A lower turnover in personal and reproduction relationships
» More self-deprecation and less satire
» Lower car speeds and more walking
» More listening and less therapy
» More thanksgiving and less intercession
» A slight reverse in longevity
» More grey and less red
» More competence and less heroism
» More virtue and less celebrity
» Above all, more silence

The door bell rang and Sir Pluto ushered in Sir Granville.

"Sir Pluto has just been delivering a master class on what he calls the criteria for measuring a cooling in the social temperature," said Max.

Granville looked at his list: "When do you think we'll see the signs?"

"I think the downturn will help."

"Oddly counter intuitive," said Granville. "I hope you're right. I am worried, however, because all the signs I see are moving the other way. I think I've one to add to your list." He wrote another item on the bottom of Max's list:

» More tolerance of difference and less tribalism

"As for claims of generosity during times of hardship, I think it's a bit of a sentimental throw-back to a notional golden age. I remember the Blitz—just—but it's amazing how many people who weren't born at the time talk about it with affection. People are now so used to being individualist consumers that it will be very hard to build up any kind of solidarity. The most difficult area is immigration, asylum, and race. I can see no way that we can give enough support to developing countries to narrow the gap such that their people want to stay there rather than coming here. It's a Utopian theory. There will always be enough outright basket cases to export more people than we can reasonably handle. It's all right for us, but for Class E males, losing jobs to immigrants is tough. Anyway, that's not why I dropped in. The first reason is that I've heard a whisper that Horace is up to his old tricks. I really don't know why. When I was his boss he was the epitome of calculated moderation, but he seems to have taken an irrational dislike to Perpetuans. It might be the anti-consumption campaign, Pluto, but you would know more about that than me. This time he says that Perpetuans are promoting pacifism and this is having a bad effect on military recruitment and morale."

"Well, we are pacifists, right enough," said Max. "We don't so much preach it as practice it, although there isn't really much opportunity for that. He has a point insofar as most of our really good work is in the poorest parts of the country where most soldiers come from, but I doubt what we say stops people in dire circumstances, wanting to prove themselves, joining up. We wouldn't really preach about it. Again, it's one of those areas where the distinction between Perpetuan principle and secular society's need to handle the consequences of imperfection is particularly sharp. It's also an area which shows how difficult it is to be a good Perpetuan. You get that old argument, 'if your child were attacked would you use violence to defend it?' I hope not, but I probably would. It's an area where Christianity has become markedly weak, tied up with the establishment. I'm sure we all could have thought of better ways of trying to deal with the Taliban in Afghanistan than invading the country and getting bogged down there. Nobody at the time seemed to think there was any alternative, and that's where matters become even more difficult for us because that invasion wasn't the civil power handling the consequences of human imperfection, it was pure revenge. The link between domestic security and subduing Afghanistan is bogus. Sorry, I'm getting off the point, but for all kinds of reasons I think it will soon be impossible for democracies to wage war. That shows the superiority of democracy. There will be adaptive throes, and I suppose Horace is symptomatic. Does it mean anything, Granville?"

"Just when you think the Government has gone as far as it can in attacking civil liberties, it does something else. It looks mad, but we must be vigilant. Remember what I said about race. The way we define terrorism on the one hand and sects, as opposed to respectable denominations, on the other, is not entirely rational. Taxonomy seems to be a weak point in the civil service which wants to sweep as much into every class as it can find.

"However, I mentioned two reasons for coming and my second piece of news is much more interesting. I like saving the best till last. It seems likely that the Dean of Alchester, your good brother, is going to be offered a bishopric."

Max gulped. "But he's a Perpetuan, how can that be?"

"Archbishop Hall seems to think that Perpetuanism might add something to Simon's credal commitments to God, but won't take anything away."

"But he radically turned against Perpetuanism after a brief flirtation."

"You've no idea what an effect the Dean had on him when he was at Alchester—he says he hasn't stopped thinking about it—and he says that Clement, during the time he worked in his private office, was far more loyal and affectionate to him than supposedly 'loyal Anglians' like Crozier. The Torans and Petrans—excuse the expression—both give him hell because they can't have all that they want, which seems a very odd way of being humble. I've heard that Bishop Crowther is furious, but I know he won't do anything because he never has had any follow-through."

"And will my brother accept?" asked Max, still incredulous.

"I don't know. He's deep is Mr Dean, very deep indeed. He won't rush and he'll be right when he reaches his conclusion. He won't be flattered and he won't be bamboozled. He won't want to be 'used' as a way of creating pressure on Perpetuanism. That isn't James' intent but there's always that danger."

"Let's pray for him," said Max. And even Sir Pluto put his hands together.

◆　◆　◆

The Dean sat in his cosy corner after saying his evening prayers. He had put off thinking about his dilemma until he had the proper time to give it his full attention. One of his almost innumerable rules of personal conduct was never to do two things badly as an escape from choosing which single thing one should do well. Ever since the amazing call had come from Schuhorn (in his last week before moving into the Archbishop's private office) he had honestly given his full attention to his list of appointments. Now, after Evensong in the cathedral and his own private devotions, he was ready.

The first question he asked himself was whether to call Max, but he decided that he should reach his own interim position before seeking advice. Whatever the conclusion it must have more of him in it than the external elements, no matter how sound each might be and no matter how well they combined. People might be able to advise him in theory, in the abstract, but only he knew fully who he was. He would talk to Max if he needed to rather than before he knew whether he needed to. He poured himself a modest glass of modest Rioja, took a modest sip, poked the rather dejected fire, and laid his silver fountain pen on top of a packet of thick, cream paper. More than an hour later, his wine untouched, he took up the pen.

> My Dear James
>
> I cannot say how touched I was—I know you do not flatter and so I will spare you this decorous self-deprecation—by the informal approach you caused to be made to me regarding my willingness, in principle, to accept the office of bishop in the Church of England. No-one can know better than you what conflicting arguments and emotions have played themselves across my consciousness in considering your request, and now, rather than the curt reply of the reluctant lover, I think you are properly owed a detailed self-examination which I hope will at the end, present you with a reasonable and rounded conclusion.
>
> Forgive me if I state the obvious, but I think it is best, to avoid any misunderstanding, to be scrupulous.
>
> We are God's creatures, created to love God and each other. The mystery of the nature of God and the existence of things and ourselves is infinitely compounded by the wondrous mystery of incarnation, at which point we part company with Jews and Muslims. Incarnation is central to Christianity and Perpetuanism. The difference is not in regard to the concept, but in regard to its sufficiency. Christians stipulate that the incarnation of God in Jesus Christ was a unique instance for all time and space. I find this difficult to accept in respect of both dimensions. We cannot specify that there should only be one incarnational instance for all time. The Genesis account of God walking in the cool of the evening—Adam and Eve's shame which caused them to hide implies that on previous occasions they had not hidden and had come face to face with God—may be a faint echo of an incarnational manifestation of the divine so far back in history that it was almost lost to oral tradition, and we cannot say that God would not "choose" to be manifested after Jesus. We are even less in a position to make any credible statement about God's manifestation in other parts

of creation. Perpetuans believe that she was an incarnational manifestation of the divine, and so did she. Yet this difference is not so radical as it might be. There was a strong possibility in first century Palestine that Judaism, so fiercely monotheistic, would accept a "loose" trinitarianism and the contemporary acceptance of multiple occurrences of divine incarnation is theologically less problematic than, say, the reception of the initial doctrine of incarnation. Within the broad scope allowed by the Church of England—as opposed to Roman Catholicism—for theological speculation, Perpetuanism would be less radical than, for example, the theology of Bultmann or Hick. On doctrinal grounds, therefore, I believe that there is no obstacle to my becoming a Bishop in the Church of England just as I have remained a Dean, undisturbed since I adopted Perpetuanism, and, I may say with gratitude, undisturbed by you.

But there is a more important matter to consider and that is the nature of the love that we were created to practice. I believe that the love proclaimed by Jesus and Perpetua is identical in its unlimited scope and "passivist" stance. Jesus did not moralise, refused to appeal to the Father to spare him from his earthly fate and expressed the unlimited nature of his love in his death. Those precise statements can also be made in respect of Perpetua. However, Christianity has somehow lost its ability to embrace unconditional, passivist, love at its core, and has "descended" into moralism. In doing so, it has been severely wounded by the enlightenment weapons it took up to combat the enlightenment such that it is severely deficient in matters of love and mystery. The question, then, is whether one should remain inside Christianity to reform it or take the apparently easier path of becoming a Perpetuan separate from Christianity, perhaps with the hope, through practising in this separate sphere, of reforming Christianity from the outside rather than the inside. On balance, however, I believe that it is better to reform from within than without and, therefore, on this second tactical ground, I could accept a bishopric without any loss of integrity.

There is, however, a further consideration. The human grasp of mystery and the dynamic of love are both directly proportionate to the intensity of the personal relationship between creature and Creator. There is no logical ground for saying this, but I believe that the Christian grasp of the mystery of God and its descent into moralism are both accounted for by its failure to make the personal relationship with God central to its purpose. The function of the incarnation of Jesus was to facilitate that personal relationship with God—which we call prayer—and the turning away from what Jesus facilitated accounts for the incarnation of Perpetua. Just as we made the Crucifixion of Jesus necessary to remind us both of our imperfection and the truth that our part in it will never impair God's love, so our loss of enterprise in seeking a relationship with God after Jesus necessitated the incarnation of God in Perpetua. None of this in itself disqualifies a Perpetuan from remaining a Christian, but I believe, in conclusion, that I should dedicate my life to helping people to develop a personal relationship with God in the context of mystery and with a strengthening capacity to love and that there are such ingrained problems within conventional Christianity that I fear I will spend all my energies trying to reform it as a necessary precondition for my mission rather than carrying that mission out.

You know, James, from our very open discussions which you have always promoted so generously, that I have long been disturbed by the Christian obsession with ecclesiology, hierarchy, and power. Of course I do not count this to your charge and I am acutely aware of your loneliness, but I am afraid that I cannot bring myself to stand at your side. I am truly sorry. Even if I am able to live the rest of my life believing that I took the correct decision, I will never be free of the pain it causes me because of the pain I know it will cause you.

In conclusion, then, in spite of the very close doctrinal alignment of the two entities, the relational over-rides the doctrinal and, therefore, with the best grace I can, I must decline your kind offer.

He wiped his pen carefully and put it back in its drawer. He smiled at the untouched glass of wine and took a deep drink. He was sorry to disappoint James who had paid him a great compliment. He toyed with the idea that God was more important than James, but dismissed it as bad theology, like saying that he was more important than a stone. It made syntactic sense, but that was all. That was the trouble with a good deal of theology. He thought he blamed Descartes and Kant and he promised himself that he would re-read late Wittgenstein. He poured himself another half glass of wine and stood in the bay window to drink it and enjoy the Close in moonlight. He did not know how long he could stay. The invitation and its refusal might destroy the status quo, but he was distracted by the sight of Lady Gowers walking purposefully across the Close towards the Palace.

◆   ◆   ◆

"Reggie," said Marianne, even before he had had the chance to hand her an armagnac, "Lady Broadparks told me that odious Dean of yours might be offered a bishopric."

"He won't accept."

"Why not? He's vain enough."

"He's only vain in respect of his integrity which makes him the Pharisee to my Publican, and that very vanity will stop him accepting. He values his ability to say to himself, and anybody else, that he's a man of integrity. He couldn't live without that. Being who I am, I can't stand his integrity. He doesn't do anything in the least bit showy, but it's always there, always threatening. It's the first thing he makes sure you know about him."

"Lady Broadparks says he'll take it if offered to form an alliance with James and his brother Max to stage a Lambeth Palace coup."

"Nonsense, Marianne. James is being absolutely honest, which he always is, but honesty is no defence or, rather, the opposite, is an almost certain guarantee of wrong headedness. James will offer something to somebody because he thinks they deserve it, but that's no guarantee that they do. Even if people 'deserve' something it might be the wrong time or the wrong thing. James might have Mr Dean as his private chaplain or spiritual director but not as a bishop."

"Did you deserve it, Reggie?"

"Not by commonly applied standards, but patronage isn't a set of individual decisions taken on the basis of merit, it's a game of chess and Schuhorn just happened to need my piece in Alchester."

"Good old Schuhorn," said Marianne, removing her shoes.

◆　◆　◆

James received the Dean's gracious, humble, and apologetic letter with sadness, but no surprise. It was just one more rebuff. Since Clement's departure matters had gone from bad to worse. The two factions in the Church were becoming ever more bitter and the Americans and Nigerians were, if anything, behaving even more badly. He had no sympathy with Janet who wanted to pick fights rather than calm critics and he had nothing at all from Crozier except impenetrable financial memoranda which issued forth regularly at the conclusion of one of his extended bouts of gloomy pouring over the figures. He was dreading the arrival of Schuhorn who was suave, calculating and impenetrable. He would never know what was going on. He was imprisoned in the classic cell of being responsible for everything and knowing next to nothing that his officials, all paid more than him, did not want him to know. It was mad, he thought, that the top level of British society had come to this The top people in government, QUANGOs and social institutions were powerless and poorly paid while their assistants were powerful and well paid whereas people at the top in banks and businesses were well paid, but claimed to be powerless.

He would have to be careful not to use prayer and worship as escape routes from his responsibilities, but he was sorely tempted. The only peace of mind he got was in his private chapel. Yes, he enjoyed his visits to parishes, schools, drop-in centres, and any place where he made real contact with real people, but these occasions were always marred by the thought at the back of his mind by the fact that they were always suggested when his people needed to get him out of the way, knowing that it was impossible for him to refuse.

"What am I to do, Doris?" he asked over a particularly gloomy dinner. "I was so counting on the Dean."

"I know you were, James, and no amount of warning from me that Simon would turn you down made any difference. It's a pity that Schuhorn isn't ordained or you could promote him to a bishopric. If I were you I would get somebody pastoral, diplomatic, and devoted to you, like Brian Sedge, to be your chaplain and Private Secretary and make Schuhorn your Chief of Staff or some other such grand title. He won't be taken in by the change of title, but he's vain."

"Brian Sedge is a good man, but this is London."

"He's a good man wherever he is and it would be a reward for long service and an escape from the dreadful Crowther."

"I wonder why he was given Alchester, Doris."

She knew. She knew James too well, and wouldn't say.

"And if Brian comes, what then? I feel as if everything is going away from me, that I'm letting the Church down. To be honest, I really only want to pray and study a little."

"I know what the mystics say, James, but there's no point doing all this praying if it isn't getting you closer to God. If it is, then listen to what he says."

"Typically good advice," thought James. He wished he loved her the way she wanted to be loved, but they did their best.

He persuaded Brian to join him and then went on retreat for a week to see if God would help him out.

◆   ◆   ◆

"And what about the Venerable Bland?" She asked, curling herself up comfortably at the opposite end of the sofa from the silk dressing gowned Reggie.

Wearily, Crowther poured himself another brandy. He wasn't enjoying it. It just passed the time while Marianne went on and on. The more she went on the less he wanted her. It had been a mistake. The small and decreasing pleasure wasn't worth the large and increasing risk. He needed to get rid of her, and the sooner the better. He should spark a row. That would get rid of her now, in the middle of the night, when there was least risk. She might get angry and denounce, him but he'd have to risk it. He should have known from the start that he would have to get rid of her sooner or later and that she would almost certainly turn poisonous. Better now when he hadn't actually done anything worth reporting. He had been indiscreet, but not reckless.

"Marianne," he said, putting his glass down rather too sharply, "I don't care about Bland, or any of them. I don't know why you are so interested in church gossip."

"It isn't gossip, Reggie, it's important to collect information to defend the Church. You know that my parish has turned heretic. It's your job to do something about it. If you won't, I need the information to do it for you."

"You mean these visits are primarily information gathering?"

"Not primarily, Reggie, wholly. You didn't think, did you—Oh God, you did!—that there was something amorous? O God, you did! I don't know who's the more stupid, you for thinking it or me for not knowing that you would. Let's face it, Reggie, how could a 'gossip' such as me not know about your tomcattery? Lady Broadparks is a good friend of old Griswald, Lord Warpley, you know. There are all kinds of stories about your sisters. Well, I've said enough.

Too much! I'd better go for both our sakes."

She put her shoes on and stood up. "And, by the way, I'll say nothing because anything I might say that would damage you because of your association with me would damage me more because of my association with you. Good night."

The insomniac Dean saw Lady Gowers steaming across the Close, head down. "Reggie will need comforting," he thought, "not because he has done anything, but be because he hasn't. We all misjudged him. We went on appearances laced with a little malice. God forgive me."

◆   ◆   ◆

James closed his Bible and looked out across the rough country lawn. He wished that being a Christian was as easy as some of his detractors said it was. For him it was to live a life in full consciousness of brokenness and human failure. He understood the rhetoric or, rather, the logic of the joy of creation—as a young man he had taken to Aquinas—but he had never felt it in his bones nor in his prayer. He had read von Balthasar with a sense of wonder, but also with a deep feeling, almost resentful, that he had been shut out from even the slightest intimation of God's glory. For whatever set of causes—incoherent and tangential or simple and ascertainable—his discipleship was bleak. It was so bleak that he could imagine the concept of the withdrawal of God. There had been another earthquake killing hundreds and, he thought, perhaps theodicy isn't a mechanism for enabling choice, perhaps it is, simply, God "showing off", defending "himself" against anthropomorphisation. This God, on that basis, was beyond our reach, but we still must reach. It was beyond our language but we must think and speak. There were many other people who adopted an identical stance, it was just that the gap which James perceived, in himself at least, was wider than the gap that others seemed to experience. Perhaps it was that very bleakness, the habits of mind involved with struggle, that had led him to suspect the gaiety of Perpetua. He had temporarily accepted what she said on more or less theological grounds—you could never be sure—but his temperament was against her. He wished he felt free to say more in public about the role of temperament in faith, but he wanted no more controversy.

He took Simon's letter from its place inside the hard back cover. He read it with a growing sense of recognition. Simon was scrupulous, but he could not help his combination of simplicity and elegance of expression being persuasive. James knew, when he folded the letter, that he agreed with everything that Simon said, but he also knew that he would never admit it to anyone else. What was left of his life would be spent labouring in the shadow of the wall, watching his brothers and sister as they played in God's sunlit fields. Looking back he had felt that there was something of the facile about her, not dissimilar to the "happy clappy" tendency but, then, Jesus probably led the singing round the camp fire.

He saw Max go past his window and turn into the building. He knocked. "I heard you were here, James, and hoped you would not mind if I had a few words with you."

"I'm a bit bleak, Max. Not good company at all."

"I can understand that. My brother's decision must have been a blow. For what it's worth—and I'm not being disloyal to him because we all have to live with what we decide—I think he should have accepted your offer. I will never tell him so, but the comfort this might give you outweighs any theoretical breach of confidence. I want you to know that our door is still open to any form of collaboration that your colleagues can accept."

"I was thinking to myself, Max, that perhaps the difference between us, in the end, is temperamental rather than doctrinal. There's a serious vein of misery in Christianity with which it's comfortable. If I'm honest, I think that Jesus was probably cheerful in the way that Perpetua was cheerful, but it's all right for incarnate ones to be cheerful. They are, after all, without sin. It is that very misery, perhaps, which draws us away from God. Instead of gift we can only see slight. We are always criticising God and belittling ourselves. I know we should not give into it, but I think I'm beyond change. I could accept doctrinal change, but I can't change the temperament of brokenness and failure. Perhaps that's why Christianity isn't attractive to young people and why Perpetuanism might be. I know there are some religious leaders who convey optimism to youth, but we wear them down in the end. Did you come to see me particularly?"

"No James. Like you, I am on retreat. I think it's always best to think about things when everything is going well rather than during a crisis. I am sure we will have crises enough but, for the time being, we are calm. Indeed that very calmness presents us with a problem of loss of momentum. I also wanted some time to think about the earthquake."

"Have you reached any conclusions?"

"No, not as such, but a direction of travel. I might be heretical, but I don't think that Perpetua's point, put baldly, that bad things happen in order to facilitate choice, is good enough. I can see the logic of it—that if you live in a perfect world you can't choose good over bad or to be Godward over, let's say, to be devilward—but we don't need earthquakes or child cancer to generate the conditions for choice. If the earth was tranquil and our health allowed us to live until a good old age we would still be different and need different kinds of care and be capable of offering ourselves in love to different kinds of people. And we would face the different temptations of comfort."

"The problem with that, Max, is that your soft heartedness does not allow you to see the 'hard heartedness' of God. You saw in Perpetua, as I see in Jesus, the softness of God incarnate which is in stark contrast, in human terms, with the hardness of God our Creator. It's another mystery which we try to simplify. How often have I heard people puzzling over the difference between the Old Testament God and the New Testament Jesus. But, Max, it's all pretty pointless. The difference is in the way we see God through history, and Perpetuanism does have one great point in its favour, it has altered the narrative of the relationship between humanity and God yet again, softened it a little, for the time being."

"You are so good and straight, James. I'm sorry it makes you so sad."

"I ought to be, but I'm the Prince of Schadenfreude, Max. Anyway, let's try to cheer up a little. How is Clement?"

"He's really stepping into my administrative shoes while I seem to be drifting into matters spiritual. I am a reasonable administrator and strategist because of my banking background, but you must have found out that he is in a different league altogether. I have never met anyone so careful not to convince himself of the rightness of what suits him operationally or temperamentally. Most administrators are fundamentally selfish, putting their own convenience and power above the corporate mission, but not Clement."

"I know. He put my Church of England mission above his Perpetuan mission when he worked for me."

"But he is profoundly unhappy because of the 'disappearing' evidence of Perpetua's life. I keep telling him that the evidence of her life should be in our lives, but he would like something written down."

"Another case of God being awkward. We never shall tame 'him.'"

Max smiled, and then frowned as he remembered something. "He told me to tell you—it sounds rather curious, but these were his words—that in spite of where he is he is suffering a kind of bleakness from his childhood Roman Catholicism which he thinks you will understand. He says you are in different places, but began in much the same place. He says that he is where he is because he longs to be cured, but he thinks you do not."

"He's right," said Hall, opening his Bible as a sign to Max who immediately took it.

When he was alone he closed it again. If Clement could climb to the sunny heights, why could he not, even within the Church of England where his duty lay? It was time that somebody in the Anglican Communion took love seriously.

◆　◆　◆

Bishop Crowther was suffering from an unprecedented succession of broken nights of wracking penitence. As with previous, single, instances, this had nothing to do with a "presenting case" such as Marianne Gowers, it was the invasion of his very self by the notion that he did not possess of himself a very self. His pride laid low, he was engulfed by his own penitence and it became so bad that he cast about for help and, after dismissing his two assistant Bishops, he fell upon the unlikely figure of the insomniac Dean whom he met as he was stumbling groggily back to the Palace after a bad night which he had spent roaming the chilly cloisters.

"I would have given you a key had I known," said the Dean. "There is a tiny door near the chapel for private prayer which you can always use. I am sorry you didn't know."

"Don't worry, Dean. I've hardly taken the trouble, have I?"

"You sound as if you are being hard on yourself and in danger of enjoying your self-abasement. Excuse my directness, please, but I would guard against it if I were you. It's a form of pride which is ironic as the abasement starts as a an attempt to check pride."

They went into the Palace and the Dean, familiar with the kitchen's appointments and arrangements, made coffee.

"Without wallowing, against which you have rightly warned me, I do feel as if I have not been a very great success as a bishop."

"Only supposing you knew how you would know if you were successful."

"Very clever, but that does not get me off the hook. What I mean by it is that I haven't made a difference."

"Forgive me, Bishop, Reggie, you and I might disagree on some points, but on this we are surely united; it's impossible for human beings to know when they have been a success and when they have not. To do so is to forget that everything is pure gift and only God knows."

"Yes, Yes! I've heard the classic Perpetuan arguments, but what I need to know—have to ask—as a Christian is how I know when I have chosen to do the right thing."

"You never do, as there is nothing so simple. That is, if you like, the burden of Christianity. The more static a system, the less agonising. Our way of looking at belief and life is that they are dynamic. You can't know that if you take a course of action twice in identical circumstances that both, in the sense we use the term, will be equally right. On one occasion you might be taking a way out that is too easy. On another it might be the most you can manage. Good people are too hard on themselves but the essence of not being a good person is not being hard enough. Most of us aren't very big sinners in a tabloid way, but most of us fall into a kind of diluted hubris where we assume, without thinking about it, that what we do is of ourselves, and we forget the idea of gift."

"Yes, that's what I'm suffering from."

"I am sad to hear, it but don't lose sleep over it, Reggie, and certainly don't drag yourself round the cloisters in the middle of the night. Just pray more."

"I don't think I'm very good at that,either. Not much of a bishop, eh?"

"Nobody's much of a bishop. Part of being a bishop—or a dean—is knowing that you're not much. It's being—or thinking that you are being—much that gets in the way. Christianity would do better to stick to humility as its chief virtue. Anyway, that's not really at the root of it, is it?"

"I'm not all that good at self-diagnosis Dean—Simon—as you have probably heard, they used to refer to my type of Christianity as 'muscular', you know, getting out there with a cross and a megaphone and not much introspection. There is a strong vein of belief amongst Torans that all they have to do is put in the effort and they will get new adherents for Christ. They seem to forget that only the Spirit gets new adherents for Christ which makes the Christian obsession with numerical success problematic. Why, on the other hand, is the spirit satisfied with so few? If news of Christ is so wonderful, why is it not more widely disseminated by the Spirit?"

"I don't know," said the Dean. "I keep having conversations where people think they know what God wants. I won't go there now. I just need to say, because I think it really might help you, that God self-communicates with everyone and our task is to get on the wavelength. Get personal with God and you will soon be better equipped to be the humble bishop I know you really are."

"That's good of you. It makes religion sound rather mundane."

"It is. It ought to be more so. The glory is God's not the Church's."

"And what do you do now that you have turned James down?"

"I live in your benevolent protection."

"I've tried to harm you up until now, but I will stop."

"God bless you, Reggie, and don't worry. In the end we all sail our tiny ships in the comfort of the proximity of other ships, and we share our Sacramental life when we come into port. That is better than the image of the Church as an oil tanker which stresses and therefore puts so much stress on people like you. Perpetuanism has brought us all to understand that it's time for a re-think. Unless Christians think that Perpetuanism is wicked or fraudulent, then it has a responsibility to consider what Perpetua said and what it might mean. The trouble is, the Church has tended to see Perpetuanism as competition rather than another resource. That's why it's infinitely more comfortable talking to other faiths rather than other kinds of Christian. I respect your zeal for doing the right thing—you put up quite a show at London Minster—but it looked more like politics than religion to me, Reggie."

"You have a way of saying hard things nicely, Simon. This is a rather conservative diocese, but I will do my best. We all keep on making the same mistakes—committing the same sins—which is why we need the sacrament of Reconciliation, but in trying to come to terms with my own weakness, I will try to be less combative."

The Dean walked across the Close as the first regulars made their way into the cathedral for Matins. He started to follow them, but then changed his mind and went home for an early breakfast. He took Reggie's change of heart to be pivotal. Alchester had been notoriously conservative. The challenge now was to ensure that Perpetuans kept the faith and resisted triumphalism.

◆　◆　◆

Cara was feeling restless. She was a member of the Perpetuan core group, but it had not made any real difference to her life. True, she had been cured by

Perpetua and she was grateful, but nobody else seemed very impressed by that. She was running house groups in South London just like she had before Perpetua when they were self-help and secular. Then there was the episode of Fidel who had over-reached himself. If anything, the Perpetuans had been so kind that it hurt more than a little resentment would have done. Fidel was working alongside her now, slowly gaining strength after his lapse, but they were still under some sort of cloud. Trina and Max were scrupulous in seeing that she was present at key meetings and always made room for her to speak, but she had nothing to say. She wasn't very clever and they all knew it—nobody pretended she was—but it was still awkward. She felt inferior.

It had been exciting at the beginning, but now the work had fallen into routine. She understood what Perpetua had meant by being open to the other, but she was getting worn out by it. "Try to say a bit more about it, Josie," she said, fighting for patience. "Why do you have such a problem with immigrants? We don't want to argue with you, we just want to understand."

"Well, he was so rude to me."

"But that doesn't mean that all black people are rude. Many white people whose families have lived here for hundreds of years are rude. What is important is that the Perpetuan response is not to answer back or even take offence. The right response is to be patient."

"But that would make them think that the way they behave was all right," said Josie. "If you ignore rudeness, they just go on being rude."

Cara sighed. "But the whole point of Perpetuanism is that you don't lecture people."

"Well, the whole place will descend into chaos. Somebody's got to keep order."

"Yes, Josie, that's what the police do, but it doesn't mean that we should judge people."

The group was becoming restless. Cara felt herself losing control. She knew that "control" was the wrong method, that she should be open, but she was part of the core leadership and she felt that she had a right to respect. She knew she didn't have a "right", but she couldn't help it. Well, if she couldn't be respected, why should anybody else? "You're right, Josie," she said. "I'm sure Perpetua didn't draw such a clear line but, in any case, Perpetua was only human." Nobody interrupted. "She might have been a good teacher, but she could make mistakes."

"So what are we here for, then?" asked Josie.

"Well, it's very good to remember a brilliant teacher," said Cara. She was too far in to turn back. "Through the ages people have formed circles to study the teaching of all sorts of influential people, and it helps us to think about big issues if they are centred round a real person."

"But what about God?" asked Bruno.

"Well, she never really said it. It was other people trying to make themselves important, saying they were in contact with God. I mean, she did say that she was God's child, but we all are. She called herself the Sacred Vessel, or the Sustainer but, as we were all created by God, we're all sacred vessels, aren't we?"

There was a mutter of assent, but no enthusiasm. People began to shift in their seats. Bruno got up. Josie followed. Within five minutes the room was empty. No tea. No fellowship. No affectionate farewells. Nothing. Cara viewed the ruin of all their hopes. And hers. She thought about calling them back, about texting them. She thought about asking for advice from Trina. She thought. But she did not have the courage to do anything. She went home, miserable.

Meanwhile, Josie had contacted people from other groups in South London. She had a story to tell. For the first time in her life she was important. What she said caused initial surprise and then deep disappointment. Trina reflected later, when the full extent of the damage was exposed, how easily people had given up their hopes.

Within days the rot was setting in all over the country. After the initial shock, Trina and Max thought that the hope which Perpetua offered would be welcome to people who were living at the bottom of the pile at the beginning of what was predicted to be a terrible economic crisis, but the loss of hope seemed to chime in with the economic times. People seemed to want to sink into a state of despondency, almost to enjoy it.

As reports came in of disintegrating and disbanding house groups, the core group felt helpless. Trina called a mini summit. The key issue was what, if anything, to do about Cara. From the beginning she was a mixture of aggression and regret. "I am entitled to say what I said," she began when she was asked to speak first, not as an accused, but simply as one of the group who had something special to say. "I am sorry that what I have said has made people upset, and I'm sorry if it's made some people depressed, but you have to tell the truth as you see it."

"Yes, you do," said Trina. "We are not arguing that you should not be able to say whatever you like, but as you are a member of the core group, it is important that we are clear from the standpoint from which you are speaking. We are all responsible for each other, but surely you can see that you cannot deny Perpetua's divinity and remain a member of the core group. We are very relaxed about what might be called orthodoxy, but there is a limit. We only have three core beliefs after all—the divinity of Perpetua, reformed, inclusive Sacramentality and the nature of love—and so it isn't much to ask. If you feel that you cannot agree with these three values we hope you will feel that you would be more comfortable not being a member of the core group. We will not force you out. We made a decision to trust you and one of the consequences of Perpetua's view of the nature of love is that we must continue to offer you our non-conditional love regardless of what you do, even if, as it appears, what you have done has caused considerable damage to our cause or, rather, God's cause."

"You can't make me resign," said Cara, defiantly.

"We have just said that," said Max, gently. "We can't make you resign, but if you have to live as a member of the core group and to live in denial of Perpetua's divinity, it will damage you, regardless, quite separate from, what it does to the credibility of Perpetuanism."

"Are you pushing me out, then?"

"No, Cara," said Kylie, "we are just asking you to think of how you will live with yourself if you carry these two contradictory positions."

There was silence. Then Father Bill said, "this is beginning to feel political in the way we are handling ourselves. Let us pray."

They prayed. During the period of more than five minutes Trina felt empty. She could not help trying to work out how to resolve the situation. She felt nothing spiritual at all. Bill was so right. She was thinking politically.

When people began to emerge from prayer, Bill asked Trina to continue. She was about to begin when she recognised that she was unfit to continue in her current "political" state of mind. She looked at Max, but he looked at Clement.

"Let us," said Clement, "be clear what we are trying to resolve. We are not trying to reach a compromise with Cara. We can't split the difference between Perpetua's divinity and her being only human. We believe that she is neither an angel nor a saint. We think that she was a child of God in a fundamentally different way from that in which we are all children of God. This is not a narrow, doctrinal dispute. There is no doubt that Perpetua simply as the teacher Cara describes would have done much good in the world, but her life would have said nothing about the nature of God's love for us, expressed in human form, which gives us hope. So, in summary, there is no compromise on this point.

There was assent, except for Cara who kept completely still.

"Then," said Clement, "there is the position of Cara as a member of the core group. Th question is whether we can withdraw her position, rescind it in some way, having laid hands upon her; or, indeed, whether she can rescind it of her own accord. The clear answer to this is negative. We cannot rescind our laying on of hands and nor can she, not for some complex ecclesiological doctrinal reason, but because we transmitted the power of Our Sister the Spirit and we cannot, so to speak, de-transmit it. Cara, having had hands laid upon her, is particularly the 'property' of the Spirit. The Spirit will take care of her and will need to do so because of the third consideration which we have already discussed, Cara's inner conflict. Our primary responsibility to Cara is to pray for her that she will be moved by the Spirit to resolve her inner conflict. She will always be a member of the core group, but she may feel that she wishes to go on a retreat or take some time off. We can and should ask her to say nothing for the time being. She knows as well as any of us how people need hope and that what she has said has weakened hope."

Cara nodded, grudgingly. She had thought that her initial pronouncements would bring her prominence in a breakaway organisation, but she had been left with nothing. She was ashamed, but could not show it. She had immense faith in the Spirit and recognised that she had lapsed in her prayer life in the weeks before her break. She had become bored with the earthly because she had abandoned the divine. She was not really grudging at all, but she did not have the resource of grace to admit openly that she was submitting herself to the Spirit.

"Finally, then," said Clement, "we must reinforce our message of hope without at any point making any direct criticism of Cara. In political terms—I know, Bill—she has broken collective responsibility, but we have to live with that. Just as we will live with Cara's doubt, she must live with our hope."

"There is no contradiction," said Stacey. "We live in hope, but doubt is part of hope."

Brian said that he would prepare campaigning material but, again, Bill intervened to warn against becoming political.

Philip, who had been used to seeing human fallibility in its most lurid terms, managed to say nothing. John almost cited Monica as an example, but thought this would not be helpful. The teleconference members simply affirmed their agreement. Trina managed to close the meeting with a prayer, but to her it was simply a form of words. She felt empty.

◆　　◆　　◆

"Geoff Brooks." said the voice.

"Who" asked Max.

"You mean you don't know who I am?"

"Sorry, Geoff, I don't."

"I'm Geoff Brooks."

"Yes, Geoff, you have said that three times now. I think we've pretty well established that you're Geoff Brooks. Shall we proceed to the next point?"

"Well, I'm Geoff Brooks." Max remained silent. "From the Number 10 Policy Unit."

"Oh yes!" said Max, sounding pleased. "I remember hearing about you from Sir Granville."

Geoff gulped. The series of incidents at the 2007 Party Conference, commonly referred to as "an extraordinary series of minor gaffes", was the lowest point of his roller-coaster career so far. He had only survived because in the turmoil after the Prime Minister had pulled back from calling a General Election he would surely have won he was wise enough to engineer a fortnight's sick leave which his doctor granted on the flimsy basis that Geoff was actually sick 365 days of the year so giving him a two weeks allowance was hardly excessive.

"Sorry, Geoff. I shouldn't have teased a telephone guest so ..."

"... It's all right," said Geoff, wanting to change the subject and get on with it. "The thing is, I'm calling on behalf of the Prime Minister, Gordon."

"Yes, I know his name's Gordon!"

"Well, to say that he is gob-smacked—no, I know, he didn't use that phrase—extremely surprised by the poll evidence of a steep decline in the country's morale."

"Yes," said Max, determined to be serious. "We are disturbed too. If hope is your brand, poor morale cuts both ways. It's your primary market, but also the evidence of your failure."

"It's an electoral liability," said Geoff, veering off his brief. "Oh, I shouldn't have said that."

"Said what?" asked Max, kindly.

Geoff cottoned on. "Er thanks. Well, the Prime Minister would be grateful for any efforts you could make to boost national morale."

"Politicians are like everybody else, more or less. They only seem to turn to religion in times of trouble. Most of the time New Labour, for all its moral strictures, regards religion as dangerously toxic. We would contest the idea that it's dangerous—most research shows that it's good for people—but w have long experience of knowing that it's not toxic. Most people seem not to be affected by it, no matter how hard we try."

Geoff, who was not equal to this level of argument, thrashed around to find a connecting point which would get him back onto his brief.

"Strange really," said Max, almost dreamily, "that politicians and religious people share the occupation of spreading hope, but whereas politicians are invariably found out, every great new dawn fading into fog and despondency, or even tragedy, we are never found out. We are a more difficult target. anyway, Geoff," he said, perking up, "we will do anything we can for the good of the country as long as we are not seen to be 'political'."

Geoff was about to give voice to his central theme that everything was political—everything—but wisely decided to say nothing. "Thank you, and I'll tell Gordon what you said about politicians being two faced—oops—confused in their views on religion."

"Please don't," said Max. "It isn't that long since you were in a spot of bother. Just report our message that we will do our best."

Geoff gulped. "Can I ask you one question?"

"Yes, as many as you would like."

"Does Sir Granville really hate me?"

"Of course not. He was amused by the tactics of the Number 10 staff, not you in particular, you just happened to be the 'presenting' person, and he told me the story with a smile on his face. He would have been very sorry if he had thought that he had anything to do with your discomfort."

"But I spilled the beans," said Geoff, a shade contrite.

"Sir Granville says that there was a remarkable series of germinations between your spilling of a few beans and the tabloid harvest. Sir Granville doesn't hate anybody. He has that priceless ability to turn anything into gentle humour."

"You lot seem rather decent, really," said Geoff, like a tiny devil peeping through the fence of paradise, wishing he could somehow switch sides.

"We do our best," said Max, his need to be generous beginning to be impaired by his need to get on.

Geoff spared him. "Thank you. I have many other calls to make in this smile-up initiative."

Max would normally have been glad to listen to Geoff for as long as Geoff wanted to talk, but he urgently needed to talk to Trina. He had been trying to talk to her since the meeting with Cara, but she had somehow not been around. He could not definitely accuse her of avoiding him, but this was the first time since they had started working together, other than retreats, when they had not talked for a whole week.

"Trina," said Max, finally finding her alone in his office. "We need to talk. Or, rather, I think you might need to talk which is why you haven't been."

"I haven't wanted to say it out loud, Max. I've been saying it to myself and trying to work out how I might say it out loud, but I have kept shying away. I'm empty. I can't feel anything spiritually. I think, finally, Miles' death has caught up with me, Miles who died for Perpetua. Now I can't feel warm about Perpetua. It might be temporary or it might be permanent. I don't know. I think I need the Cara dispensation of being allowed to say nothing for a while. The rest of you will need to carry on the work if you think it's worth carrying on."

"You mean you don't think it is," said Max, before he could check himself.

"I don't know," said Trina, on the verge of tears. "I just don't know."

Max calmed himself. "But in this crisis we need you."

"That is what makes it worse than it might otherwise be. My head completely understands. I can still put all the arguments, say all the words, but they are empty. I would be grateful if you could call a meeting so that we can lay hands on Marta. I want to keep a proper balance. Then you can tell the others that I am going on an extended retreat."

"I think we need to make a statement about hope."

"I agree, but it would not come right if I were to write it. I trust you to say the right things, but I suppose you will want Clement to write it."

"After you, that would be the next best thing."

Next day, Trina, Max, Brian, and Clement laid hands on Marta who was attended by Perpetua acting in the capacity of an episcopal bridesmaid. Afterwards, when Trina had left quietly, Max said, "Trina is suffering from what looks like a delayed reaction to Miles' death. She is suffering doubts about her faith and has gone on an extended retreat."

"Doubts are a part of faith," they said, almost in unison.

◆   ◆   ◆

It was the early Spring of the year 2009, more than one year away from a General Election as late as it could be and therefore a year away from the end of the phoney war and the beginning of the unfolding of the truth about the desperate state of the nation's finances. When politicians deliberately hide the truth their main accomplices are the people, who long ago made a solemn pact with politicians that they would prefer to have politicians who would not tell them the truth, in exchange for the right to grumble about them rather than having politicians who did tell the truth. If politicians broke the pact by telling the truth they would be punished with electoral annihilation.

In mid-March, when the markets hit rock bottom, the gloom was deep, but it was the terrifying gloom of uncertainty rather than the shock of knowledge which had soon passed. Had the people not made such a solemn pact with politicians they would have been spared more than another year of fear, but the pact was unbreakable. Any party that dared to tell the truth about the fiscal crisis and the need for higher taxes and lower public expenditure would be wiped out. So the people looked forward to another year of fear and, as if to ward it off, they lived as normal a life as could be expected except that, against the wishes of the Government, they cut their spending moderately and increased their savings. The rich, as usual, felt nothing. The middle classes, for the time being at least, felt nothing, although they were always alert to the advantages of victimhood and could rely on their media champions to dissect and exaggerate their plight. The poor felt the scourge of rising unemployment, and feared the worst, but they always did. That was their lot. Sympathy was wasted on them.

Kylie, who had grown to love the gentle ways of the south coast counties, did not find it hard to locate large and increasing patches of poverty amongst the wealth. In many small, pretty market towns horribly cut in half by roads, all seemed well, apart from a growth in the number of charity shops as retail migrated to out-of-town supermarkets, but on the edge of many of these towns were public housing settlements—estates was a silly word—where there was terrible poverty which often led to degradation. It was to such places that Perpetua had most wanted to bring hope and the first places to abandon it.

"I need to understand the problem," Kylie said to a group of mothers, freed from the incessant care of their young children by the provision of a creche supervised by some of the local Guides, including Mark Price. "I need to know why you gave up so soon."

"It's like this," said Kat, the unofficial leader. "When you are poor you become a guinea pig. They try all sorts of experiments on you about how little you can live on, where the balance is between collecting benefits and being forced to take a lousy, badly paid job, and what they can 'give' you without giving you money. This place is full of projects and initiatives, but we're still as poor as ever. We know that when the Government's cuts come, as they will, we will suffer the most, even though we had nothing to do with the banking collapse and even though we gained nothing in the boom from windfall profits on houses, de-mutualising banks, stock market speculation and all that. They'll put up VAT which hurts us proportionately more than rich people. They'll cut benefits in real terms while the number of jobs open to us is falling. They'll narrow benefits criteria, and although they might only be of limited use, they'll pull all the initiatives. They'll turn a blind eye to all but the fattest bonuses. They'll make a load of noise about immigration without stopping it, which means a further fall in the price of labour. They'll just play a game of musical chairs with the people who caused the crisis. We're used to this. Mostly it's not our fault that we were born in lousy places like this and haven't got the education or determination, or whatever it is, to fight our way out. And how should we? They don't want us, they don't like us, and they don't trust us. We don't belong. We're treated like blacks.

"Just occasionally, we let our guard drop, and we dare to hope. We dared to hope when Blair took over from Thatcher, but it came to nothing much. Yes, we did gain a bit, but the gap still widened between us and everybody else. Yes, for a while the number of people defined as in a state of poverty fell, as if that was the most we could expect. I suppose we were supposed to be grateful.

"And then Perpetua came and we hoped again. She said we could take control of our lives and the most important thing was that all sorts of people began to talk to us properly in house groups and, yes, they helped us loads, but we helped them, too, which was even better. Then one of her top people—Cara, wasn't it?—says she wasn't what she said she was, and here we are, waiting to be beaten up by the next government, whatever sort it is, and we've lost Perpetua."

"We disagree with Cara when she said that Perpetua was not God."

"So you think she shouldn't have said it?"

"That's not quite the same thing, Kat, although I don't want to split hairs. If you trust people—and you want to be trusted—then they sometimes say things you wish they hadn't said, but you don't go round telling them off. You just learn to put up with it."

"So you don't agree with her? You think Perpetua was the real thing?"

"Yes. I realise that this has been a terrible blow for you, and I also understand that when you're down all the different difficulties in your life merge into one big problem that you can't sort out and it leads to a smothering kind of depression. I would ask you to remember what Perpetua said and to try to separate the big problem into bite-seized pieces, or strands, and to solve the bits you can solve, and then see what's left."

"I really want to. I really loved her. It's just so hard picking up again. It isn't just difficult to help ourselves, you know. When we do a tiny thing that's good, like putting on a bit of a play with the kids, nobody notices. It's not that we want a lot of thanks—we won't get it—but it would be nice to be noticed. She noticed. Even that strange bloke Miles noticed when he came here on what he called a 'mini mission'. One of the reasons we worked so hard with Perpetua was that she noticed everything. Will you?"

"No. I won't notice everything. I'm not perfect. I'm not God like Perpetua is. I'm just me and I'll try to notice, but I'll miss things. So you're left with me, and the Spirit. I really believe that's enough, in spite of my weaknesses."

"We'll try. We really did want her to be God. We really believed it. It's so easy to lose heart, it really is."

"Yes. It's much more difficult to build than knock down, particularly when most of your experience is of people knocking you down rather than building you up. How can we expect you to be constructive when people who are more powerful and better trained than you fail to be constructive about you and teach you the skills to be constructive?"

The sympathy helped. The mothers seemed determined to try. Kelvin came in and said, "they cut the tropical bird project I was on. I finished."

The women moved to comfort him, but that only made him cry, and then they all began to cry over one more wasted life and one more wage not coming in. Kylie cried a little, too, but then sat quietly until they had finished, not wishing to intrude. It was not professional detachment, but the feeling that, as a guest, she should absent herself as much as she could without going away.

Mark Price came into the house and this gave Kylie the chance to slip out of the room with him, though not away. "It's Kelvin," she said. "You remember, the one Perpetua helped to find a new life by studying tropical birds. He was promised a modest job in a project but it's been cut."

"There comes a time," said Mark, wearily, "when the accumulation of thousands of small pieces of help reach a critical point and the capacity to help collapses. But that point has not yet come. It's so much easier and cheaper to keep people alive with wages. Helping on a one-off basis takes so much time and doesn't produce enough money. As I say, we're not at the tipping point yet, though it won't be long. We can persuade Mothers Union secretaries to invite Kelvin to talk to them, bringing all his lovely drawings. Strictly speaking, they only make donations to charities who send speakers, but I've got a discretionary fund and I'm sure many of my Perpetuan and Church of England colleagues will be able to do their bit. You never know. It might lead to something. It's not much. How do we do this? You know how bad I am at saying the right thing."

"Thanks, Mark. We might see if Max can set up a discretionary fund and find somebody to run it."

Kylie went back into the house and found the women solacing themselves with tea. "I've found some little things for you to do, Kelvin. Talking about your birds and showing your pictures. It won't make you a millionaire, but it will be a start. I didn't know till now that you had drawn all the pictures. I think you will find that there are many ladies who will be happy to buy them, so concentrate on that. Sell one picture and buy some materials, and so on."

All over the land, similar sad, little scenes of shattered hope and patchwork care were taking place. Savings that had been fought for, against the odds, against the sharp pangs of desire, the gnawing of want, peer pressure to acquire frivolous items, and the pressure of family and friends for what were always depicted as life or death scenarios, were swallowed up in a minute by the catastrophe of unemployment. Projects that had been described as indispensable were slashed to the bone, and then the bones were broken. Training budgets that had been ear marked for manual workers against the stiff competition of universities were withdrawn. Charities that were stretched to the limit in the good times were stretching even further while their revenues sagged. Generous souls who had made solid contributions to charities and were always ready with extra bits and pieces found that there were no more bits and pieces and the solid contributions had to be trimmed. Only the rich stayed rich. Everyone else became poorer, many resisting to the last the temptation to compete for resources, preserving solidarity at high personal cost. It was a matter more of doggedness than high principle, more out of habit than hope of reciprocity.

In the midst of this grinding struggle the corrosive news of Perpetua's fall was just one more straw. Not a final straw because for the poor the idea of a final straw is illusory. With each blow there is a sense of the final straw, but they stagger on until the next blow falls, and the next, until they sink into one kind of oblivion or another. Nothing so esoteric as the disappointment of spiritual hope could ever be thought to be a final straw; it was just one more thing, for there always was just one more thing. The damage was not so much in what had been lost—for it was little enough in the scheme of things—but the pain of a door slammed, a face slapped, a back turned. All the time, the men in suits went into the city they had almost ruined, oblivious of the details of the damage to millions of individuals, and did what they had always done for ever bigger salaries and bonuses and not a scintilla of solidarity, their nearest contact with the poor being the waiters in their starred restaurants.

Perpetua's followers needed to re-group, not just for the sake of their movement, but for the people they existed to serve.

◆   ◆   ◆

Clement, a follower of Perpetua, to all Perpetuan Guides.

Sisters and brothers before God, through Jesus Christ our Redeemer and Perpetua, our Sustainer and God's Sacred Vessel, in the power of Our Sister the Spirit, grace, reticence and calm be yours in the full knowledge that we all shall be saved and be enfolded back into God's infinite love under the promises of Jesus and his sister Perpetua who gave up their divine incommensurability so that they might be with us as guarantors of the promise.

We who are gathered here in London where Perpetua lived and prayed, endeavour to live the life which she enshrined and we pray for all of you daily so that we all might be strengthened in the Spirit. We thank God through Jesus and Perpetua for all the work you do and, even more so, for each word you do not say and each action you do not take in the exercise of moral, physical, psychological, or spiritual power, so that you might be ever more free from temptation to dominate, leaving yourselves open in love to those around you, beset by doubt and trouble.

I am writing to you on behalf of us all—although any infelicity in what I say and how I say it should be attributed solely to me—so that you may be strengthened in these times of trouble. It cannot be denied, sisters and brothers, that we have been set back by the extensive coverage of the view that Perpetua was not a manifestation of the Godhead in human form but was simply a remarkable human being. We are sorry that this belief has been received with so little searching. It has taken such courage for many of you and those with whom you work to face up to the presence of the divine in human form, first in Jesus and now in Perpetua, that we are sorry if such courage has been so quickly dissipated. We hoped for greater caution and greater effort.

Not that we would wish to be misunderstood. We absolutely accept that doubt is an intrinsic part of our human condition; that it is part of our necessary imperfection. Some of us have the fortune—whether it is good or not is another matter—to fall in love early in life and never to waver from our love of the beloved, but most of us only find love through pain and retain it through struggle. Such is the way of humanity in its love of God. Just as we often wonder whether we are doing the correct thing, or whether in doing the correct thing we have disrupted some aspect of our lives, so we should properly wonder whether our faith in God is a true part of our selves or whether it might have been a posture, a measure for achieving therapeutic inner calm or simply a habit of life. There is nothing virtuous in having to struggle—it is part of our condition—but those who escape such trouble might, conversely, be subject to the danger of comfort, of self-satisfaction, of being spiritually becalmed. It is therefore important that we should all be scrupulous in our self-examination to ensure that our relationship with the godhead, through Jesus and Perpetua, and in the power of Our Sister the Spirit, is a right relationship and that we do not evade the problems and seek to paper over the spiritual cracks. We are, in other words, bound by our promises to ourselves to question our approach to God to ensure that it is honest in the full knowledge and understanding that we are in the Spirit. So, although we are sad that the faith of many in Perpetua has been shaken, we accept this as a part of our creaturely condition.

Now, having said all that, we are particularly aware that many people are beset by earthly problems and that they are in need of spiritual strength. It is therefore unfortunate, from a human perspective, that the secular and spiritual crises should have occurred simultaneously in what experts foolishly call "a perfect storm", but this is no "perfect storm" as long as we remain confident and trust in the Spirit, on whose behalf we all act, to achieve God's ends whose detail we cannot know.

It is therefore absolutely essential that we devote as much time as possible simply to being with people so that we can absorb their troubles, their doubts, their sorrows, their uncertainties, their setbacks, their fear, and their doubt. We are not there to preach a doctrinal Gospel of Perpetuanism but to live humbly like her, always open to the other. In that way, and that way alone, lies hope.

It is often said that doubt is the opposite of hope, but they are even more closely allied than two sides of a coin. Hope is our down payment from God in the Resurrection of Jesus and the re-manifestation of Perpetua and doubt is the collection of small change we carry when we encash that down payment. We must all accept doubt instead of denying it, for if we do not doubt, we have not encashed God's down-payment to us, but have left it, like the buried talent, denying the life of choice and risk which creatureliness entails.

Accordingly, although we would not wish in any way to issue instructions to you all, living as you do in different circumstances with different kinds of house groups, we would encourage you to introduce the three topics of doubt, hope and prayer into your discussions so that our friends will be better able to deal with the current and, apparently worsening, crisis.

The peril of doctrinal discussion, such as that which concerns the divine nature of Perpetua, is that it, paradoxically, anthropomorphises the terms of the discussion as we become heroically tangled in the effort to wrest language from its moorings to give wind to the sails of God. Such dangers must be encountered, but only if we all live in the Spirit and pray that we all may be strengthened by the doubt that which is part of hope, just as fruit is part of a fruit cake, rather than being weakened by doubt, thinking of it as a fungus that attacks a fruit cake.

In this time of doubt, never forget the centrality of our personal relationship with the Godhead. Prayer is our only true defence, in a crisis, against despair. Prayer is never easy, but we must all persevere so that we may occasionally experience that glimpse of the divine, that inner illumination which gives us the strength to go on. Only God our Parent knows every child, and every child must try to be thankful for creatureliness and seek to do God's will, discerned in personal prayer and collective sacrament.

Above all, never cease to love one another in meekness and patience, building up one another in prayer and solidarity.

Our prayer and trust go out to all of you as we wait for you to come to us, so that we may, in turn, receive the pain that has been passed on to you. We are all working hard for the same end but we particularly appreciate your work at the "sharp end", your "heavy lifting", and your unstinting patience.

We remember you all in our prayers and pray that you remember us who are here to serve.

◆   ◆   ◆

Although the precise meaning of Clement's letter eluded Geoff Brooks, he was sure that he had not so much gained a feather for his cap but at least had earned the right to wear it again. At this point in the political cycle, the Government was divided into three factions of equal size. Firstly, there were those who were jockeying for position after losing the General Election and framed their words and actions in that light. Next came those who had given up hope of winning and were just serving out time, cashing whatever chips they had to be cashed in with those for whom they had done favour. Last were those who went on governing doggedly because it was their duty or because they wanted to enjoy it as long as they could. Geoff was not sure which of these groups he should concentrate on. He was thinking over his options in the Committee Corridor of the House of Commons when Sir Granville spotted him. "Ah, Mr Brooker."

"Brooks."

"Mr Brooke."

"Brookes."

"Sorry, it was Dickens and then George Eliot that set me off. Brooks, yes; the Party Conference. What are you looking so nervous about?"

"Well, it's like this."

"Nothing ever is, Geoffrey, is it?"

"Yes. No. Well. It's like this. I've been on a charm offensive—as they call it ..."

"... Nobody better, Geoff ..."

"... to persuade your friends the Perpetuans to boost national morale."

"Very good. We're an optimistic lot except for Philip, up North, who can't help taking something of a gloomy view of human nature."

"Anyway, I've been doing this charm thing and, as you probably know, Clement's written this letter. It's a trifle impenetrable, even if you've studied sociology at Brickton Uni, but we get the message. Anyway, who should I carry it to, this message of hope: the fencers or the lifters? They are the only two options."

"Yes, Geoff, but they are politicians. You are a junior to the Prime Minister, attached to the Cabinet Office. If I were you I would get very firmly stuck to the Cabinet Office. Then you will still be around after the Election, and whatever they cut, they won't cut there, you know, it's too near the PM."

Sir Granville was about to go when a thought struck him. "By the way, Geoff, a word of advice, because you really did me a favour when you showed me I could no longer stay in the Government." To his credit, Geoff blushed. "Stay away from Griswald, Lord Warpley. He was against you over this initiative and his star's waning. His do-good image is wearing a little thin. You should have heard what he used to get up to with—I mean alongside—Bishop Crowther. Quite colourful. Nowadays they call it 'flamboyant'. Like criminals who can't resist returning to the scenes of their crimes, people like Crowther and Warpley, who lead rather racy lives can't resist moralising."

◆ ◆ ◆

Fortunately for Stacey and Father Bill, still in a period of extended honeymoon, Stacey's duties on the European mainland allowed her to come home frequently. They missed each other, but each had important duties within Perpetuanism which rendered their sacrifices more than tolerable.

Bill was still unofficial guardian to the core group, but he was now taken up with the construction of the shrine to Perpetua in Saint Simple's. This had been the cause of an intense discussion between the couple which they honestly represented to the group. Stacey's evangelical upbringing had made her hostile to religious art, decoration, ritual, and iconography which she had learned to dismiss under the general heading of Popery.

"Let's start at the beginning, then," said Bill, pouring a glass of red wine and lighting his pipe, ready for a long session. "What's wrong with Popery?"

"Well, we were taught that the Roman Catholic Church was idolatrous, that it worshipped Mary and other saints, and that the people even worshipped their own priests?"

"Were that true, it would be very idolatrous indeed, but can we take such an immense body of people to be so foolish? The root of much Roman Catholic piety and practice, the frame of reference, is based on the idea of intermediaries, intercessors, and the place you find this most prominently is in the Gospel of Saint John which I think many Protestants don't read often or carefully enough. Jesus—the Son—is, classically, and according to his own testimony, the intercessor or intermediary between us and God. Roman Catholics have added saints, particularly Our Lady, Mary the mother of Jesus. It's all a natural consequence of the doctrine of incarnation. Roman Catholics don't worship saints, they hold them up as examples of holy living who are now 'in heaven'. You might ask why Jesus isn't enough to which the answer is that, in a way, he's too much. Mary, being immaculate, is also a shade too much, but at least she bore a baby. Saints are much nearer to us. If you want a bridge—and incarnation is a bridge—it has to have two ends each of which reaches a bank. I often wonder whether Protestants have any notion at all about bridges and salvation."

"All right, Bill. I see your point. But aren't shrines superstitious?"

"I suspect that question has more to do with your being an American than a Protestant. You're not old enough as a country to have developed shrines like Lourdes, Compostella or, most notably, the places associated with the life of Jesus. The important point here is that incarnation necessarily creates links between person and place. We can't be sure of precise flag stones where Jesus placed his foot but the nearer we get, the more intensely we feel. That is why so many Christians—not only Roman Catholics—go on pilgrimage to the Holy Land. That is why what we do here is going to be so important. We have an incarnational location of immense power. We know that Perpetua walked here, that she said her last, sustained prayer here before she went to her death, and that her body was taken up from here into 'heaven'. The whole point about incarnation is that it frees us from our terrible struggle with abstract monotheism, and gives God flesh and, incidentally, collaterally, places of worship with a deep significance. Pilgrimage isn't just metaphorical. One of the problems for Christianity is that it has bought the enlightenment agenda and turned itself into a set of rules, or ideas, instead of sticking to the traditional, Roman Catholic idea that God is a mystery and our holy life is personal, that the truth of what we believe can never be separated from who we are because truth, as distinct from fact, is personal and not empirical."

Stacey had problems absorbing what Bill said, but she knew the narrowness of her own upbringing and the breadth of his wisdom, and she was happy to trust him. When Bill began to consider the nature of the shrine what Stacey had said had a great influence on his vision. He wanted a strong sense of place and thought that a simple approach would best generate this. The focal points in his church were the nave, chancel, and vestry. The first two locations were part of the body of his square Barry church, but the vestry was a closed-in box South of the chancel. Because it was a Barry church the heritage industry, indifferent as always to the central purpose of a religious building and only interested in architecture and art, put up strong opposition to the changes he proposed, particularly the inclusion of the vestry in the main body of the church through the removal of its walls and the re-location of the organ. Such were the delays engendered by the objectors that Bill consulted Max and his lawyer friend Adrian, who agreed that the sensible course of action was for Bill to proceed and risk being prosecuted. "Our primary purpose is God's mission," Max said, "and no secular authorities should get in our way. If we are punished, then that is God's will for us."

Adrian looked doubtful but did not demur.

Max had raised enough money for what was, essentially, a cleaning up operation. The walls were repaired, cleaned, and whitewashed, plaques were relocated to a small chapel, ugly church pews and other furnishings were replaced by modern, simple chairs. Except for the removal of its Northern and Western walls, the vestry was left intact, with the red choir robes placed precisely where the body of Perpetua had been laid.

The whole of the core group, including Thomas, Sarah and Simon, celebrated the Sacrament of Union and Father Bill preached a sermon about incarnation.

Bill and the group had hoped that the shrine would be a place of solace and encouragement for Perpetuans, but almost immediately it became a noisy, crowded place of pilgrimage where people wanted not only to be where Perpetua had been, they also wanted toilets, food and drink, and a souvenir shop. Although they had risked the wrath of the heritage lobby over the inside of the church they would not do so with respect to its lovely exterior, so Max acquired land across the street where a shortage of public money had led to the abandonment of a new house building project on the site of the demolished tower block. Plans were drawn up for the extra facilities for the shrine, together with low cost housing for the rest of the plot.

Everyone except Bill was astounded at the hundreds of thousands of visitors who came to Saint Simple's now that it was one of the top ten "must see" places in all the London guide books. Bill, who always had a very secure sense of the concrete and the emotional, had known from the start that his plans would bring great benefits to those in search of God he had not seen it as the turning point in the fortunes of Perpetuanism. Although her ideas commanded great loyalty among followers who struggled to live the life she advocated, what secured Perpetuanism as a permanent feature of life in England and beyond was its possession of a physical place where Perpetua was known to have been. There were many others which had similar claims and soon these were being turned into shrines. Although Perpetua's life had not been methodically documented, there were many people who remembered her presence in streets, squares, hospitals and factories. Within two years of her death, the Church of Perpetua could claim more than a thousand authentic locations. Max and the core group fought against the designation of Perpetuanism as a Church but they ultimately had to give in. They might have scruples but ordinary people were not attracted by the vague designation of a movement, and they knew what a church was. This was a minor, rather abstruse, setback compared with the massive boost in numbers and self-confidence; but there was one great sadness. Trina had been in retreat for two months and had ceased to communicate with Max and the rest of her colleagues. They wondered whether, struggling in doubt, she would ever return to them.

◆　◆　◆

Trina sat on the window seat of her room in the early afternoon, in the late spring sun, protected from the east wind, characteristic of the new climatic age. She turned over the pages of a fat booklet accompanying a box of Bach Cantatas, recalling the observation of Angela Tilby that in Bach humanity comes closest to the fusion of *Mythos* and *Logos*, and she felt that she understood for the first time those who said they were deeply moved by religious music even though they did not believe in God. Bach was all she had to hang onto.

For weeks she had hung on grimly, out of loyalty to the group, but after the Sacrament of Union for the dedication of the shrine of Perpetua at Saint Simple's, which she had concelebrated almost in tears, she knew that she must get away, not just for a few days of retreat, but for as long as it took. Now it felt as if it would take forever.

The decline of faith had been like the steady deterioration of a tapestry. First, the vibrancy and colour had gone. She could still see all the outlines of Perpetuanism's structure and form, but there was no life. It was as if the music had retreated back onto the page. She knew how it must sound, but it only played mechanically in her head. It was as if food had kept its texture, but lost its spice and its sweetness. She knew what each item was supposed to taste like but it possessed none of its peculiar savour. Most of all it was as if all the different strands of her life and thought had turned grey. Ever since she had met Perpetua she had tried to hold on to the idea that one believed and acted for the thing-in-itself without expecting any reward. Now she felt dragged down by the struggle to act and believe when it yielded no satisfaction. She was being forced to try to live as she had advised we should all live. She did not complain. One must be prepared to endure what one advocated. She wished she could feel pain or regret, any emotion to enliven her grey, mental topography. She did not rage, or even complain; she endured. She thought that words would give her solace, but she did not care for the people in the books she read nor, to her surprise, in the books that she re-read. She remembered being devastated for more than a week by the

death of Stephanie in *Still Life,* but it did nothing for her now. She read the death
of King Lear with an almost clinical attention. At least there was still Bach.

Then the formal structure began to disintegrate, the lines of belief and the
definitions of conduct began to blur. She did not know what she believed any
more or, rather, she knew in very general terms what she should believe, but the
subtlety of approach and articulation leached away. When she set herself the
exercise of writing a list of Perpetuan attributes they began to assemble themselves in no particular order. There was no longer a sequence, a narrative, a set
of preconditions necessary for what followed. She could say that she believed in
Perpetua, but it was simply a shell of a statement lacking content. At this point
her mind would not accept complex propositions of any kind.

Then the fabric itself began to disintegrate as stresses snapped threads, laxity
caused threads to lose their tension and loop out, and all kinds of rot and fungus
attacked what was left until she could not recognise herself. It was then that she
despaired of ever being able to put it back together again. She began to be confused about what part God would play and what part she must play. Was God
the canvas and was she the embroiderer, or was that wrong?

She still stuck doggedly to what was left, the single, though abstract, idea that
God would return. She did not know why she had been abandoned, why her
inner self had been so horribly debilitated, defaced, and then ruined, but God
would return. Her lifeline, the only thing that kept her sane, the only thing that
gave her the strength to believe that God would return, was this box of Bach
Cantatas. She clung on to the idea that the essence of existence was a fusion of
Mythos and *Logos* and she recited it like a mantra, frightened that if she stopped
for too long she would never get it back.

She turned the pages, torn between Cantatas 82 and 170 and chose 82. The
one human being she had managed to stay close to during the struggle was
Mary. Even when Jesus and Perpetua had gone, Mary was still there, puzzled at
Simeon, distraught at Calvary, quiet in the upper room awaiting Pentecost. She
understood why Christians throughout the ages, up until the enlightenment—
and beyond it in the case of Roman Catholics—had stuck to Mary for safety and
comfort.

She might be inarticulate and bereft, but she could see through all the tangle
and mess of *Logos* that salvation lay with *Mythos.* She could understand the
mathematics of Bach and her intellect loved the patterns, but he had the genius
to infuse mathematics with God through himself. *Ich habe genug.* No, that was
self-indulgent, melancholic. She was not there yet. She was still a Marian specta-
tor and not an alter ego.

She was not left entirely alone during her period of trial. The Guest Master
had gently advised her to submit herself to a Spiritual Director and she had been
given Brother Stephen who barely said a word. He listened to her and soothed
her as if she were an injured animal. She asked him questions about her condition, but his only response was that the Spirit would be with her; that God never
set anybody a test for which they were not given the appropriate material. When

she asked him to advise her, he simply said that a Spiritual Director was not really a director at all, but a friendly ear.

She changed the disc to Cantata 170. "Only you can strengthen my weak heart", she said. "Only you." The alto sang so sweetly, plangently. It was that voice which kept her heart alive. Somehow, when all the meaning had ebbed away, there was still an aesthetic that touched her heart. She played 169, 35, and 200, and then sat in silence, waiting for something to happen, as if she expected the Holy Spirit to arrive any moment. Nothing happened. She watched the light fading and was about to console herself with a cup of tea when there was a knock on her door.

It was Cara. "I didn't want to disturb you, but since you arrived you have become more and more pale. I have kept out of your way for fear of upsetting you, after what I did—I won't go into what's being happening to me since I came here, it's not the right time—but it looks as though nothing that anybody does can make you worse, and might actually make you better."

"There is no point being long winded about it. I have lost my faith."

"I'm no theologian nor cleric but my guess is that you haven't. It is much more likely that you are expecting too much of yourself and have become over scrupulous in an area which doesn't profit from too much detail. The sensible thing to do—and when you're down, doing the most sensible thing is the most difficult—is to tell yourself what you've told everybody else. I can almost hear you telling people that doubt is an integral part of belief. I know that, since what I did, Clement has written a lot about this and that the whole core group accepts what he says. I wonder—although, as I said, I'm no expert—whether over scrupulousness about one's articulated personal belief in God isn't a form of pride."

Trina flinched.

"I don't mean to hurt. I really don't. But—again, I don't want to talk about me now—I think I have found out while I have been here that I was too concerned with coherence and not concerned enough with simply living as a creature. My memory of Perpetua the woman was over-riding my perception of Perpetua, our Sustainer, and God's Sacred Vessel."

"But it isn't Perpetua, Cara, it's God, the whole thing. It hasn't been dramatic, I don't feel like slitting my throat, it's just gone."

"But something else has gone, Trina. I have never seen you with a pile of books lacking book marks ever before. What happened, did God leave first or the books?"

"They left together, in parallel."

"That's good, then. Had God gone first, leaving the books behind, I would have worried that you were in denial. If, on the other hand, the books had left first I would have worried that you were falling into depression with God as collateral damage, but as they have left in tandem I am encouraged to believe that you are simply over-loaded with patches and bug fixes and need a re-boot."

Trina could not help smiling. "How do I get that?"

"You try to forget everything you have ever placed a value on and judge things for themselves. It's assigning value that obscures clarity. I'm not a theologian, but I know this from my experience of being cured by Perpetua. For a long time the only thing concerning Perpetua that I could think about was my cure and how I valued it. For me the breakthrough came when I began to think about her for herself. It was only a couple of days ago, so the experience is still fresh. for two years I was nothing but a cure. That's what defined me. That's what I placed all my value upon. Then, earlier this year, I wanted to stop being dominated by the cure and go back to being myself—of course, that was silly—and that led to the necessity for changing the value I set on Perpetua. The only way I could rid myself of the burden of the idea of the cure was to persuade myself that it had not been a miracle, but some kind of coincidence."

"Strange," said Trina, "because she was always deeply wary of her own mighty acts."

"So I made myself believe that Perpetua had not cured me. She was no longer God and I was no longer a miracle. We were both women. I looked at her and I liked her. If she wanted, she could look at me, but only as an ordinary woman. Then I thought, 'there's no such thing as an ordinary woman'. I began to look at everything around me—its structure, its detail, its purpose. It was the sheer wonder of structure and aliveness that gripped me."

"Mythos and Logos."

"Whatever. The thing is, it's the combination of structure and feeling that makes us what we are. You have to start accounting for it. Then it didn't matter whether or not Perpetua was God. All I knew was that somebody had to be, and knowing that was more important than knowing who. I have sometimes wondered in the past few days whether Jesus is not just a little distracting when we are trying to get our heads round the Creator. I know all that you have said about the concreteness of incarnation, but we can become too familiar with the stories in the Gospels and perhaps I have become too familiar with the idea that I walked down the street with Perpetua. This has damaged my focus. Anyway, I thought I would drop in and see if I could cheer you up just a little, superficially. My change of heart about Perpetua isn't very important in the scheme of things."

"But, to you, you are the scheme of things. There is no scheme of things without you to see it. No, I don't mean that nothing exists unless you exist—the tree doesn't fall if nobody sees it nonsense—but there's something quite different between a structure in-itself and a scheme. Only sentient phenomena have schemes whereas all phenomena seem to have structures."

"You see, you are talking like a real person for the first time in weeks, quite your old self. I will quit while you're ahead and see you soon, when you ask. Signal to me in chapel."

They usually ate dinner in silence with a monk reading from a pleasant, mildly informative book. Tonight it was an account of the conception and architecture of Fatepur Sikri and its sad abandonment. "They didn't precisely forget about water," she thought. "I suppose they were counting on unlimited slave labour. It's amazing what we count on. Even clever people count on some very strange things happening." She felt something knit.

At Compline she stopped over "Oh Lord, support us all the day long" and did not re-connect with her surroundings until the other guests began to leave quietly.

Back in her room she reached for the Bach and then stopped herself. For the first time in weeks she thought she could manage with tea and silence. "All the day long," she thought, "not just when I need something or when I am puzzled, not just when I have thanks to offer or joy to experience, it's in the interstices of my self-that the Holy Spirit operates. All the day long. That is surely the wonder of it. Perhaps it's another case of anthropomorphising God, like Cara said, but in this case maybe there's too much Creator and Redeemer and not enough Sanctifier in my system. System? I can see what Cara meant when she said that the incarnate can obtrude and become, if you like, normal, leaving the wonder of God out of it, but the wonder of God can ensure that we are aware of all the dimensions. There wouldn't have been incarnations if they were bad for us. To-morrow, I will begin to reconstruct."

◆　　◆　　◆

Trina to all her beloved followers in Christ and Perpetua, born of the Father and alive in the power of the Spirit, peace to you and Grace from that wondrous reality which is our God.

I have been moved by Clement's letter to all of our Guides and by my own personal experience of doubting God, to write to you all on the subject of the wonder of God in creation.

For many of us who are employed in daily activities concerning God, as "professionals", if you like, we are always in grave danger of losing the wonder, as are those who see God purely—or, paradoxically, impurely—as a philosophical proposition. It is, incidentally, one of the saddest cultural instances of disjuncture, that Mr Hawkins should be one of the best people in the whole of history to explain and enjoy the wonder of our world while not seeing God in it.

Often that wonder, of the fellow human being, the flower, the sunset; and also the humanly factored wonder, through God's grace, of *The Tempest*, the Mass in B Minor, the *Pieta*, or the *Comedia Divina*, is obscured by the discussion of what we call theodicy. I will start there, clearing the way for a better discussion of the glory of God in creation.

I know I have said this many times before but, as it seems to present people with such an intractable problem, I think I need to say it again: there is more to being than the good and the true. We do not understand the ways of God. We can say, as I do, that imperfection is a necessary pre-condition for choice and that suffering is, in a sense difficult to articulate, the price we pay for choice. To that extent, I would say that illness and what people call "evil" are related imperfections. This is not enough. We have to accept that we do not understand the ways of God and subjecting God to the judgment of laws humanly made is futile. The world's viability, its integrity, its sense of itself as separate from the Godhead, perhaps even requires that it is not perfect and that God does not "descend" to tame volcanoes or quell tsunamis. That integrity, too, surely means that although God might occasionally intervene in human affairs to cure an illness—Jesus and Perpetua both undertook such mighty acts in the name of God— our normative existence and our normative relationship with God require us to be ourselves and to judge ourselves as ourselves.

Our way of understanding God is through what Christians have termed the "three persons" of the Trinity. The Perpetuan understanding of God flows from the Christian tradition, but attempts to "escape" from anthropomorphic ideas of judgment, atonement and discriminatory salvation which, in turn, reflects both on its understanding of creation and of the Holy Spirit.

While admiring many created phenomena, the Christian tradition has flirted dangerously with the idea that the physical is inferior to the spiritual, corrupt or even evil. This is a very strange response to God as Creator. How could God have created something corrupt or evil? Christians might respond that the real problem is that—using the story of Adam and Eve—we were perfect and have fallen, tarnishing the earth. It is true that everywhere we look we can see evidence of earth's tarnishing, but that is the effect of our choice, not the hand of God. To be a creature is to be imperfect. That is the significance of the story of Eve. The physical is our means of being children of God on earth, as Theresa of Avilla said, "God has no body now but yours". The Perpetuan tries hard through holy living and openness to the other to celebrate creation by ranking it equal to, but different from, our spiritual selves, being so integrated that we must, reflecting incarnation, be both physical and spiritual to be human. That is the great message of the incarnation, that Jesus and Perpetua, in choosing to be both human and divine, confirmed our own duality of nature in one individual person. Seen from that perspective, physical creation is something that we should celebrate in every moment of our lives, giving thanks for who we are and having been given the privilege, in pure gift, of the ability through our life in this world to love God and each other.

The epitome and the climax of God's creation—in respect of our known universe—is the gift of incarnation. Again, we love and respect the Christian tradition of following Jesus, but we simply affirm in addition that God's relationship with creation is dynamic, that there is no stopping point, that the Godhead might have been manifested in human form before history— even myth—began, and incarnation might happen again. Perpetua affirms our deep commitment to the earthliness of God incarnate. The physical manifestation of the divine is the most amazing phenomenon of creation and raises the puzzle of how, in this light, God could ever have been thought of as the divine watch-maker. The least fascinating and enlightening aspect of the creation we know is its uniformity, predictability, empirical aspect, and consistency of performance. Fascinating though it is that generations of animals migrate across the globe only for their offspring to return to an exact spot, this is nothing compared with the enlivenment within us of the divine grace, our intimations of the divine, our glimpses into the mystery of God, and our living as children of the Resurrections of Jesus and Perpetua.

In turn, our wonder at creation and its epitome in Jesus and Perpetua should lead us better to understand the driving power of the Spirit in creation for it is our Sister within us who helps us to forge the appropriate creaturely bonds with the physical and the spiritual dimensions of createdness, within ourselves and between ourselves and others and most fully in our relationship with God. It is because creation is sacred that we are a Sacramental people. We cannot love God as we should without using physical elements to recall the incarnational nexus.

Having discussed the broader points, I want you to learn from my own particular predicament. After two years of trying faithfully to follow Perpetua, I began to doubt her divine nature. I became bogged down in a theological-type discussion about how much difference it made whether she was divine or not. I came to the conclusion—as I would call it—that she was a wonderful woman but that there was no God. I wanted a different answer, but my mind and spirit would not yield it. I became, at the same time, lonely and calm.

Then, with the help of Cara, who has also expressed her doubts, as you know, I came to see that God is not a doctrine, but a presence in creation. I think, more than anything else, it was the music of Bach that helped me back to seeing this but it might have been a clump of bluebells or the tide running into a bay. For me, createdness became totally inhabited by the sacred. That might have been the reaction of a playwright of ancient Greece or a poet of the Romantic age. In seeing the divine in createdness my whole person leaned towards God as the personal, in Jesus and Perpetua, for the Holy Spirit had not abandoned me but had hovered as I speculated and laboured until such time as I opened myself up again to incarnational perception.

The crucial episodes that came to mind were not the miracles nor the teaching of Jesus and Perpetua, but the final acts of each of them. This is where I discovered in myself, where the Spirit resides, the true meaning of the Sacrament of Union as a re-living of the deaths of Jesus and Perpetua. These were not exercises in accountancy nor revenge. These were not the arbitrary settlements of an anthropomorphic God. These were acts which said that divine love will never be impaired. We will not be "punished" for our imperfection, that the earth is what it is and we are blessed to live in it in the true knowledge of good and evil, joy and suffering, experiences unique to us, denied to the angels and denied by the Godhead to itself. We are the only creatures of whom we know who are so blessed, so blessed in imperfection, so supremely ourselves in brokenness.

It is my loving hope that you will all learn from my experience and not be frightened of those times when you doubt the existence of the divine as an integral part of who we are. We are to be ourselves and, in being so, the Spirit will never abandon us.

Gladdened by the vigour of renewal, I have decided with my colleagues that we will go forward in constructive engagement so that all may not only know the good news in their intellects, but also in their hearts, that we are destined to be enfolded back into the divine love and that while we are here we are to live the commitment and practice of love for which we were created. Not as inhabitants of a divine ante chamber, but as joyful beings-in-ourselves.

◆ ◆ ◆

Bronwen, who felt somewhat disoriented as she was the only London-based member of the core group who had not known Perpetua, struggled to come to terms with Trina's letter. She had come into the movement from nowhere—a "religious virgin"—because she thought that her life needed shape and purpose, a sense of direction and, most of all, a sense that she was doing what was right. She was chosen by the core group because it felt that it was becoming too inward looking. She had rejected Christianity because her need to do right did not involve imitation or judgment. She had been attracted to Perpetua through what she had heard and seen, but she had not considered the issue of the "greater God". Not that she had agreed to be a member of the core group without a great deal of thought, but she had not been sent on a long course or put to the doctrinal test. Why was it, she wondered, that the Godhead, designated the creator in love, the incarnate manifestations of Jesus, Perpetua, and the Spirit, should be understood as four things in one rather than simply being four ways of looking at the same thing? Couldn't you hold up all the best jewels and they would catch the light in a myriad of ways? The insistence on "personhood" in the Godhead seemed to complicate matters. Yes, she understood that God is innumerable—a point which seemed to escape many theologians—but the different phenomena might be explained without the complexities of multiple natures in single persons. What would it mean if God had simply appeared "through" Jesus and Perpetua as agents rather than their being part of the Godhead? Or were the incarnations a form of reversible caterpillar to butterfly? In short, although the Perpetuans were not doctrinally very exact, Trina's letter had set Bronwen off on a train of enquiry which seemed to lead to the opposite place from that intended. Instead of wonder, she experienced bewilderment.

"We've got reality and metaphor," said Trina, "as two different ways of understanding the Godhead and it helps not to get the two mixed up. The earth we live on and the universe we live in are not metaphors, nor are they meta-realities. We are not dreaming when our wakeful eyes see the morning sun. What we experience through our senses is reality, the reality of creation, and all that we know we know through these senses. Even mystics know everything through their senses but their skill is to be able to re-calibrate their senses radically. Through prayer we do this gradually and in small ways. So our existence is real and it is existence within the loving will of the Godhead. My idea about wonder is that it need not have been this way. God is self-sufficient. We are the result of an overflowing of love—although, of course, you can't overflow when you are sufficient-in-yourself—and that is the wonder. As for metaphor, we use that, as I have just demonstrated, to try to talk about God, but the problematic nature of what we are trying to discuss does not mean that the subject of the discussion is problematic. For instance, ordinary people find it difficult to discuss how electricity functions, but it doesn't mean that it doesn't or that we have serious doubts whether it does. Finding difficulty in discussing the incommensurable doesn't call the existence of God into doubt, it simply, and properly, reminds us of our limitations."

"So," said Bronwen, "let me try to get this right. The reality of the Godhead is demonstrated by the existence of the universe and its creatures?"

"Yes."

"So, as the Jews were clear about this, why did we need Jesus?"

"Because there is more to creation than its createdness in love. Our history has been a struggle to understand creatureliness and Jesus helped us to do that, but that help became dissipated over time and so Perpetua came to give our understanding of creatureliness a boost."

"Couldn't saints do that?"

"No. Not really. Only God can be a bridge between Creator and creature. Saints are very helpful in showing us how to lead our lives, and particularly how to worship, but God didn't just want us to take their word for it. It's God's word that counts."

"That seems a bit over-the-top."

"Yes God is over-the-top. That's the point of Godhead."

Bronwen thought about her exploration of Christianity. The people she sought help from were all gentle, pastoral people, suspicious of fanaticism or even the expression of emotion and they were very uncomfortable with people they called "happy clappy". But those people, who said they were born again, were full of wonder. Her mild temperament, which favoured the cool Anglicans, and the wonder of Jesus, seemed to be in conflict. Perhaps Perpetuans would offer wonder without fanaticism and high emotion. She thought that people wanted wonder but they also wanted comfort. Somehow the God of the Torans was too overpowering, seeming to close down the fundamentally creaturely attribute of choice. Perhaps her way of being a faithful Perpetuan would be to use her senses carefully to gather experience of the wonder of creation. She thought about the rhythms of the land and how they had seemed to help people to apprehend creatureliness. Suburbia was an unhelpful starting point. A massive dietary choice presented itself all year round, so there was no sense of the seasons, and no need to fast before Christmas and Easter. Private and public transport had played tricks with time. Weather was an inconvenience, but not a matter of life and death. The whole environment was flattened and bland. No wonder people found it difficult. They needed a form of eco-Perpetuanism. She would try to articulate it. In the meantime, she often looked at her grandmother's engagement ring and took to collecting interesting pieces of glass.

◆   ◆   ◆

Cara had never been happier in her life. She was happy enough that she had found her way back to Perpetua without doing too much damage on the way, but she was even happier that she had brought Trina back to Perpetua. She was not sure of the process that had taken place between them, but she knew—wanted to know?—that had she not been there it might have been much more difficult for Trina. On the surface the key day was when she visited her while she was playing Bach, but Cara thought that the actual, real moment within that wide discussion was when she said that Trina's doubt was a symptom of pride. It was a hard thing to say, but Cara knew that her own failings and those of her partner, Fidel, could all be traced back to pride which to her was the denial of creatureliness and affirming—no matter how—that you were part of or an imperfect replica of the Creator. The problem for humanity was that it was not content to be a creature. It kept trying to be God. This was a harsh charge to level at Trina, but it was the besetting weakness of us all. Cara, with her Spanish Catholic upbringing knew all about the devil prowling around, the sins of imagined sex and imagined falsehood, the sins of omission, the sins of idleness and yet, when she looked back, she knew that the children were little innocents compared with the nuns who preened their piety like the Pharisee in the temple. The pride of the religious life was much more dangerous to the soul than the life in crowded tenements, in the tatty streets and the scruffy markets where there was little room for pride and a constant reminder of humility and helplessness. They used to say that you never saw a nun without a paunch and a car. Pride was the sin of the church which was kept under the cloth by the practised voice of pastoral platitude. They only cared for you in the way they did because their pride led them, without thinking, to operate on the basis of a power relationship into all their pastoral work. You could always please a priest if you were sick, weak, or a child, but priests didn't like people who were their intellectual or theological equals. They took it really badly. Cara knew that all humans were imperfect and that priests and churches could be no different, but she had a peculiar suspicion of clerical pride and she had seen just an inkling of it in Trina whose scrupulous examination of conscience had became just a little self-conscious and self-indulgent.

Cara was still profoundly uncomfortable about what she had said, true though it was. They didn't quite avoid each other, but they always found good reasons not to be in a room alone together until one day in early Summer Trina sought Cara out and said, "I've been wrong. I know what you said was right and I know that you have been in pain because you told Marta, but I wish you had said something to me. I know I should have said something to you, but I didn't quite know how, so I said nothing, and I presume you were in the same predicament but it doesn't help either of us to burden Marta. This phrase about sharing burdens applies to mutual agreement, not imposition. It's a strange thing with human dilemma that the more people share it the greater the total content of dilemma there is out there. It doesn't divide like pie. Anyway, that's me being harsh. The main point is that you were right, and I know you were right. Far from needing to be forgiven, you need to be thanked."

Cara told Fidel what had happened. "The thing about Trina," he said, "is that she's always like that. When I went off the rails she was very forgiving and she didn't tell me off or say how bad I had been in a quantitative or qualitative way, but she did explain how she sees things. It's close to being a preacher after all, but just the right side of the line."

They'd had their troubles, Cara and Fidel, and no doubt they would again, but they enjoyed a kind of comfort in their struggles and their house groups flourished. Cara knew that any credit she took for bringing Trina back was in itself a sin of pride, but she could not help it.

◆   ◆   ◆

The mission to the people of Stumpy Knoll could not help but be anomalous. Philip had been a rather moralising pastor who had come to Perpetua through her own visits, the martyrdom of Dexter who had worked miracles in his church and the more recent martyrdoms of Father Joe and Wayne who had brought the word after the death of Perpetua. Thus it was that, outside Saint Simple's, this was the most important Perpetuan site in the world named, in an uncharacteristically Roman Catholic manner, Perpetua the Sustainer and the Holy Martyrs.

Then there were the girls. Lucie and Stella had become leading celebrities throughout the North of England, arranging missions and revival meetings which Philip should have been proud of and which filled the Christian clergy with envy. People remembered Perpetua's and Dexter's mass feeding miracles and the girls were strong on spiritual food. They also had the enthusiasm of the cured drug addict and sex worker. They had come to enjoy recounting their lurid tales and their dramatic escape. On occasion, they also liked to tell the story, which made Philip extremely uncomfortable, about the night that Perpetua had first come to the town and had sat with them when Philip wouldn't come close. The story was well meant, illustrating Perpetua's virtue, but it could not help but make the good Philip uncomfortable, although he never mentioned it. Matters, however, came to a head not over anything so personal nor trivial, but over sermons they were preaching about their history and its implications.

Philip did not mind their story being told, although the somewhat lurid style of its telling made him feel uncomfortable, but he felt that he had to say something about the implications. "I really don't mind, you know, even if you do have a bit of fun at my expense—it's not that at all—and I don't mind you telling your story in your own words—there are really no better words—but you go a bit far in saying that you have been completely healed by what happened to you."

"But we have been. We're not addicted any more and we don't carry on our old trade. We have high neck lines and low hem lines," said Lucie, still managing to look seductive.

Philip winced. "But don't you see, nobody is completely healed. We are all broken."

"Well, I know what you mean," said Stella. "We're all sinners, but we needn't make too much of that. We can't go into the estate behind the chemical plant and tell people that they're all sinners—that we're all sinners—because that will turn them off completely."

"I don't mean you to tell them that they're all sinners, but I do want you to say—if you believe it, and I think you do—that as God's creatures we all fall short, but that we're forgiven and can rely completely on God's unlimited love."

"They don't understand that sort of thing," said Lucie, "it's a bit, well, pious and philosophical, you know. They don't really feel God's love on the estate, but they do understand it if you give them material help and encourage the kids not to steal and mess things up."

"And anyway," said Stella, "you know that we're up against that 'Fresh expression' thing that the Vicar of Saint Chad's is promoting, all banners and orange juice! He gives people a good time, you have to admit, and we have to pull out all the stops to keep up. He tells them that they need to repent and that puts them off, even with the orange juice and banners, so our line is to say that God will fix it."

"Which God will," said Philip, struggling. "But he won't fix what we can fix. That was Perpetua's point."

"Well, that's all right then," said Lucie, triumphantly.

"I mean yes. Let's start again. God will ensure that we are all loved, but God won't watch us mess things up and put them right, like magic. So you're right to help people to fix things. We are here to do our best, spiritually, for ourselves and each other, but it will always be a struggle and we will never quite get it right. You can see that, can't you?"

"Yes," said Stella, looking wary.

"The point to bear in mind is that we are all broken, which is why it takes a lot of energy and courage to make proper decisions."

"But why would God make something that was broken?" asked Lucie.

"Because if we were perfect there would be no point, would there?"

They looked puzzled.

"If we were perfect we wouldn't turn to God, we'd be with God, but God wants us to turn towards our Creator and to be brothers and sisters of Jesus and Perpetua because that's what we were made for."

They still looked puzzled. Philip was floundering.

"I know it's not easy. I'll try once more. God made us in love so that we could love God and each other. He gave us free will, as its called, choice. Every time we make a wrong choice as the result of the gift of freedom that we were given, it hurts God, and we shouldn't hurt the Creator who loves us and Jesus and Perpetua who died for us."

"Got it!" said Lucie. "I can see why you wouldn't want to hurt somebody who loves you, and Perpetua did love us. That's only fair."

"But I didn't think God could suffer," said Stella.

"Well, God doesn't suffer in the way we do, I'm sure, in the way that Jesus and Perpetua suffered, but it's hard if you're pure love to be rejected because you don't know anything else but love. That's what you are. You can't see how anybody can be different. I know we were made with freedom, but I suppose God just hoped that we'd use it well and when we didn't, prophets and priests weren't good enough so he sent Jesus, and when we got tired of thinking about Jesus he sent Perpetua."

"That makes sense," said Lucie. "So what we will say is that Perpetua loved us and wanted us to love her and it's only right that we should."

Philip wasn't sure that was ideal, but it was the best that he could do. He had a very deep sense, from his days as a Pastor, of total dependence on God and his own brokenness and although Perpetuan and Dexter had weaned him off fatalism and moralism, he still found it hard to understand the joy of God. He somehow felt that Christianity had turned sour and he was part of the result. Part of his brokenness was his inability to help people to experience the joy of God's love. He leafed through his Bible and the few texts of Perpetua that were kept in the back of it and searched for something that resembled joy and found something she said in reply to an interviewer's question, "yes, we will all be 'saved', as you put it. So the point of being good, or worshipping God, or imitating Jesus—and me—is not to improve your chances of being saved, but to experience the utter rightness of being a creature created out of love to love. If you think that the purpose of religion is to give you some sort of advantage in the heavenly stakes, you have misunderstood, but it is not your fault really. Jesus brought—and I bring—good news. I just wish people could get that far."

Philip still felt broken, but he promised himself that he would try to focus on the good news.

"Tell you what," said Stella, "we will just try to be like her, loving, but not judging, listening and preaching less."

"And," said Lucie, "we'll try to help people to be contented, even a little happy. Will that do?"

"Yes," said Philip, almost warmly, "that will do very nicely."

◆ ◆ ◆

At last, after fiddling at the edges since new year, Monica was having a complete overhaul. She looked at the cover of each book as she put it on the reject pile with a sense that she ought to savour the moment, that she should somehow feel sad, either because they were old friends or because they should not have been and had wasted so much of her life—but she felt neither. She was just filled with annoyance with herself that she had ever allowed herself to be carried away. The only items that caused her to stop were those which dealt with the war in Iraq. She remembered with delight the day that she discovered that there were Christians who agreed with the militants that the traditional Christian doctrine of the just war didn't hold up, but most Christians didn't seem all that bothered either way. She went on all the demos and met some nice Christians, but she thought of all those who stayed at home. At least Perpetuans were clear on this point: there was no justification whatsoever for any kind of violence, pre-emptive or retaliatory. The civil power could wage war, but Perpetuans would not take part, and if the majority became Perpetuans then public policy would turn against war. At least this was clear; much better than the leftist mumbo jumbo about the deeply discredited United Nations, and the ranting against precision weapons which had been developed to make mass destruction less "necessary". Ultimately, leftists were just anti-American. She couldn't see the merit of supporting people who were oblivious of the plain fact that it was impossible to calculate the numerical balance between the slaughter of Muslims by Christians and vice versa and she despised the concept of estimating guilt according to a head count, or even the rather silly playground spats about who started it. Whoever started it, the conflict was usually the result of the "plane crash" phenomenon whereby nothing went badly wrong unless at least three safety mechanisms faulted more or less simultaneously. Anyway, she thought, Muslims had mostly killed each other. One last look and the Iraq books went into a box.

Steve was helping her to put the books in boxes and take them out to his van. "Don't look so upset," he said, "when you're doing the right thing."

"It just makes you feel old when you've spent twenty years of your adult life chasing after the wrong thing."

"I know. I don't understand now how I could have cared more about computers than people, I don't understand how I could have been such a prat when Dexter came to see us. I'm smiling because you changed me and I've no time to waste thinking about the time I wasted. I'll take these books out when you've given me a kiss."

John, sitting on the church steps in the June sun, watched Steve shuttling between the house and the van. A couple of women in the house group had accused him of being anti-lesbian because he was so pleased when Monica and Steve got together, but he said, "I would have been equally happy if Monica was having an unhappy relationship with Steve and had found Mary, or whoever. It's being yourself." Monica nodded. "A lot of positions I have taken have been about attention getting, and I don't know which came first, Perpetua or Steve, but they make a fantastic pair of companions for me."

John strolled over and looked at the books. "As an academic," he said, "I reckon that just about all of these are operatively out of date though they might interest an historian. If this crisis gets much worse—and everybody says that it will—then they will be even less relevant. I was always uncomfortable with the massive welfare state. As a Perpetuan I think it's far more important to give voluntarily than be forced to give for a state fix. Don't look at me like that, I'm not a Tory, I recognise that society has to tax people for social purposes if they're too mean to do it themselves. Tories, and Republicans, are against taxation because they are selfish. They have turned their personal selfishness into a supposed virtue called liberty. But taxation doesn't stop you being selfish. It's rather the same with choice. People are always going on about choice—the choice of whether or not to contribute to society, the choice of a pregnant woman whether or not to have her baby, the choice of a school, but choice isn't a moral issue, it's a power issue, it's about how much leverage you've got. It's not a right it's an assertion of individual or collective power."

"Perpetua was always going on about choice," said Monica, a little testily.

"Yes, but that was about exercising moral choice, the choice over how you choose to love and not love. She wasn't going on about schools or chocolate. It's as well to get this straight. Perpetuan self-determination is about exercising your free will to love or not love God. It's got nothing to do with power." He looked again. "I wouldn't throw that out with the rest."

She looked over his shoulder. "I just wanted to make a clean break from all my old thoughts and interests."

"I don't think you ever can and, besides, surely your experience isn't uniformly redundant?"

"I suppose not."

"I mean, just because I weaned Steve off his obsession with computers it doesn't mean he doesn't use them any more. In some ways the breach can be as fanatical as the adherence. There is a lot that we can learn from socialism, even though, like every other movement, it has its fringe fundamentalists. At the university I really miss the Marxists, they were so passionate and fisiparous, all bravado and betrayal. Today students only seem to be interested in their future careers and incomes. If there were more socialists there would be fewer grumbles about student finance. Their loans, after all, are simply a differently formatted graduate tax. When I was at university in the late 1960s we did some really silly things, but we were passionately against dictatorship except, of course, that some of us were myopic about the Soviet Union and its allies—and we really did want to help developing countries. Perhaps our greatest achievement has been to make the elimination of world poverty axiomatic, even if the implementation is half hearted. More fundamentally, very few students nowadays know anything about Karl Marx and only a handful have ever read him. If I were you I'd hold on to that very fine Marx reader. The difficulty isn't in the economics nor the philosophy, but with the language. He shares a peculiarly opaque German style with Hegel and Barth. They could all have done with good editors, but the old Jewish sharpness shines through. Apart from its intrinsic value, we all need to know about things that are outside our usual frame of reference. Today people more and more stick to their own communities of lifestyle and practice. The ignorance of those around us is truly shocking. Look at the terrible clash in the Christian church over homosexuality. Nobody is listening, few are studying, and the factions just want everybody to be like Africa or like America. If you study different ideas you are likely to be content to let them be. Another thing, learning about difference helps us not only to benefit from failure, but also from success. Nineteenth century liberals, for all their virtue, would have been incapable of the heavy lifting required to humanise capitalism. I'd keep that Montesquieu as well, that Vico, and Edmund Wilson's *To the Finland Station*, but, above all, I'd keep Brecht."

He re-packed a box with books that had been discarded and carried it back into the house. Then he returned to his station on the church steps and watched the progress of the move. So much of his life and Monica's since they met seemed to have been concerned with the nature of treachery or, at the very least, of being let down. Was it expecting too much of others that they should keep their promises and be consistent in their pronouncements? Surely the wrong question. What stopped people being true to themselves in situations where others were not seeking to impose on them? That was a better start. They hadn't been betrayed so much as expected others to conform to what they thought was right. There was a good deal of inconsistency and muddle, he thought, but little enough malice. If anything, there was too much emphasis on consistency in areas where it didn't work. Monica and Steve would make very fine Guides. At least they knew what to expect. In the meantime, he had to square it with Monica's Rector and then find her a place.

◆　◆　◆

Simon looked out of his window at the Fairview Hotel, remembering the time when it had been a place of broad lawns and brown soup, the car park full of mission vehicles from up country. Now it was all built up, burgered and enclosed in a steel ring of flashy people carriers, but these were small concerns compared with his fear of being arrested, tortured, and murdered. He had been careful in his preaching of the good news of Jesus and Perpetua to steer well clear of controversy, but the Spirit had, unfortunately, told him to go to Uganda where he knew he would be in great danger.

After checking out, he met Samuel on the front steps and they drove towards Westlands to find a quiet parking spot.

"How are you?" asked Samuel when they had parked in a quiet street.

"Very frightened."

"So why must you go when you are needed here? We have no need of martyrs. There are enough of them already."

"There is a difference between wanting to be a martyr and being one collaterally. You have grown well in the faith, Samuel, and will look after matters very nicely. There are tribal tensions, but what we have to say is reducing them. Our only real enemies are the people who want the tensions to persist and, of course, the Torans, but there is nothing we can do about them except to be patient and hope that their violent words do not turn into violent actions."

"That still does not justify your departure, Simon. If you go to Uganda and are killed in a day, what good will that have done?"

"I will never know, Samuel. It isn't about knowing. It's about doing God's will. If I go to Kampala, and die within 24 hours, as you say, I might have tended one person who becomes like the mustard seed."

An Ascari looked at the car threateningly, and they drove away, finding a secluded spot in another street.

"That's unfortunate," said Simon. "The more places you stop, the more chance there is of being remembered. The people in the Fairview are all right because they have this long, Polish tradition of hating the police, but there aren't many places like that. Where were we? Ah, yes! The mustard seed. It may be that I don't manage to find a mustard seed, but I don't expect to know. God is great and God is good. We really must not be utilitarian about this, trying to calculate the good we do through God's grace against the trouble we undergo. It's forgetting the 'through God's grace' clause that we get into trouble. So, Samuel, I am not here to calculate whether my death is worth this or that result. I just have to go because that's where the Spirit would have me go."

"I try, Simon, but I'm not very good on this idea of the Spirit."

"Don't under estimate yourself, Samuel. Your spirit is in the right place, you just need a little more technical honing to get the common vocabulary; but that's less important than being right in your spirit. You tend to say that God has said something, and I tend to say the Spirit has said something. The difference doesn't matter.

"Anyway, I believe that the Spirit is calling me to Uganda. This sort of 'calling' talk is often human beings bamboozling themselves into believing that God wants for them what they want for themselves but, believe me, Samuel, I don't want Uganda for myself. When I pray the people of Uganda keep rising up before me, asking for the good news to be brought to them. I feel that they are being torn apart by futile controversy and they want some calm. I am to take it to them. You can drop me at the bus station and I'll go to the airport that way. Nobody notices the people who ride in buses."

As he felt the fear mounting, he was almost grateful for the tedium of the airport procedure and for the bumpy flight over Lake Victoria. Kenneth met him, bundled him into a car and drove him to Jinja.

"As you know, my first task is spiritual insurance, Kenneth, so we will gather the people together and I will celebrate a Sacrament of Commitment for you and your five Guides and then we will celebrate a Sacrament of Union and of Response for all. Then I will feel more secure."

Emotion was high during the Sacraments but it reached near hysteria when Father Ambrose came in quietly and said that the police were outside. He said that they had agreed to wait for half an hour until the service was over and then they only wanted to talk to Simon. He had brokered a deal which meant that all the others could leave in peace.

Suspecting that something like this would happen, Simon had left his homily until the end of the Sacraments. "Brothers and sisters. I do not have much to say. You are better acquainted even than I with the ways of your police force. We have to admit to ourselves that in all probability we will never meet again.

"I therefore want to leave you with the good news of Jesus and Perpetua so that you may be comforted if the worst happens, always supposing, as I don't really, that death is the worst. I am frail enough to want that death to be as swift and painless as God will grant. It is so strange how religious people are hardly more immune from the life force than others. We long for heaven and yet we do not want to bid farewell to this physical creation which we have so tarnished.

"The good news is that we will all be enfolded back into God's infinite love. This lie of struggle and toil, of craft and cruelty, is the theatre where we may be part of God's drama, but we will all, ultimately, cease to play our separate parts and will be part of the infinite love from which, and for which, we were made.

"There will be a temptation for some to retaliate, but you must see that this does not happen. Keep your focus on the good news and subordinate everything else to that. Our colonial masters often used to praise hardship on the grounds that it hardened us for heaven, but I would not be so foolish. There is nothing intrinsically good in hardship and pain, but neither is their anything bad in them. They are part of our condition and we must accept for ourselves what we would struggle to spare others. That is the nature of solidarity.

"Never forget the smile of Perpetua. Never forget how she loved and encouraged. Never forget that you are her sisters and brothers, and never forget that she brought news for all, no less for the poor than the rich.

"God bless you."

Some of the people tried to restrain him as he walked slowly and purposefully towards the door. "I'm sorry," said Ambrose, almost in a whisper. "I got everything else guaranteed but you. From today I will unite Perpetuans with my Catholic flock to make a new beginning. You, and she, deserve nothing less."

As he walked through the door, Simon smiled at the thought of the mustard seed and seated himself in the back of the waiting police people carrier where he was joined by an officer on either side and another with a gun next to the driver. He knew that asking questions would be worse than useless. The question "Why am I here?" is not only futile, but a goad in a chaotic place. He handed round the cigarettes which he had brought for this eventuality. Cigarettes kept conversation and physical restlessness to a minimum. When he had handed the cigarettes round to show his goodwill, he handed the packet and lighter to the officer on his right. He asked quietly whether he could move his hands as they had not bothered to handcuff him. He indicated his small case and asked the officer to take charge of it and the money he extracted from his trousers pocket. Best to arrive with nothing at the police station.

The officer said, "is this a bribe? It won't save you."

"It's a gift. We both know I won't need anything any more."

When they reached Kampala he was immediately taken to a senior official dressed in a dark suit. He sat and waited for the other to begin.

"You are accused of spreading propaganda in favour of homosexuality and, therefore, of undermining the post-colonial integrity of this country by introducing decadent and unmanly practises. What have you to say?"

"Nothing."

"You know that I can decide whether to have you tortured or killed?"

Simon nodded.

"And still you say nothing."

"Nothing I say will make any difference. You have made up your mind."

"And you do not want to try to change it?"

"Perpetua always wants us to say things that will help and encourage people, but it is up to them to change their own minds. How could it be different? You can't actually change anybody else's mind, it's a kind of linguistic nonsense."

"Are you trying to be clever to make me look stupid?"

"No, sorry. I'm half talking to myself. But can I ask you one question? Not that the answer will make any difference to my life but it may change you?"

The man nodded.

"When there is so much civil war, poverty, and disease in your country, why are you so concerned with homosexuality?"

"I am becoming very tired of this question from imperialists, but it makes me angry when I hear it from Africans. It is obvious. As you are going to die I can be honest as you will never repeat this. There is nothing we can do about poverty because the system is the way it is, and that's our fault. There's nothing we can do about disease for the same reason. We can blame poverty and disease on the imperialists, but everybody knows we are lying to ourselves. The poverty and the disease are largely the result of the civil war that's also our own fault. But the one thing we can blame on the West is homosexuality and HIV/AIDS. It is our form of bread and circuses. It is what stops our self-loathing becoming unmanageable. It would not matter at all if the Americans just let us rant while we let them bugger each other to their hearts' content, but they want to establish their moral superiority by asserting their liberalism. We strike back by asserting our moralism. They brought us the Bible and, look, we live closer to it than they do because of our physical conditions. We have gained our point."

Simon was so interested that he forgot his surroundings altogether.

"I can see that, but I'm not a homosexual and I've never preached in favour of it in Kenya. I have only been here a few hours and you can't know what I said at Jinja."

"I know, but we can't have your brand of Perpetuanism with its moral pacifism subverting our culture. We can't have peace and quiet and a cessation of violence. The homosexual point is a pretext. To us you look like late 1960s California and we don't want that here. I don't want to be unduly cruel because, as you say, you haven't done anything, really. What I need is the publicity not the cruelty, so you will be obliged to make a broadcast admitting your homosexuality, explaining how the whole of the West is corroded by it, responsible for HIV/AIDS, and recanting your own personal immorality."

"It is so kind of you to make things so easy, but I can't do that."

"In which case you will be tortured and die a slow and painful death."

"But that's no use to you if what you want is the publicity."

"You are not frightened of pain or does your Perpetua give you immunity?"

"Just the opposite. I'm very frightened of pain and she makes me more, not less, human."

The man looked bored.

"There will," he said, "be plenty of others" and, with that, he killed Simon with a single shot.

◆　◆　◆

Thomas emerged from the Mass Transit subway into Harvard Square and felt disoriented for a moment as he looked for the familiar landmarks of his student days. The Wursthaus and many of its companions had gone, together with the subway car sidings, to make way for a traffic free zone of small cafes and shops. He walked across Harvard Yard to the Kennedy School of Government. The medium-sized seminar room was packed. Perpetuanism had gained a foothold in the University, notably in Kirkland House and Radcliffe. Thomas was a noted broadcaster on religion and ethics, and his love and knowledge of the Bach Cantatas which formed a key element in his Sunday services was—to misuse a word—legendary. There had been an initial proposal for a panel discussion, but he had said that he did not want to be drawn into artificial confrontation as there was quite enough of the real thing. He agreed to give a short talk and then answer any questions. What he said was later posted on the internet.

> Thomas to Harvard—Science and Happiness
>
> In a way, Perpetuanism needs no apologia. In a country such as ours where people are no more than ridiculed for their religion, any new doctrinal position is free to operate in the market, but there has, of late, been such an aggressive attack upon religion by people from parts of the scientific community that religion in general is in need of an apologia.
>
> This is not the time to mount a broad defence across all fronts, and so I simply want to concentrate on one aspect of the lack of dialogue between scientific atheism and religion, namely, that element of the United States Constitution which cites the pursuit of happiness as one of our corporate goals.
>
> I should start by saying that I do not contest any of the current, major scientific paradigms which represent the best of what we know. A little humility would go down well, but, given science's massive achievements, it's a bit too much to ask. Humility might also lead this segment of the scien-

tific community to ask why so many of its members, now as well as in the past, found no conflict between science and faith in a supreme being. We all have our various differences with Plato, Aristotle, Aquinas, Mahomet, Maimonides, Newton, Descartes, Leibniz, Kant, and Hegel, but to dismiss them and the countless people who have believed in God as irrational, or even gullible and stupid, is a piece of intellectual arrogance.

How do the achievements of science relate to the achievement of happiness? On the surface, the answer should be a resounding positive. We are healthier , wealthier, and live longer than any previous generation. There has never been a generation so well—I was going to say educated, but I will stick to the less ambitious—informed. Surely this is what the founding fathers meant by happiness, the harnessing of individual and corporate effort to improve life and life chances for citizens.

Somehow I doubt it. Now I am not going to fall into the "misery trap" of saying that better health, more wealth, and almost unlimited opportunities to learn are not beneficial, but the question is whether these things make us happier. The statistical information is interesting. It shows that when very poor people achieve a slight uplift in their life chances they become happier, but once they achieve average income and wealth, additions do not affect their happiness rating. If anything their consumption is a form of displacement activity that operates like a ratchet, resembling substance addiction.

So what does this have to do with science? Well, I might be caricaturing just a fraction—though not much—when I say that many scientists, particularly aggressive atheists, say that we only know what can be empirically demonstrated. I say that this is a slight parody because some of these people will tell you that they cry at the opera, but then they rather spoil the effect by saying it's some neural-chemical phenomenon. They have come so near to the truth and then veer off.

Their chief social argument, it seems to me, is that however bad things are now, however unhappy we might be because of the ravages of cancer, however guilty we might feel about our oil consumption and pressure on the environment, however puzzled we might be about mass murderers, and, on the other side, however frustrated we might be that some children seem to learn better than others, that genius can't be identified and bottled. Even between zygotic twins, there are such radical differences that one might be an alcoholic and the other a happy, moderate drinker, the future will fix it. Science will produce an answer. The "progressive" political and atheist scientific community offers jam tomorrow, but, of course, that is what they accuse us of, which accounts for Marx's characterisation of religion as the "opium of the people". I want to show that Christianity has rather overdone the idea that earth is simply an ante chamber to heaven whereas Perpetuans believe that the Kingdom of God is here and now in its putative form.

But, to return to science. Look at the genome project. Do you suppose it will uncover a genetic locus for happiness? Well, it might, you see, locate the place which can be suppressed or stimulated to make us feel good, but feeling good isn't the same as being happy.

Because, with the aid of science, we have transformed our culture from mystery to measurement, we think that happiness is measured by our intellectual, physical and material possessions. And, because of liberalism, we tend to think that happiness is individual or, at best, familial. We have fallen into a profoundly narrow, selfish form of measurement and, if we go on this way, the social solidarity which guarantees our privacy will break down. More fences and guard dogs, less security.

This is where I want to introduce Perpetuanism. It shares with Christianity the idea that creatureliness, behaving as we were created to behave, makes us happy. Unlike much contemporary Christianity, we say that behaving as creatures does not only make us happy, it is our natural state. We were made to be happy and to love the Creator, and when we stop loving the creator our happiness is affected; it is what Christians call sin. Christians, too, hold that we were made to love the Creator but they rather spoil this by saying that we are intrinsically "fallen" and "sinful" or corrupt. It is not logical to want to love a Creator who has made you "corrupt".

The connection between my remarks about atheism and Perpetuanism is that as atheism cannot begin to consider the idea of a creator, it automatically shuts itself off from the concept of mystery and the concept of the search for inner, or spiritual, happiness. It can understand the idea of trance, but it cannot understand the idea of God as a personal phenomenon, so there is no relationship involved in what it might own to as not physical.

The idea of spiritualism separate from the idea of a personal God is widely accepted but, again, because it is a matter of individual choice, an option exercised in private, it resembles consumerism. People say that they can choose their own spirituality, but we can't choose our own Creator or our own Holy Spirit. We can choose whether to establish relationships with the Creator through Jesus and Perpetua but our starting point is that we believe that we are creatures of the Creator. No amount of dialogue is going to change anybody's mind about this on either side. We ought to be more realistic. Christianity has become rather obsessed with arguing against atheists. We believe that it's simply best to say what we say, to bring the good news that we were made to be happy and help people to open up channels which will result in their establishing personal relationships with the Godhead. We can talk in human language, but only the Spirit can infuse belief.

Now this is all a little abstruse, but I want to leave you with three final thoughts. First, it makes sense for Perpetuans to focus on what makes us happy instead of protesting against the society in which we live. The long American tradition of pursuing happiness and an equally strong Christian tradition of regarding happiness as somehow un-Christian, seems to have achieved the very un-American phenomenon of a draw. Perhaps it would be better understood as a paradox, that the pursuit of earthly happiness doesn't make you happy. Science also seems to have created up-sides and down-sides which, arguably, have also played out a draw. The tie breaker is surely the pursuit of happiness in our proper creaturely state.

Secondly, scientific atheists are fond of berating the great religions for many of the world's ills, but where it has had a monopoly the results have not been very good. If they are as empirical as they claim to be, atheists should look at the evidence of their achievements as it relates to happiness. Believers are not ethically superior to non-believers, but we do have a broader and deeper notion of why we are here. Science is not enough and, in a way, God isn't enough, but you don't have to choose.

Thirdly, and finally, in a really profound way, most of the questions we think of as absolutely fundamental to our existence aren't that at all if we are simply investigating them to extend our own knowledge. If you want to help starving people in Africa it doesn't matter whether there was something or nothing before the big bang, but if you believe in a Creator it really does matter because the people of Africa are not only your fellow creatures, they are also children of God. Although we fall short, justice isn't optional. Perpetuanism will continue to be interested in big scientific questions, but we will always be wary of being drawn into an agenda which does not improve the relationship between the Creator and creatures. We need to be careful to play at least some of our games on our own turf.

The session then moved to discussion.

"I am what you might call a friendly atheist. I don't think the aggression and the ridiculous claims help, but I can't get my head round the idea of a creator entity you call a being."

"I know," replied Thomas. "The problem is that you think it's an idea and I believe that it is a real being. What puzzles me, given that you have a problem with an idea and I have a strong commitment to a belief, why are some of your co-believers so aggressive, as if religion threatens something? They don't think that Shakespeare or Bach threatens them. They don't mind all that much if people in fiction influence the lives of real people more than other real people. All that I can gauge from what they say is that there is a danger that we will lead them to be credulous or to believe in myths or nonsense, but atheists believe in all kinds of myths and nonsense. It's part of the human condition to re-write your individual and collective history. It's the way we survive and the way we justify aggression. It's the way we reinforce our prejudices and justify partiality. I can quite see why people are frightened when people kill each other in the name of religion, but that's no different in degree from people killing each other in the name of Marx or Hitler."

"I'm not so friendly. Doesn't this mystical obsession cloud reality?"

"Well, it certainly queries empiricism, but if it's as foolish as you say it is, what makes you so worried about it apart from your concern for clarity. Always supposing that there is any such thing as clarity. There is such a thing as paradigm and the set we have at the moment is better than the last set and not as good as the next set. Science is correct to the extent that it is more likely that new paradigms will be superior to old paradigms than the other way round. The real question here, however, is what do you want clarity for? What's its purpose? Yes, to make things clear, but they aren't. A paradigm is an internally consistent set of axioms, but your axiom is empiricism and mine's God. We need to go further. You are equating reality with empiricism; if it isn't empirical, it isn't real. That is a very primitive, crude paradigm which might relate to stone and to stoniness, but hardly to people."

"So why Perpetua rather than any other form of God?"

"In many ways this is the big question. We are accustomed in history to see religions and factions within religions competing for space and power, so that issues are reduced to matters of order and obedience. That's what the gay issue is about in Christianity. It's not a humble discussion about the mystery of person-hood and the primacy of God, it's about who imposes what rules on the basis of which interpretation of Scripture is 'right'. This is clearly a nonsense and it's what led me towards Perpetua. Let me stay with the gay issue for a moment. It's not the most important dispute in this world, but it's the one a lot of us know about. It's the one that drove me out of the Episcopal Church.

"Establishing a two-way relationship with God is admitted by most Chris-tians to be difficult. Our means of making it easier are Scripture and Sacrament, but because they are hybrid constructs, respectively of the Holy Spirit and hu-manity and Jesus and humanity, they are as difficult in their way as the hybrid construct of prayer. As we find it difficult to get to grips with hybrid constructs, we have to own that we ourselves are hybrid constructs, too. Many Christians describe humanity as being dual, consisting of a body and a soul, but Perpetu-ans, and some Christians, believe that the two are integral and that in other words we, too, are hybrids, not in the way that Jesus and Perpetua were hybrids, but hybrids nonetheless. Now if we are hybrids, our personal meaning and our relationships with God are deeply problematic, but many Christians want to reduce this mystery to a reductionist position, a kind of fundamentalism mir-roring atheistic empiricism, just as they want the meaning of Scripture and/or Sacrament to be cut and dried. In summary—and I'm sorry for going on for so long—the flaw in the empirical position which you characterise as giving clar-ity, is that it thinks about paradigm instead of thinking about what cannot be reduced to paradigm. They both have their spheres, but they don't interfere with each other. The classic statement is that Darwin's paradigms do not contradict the Creator mystery."

"Yet ignore the evidence shows that as science advances, religion retreats."

"Because it has produced so many great social gains, science has enjoyed massive prestige for the past 300 years—and I would have to say that in the West at least, religion has transformed itself from conforming to affirming—but this has nothing to do with the question I initially posed. Has the triumph of science over religion made people happy? It might be objected that this is a strange test, but I have already shown that in Perpetuan terms it is the crucial test. If it is not the purpose of science to make people happier, what is its purpose? If the reply is that it exists to make people physically and mentally better off, we are not far from saying that the only thing that distinguishes humanity from animals is pattern recognition and its special application in language. It is my guess that if more of us believed that that was all we were worth, the suicide rate would rocket. One more, please?"

"You Perpetuans are pacifists, so what about our boys in Iraq and Afghanistan?"

"We are pacifists for two fundamental reasons. Firstly there is the Christian position that it's not evil to be hurt by others. I know this is difficult, but that argument rather defuses the question 'if it was your own child being attacked, would you defend it with violence?' The only logical answer is 'no' because the child is not right or property; it is gift. Secondly, the Perpetuan argument is that the use of violence is an extreme form of the use of power which is, in turn, an extreme form of the operation of earthly judgment. We don't deny this to the civil powers, we simply deny it to ourselves. So, you might ask, what if there are millions of pacifists, to which the answer is that waging war would become less easy. I recognise the huge pain caused on 9/11, but you all know, deep down, that whatever the temporary temptation, the answer was love. On a quite different tack, however, if the civil power is to wage war it ought to think through the consequences. The world would still have wars if the great powers spent all their armaments budgets on social justice—and no doubt we would think of new ways of denying our creatureliness—but we can only do what we imagine. Almost all wars, like almost all crime, result from antecedent wrongdoing. Which brings us back to happiness. I can't see how waging war increases human happiness. You would reply that being a victim of violence does not increase human happiness, but I am not sure. There is a quite proper happiness from doing the right thing by God's grace. God bless you."

Thomas met Sarah and Gregory outside the hall and they walked back across the Yard to Kirkland House where Thomas had SCR privileges. "I thought you did well on the war," said Sarah. Gregory's face twitched and put itself right almost imperceptibly.

"It isn't war, really," said Thomas, "it's this dreadful need to be active, to do things, to fight or to feed, to judge and to advise, to run and to fidget. I'm not nostalgic. When we were hunter gatherers we had no leisure to sit in the mouths of our caves thinking about the meaning of the universe, but the point is, we are not hunter gatherers. Indeed, I'm coming round to the view that there was a pre-historical incarnational manifestation. The way global history starts to change radically, as far as we can tell, around 8000 BCE indicates that there was a very important shift in consciousness which took perhaps 5,000 years to spread round the inhabited world."

"Fascinating," said Sarah. "That might bring us closer to some otherwise far off people and ideas."

"It might, but the more I think about it—and here's a paradox—the more I am not sure it's worth thinking about. What Perpetua taught me, for all her presence, her being there right in front of you, was that faith and prayer are by far the most important things. Christianity, with the possible exception of the Greek Orthodox, has got itself into a terrible intellectual tangle by buying into the enlightenment and playing all its games on the road."

Gregory sat quietly while Sarah and Thomas talked a little more about faith and philosophy and then he said, "none of us knows how powerful faith can be.

Sometimes it's even more powerful than we want it to be. Faith once coursed through me so powerfully that I was hardly human, but I suppose it's the opposite for most people. I suppose it's super faith that worked through Jesus and Perpetua and, in a more limited form, works in saints."

"I don't know," said Thomas, looking curiously at Gregory who had never before offered anything like a theological statement, but stuck to the pastoral.

"Neither do I," said Gregory, "but I am so grateful to have been left with slightly less faith than I need. That's precisely the right state to be in."

They parted at the Harvard subway station. Thomas went downstairs and Gregory and Sarah walked up Massachusetts Avenue until they reached Gregory's car. They were turning into the parking lot when Gregory was called by a pathetic figure hunched in a doorway. "I'm dying," said the man, in a weak voice. "I'm blaming no-one. It's my own fault, but I'm dying. Only the Lord Jesus can save me and it's probably too late for that. Do you know how to pray? I used to be a Catholic."

Gregory knelt down and put his hand on top of the other's wasted arm. The man stood up, as if transformed.

Gregory was on the point of violently pulling away when Sarah said, "It's all right, Gregory. I know. My mother is one of the people you cured."

The man took Gregory's hand and almost broke his fingers, so strong was the grip. "It's a bloody miracle!" he shouted.

"All right," said Gregory. "Thank God, but not so loud. Remember, that's your one chance. Don't celebrate your wonderful cure by going to a bar or getting a fix." To Gregory's relief, the man sloped off to find his friends.

"It's all right," said Sarah. "I know, and Thomas knows. In fact, most people in the movement know but, remember, the whole key is that we don't judge. Drop me at MIT and go home to your lovely wife and be at peace. You're a good man, Gregory. Nobody knows how good. Nobody knows how good you have been since you came here. Nobody knows what you went through with what we might call your surfeit of faith. How should we know? Oh, by the way, Max sent you a message through me, knowing you would be out of town for a few days. He said that Sir Pluto—what a very strange name—has tidied everything up and is about to become a full Perpetuan."

Gregg smiled.

◆   ◆   ◆

Sir Pluto had indeed been putting his affairs in order, not in anticipation of imminent death, but quite the opposite. He had finally decided that flirting with Perpetuanism was an irresponsible position. Max was trying to be both a spiritual leader and Perpetuanism's chief administrator. "I'm not really up with the spiritual bit yet," said Sir Pluto to Max, "although I am very close to old Hawthorne and I am sure he will give me some help. What I have done, as you may know, is to withdraw from any role in Hypo. I have transferred all my shares in all my companies over to the movement and would be grateful if you could dedicate some of them to paying me a modest salary."

"What about Annie?"

"She wants to be a Guide, if you'll have her, working in Grunge Park. She became very committed to it in the Partnership."

"What about the campaign for the self-regulation of consumption?"

"The down turn is about to hit us really quite hard. I don't think it will make very much difference at the top end, but it will at the bottom, and we do notice that those very near the bottom are proportionately more generous than those near the top. We have—or, rather Annie has—changed consumption patterns to a really quite remarkable degree within a year, by almost 5%, which is why the shares are looking somewhat peaky, but we have only recovered 2% of that saving into contributions to those who are hit by lower consumption. It's something, of course, but not enough. I was hoping you would put some funding by to establish a trust to promote social justice and lower consumption. I will leave you to work out allocations. I've left you a list of suggestions, but there's absolutely no pressure: Saint Simple's Shrine, Perpetua and the Martyrs, the Transfiguration Chapel in the City, foundation arrangements for Guides, a social justice fund, we're becoming quite a church!"

Max winced.

"Only joking, Max. We've got to have the foundation funding so that our people don't spend all their time fund raising for Guide salaries. Structure is inevitable, but it's fine as long as it doesn't become the raison d'etre. The next big problem we will need to solve is how to prevent that from happening. You would have thought that Christians would have worked that out before they were swallowed up by the Empire. It was just too much to get from Jane Austen's parsons to Doctor Livingstone."

"You of all people," said Max, smiling, "ought to know that people who are fighting off the competition are the last to see the big strategic picture. They just become obsessed with the details of slighting and being slighted. Ever since the Reformation Christianity has been a long and woeful tale of nasty tactics and no strategy. So you see, they were so worried about holding their own, they couldn't imagine being top dog."

"And do we need to?"

"I think not, Pluto. If we are faithful to our principles we will continue to be non-combative, which means that we will be the whipping boy of the strong and the refuge of the weak, which is how it should be, but that's no recipe for building a strong institution in the conventional way. Neither do I mean by this that we will be some sort of internet phenomenon. We will always place the highest value on personal contact. You can't be open to others by offering them a place to send emails."

"There's always a problem with organisations getting worldly."

"That is why it is particularly appropriate, Pluto, that you, as a former worldly person, can stop us going down that route. Meanwhile, I think I will follow the Perpetuan custom and write a letter."

> Max to all Perpetuan leaders and Guides.
>
> Now that we appear to have settled after a number of upheavals, and now that faith in Perpetua is growing steadily in many places, it seems right that we should consider our position as it is always best to attend to serious matters in relatively good times rather than waiting for a crisis.
>
> As you know, I have served for the past two years, since the death of Perpetua, as a sort of Chief Executive, part of that time as one of the core group, but we have agreed that we should appoint an official administrator and that I should devote my time to mission in London. As a farewell to administration, we thought it right that I should write a few words about what I have learned and how we should proceed.
>
> There are many dangers in becoming transfixed with buildings. There is a terrible temptation for groups of people to identify themselves by acquiring or, better still, erecting a building. What begins as an act of vanity soon turns out to be an act of folly because of the cost of borrowing, the obligations of repayment and the subsequent maintenance burden which not only comes to dominate the affairs of the group, but also prevents them from using their resources for the good of others. Granted, our way of conducting ourselves might be interpreted as putting ourselves first, but I hope that it will be seen to be modest and practical.
>
> The core element of Perpetuanism will continue to be its house groups. These will consist of people of varied backgrounds and talents and we hope that you will always ask a Guide to help you if it seems that your house group is becoming too exclusive and monochrome. We have all agreed that we should acquire places of worship for our major Sacramental celebrations, but we urge you all to be realistic. Our general rule is that we should save to acquire buildings and then establish a foundation for their upkeep so that subsequent generations are not burdened with our debts. The leadership group has established a small corporation to handle our central finances. Firstly, we have foundation finance for our only two shrines, Saint Simple's in the South and Perpetua, Our Sustainer and the Holy Martyrs in the North. Secondly, we have foundation funding for a core leadership which must not exceed ten and an administration budget that must not exceed one half of the leadership budget. Thirdly, we have foundation finance for a small number of Guides who will begin their operations in deprived and rural areas, but we do expect that the requirements for all house groups to be varied in the income, wealth, and talents of its members will draw in finance for shared Guides once the groups are established. Finally, we have a small fund to pay for Guides on the undertaking of a collection of house groups that they will raise the foundation funding for them.
>
> We can insist on none of this other than for ourselves as a leadership group, but we urge you to be prudent and modest in all that you do. We are not a heritage society nor a cultural institution—though we value both—

but are dedicated to God's mission to bring the good news to all people through the life and teaching of Jesus and Perpetua.

I can only speak for ourselves when I say that we have tried to assemble a leadership team with a variety of gifts, but all sharing in the belief that we should be modest, that we should facilitate what you think best for your groups and Guides, and that, above all, we should refrain from issuing orders. This letter is the "heaviest" it will get, but we did think it right to issue some "light touch" guidance in this letter as it would no doubt have filtered down through your Guides.

We thought it might help if we were to say a little about the qualities of the people you might propose as guides. Firstly, to lead a good and holy life, modest in disposition, not apt to be angry or ill tempered, is a necessary, but not a sufficient condition.

Secondly, we believe that for Guides to be effective they must, above all, be comfortable within themselves so that they do not suffer from a lack of self-esteem which is the root of most balanced and constructive facilitation and prudent leadership. To be a Guide is not a right, but is a vital form of service and for this we need people who are fitted to serve. We will deny no calling, but we cannot undertake to recognise every calling.

Thirdly, a good Guide should not judge, but should listen and encourage and, in the life of the community, should always make room for the exercise of all the talents of others for, to quote what might be thought to be a trivial example, there is little point trying to stage a musical event in a small community if its chief talent is in circus skills. Common management terminology talks about leaders being "team players", but we would prefer to describe them as talent spotters, trainers, and facilitators.

Finally, Guides should regularly, conscientiously, and scrupulously examine their conduct as an integral part of their prayer life, seeking always to be balanced in their self-assessment and proportionate in making amendment. Guilt and exaggeration are as damaging as refusing to take responsibility.

From these few words we hope that you will see that we are determined to practice the modesty and restraint that we advise. We must learn from previous generations which have become burdened with buildings and bureaucracy. They have also become hopelessly entangled in chronic questions of order and it is to that point that we finally turn.

The purpose of a church, or movement of any kind, is to facilitate the personal two-way relationship between God and its members. We believe that its two functions are: to preach the Word, as set out in the Christian scriptures and further works concerned with Perpetua, shortly to be advised, and to celebrate the reformed Sacramental rites. We shall, in due course, issue a reading guide to Scripture which will advise how it should be approached, but we will not issue any guidance on the merits of conclusions reached. We must trust that those who reach conclusions inimical to Perpetuans will know this through the gentle encouragement and comment of their house group colleagues.

We will also issue a handbook of guidance on the celebration of the Sacraments and trust that regular, comradely, and informal meetings of

Guides and attendance at major celebrations where many are present will ensure that practice is kept with the very wide bounds we will advise.

The chief purpose of order is to impose standardisation. We believe that there is no requirement for us to establish a structure to enforce order. If, however, there are any major disputes we hope that the parties involved will begin by trying to resolve the issues themselves. We are happy to be a forum of last resort, but in that case we will only issue guidance. It is for people in disputes to settle them. We will not resort to the use of external force. No dispute is ever resolved by force; and no community is ever created by the imposition of order, but is, rather, generated by voluntary, mutual and loving assent. Power seeks to eliminate a difference through diktat or to eliminate one of the parties in the dispute. Neither course of action is acceptable to us.

It might be argued that such arrangements as these are a recipe for chaos. To say this is to express a lack of faith in God's creatures. We have faith, through Jesus and Perpetua, in our people and believe that the more responsibility they take upon themselves, the better. There will no doubt be a good deal of doctrinal and liturgical untidiness, but this is a small price to pay for the elimination from our arrangements, as far as possible, of the exercise of power. We are not, in any case, a movement primarily concerned with doctrine and liturgy, but, rather, with the living of holy lives in love, the faithful and open-minded reading of Scripture and the celebration of God's gift to us in Sacrament.

We recognise, brothers and sisters, that to live a life of Perpetuan love, with its emphasis on facilitating the freedom of the beloved, is to ask a great deal of us all, and to give ourselves the best chance of being faithful to Perpetua, we must rid ourselves of all encumbrances so that we remain totally committed to our purpose. Our chief enemy is the temptation to exercise power, even through such positive acts as feeding the hungry and caring for the sick, and so we must always be wary.

All our care and love goes out to you.

Max

◆   ◆   ◆

Although his change of lifestyle did not come as a total surprise to his friends who had watched his progress carefully since his involvement with Perpetuanism and his marriage to Annie, Sir Pluto (who had dropped the title and was in the process of changing his pagan first name to Gerontius as a tribute to his quirkily musical father) could not escape a certain degree of raillery.

He called Randall with the news. "I'm calling you to say farewell."

"I'm a journalist, Pluto—er, rumoured Gerontius—so you see I already knew. In fact, I was going to call you to ask for an exclusive."

"It's yours for old times' sake Randall, if there's anything that such a serious paper as yours might find newsworthy. By the way, how's Nina?"

Randall gulped at the twin jibes. "She's changed from being an action-based therapist into being a talk based therapist."

"I suppose it comes to us all, in the end. What can I tell you?"

"Well, Pluto, let's put the idea of an exclusive to one side for now. Is the paper going to continue to be independent?"

"Yes, of course, Randall. I've negotiated a deal with the new proprietor that you can operate under precisely the same conditions of independence as at present."

"So who is the new owner?"

"And you such a news hound! Why, it's Vespasian Crow of the Raptor Group, a very staunch advocate of press freedom. I shouldn't say this to you, Randall, as a new Perpetuan, but you have been so faithful that I wish you joy of him."

Gerontius reluctantly agreed to a little celebration of his changed state with a few male "friends". Whoever chose the list—he suspected Max and Annie, but neither would say—had a wicked sense of humour as it included Lord Warpley and Horace Strider. He was consoled by the presence of Sir Granville, ever the gentleman scholar, and Gwyn Evans, the funniest man in a QUANGO.

Gerontius thought he had better make a start with his more touchy celebrators so he sought out Lord Warpley. "Well, Griswald, how's the political weather in their Lordships' House?"

"Pretty dull, really. This lot are completely blown out and there's no rage, genuine or synthetic, to be had."

"I'm pleased to hear it. I thought at one time some of that rage might have been pointed in our direction."

"Don't believe it. Religion, of most sorts at least, is good for the soul. We will need all the help we can get as society becomes ever more secular."

"So I can take it that you are dropping your campaign for 'orthodoxy'?"

"Oh Pluto, of all people you should know better. That was just a little device for getting me onto a couple of boards of trustees where I needed to be."

"So much for society. So you would subvert Perpetuanism for your own personal ambition?" thought Gerontius, slipping back into his old ways, but he said, "I think we all know that it doesn't really work that way. I will be happy if you just stand back and wait before passing any kind of judgment."

Horace Strider did not wait to be found. He came across to Gerontius with a real spring in his step.

"Horace, you look so well."

"It's being out of office and less than a year from being out of Parliament. The day that the expenses scandal broke—I was in it no more than the average, you know. Silly, really, because I didn't really need any of the money—but that day I told my constituency chair that I was off. I told the PM that I'd hold on to Trade if it was all the same to him as a favour, you know, but there would be no new policies. The officials were welcome to massage anything they liked. He didn't want a by-election so he would have to put up with it, but that's just what he didn't do. He said he wanted somebody ruthless who would wreak havoc to prepare for the opposition coming in. As it is, I've got the Chair of the Leicester Black Stripe Association which involves me picking up £40k a year for eating pork dinners and opening my address book. Then there's the Date & Walnut Importers Federation which is another £30k plus some very pleasant trips overseas. Very pleasant. Mrs Strider doesn't like air travel, you know. There's the Porcelain Guild coming in at £50k per year. All in all, it's very tidy, and all sorted out before the expenses scandal really hits home."

"I think that a couple of those were mine, you know."

"Well, they are in good hands."

Gerontius moved on smoothly to Theodor Schuhorn. "How are things with poor Archbishop James?"

"All right," said Schuhorn, looking past him in case somebody more important was coming in.

"And what about your good friend Crowther?"

Schuhorn swallowed. "He isn't my good friend, as you put it. An Appointments Secretary doesn't have friends; quite the opposite. I simply needed somebody who could run a decent administrative machine to get hold of Alchester and Crowther was available, more than that, was very anxious."

Having done his duty, Gerontius settled down with Sir Marcus Gowder and Sir Granville.

"So what does it mean in the grand scale of things?" asked Sir Marcus, his customary encouraging softness hiding his towering intellect.

"It's hard to say," said Gerontius. "History is littered with sects that have flourished like comets and faded, but I like to think—don't we all?—that the short lived wonders have been largely based on deluded ego. It isn't that simple. Clearly, if religion is to survive in our kind of what we call 'sophisticated' society it's got to move away from clerical strangulation, whatever it claims. You can't have a population where up to 40% go to university simply turning up for threadbare liturgy and a poor sermon. Whether God is three persons or four, or whether Jesus is two natures in one person are fascinatingly abstruse issues, but hardly crowd pullers. There's no point saying that numbers don't count. If you are told by your leader to go and tell the whole world about the good news of Perpetua, how many you tell does count."

Sir Granville looked pensive. "I suppose that the general interest in what Christians contemptuously call 'pick and mix spiritualism' at least tells us that people are looking for something that is not doctrinal. I think it's the doctrine that has got in the way of the love. Let's say, Gerontius, that we think that Jesus really was God, and that Perpetua was God too. That's wonderful, but we don't need all the Greek and Latin, do we? Sometimes I think that Evangelicals who say that Jesus loves us are as nearly right as you can get, but then they spoil it by saying how wicked we all are and they, consequently, advise good behaviour on the basis of divine threat, which doesn't leave much room for love."

"The grand scheme of things?" urged Sir Marcus. "It's difficult enough sorting out cosmology and religion—I like Teilhard de Chardin—but mustn't we simply be content to try to be happy and help others to be happy?"

"It's difficult enough," said Sir Granville. "But we don't want to confine ourselves to utilitarianism."

"Mt guess", said Sir Marcus, sadly, "is that the Jews would have settled for Jeremy Bentham in 1939."

They were joined by Schuhorn. "What do you say about the grand scheme of things, Theo?" asked Sir Marcus.

"I think that James will turn out to be one of our better Archbishops."

"So he may, so he may. But what about the grand scheme of things?"

Granville came to the rescue. "I suppose in the very long run we will either evolve into pure intelligences or we'll be extinct, but that doesn't help us work out what to do now, Sir Marcus, although I am attracted to a less rigid and more flexible society. It leads to individual cruelty and greed on a scale larger than a twentieth century state could allow, but, then, it was those very states which brought about two massive world wars and somehow persuaded their young men that these states-in-themselves were worth dying for. On balance, I like Handel's generosity and Bach's creative scope rather more than I like Shostakovich's agonisings and Stravinsky's barbarism. In spite of what we say about individual freedom, we have wrung individualism out of our major societies. We don't like people who stand out. Everybody has to be the same apparently in the name of 'political correctness', but actually in the name of letting the state get on with it. We have got consumerism to satisfy the Juvenal requirement, and after that, it's flat, a suburbia of the mind. That is why I loved Perpetua so. If she had lived 300 years ago and said that people of different classes should mix, she would have found herself among friends in the Royal Society. If she had said that what counted was your individual choice, she would have found friends in philosophy and politics, and if she had said that we must re-engineer religion, she would have found friends even in the established Church. But what do we have now? The class divide is widening and deepening, and nobody is really bothered to do anything about it. Lip service is paid everywhere to choice, but it's usually about school places or hospital treatment, or cars, it's not about political ideas. I think we would agree that there isn't much that divides the three major parties, and, as for religion, it's got horribly stuck in its ways. There are a few weird suggestions about the impact of the internet and some interesting theology of brokenness but, it seems, the big questions are closed. That's why Perpetua would have been important, even if she hadn't bee an incarnational event."

"That's pessimistic, for you, Granville. I wonder," said Sir Marcus, hopefully, "whether science will help us out?"

"Well, if it's the Hawkins sort it won't," said Schuhorn. "The problem with science is that it's only really responsible for itself. I know you can't stop scientists finding things out. You can't put embryo technology back into its bottle, but these fellows should occasionally reduce themselves to demotic speech and explain what they're doing."

"Like churchmen," said Sir Marcus, coming close to sarcasm.

"Come," said Sir Granville, in an attempt to lift them. "Perpetuanism has much to offer us and, at the very least, it will stir us up just a little. I have thought for some time that we were about to lave the terrible period of the central state—from Pitt the Younger to Blair—and go back to a mercantile age and Perpetua can do nothing but help that turn of events."

Gerontius looked solemn. "I hope you are right. The use of state power to suppress civil strife is illusory—look at Yugoslavia—but can we face up to our own weaknesses, recognising that civilisation is skin deep?"

"Too big a risk," said Schuhorn. "The Church and the public schools and the governing classes have all come in for a lot of stick from 'politically correct' commentators, but you wouldn't want to live in a society with no church and ill educated, corrupt civil servants. Try the Russian oligarchs!"

Sir Granville looked affectionately at Sir Marcus who was, as usual looking rather disappointed with the discussion he had started. "Never mind, Sir Marcus," said Sir Granville, seeking to rally him, "your scientific grand scheme of things is a fascinating subject of enquiry which doesn't in the least threaten our theological grand scheme of things where we each think we are blessed to be God's children. You might want to arrange some seminars which aren't confrontational, but are more like dialogues. I could start on our social incapacity for conversation, but it's getting late and you don't want that now. Where are you going, Pluto—er Gerontius? I could do with having a few words."

"Come home and see Annie."

Sir Marcus walked slowly back to his little, paper strewn flat off the Grand Parade, Schuhorn walked across the river to his elegant, immaculately tidy apartment in the Archbishop's Palace and Granville and Gerontius prepared to walk North to his unobtrusive, but exquisite, terraced house by the canal.

On the way out they passed Gwyn. "Terribly sorry we didn't talk," said Gerontius, "but I got completely entangled with God and science."

"I'm fed up with God and science," said Gwyn, "particularly God."

'Yes, I'm sure you will be a—er substantial—footnote in twenty-first century history if, as I hear, your report is going to attribute a major communications breakdown to God. There's something incongruous about the great communicator—God, I mean—being accused of subverting the system but, then, I blame your explanation on that other great communicator, Mr Blair. You never should have fallen for it, Gwyn. It was just his joke."

"Llook where it's left me! Brookes says I'll be offered the Religious Broadcasting Council instead of a the big banking regulator job I want."

"Don't be so churlish, Gwyn, the Religious Broadcasting Council doesn't pay as much as DIM, but it's better than nothing. Anyway, would we really want banks to be regulated by people who know nothing about banking?"

Annie saw that they had not finished their business, so she brought a soda decanter and an ice bucket, and withdrew. "What is it?" asked Gerontius.

"I won't keep you long," said Granville, "But I thought you might like to know, in confidence, that Schuhorn, who spoke so warmly of Archbishop Hall, is briefing against him in Downing Street. It might not come to anything, but you might want to put in a word if you want to keep a relatively friendly Archbishop. You never know who you might get."

"You never do," said Gerontius. "Having had three in the space of two years, the best of whom was the first, options are running just a little thin. I mean, sending Crowther to Alchester was scraping the bottom of the barrel, wasn't it?"

"Theologically and morally, yes, but James left behind a bureaucratic Augean stable in Alchester and he's been busy presiding—or, rather not presiding—over another at Lambeth Palace which is why Schuhorn was put in there after the departure your efficient friend Clement."

"I'm a Perpetuan now you know. I can't go around lobbying and throwing my weight about."

"We'll just have to put up with it, then," said Granville, sighing somewhat theatrically.

Gerontius brought Annie into the room. "You could have stayed," he said. "Sir Granville and I have no confidences from you."

"I have no doubt, but if it's politics—Church or state—I prefer to go on with my studying."

"What are you studying?"

"Ethical economics. I'm about to plunge into the Grunge Park Partnership full time now that Gerry has some new responsibilities."

Sir Granville walked south in the Summer twilight and settled down with a final brandy and a new edition of *Tristram Shandy*, with Handel's first set of Concerti Grossi playing quietly in the background.

As soon as the door closed Annie was about to speak when Gerontius said, "you're pregnant."

"How did you know?"

"I learned to notice the characteristic facial glow in the maternity department, even on the faces of poor, ill-nourished girls. I noticed it this morning, but as you had a medical appointment for 'nothing much,' as you put it, I thought I would leave it until this evening."

They sat, companionably, listening to Keith Jarrett's *Koln Concert*.

◆　◆　◆

The next morning Annie went down to Grunge Park for the first time as Head of the Partnership. Nothing looked very different. Some of the burned out buildings had been patched, but most of them stood neglected and empty. The community centre was a useless eyesore. The Hollow was as depressing as any open space supposed to be a play area could be, except for the plot, just in front of the Centre, looked after by Marta, where Dexter, Miles, and Will were buried. Annie stopped and wondered whether her calling to mind of Will was a genuine pulse of emotion or a ritual gesture but, then, she thought, there is something important about ritual gestures. Poor Will. Even though he had never lived for journalism, he had died for it.

She visited Kish's mother. "How are things?"

"No different."

"What about Kish?"

"No different. He still has the gang and they still run the patch and do the deals. At least they don't use violence. Anyway, not routinely like they used to."

"So Perpetua made no difference?"

"I'm not saying that. Not even Perpetua herself could change these gangsters into choir boys but, for all their misdeeds, she is there for them. She shines like the moon which makes operating secretly in the dark more difficult, and occasionally they have to stop and look. They will never forget her and they know that they should reform in line with what she said, but not even the woman herself could change something so fundamental as this. It's all very well for commentators to say that they should stop dealing drugs and do something else, but what else? I know drugs harm people, even destroy their lives, but where's the regret? If you're born here your life gets destroyed anyway? Drugs are mindless. Grunge Park is mindless."

"This sounds desperate. I don't suppose there's much we can do if Perpetua couldn't do it."

"Just go on doing what she did. Run the risk of telling people they can do better. Look at Kelvin, selling his nice pictures to fancy ladies. He's got a small place in Excelsior Gardens. Everybody who can moves out of here." Kish came in. "So what are the Partnership going to do for us?"

"What do you want it to do?"

"Don't know."

"So how can we know?"

Kish came in. "Still trying to change the world? he said. "I thought your Perpetua would magic it all away."

"You weren't listening, Kish. God doesn't make social policy."

Annie called out to Calib and Ruthie as they walked past the window.

"We're just the same," said Calib. "Clever but captive. Now Ruthie's pregnant we don't know what to do. We need to do something. We thought of an abortion, but we want the baby. We need to protect it."

"As long as you know what you want," said Annie. "That's more than 90% of the problem solved. I can't work miracles. I won't load you with cliches. I can do two practical things. Firstly, Kish, I need you to promise, for the sake of the baby, that you and your people will not try to deal with Ruthie until her baby is two. Secondly, it's terribly anti-Perpetuan because it's a bit limiting, but I can use some of the Hypo lower consumption funding to give you enough vouchers to eat properly."

"It's true what they say about women having babies to get care," said Calib. "You wouldn't have offered vouchers if she wasn't pregnant."

"I would, but every time I have asked you before about what you want you have just said, 'the next fix'. Don't get aggressively victimised with me, Calib."

Ruthie tried to pull him away.

"Never mind," said Annie. "I can take it as long as you look after Ruthie and the baby. It was a form of protection, wasn't it?"

"Yes, sorry," said Calib, looking at Ruthie and then at Annie.

"And what about you, Kish?"

"All right."

As she was walking back towards her deliberately scruffy car, she almost bumped into a prettily dressed young woman. "Don't I know you?"

"I don't think so."

"Yes, I do. You were the girl who attracted the unpleasant attentions of our security guard at Hypo. Beth isn't it?"

"Yes. I should have thanked you."

"So what are you doing now? It looks to me as if you're model material."

"You're very clever. I went to college to do a multimedia course, but it didn't work out right. They didn't like my assignment."

"Why not?"

"It was about Perpetua and they said it was fanciful.."

"I would love to see it."

"I lost it somewhere, and, anyway, I'm a model now."

"Good luck."

Marta crossed the Hollow to where Brod was slumped on a bench.

"Soup," she said, like a pigeon.

Brod stirred. "Bloody cabbage water."

"No blood, just good, honest Polish cabbage!"

"Where'd you get that from?"

"Look."

"Can't see anything different to English cabbage."

"No. Saint Look make me bring soup."

"Does he now?"

"Well, Look and Perpetwa, really. She like to see you grumble. Think it very funny."

"So where is she now?"

"At grave with flowers."

"I wish I was in it."

"Eat your soup and then see what you wish."

"I wish," said Brod, "that I could get out of this. I am so lonely since I lost Max, but I am glad he got out. I wish I could remember the evening that Perpetua died when Max tried to help. I wish I could remember, but I can't and that's the worst thing of all. How can you live with the thought that you were within feet of God and were too pissed to notice, let alone do anything? It was bad enough before, but now I can't get this out of my head."

"You close to God now," said Marta. "You can't get any closer, really. All the time we are all close to God, but not realise it."

"Sophistry," said Brod.

"Don't know word, but God very close to all of us. Just look. Even in this scruffy English place where even the sky is scruffy, still, God is."

Perpetua came over to Brod and patted his head as if he was a toy bear.

"Growl, Mr Brod," she said.

Brod growled wearily, but even that paltry effort gained him praise.

"Now you see," said Marta, "God really is with us."

"Christ has no body now but yours," said Annie, sitting next to Brod.

◆　　◆　　◆

"I'm sorry about your uncle, Rory," said Annie.

"Yeh. Holy queer martyred. Funny."

"You don't improve, Rory."

"No he doesn't," said Olly.

"So what are you doing these days?"

"Bits and pieces," said Rory. "She knocked the stuffing out of us, really. We can't forget that night and what we did."

"Do you mean you've given up the porn project?"

"Not really," said Rory, "but there's no fun in it any more."

"It's what we did, though," said Olly. "We never should. It was pointless and stupid. It didn't get us anything except guilt. We've had fights about it, but needing to remind each other and working out who carries what blame keeps us together."

"Guilt won't help."

"How do you get out of that, then?" asked Rory.

"Working your way out. Loving your way out. Guilt will just get further in."

"We know the theory," said Olly.

"There's practice as well in the way your Uncle Joe lived and died."

"Don't talk about him."

"Another thing for you not to talk about. Like the porn. That's a way of not talking about the beauty of real sex because you're frightened of vulnerability."

They walked away together, not looking back.

◆　　◆　　◆

Brian was back in his old Grunge Park headquarters. "What's all this about?"

asked Annie.

"I didn't like central London, but after Jim's death I asked if we could re-locate. The central London office wasn't the right place for keeping in touch with the people. As you know, Max wanted to get us out of that overblown headquarters building."

"So this is all that's left, Brian. It doesn't look like much."

"It isn't. We've only got a few stills of Perpetua now. All the moving pictures have gone and all the scripts they had at the headquarters went in the fire. I wouldn't be surprised if the pictures don't go soon and we're left to carry on the idea. That's what she wanted, but it does rather blunt the incarnational impact. Jesus and Perpetua, being Gods, could have ensured much better record keeping instead of relying on Our Sister the Spirit, but they must have had their reasons. I suppose that the key thing is that we aren't supposed to have God on a plate or, really, it wouldn't be God at all. We spend our time now following people who are struggling to make Perpetua real for them and, actually, the pictures don't make all that much difference. I love to look at them, but I will just have to be resigned to their disappearance."

Suddenly his face changed. "No. It's just so cruel I can hardly bear it. I think I understand the purposes behind it and I try to be loyal about it, but it hurts so much. Every day when I come in I fear what will have disappeared in the night. Think about all that has gone. Her televised death, the rally on Palm Sunday, her television Christmas and Easter, all those healings and little sermons, the chil-dren's choir, little intimate moments with us when somebody took a few casual pictures, and then there's the theology work old Hawthorne did for us which went up in that fire with most of the other documents. It's just so hard. I thought the whole point of incarnation was that it made God concrete. Well audio and pictures are concrete and they're all going."

"I know," said Annie. "We're all upset."

"There was a rumour for a while that some journalist was writing a book but that's faded."

"Oh dear, yes."

"It's so hard. There's video of Dexter's death and a few pictures taken on mo-biles, but it isn't the same. Maybe that will go too."

"I wouldn't be surprised. I don't think of Will's death as often as I should and I'm not sure whether I would want to see the pictures, but I remember being down here when Perpetua was performing her great Sacrament of Response. It would have been so good to have that. It was her smile."

Brian knelt down and Annie followed him. She was getting used to prayer. After almost five minutes' silence, Brian said, "the Spirit is with us. We must be strong. Everything is for a purpose. We must hold on to the spirit of what she said which is beyond doubt. It's hard. It's so hard. But we must persevere."

They got up and went over to the computer desk. There was a message on the screen: "You can keep everything that is left. It's my kind of rainbow."

◆   ◆   ◆

"I thought I better tell you, Prime Minister, that the report into the disruptive incidents on Christmas Eve 2007 and Easter Sunday 2008 draws no firm, conventional conclusions. Common to the two sets of incidents is a person known as Perpetua who, some allege, exercised power over the networks in order to appear on them. Of course both incidents took place during Christian festivals, but we can draw no conclusions. Fellow regulators in the United States and Europe have reached the same inconclusive point."

"Thank you, Gwyn. What does it mean?"

"Well, Prime Minister, I don't like to say this, but it's my duty. I used to say similar things to Tony and he just smiled down the phone, so here goes. It just depends on the public mood where the ridicule falls. It's August, everybody's on holiday, the 'silly season' is in full swing, but the expenses scandal is being kept well stoked with daily revelations. I mean, people might say that DIM, the BBC, and regulators are stupid. Believe me, Prime Minister, I would be happy to take the flak if it could be directed at me. I've been at DIM for five years and could do with a change to some other, bigger regulator, probably something in finance as it's in a shambles and needs sorting out."

"I'll think about it, Gwyn. For God's sake get on with it."

"Or they might think the whole thing is a holy joke, which isn't likely, but we can pray."

"You're getting flippant. Just get on with it."

"Or, and this is the problem, and you knew it was coming, they might just, irrationally of course, blame it on the Government."

"I'll ..."

"Calm down, Prime Minister. Bad temper and bullying aren't going to help."

"I thought I could rely on people to sort these things out."

"Look, Prime Minster, you're religious, I'm not. You believe in the supernatural, I don't. Now if you believe in the supernatural, as you do, what's so odd about assigning some inexplicable events to supernatural causes?"

"Don't' be so f...ing stupid ..."

"Look, before we go on, stop swearing. It's unbecoming of a Christian."

"If we say that something we can't explain is caused by supernatural forces we will be ridiculed."

"Not by the millions who go to church, mosque, and synagogue, surely."

"You just don't get it, do you Gwyn. Now listen. There are millions of people who believe in God and go to church and other places of worship, but they don't expect God to interfere in human affairs except when their dog's sick."

"Very good, dog, human affairs. Very good."

"I'm serious, Gwyn. People like God to be very nicely kept in his church or his mosque except, as I said, when they want something personal fixed. They might pray for the victims of earthquakes, but they don't expect earthquakes to stop. They might pray for peace, but they don't expect to get it. They pray for the sick and don't think there's a high percentage chance but, what the heck, it might just work now and again. Praying gives you a good feeling, you know, that you've done the right thing for your sick aunt, but I say again that they don't want God roaming around the world interfering with broadcasting systems. We were just lucky that the first incident took place at midnight and that there were no big matches on Easter Sunday. They don't want God roaming about at random, so if we say he is, that will be even worse. There are plenty of people who like God because he justifies the exercise of all kinds of power. Right wing papers think God's great because they picture him in precisely the opposite way from gentle folk like old Hawthorne and that nice Perpetua girl we were talking about, but they wouldn't want him in a Government report."

"Quite, Prime Minster., but as I've signed the report with God in it, we're left with a rather tricky situation. If I delete God we'll have a limp report that says we don't know."

"Well at least that's more honest than the f...ing bankers who said they did know."

Gwyn let it pass.

"Is there a European line?"

"Not really. It wasn't Eurosat or anything like that. The Christmas incident was purely domestic, in fact it was confined to the BBC, so we've done our best to leave it there. Everyone likes watching the BBC, but most of you lot hate it; so that's fine. The second incident was global, and far too big to blame on anybody in particular. The sun spot level was pretty normal so, as I said, we're in a fix. It's God or nothing."

"Well, it will be just one more thing that Tony left in my in-tray, then. No wonder he smiled so broadly when he said goodbye. He claims he didn't see the banking crisis coming, but I suspect that he did. Ever since I took up my place here I've been dogged by his in-tray and terrible bad luck. And now a global communications freak incident. You know what, Gwyn, I'm glad you briefed me, but there's nothing I can do to get the press off my back so you better take the blame yourself and resign. It won't be perfect, but it's the best i can do."

"Very noble, Prime Minister. we know where the buck stops, then. but there's a price."

"There always is. What's yours?"

"Three months' gardening leave to get my handicap back under ten and the Vice Chairmanship of the Banking Regulation and Audit Commission, or whatever you're going to call it. I don't know anything about money, but I know when the king's got no clothes and, barring acts of God I can generally manage."

"It won't be easy to deliver, politically. It's a touchy area."

"Leave tomorrow's touchy area until tomorrow and deal with today's touchy area today. Do we have a deal?"

"Well, Gwyn, I am not sure that we do."

"Well just tell that nice man at the Bank of England what I propose and he can think it over."

"Do you mean you don't trust me?"

"Of course I trust you, but with so many acts of God about, you can't be too careful."

"I'll speak to him. ... On the other hand, I've got a much better idea. What about the Religious Broadcasting Council? After your report, you'll have some credibility there! That's it. No more bargaining.

"Deo Gratias, Prime Minister."

"What's that, Gwyn?"

"Oh, nothing. You're what they call a Protestant, aren't you? Just some Latin I picked up from Tony."

◆　◆　◆

Quintus Sneer, who, as an act of penitence, had stubbornly refused to change his name, and Chris Smoother were having problems working out a line on the DIM network breakdown report. "I don't ever remember somebody resigning before because of an act of God," said Chris. "I mean Gwyn Edwards is hardly one of God's representatives here on earth. He tried to abolish the religious broadcasting requirement until Lady Broadparks dug her heels in."

"He also tried to exclude the broadcasting of Christian material as a public benefit when the local radio regulations were being drafted. He had the cheek to say, I remember, that Islamic broadcasts might improve 'community cohesion', but that there was no social value in Christian broadcasting. Well, for me that's a perfect example of discrimination. My current test for Christianity's treatment in the public arena is to ask, 'would you do that to Islam?'"

"The thing is," said Quintus, "that this gives us a chance to tell our own story. DIM says that communications were disrupted by an unspecified act of God. We will specify by saying that Perpetua, the fourth person of the Godhead, performed her acts in order, in the first instance, to remind British people about the true meaning of incarnation and, in the second instance, to proclaim her own Godhead in the act of re-manifestation after her brutal death."

"I'm not sure anyone will print it."

"They will. It will be quite a novelty. It's a bit counter-intuitive, but so far my contacts have told me that it's a nice change from slagging off the Government. After all people know that the Government can't be held responsible for a global communications freak event, and the brighter ones think that Gwyn has resigned to take the flak and also to feather his own nest. They say he's been getting bored at DIM and worried that a new government might clip its wings. Anyway, I think we will be pleasantly surprised."

"I hope you're right."

"It's so nice," said Quintus, smiling and leaning back in his chair, "to be able to tell your own story, good and straight, without reference to anyone else. No slagging off, no settling scores, no snide remarks. I've done my fair share of bad things, Chris, I've a lot to make up for."

"Don't be too hard on yourself, Quintus. The thing that journalists get wrong most often—and they get plenty wrong—is the estimate of their own importance. In the end, did you really make any difference in the Little Phil Mac case? You spent a bit of money, you slagged off the foreign police, you oscillated between blaming everybody but the parents and then blaming the parents, you sold a few more papers, and she still hasn't been found. I'm not excusing you, but don't be too hard on yourself."

Quintus settled even further back in his chair. "I will sit here in as calm a state as I can muster for ten minutes and then I will write you a draft of the act of God story. "She had such a sense of humour; but I really wish I could have got her on page three."

Smoother smiled and let it pass.

◆　◆　◆

Janet Burns was at the end of her tether. She had tried to interest Schuhorn and Archbishop James—in that order—in the act of God story but all they wanted to do was to deny that such things happened.

"It's like trendy vicars," said Schuhorn. "People will just laugh at us."

They had been wrong. To her great annoyance the Perpetuans had cashed in, talking about Perpetua as being the God that performed the act. They said that normally human beings were expected to fix things that God had equipped them to fix, but God couldn't be circumscribed. Perhaps, they said, Christians had been a little bit too apt to make rules by which God should be and live."

"There's no recovery now," shouted Janet at Schuhorn. "We're lost forever."

"Don't be a drama queen," said Schuhorn, patronisingly, deliberately making things even worse. "The Church of England is, above all, an institution that believes in balance and moderation."

"I thought it believed in God."

"Ah yes, very clever. Of course it believes in God, but in a very English way. I gather you are a Scot. They do things very differently up there, you know. Lots of passion and enthusiasm and that sort of thing."

"If you go on much longer like that I will resign."

Schuhorn, who hadn't been told anything he didn't know was anxious to bring about that event, so he proceeded with provocative calm. "We don't go quite so far as to say that God is English—which is a sort of Holman Hunt extravagance—and we don't precisely believe that in ancient times Jesus walked upon England's mountains green. We certainly rule out the possibility that he encountered any dark satanic mills, but, still, we accept, as any national institution must, that our notion of God necessarily involves a cultural element."

"But there are many cultures in England. You can't have a single view of God."

"No indeed. We accept a variety of views, within limits, which we hardly need to commit to writing. Some people think that the Church of England is a serious religious organisation—you know, like the Vatican—but it isn't any such thing. We have had our stability disturbed lately by what I can only call Calvinistic and exhibitionistic influences—largely, but not surprisingly, from North America, but of Scottish origin!—and we must—er—pray that these subside. The Calvinism has led people to forget their manners. There is far too much feeling and far too little courtesy, as if what they believe justifies disturbing the peace. The exhibitionism, on the other hand, involves people talking about their homosexuality. I mean, there is nothing to be ashamed of—the Church of England has a long tradition of clerical homosexuality—but it's as vulgar to discuss it as to discuss how much money you've got."

Janet was stuffing papers into her briefcase.

"Not going, are you? We were having such an interesting discussion."

She ignored him and went on packing.

"I thought you wouldn't understand, but I did try to explain," he said, sounding aggrieved.

She left, closing the door with a sharp, but not violent, tug.

Schuhorn examined the remaining contents of her desk and disposed of them, meticulously saving what he could for future operations. James came in.

"I saw Janet walking out. She looked a bit grim."

"I think—although she has said nothing formal—that she intends to seek pastures new," said Schuhorn, with a straight face.

"That's a pity," said the Archbishop. "She wasn't the easiest of creatures, but we do need a period of stability; too many Archbishops in too short a time."

"Well, if it's any consolation to you, Archbishop, I have no intention of leaving for some time yet."

"Very good," said James, equally straight faced. "How did we get on over that DIM report? Very strange, don't you think?"

"I think we did extremely well to steer clear of it. The Perpetuans went in feet first, of course, but it won't do them any good, you know, all that posturing. We managed to avoid saying anything to anyone. That is why Janet and I were having a little chat."

"A little chat, was it?"

"Indeed it was. I am afraid it was a case of her impetuosity and my imperturbability. I had to insist on a calm and measured approach. If there is nothing constructive to say that will further one's cause, then it is best to say nothing. We have already seen peaks and troughs in the Perpetuan graph. I venture to say that there will be more and more troughs than peaks. We need simply keep our counsel and wait. They have some very strange coves, if I may say so, in Rome, but at least they understand the art of saying nothing."

James was not so sure, but he let it go at that. He disliked Schuhorn intensely but he needed him to steady the ship. As James disliked being in his company and as Schuhorn's greatest wish was to be left alone, the arrangement worked tolerably well. Schuhorn ran the Church of England and Archbishop James took care of the church of God.

Doris was not surprised when he told her his news. "Schuhorn is the cuckoo in the nest, James. Just be careful you're not the last bird to be tipped out."

"I'm safe, Doris. He's so hated on the Appointments Commission that he won't be able to influence the choice of my successor, if it survives that long, so we are both relatively content with the devils we know. Besides, I tried my best, but Janet was more of a trial than an asset."

"True enough. It's very awkward when people think they want something—like professional media expertise—and then find that they don't, when all they want is to please themselves."

"Quite, but I'm not in that camp. I want people who work with me rather than people who just happen to work where I work."

"Never mind, James. It's better that she's gone. I know you had to take this job, but you are right to concentrate as much as you are allowed on the spiritual dimension, leaving the administration to Schuhorn. The only major outstanding issue is how you manage the Grand Synod. Schuhorn's snooty bullying won't work and neither will your gentle persuasion. It's such a pity about Clement and the Dean. Mwanga's such a fine orator, but he's not all that good at working the tea room, so to speak. I think you should talk to Damian. You remember, he was an intern a couple of years ago and then he went to some ecumenical forum where they say his drafting and theological arm twisting were superb."

Lady Broadparks, who had been at School with Doris, dropped in for a drink after one of her regular *tête-à-têtes* with the Chief Constable.

"How are things out in the country?" asked James.

"Pretty good, really. We've lost a few to the Perpetuans, but that was to be expected. Most people are happy to stay where they are except the youth leaders who say that Perpetua has great pulling power. I've even heard her described by both sexes as sexy, and the Perpetuans seem to be picking up most of their new recruits from unchurched people which does us no harm at all."

"So, what should we be doing?"

"Oh James, the trouble with people like you is that you always feel that you need to be doing something. Thank goodness you've got Schuhorn to keep you damped down. He's an unpleasant man, as I'm sure we all agree, but that doesn't stop him being right. We need time to reflect and settle down. There's no real hurry. The Perpetuans are going off doctrine, so I've heard, and so we might find a modus vivendi. We don't need full merger or full schism, you know. That's the sort of thing that your Damian could do for you. The people in the pews don't want any more upheaval. They've got too many prayer books and hymn books, vicars are tied up in regulatory knots, and then there are all of those silly Synods. There are a few worries about people being forced to mix with the kind of people they don't really get on with, but, as you've said before James, we do have to make an effort to make contact with the poor."

James sipped his sherry, a little unhappily, but when Lady Broadparks left, he relaxed.

"Don't worry, James," said Doris. "You just stick to your beliefs, trust in God, and let the rest take care of itself."

◆   ◆   ◆

Varnish, Hawthorne, Cardinal Podric, and Damian met, courtesy of Gerontius, in a private dining room at Booth's, a restaurant in the vicinity of London Minster that specialised in boarding school food for grown-ups. Damian explained to the three that he had just been appointed as the Archbishop's Private Secretary and that he hoped they would not mind if he took a few notes of their informal discussion. The Cardinal, within weeks of his retirement, and the two former Archbishops were relaxed and ate their dinners with restrained relish, toasting Gerontius for his customary generosity and recognising his supreme tact in staying away. Once the dessert, cheese, and port had arrived, they turned to the matter in hand.

"As you know," said Varnish, "Archbishop James has received an approach from the Holy See, in the strictest confidence, to explore what kind of posture should be adopted to Perpetuanism which has begun to make its mark in France and the Benelux countries. His Holiness notes with regret that this sect—or perhaps heresy—has taken its strongest grip in England and so he looks to England to lead the counter attack. He believes—and I think Damian shares this belief— that we should try to reach an informal consensus before the Archbishop and the new Cardinal take the final steps towards a joint, public pronouncement."

Damian nodded his assent. "I think we might all agree that a little distance from 'the fray', so to speak, might be helpful. Where shall we start?"

"I think it might be best," said Hawthorne, "to clear the ground by reminding ourselves what the issues are which divide Christianity from Perpetuanism to see whether they are any greater than the issues which divide us from each other. We might then be able to settle the issue of sect or schism, heretic or separate faith."

Varnish, who was not sure why he was there, nodded, as did Podric. They could safely let Hawthorne get on with the theology as they were only needed for the politics.

"The key issue is the nature of the Godhead," said Hawthorne, "where we more or less agree. Remember, the Greek Orthodox Church does not agree with Rome over the filioque clause and some Anglicans find themselves closer to the Greeks than to Rome."

"There's no denying the difference between three and four," said Podric.

"True," said Hawthorne, "but we might make the case that Jesus and Perpetua are the same substance, but different persons."

"That sounds a little outlandish," said Podric.

"No more outlandish, I would suggest, than saying that Jesus had two natures in one person, or, for that matter, that an eternal Holy Spirit 'proceeded' from the Father, or from the Father and the Son, depending on your persuasion."

"But that's settled in the Creeds."

"Well, the first part has certainly been settled since the fifth century, but the procession of the Holy Spirit is still in dispute, as I noted a moment ago. I am sorry if I introduced a red herring. The point we need to hang onto is, perhaps, the one which I made about Jesus and Perpetua being of the same substance with each other, just as Jesus is of one substance with the Father."

"But that would make her God."

"Precisely."

"But she isn't."

Varnish helped himself to another largish port.

"The question is not whether you believe that she is or she isn't," said Hawthorne, carefully. "The question is under what conditions could she be. In other words, is there a way in which another incarnational event could take place within our understanding of God. It's not even a matter of whether it could take place. With God anything can take place, which is why the Trinitarian doctrine is somewhat puzzling, but the question revolves around our understanding. Can we find the language?"

"But if she isn't God, do we need to find the language?"

"If we want to be faithful to God, we need to test the boundaries of what we can say."

Podric, who had been trying hard to contain himself, could not help saying, "but there are propositions of which we should not speak."

"There," said Hawthorne, "is the difference between theology and doctrine. Let me, for argument's sake, grant the Pope's position on doctrine. That would still leave us all free to pray about, and study, theology."

Podric looked nettled, but Hawthorne was an old friend and this was, after all, familiar ground. "So," said Hawthorne, trying very hard to be gentle without losing momentum, "there is a discussion to be had about whether a claimed incarnational event could be contained within our framework of understanding about God. My conclusion is that it can which, in turn, means that we would have to consider Perpetuanism to be a Christian denomination, sect, or even, in your language, heresy. I think it would be hard to say that it is a different faith altogether, like Islam or Hinduism. Perpetuans, after all, believe everything that we fundamentally believe with the one addition which, I think, we could theologically, and even doctrinally, accommodate, that there is a possibility that Perpetua is of one substance with the Creator, Redeemer, and Sanctifier, as the Sustainer."

"There's potential there," said Varnish. "I 'presided', if that's the right word, over a sterile period when I tried to impose something I called 'orthodoxy', but I have come to see that I was misguided. I'm not much of a theologian, as you know, but I do believe that our understanding of God has to be dynamic. The question I ask myself, pragmatically, is what harm would it do to our faith to accommodate Perpetua?"

"Well it would be wrong," said Podric, flatly.

"But that isn't the question," said Varnish, uncharacteristically intense. "The question is what harm would it do, not whether we believe it to be true."

"You can't just pick up and put down doctrines on a utilitarian basis!"

"I truly think you can. Theology is active within us, Doctrine is usually a collective reaction to a challenge. So somebody says to me, 'what about four persons in the Godhead?' and I reply, 'well, traditionally there have been three, but that might be for very profound reasons which accorded with the times, or it might just be that the Greeks were wedded to the number three.'"

Podric looked aghast.

Hawthorne, though he welcomed the down-to-earth intervention from Varnish, thought he better take up the argument again in his less earthy style.

"If the core of what we exist to undertake as creatures is to worship and love God and each other, and if multiple incarnational events assist those ends, then there cannot be anything harmful in them."

"But the sacrifice of Jesus was supposed to be full and final."

"I think, as it came from God, it would have to be full. Nothing that comes from God, I suggest, can be anything other than full, but, equally, I find it hard to apply the word 'final' to anything that God does for us. After all, 'only begotten' could mean only begotten so far rather than only begotten for all time."

Podric looked flustered.

"I'm sorry," said Hawthorne, gently, "I'm probably taking this a little bit fast. I don't mean to be unkind."

Podric knew he didn't.

Damian said, "I think I might be able to help. Can we not say that the consideration of Perpetua as part of the Godhead is theologically conceivable—excuse the pun—but is doctrinally problematic and should therefore be subject to the usual Catholic process of reception which, I should remind us, involves 'bottom up' doctrinal reception, as exemplified in the Assumption and quite opposite from the erroneous view of Petrans that doctrine is proposed 'top down' for reception."

Even Podric found it hard to disagree. "As theology always precedes doctrine, we could go that far, at least in a private communication with The Holy See," he said, feeling his way.

"And, after that," said Hawthorne, "Sacramentality is relatively simple. There are wide disagreements in the Christian fold about the number and nature of the Sacraments. The only radical departure proposed by Perpetua is in the sacrament of Response and, although this is hardly the point, I must say that I rather like it."

"So do I," said Podric, surprising himself. "It says something about broken-ness which badly needs saying. Before the terrible trail of paedophile scandals ends—and please God it will—we are going to have to think a great deal more about brokenness in service."

Damian took a note without troubling the three men: Christianity should consider Sacramental innovation with a degree of openness; the Perpetuan con-ception of the Sacrament of Response speaks particularly to our times.

"So," said Varnish, pleased that the discussion might be taking a practical turn, "if we can theologically conceive of Perpetuanism being within the Chris-tian fold as ..."

"An extension of", said Damian, helpfully.

"... an extension of the Christian fold, thank you, then we must treat it in that way rather than as another faith, which means we can forge ecumenical part-nerships with it. But not those rather stilted affairs we have with the Methodists and, forgive me Cardinal, with the Roman Catholics. We want something true, and resonant and dynamic."

"I am not sure we could go that far," said Podric. "But I can say this, although you mustn't write it down, Damian, if the Anglican Communion can see its way to forging these partnerships on a firm theological and on an exploratory doc-trinal basis, I have no doubt that Rome would gratefully follow. In due time..."

Damian wrote: On the basis of the discussions on the divine personhood of Perpetua and the nature of Perpetuan Sacramentality, traditional Christianity should forge deep, loving and dynamic partnerships with Perpetuanism, par-ticularly for the study of the nature of Godhead and the gift of Sacrament. The Anglican Communion is well placed to play a leading role in the formation of such partnerships.

"But the Grand Synod threw that idea out," said Varnish.

"Yes," said Hawthorne, "but, blaming nobody, we rather rushed at it. I think that if Podric is prepared to say, publicly, that Rome is not against us, but is, let us say, naturally cautious, we might command enough Petran support to carry the day. Naturally, we don't expect any support from the Torans, but there are enough good, solid Medians to form a nucleus of support. As Varnish said, peo-ple don't want upheaval, they just want to get on with their spiritual cousins."

Varnish waved the bottle of port vaguely in Podric's direction as a matter of good form and then emptied the remains of its contents into his glass.

"Didn't you write something about Perpetua while you were an intern?" asked Hawthorne.

Damian blushed. "It was supposed to be a thesis, but it was no good. I thought I might revise it but I gave up on it."

"I would like to see it."

"You may, if I can ever find it. Perhaps when I move into a new flat."

Varnish emptied his glass.

◆   ◆   ◆

Gerontius and Max thought it had been money well spent. As they sat, companionably silent, on a bench overlooking the canal, Gerontius thought of the baby and the world into which it would be born. On balance he thought that the Perpetua Epiphany would make its chances slightly better. He was under no illusion that any religion had much effect on the basic human drives of lust and aggression, but since he had come into contact with Max and his friends he had seen innumerable acts of kindness, small and great, but, more significantly, he thought that the very positive emphasis on "negative love" was the best antidote to aggression.

Max never went a day without thinking of that terrible evening when he had been unworthy of his God. He would never fully achieve a sense of self-esteem which, he understood, was an essential part of growth, but the miracle was that his failure had led him to understand that any lack in his own self-estimation was nothing compared with God's love for him.

Their contemplation was disturbed by the approach of a jogger. "Good lord," said Max. "It's Driver, the man who forced through the deal which turned me out of the bank."

The man stopped. "Max. It's you! I'm so glad to see you—no, don't interrupt or I'll completely lose heart—because I knew I would never have the courage to find you deliberately, but I've prayed—really prayed—every day that I'd come across you to say sorry. I have to take all the responsibility. It was nothing you did. It was ambition, unadulterated ambition, on my part. Because I've kept tabs on you recently, I know you won't gloat, but it did me no good in the end. I rose in the new corporation until I lost all objectivity. I allowed our dealers to go beyond all sensible limits. Then, you know what happened. I know myself better now and I'm truly sorry."

"What are you doing now, Guy? You don't look too bad for a crash victim."

"I set up a small business, just like I always wanted to do before my parents pushed me into banking. I'm a graphic designer at the artier end of the market."

"All right," said Max. "I've half forgiven you, but I will forgive you completely if you design a brilliantly elegant, but simple, logo for a movement that believes that there are four 'persons' in the Godhead."

"Done," said Guy, holding out his hand.

"Don't I kow you," asked Guy, looking at Gerontius.

"I thought you would never ask. I—you don't mind Max knowing, do you?—talked you out of throwing yourself into the river," he said, turning to Max. "It was part of our initiative to get city types to do some voluntary work in deprived areas within two miles of their offices. I was out one night talking to a couple of homeless people when I saw him behaving strangely. I don't need to say any more."

Guy looked temporarily put out but soon regained his poise. "Why should I feel upset," he said, "when I would have been dead but for you?"

"We're all dead but for each other," said Max. "Here's my card when you have a prototype."

Guy, familiar with Max's ways, waved at the pair and ran on.

There was plenty to talk about, but the two men sat quietly for a while. Max was not sentimental enough to be grateful for Guy's selfishness, but was grateful for where he was. There were all kinds of speculative strands which ran something like: "If Guy hadn't shafted me I would never have encountered Perpetua and never have met Marta," but he thought these were rather pointless.

"You never know what a difference you can make," thought Gerontius. "There were doubtless many factors which persuaded Guy not to jump, but I was one of them." And, as if embarrassed by his act of caring, he settled back into the Perpetuan love which is silence.

◆　◆　◆

Stacey and Bill sat in loving silence on the steps of Saint Simple's, watching the departure of the last pilgrims of the day.

"It's strange," said Stacey. "I was brought up to condemn shrines and such like, but I'm getting used to the new set-up."

"There isn't much point in incarnation if there's nothing earthly to remember it by. God is difficult enough without depriving people of contact with the divine where it's available."

"But what about the loss of all the films and documents?"

"I'm terribly sad about the films, but I am not so worried about documents containing doctrine. It's not fashionable to say this, but I think that it is vitally important that our emotions are engaged in worship and in our love of God. I want people to share my passion for and my passion with God. We have become prisoners of the intellectual, added to which the English are somewhat reticent. We don't really like charismatic services, but that is, I think, why we find our relationships with God so difficult. We cut a piece of ourselves off from the relationship. It's as if I only loved you because, objectively speaking, from the point of view of a painter or photographer, you look very beautiful, and although that is important, it's hardly the point."

She stayed silent, knowing he had more to say and wanting to hear it. Some people might have thought that she was something of the "little wife", but she had greater inner strength, part of which lay in knowing when to say nothing and when to say something that counted.

"In the past two years, since she died, we have gone through all kinds of crises, but most of them have been of humanity's making—crises about perception, doctrine, money—but we haven't had a crisis of love and that is because we haven't held back. What gives me so much joy is seeming apparently phlegmatic people given new life through Perpetua and then celebrating it. Who would have thought, for instance, that Max had been a banker or Gerontius—as we must learn to call him—a multi-millionaire? Look at the pilgrims who come here in all conditions of hope and fear. Look how they leave."

"That is what I have learned, Bill, watching those people. Martin Luther was either wrong—or misunderstood—when he denounced works as necessary for salvation. I understand now how you can't really be involved with God unless you are involved with all of God's children, but Perpetua has helped me to listen more and counsel less."

Bill got up to check that everybody had left before closing the gate. Stacey followed him and, without a word, they went into the shrine to pray.

She looked at all the presents that had been left for the beautiful young woman who had died a terrible death: the soft toys, cheap jewellery, flowers, candles, banners, and even t-shirts. She couldn't help rising from her knees to re-arrange the gifts in a more pleasing array. What had been given in a random state could be made into a reverential whole, her own Sacrament of Response, taking that which is broken and vulnerable in people and knitting it into worship.

◆　◆　◆

The ecumenical report on the relationship between the Anglican Communion and the Perpetuans was greeted warmly by the Grand Synod. James made a more than presentable speech, crafted by Schuhorn, elaborated by Hawthorne, re-crafted by Schuhorn, and then simplified by Damian. Cardinal Podric sat reassuringly in the gallery to receive a warm retirement tribute and to listen gravely to the debate. The Petrans and Medians formed a solid phalanx against the more strident Torans, and, as such ecumenical documents were remitted to venerable bodies rather than voted upon, nobody was embarrassed.

James felt that he had finally come home after a long period of indecision. He saw doctrinal difficulties ahead, but as an experienced professional churchman he saw such difficulties as a not unwelcome part of his remit. He had spent many happy days on strange campuses hammering out ecumenical statements and, compared with some, such as the issue of Anglican Orders, this one would be relatively pleasant. He knew that he had been lukewarm to Perpetuanism for a while, but he consoled himself with the thought that he had never been openly hostile. There had bee the orthodoxy drive in Alchester, but it had hardly been successful and had hardly received any attention. Brian Sedge, he knew, would say nothing that might hurt. As he gathered up his papers, he saw Doris standing between Podric and Damian.

"You want that young man on your staff," she said. "He will go a long way. He was telling me some fascinating stories about Perpetua and Hawthorne. Quite a mimic. He says he has some papers about her."

"I know. He says he can't find them."

"Not for a man, perhaps, not even for a brace of Archbishops, but for a lady."

"Let us hope so."

Meanwhile the Grand Synod embarked on yet another of its seemingly interminable debates on women bishops.

◆   ◆   ◆

Crowther sat in the Dean's "comfy corner" with an ample gin and tonic in his hand. The Dean sat opposite with a white wine spritzer.

"So that's official," said the Dean. "We've always got on pretty well with the Palace and this only confirms the line we've taken. I would say, quoting from the document, that we already have a 'deep, loving and dynamic partnership' here between Christians and Perpetuans. I admit that it is somewhat irregular that I should continue to hold the office of Dean and occupy the Deanery when I am a known Perpetuan, but the experiment suited James when we shared our Partnership here and it seems that it suits him as Primate. I no longer draw a salary from the Church, but I am naturally open to suggestions about my residence."

Crowther was content to leave things as they were. He knew and valued the Dean's discretion. A gossiping Dean or, worse, a Dean with a gossiping wife, might have done him grave damage. The episode with Marianne Gowers was over, but he could not honestly promise himself, in spite of his increased attention to private prayer, that there would not be another. He took a strong pull on his drink noting with appreciation that the Dean could tell his bitters from his lemons. This was another advantage not to be overlooked. Wholesome male companionship might serve to keep him out of harm's way. Still, he thought he better make a mild show of impartiality. "I don't suppose the Chapter has anything to say on the subject?"

"I would be happy for you to raise the matter in my absence. I would not want to be conflicted."

Crowther bristled. "Damn nonsense, all this stuff about conflicts of interest. You can't regulate for honesty, integrity, trust, and courage."

"Thank you, but I wouldn't want them to be embarrassed if they wanted to make a change."

"I will see to it, then."

The Bishop, warmly ginned, was walking across the close when he saw a very pretty young woman dressed, more was the pity, in a severe business suit. "Good evening," said Crowther, performing the vocal equivalent of flourishing his hat.

"Good evening, Bishop," said the lady.

"I don't think I've seen you in the close before."

"You certainly haven't, as this is the first time I've ever been in it. How beautiful it looks in the evening sun. Isn't late July glorious?"

"It is indeed," said Crowther. "But," he thought, "not as glorious as you."

"I hope to become very familiar with these beautiful buildings," said the woman. "I would certainly not want to advance my case in an unethical way by discussing it with you on a one-to-one, informal basis, but I do hope that I will get a good hearing tomorrow."

Crowther started. "Ah! You are one of the two candidates on the final short list for Diocesan Secretary? So, as the other candidate is a man, you must be Claire."

"Yes."

"Well I suppose it would be a little irregular for us to be seen together in the Close on the evening before your interview. I mean, what's-his-name—Augustus—might object, but nobody could object to a presentable and modestly dressed young lady accompanying the Bishop into Compline. Now we've got a comfortable alibi we can talk more freely. What made you apply to work in such a sleepy backwater?"

"I hope I am not behaving incorrectly," said Claire. "I saw the writing on the wall in the public sector and, to be frank, wanted to get out before the real squeeze on pay and employment."

"That's not at all what you're supposed to say, so this is a good chance to rehearse. You're supposed to say nothing about money and mortgages. You're only supposed to tell us how much you want to do the job and how committed you are to making God's mission in the world easier to accomplish."

She blushed. "Well, there is that, too. One reason I decided to apply was that I became very interested in religion when I was assigned to look after—well, to keep a watch on, actually—Perpetua. I thought that I might try ecclesiastical administration to see whether it is as fascinating as I suspect it is."

"You knew Perpetua very well, then?"

She blushed again. "Well, actually, I knew her better perhaps than I should. I was going to say better than she knew, but that's not true. She knew I was watching her and so she fed me material in the hope that I would spread it for her."

"And I suppose you wrote reports?"

"I did write short reports and, then, when I knew that I was going to resign I wrote a round-up report."

"What happened to it?"

"I don't know."

"Did you keep a copy."

"No, that would have ben highly irregular."

"And we don't want anything irregular in administration. Dear me, no."

In spite of his many good points, Augustus failed to secure the job of his dreams. The panel were split over the relative merits of his ecclesiastical knowledge and Claire's distinguished administrative record, but, as the Bishop had the casting vote, Augustus never stood a chance.

On Saturday morning the Bishop saw Claire walking through town in black cycling shorts and a baby pink halter top and put himself on guard against temptation.

The Dean, feeling just a little lonely and disappointed at the thought of returning to his gloomy Deanery, also saw the shorts and top and firmly resolved, as an act both of kindness and duty, to guard the Bishop from temptation.

◆   ◆   ◆

Castlegate and Aleford were sitting in Church House waiting for the Bishop to arrive when a message came that he was detained elsewhere.

"I wouldn't want to know where or with whom," said Bruce.

"You don't usually have the choice," said Hilary. "He doesn't exactly cover his tracks."

"It's a scandal," said Bruce, winding himself up.

"There are so many scandals if you're a Toran," said Hilary. "It must be a devil of a problem to know where to begin and end."

"Well, it's a shame we have to begin with him and you."

"That's what I mean. There are scandals from the state of the poor to the state of our finances and all you can think about are supposed private sins."

"I thought you were a man of principle. It seems to me that you're going soft."

"Yes, Bruce, I'm going soft. Precisely that. I've tried to be hard in my own defence and in defence of the things I stand for and all that it does is make me angry, not a good starting place for a Christian, let alone a bishop. I'm going to try some of that Perpetuan love."

"Never!"

"We've all got our weaknesses and the more we concentrate on our own and the less on others, the better. If we combine Perpetuan love with the Church's love of process we might be able to make progress without squabbling."

"Never!"

◆   ◆   ◆

Meg and Kylie were sharing a cup of coffee before her departure for London.

"Do you have to go?" asked Meg, knowing the answer, but not knowing how else to keep the conversation going until it was time for farewells.

"I really do want to go, I'm not just saying it. I have enjoyed my time here enormously, but I've been visiting for more than two years now and I am looking forward to crossing the Channel. Just think, when I first joined Perpetua I didn't think I could really speak English properly and now I've finished my French classes with a respectable pass. Stacey can come back to England full time to help Bill with the Shrine, and, anyway, you've got Clement. He was happy to stay where he was for a while, but he was really grateful when Gerontius agreed to take on the top administrative post. He says he's a decent administrator, but he really wants to be a theologian. He wants, he says, to exploit the Perpetua phenomenon to work out ways of helping us all get closer to God."

"I know, we are very lucky to have him, but you are the connection with the real Perpetua."

"I know, but you would be surprised how quickly it all fades, particularly when there's so little documentation left. I suppose she must have wanted it that way, but it's sad. I suppose she warned us to work hard at being close to God through her, like developing a muscle, but a bit of instruction manual would have helped. Still, I mustn't complain. Whoever said it was going to be easy to be a follower?"

Meg didn't know whether to commiserate or to try to be encouraging, so she confined herself to pouring the last of the coffee into Kylie's cup.

"But Meg, at least you have the memory of your mother's extra months. I still feel embarrassed when I remember it. So many atheists go on about miracles when people inside religions don't rate them, really, but I can't get away from it. Your mother wasn't the only one. I don't know how doing these strange acts fits into the whole picture but Clement says that these are like little boosters and they will fade away as the Spirit is manifested in more regular sorts of ways."

Unable to sustain any more conversation, Meg looked meaningfully at her watch and Kylie read the signal and rose to go.

"I want to thank you, Meg. I know we will meet again. You have ben very kind and I'd only say it to you privately, but you've been the kindest even though I know you're just about the poorest person in the Living Water group. I have felt comfortable here, not over-pressed and happy to share what little you have. I often feel that the poor would be much happier if people would be willing to share what little they have. It's not being able to give that damages self-esteem."

Meg blushed. "Well, I'm lucky. I like giving and there are people around me who understand my need and don't press their economic superiority. Well, no matter how little we have, we can always pray for each other."

"Pray for me, Meg. I'll need it. I'm not exactly frightened of going to France and other places, but it's even more daunting than the first day I came here, the day after Perpetua's re-manifestation."

"I remember. I say that things will never be the same again, but I'm not sure of the extent to which they will really change. I mean we've had plenty of discussions in Living Water about Sacramentality, liturgy, and doctrine, but it looks to me as if things will settle down. That would be a pity and a sadness."

"We will end on an optimistic note. Our Sister the Spirit will be with us."

She wheeled her small suitcase up the road until she reached a turning. "Ah,

Keith, I hoped you would be there with your motor bike. That's how we first encountered each other, but things are so different now."

"Well, in the grand scheme of things I don't suppose they are, but when we first met I could never have imagined becoming a house group leader, and elected at that."

"Nothing less than you deserve. You have been very brave to speak truth to brain, so to speak. I am sure you must have found it daunting in the early days, but you didn't give up."

"It was Clement, the cleverest of the lot who made me comfortable. I suppose you have to be clever to ask as many questions as he does and to know how to pitch them to somebody's level. We were brought up to believe that asking questions was a sign of weakness, but I have learned that it's a sign of strength. After all, clever people always seem to be asking each other questions, and asking each other favours whereas dull people, like I once was, think that what counts is self-sufficiency. Clement would ask about football, how the motor bike worked, what beer they keep at the Bear, and how the economics of a micro brewery work. Then, gradually, you would find yourself talking about what worries and frightens you. One day I found myself talking about dreams. Another day about the time I almost killed someone in a stupid fight. Then, one day, he just said, we're having a special discussion between the two spin-offs from Living Water about addiction and its possible links to poverty and I think you are the best person to lead it. I've only one piece of advice, he said, as we are supposed to keep advice to the minimum; don't let people get sentimental or talk about what they don't know about. That's what turned out to be fascinating because many of the really smart people didn't know anything about addiction, but there was one whose daughter has actually got trapped, in spite of her university education, so that made it more difficult to generalise. The thing they found most difficult to get hold of was that there are worse things than addiction, like what causes it."

Kylie had never heard him talk for so long without a break. There were plenty of trains.

"Then there was the service at the church with Father—er Guide—Mark. Instead of it being just the usual people who go there, like it was when we first went up there, remember, when you first came and ..."

"... Let's not go into that, Gordon."

"Well, when we went there this time you could see that the house groups had made such a difference. Mark still likes to have church every Sunday, in spite of the house groups, but you could see about forty people from the social housing who are now in six different house groups. That's just amazing. He allowed 'Lippy' to read from the Bible, even though she hasn't been to one of those test sessions. Afterwards the regulars didn't all huddle into groups. I mean, you couldn't blame them for wanting to be with their friends, but Helen is quite fierce about getting people to mix. I suppose we might have clustered in our own house groups, but she wouldn't allow that either."

Kylie smiled. There was a certain amount of Perpetuan influence in the social changes in the village, but she knew that Helen would have been as she was in any environment.

Keith noticed the silence. "I see your suitcase. I suppose you're leaving now."

"Sadly, yes."

"All right. There's nothing I can do to stop you. At one time I would have grumbled, but now I know there must be a good reason. I'll tie your little case to the back and take you on my bike."

◆　◆　◆

Violet and Ronald were dressing the church for the Harvest festival. "They come round quicker every year," said Ronald, honouring a dialogue that had gone on for more than 30 years without variation.

"But," said Violet, doing the same honour, "you will see many more yet."

"I don't know that I will. We never know when the Lord will call us and so we must be ready."

"Well, you're always ready."

"Not that we do what we do by way of insurance. I know Jesus told us to watch and pray, but we ought to be as good as we can for it's own sake—My God I Love Thee not because—or for the sake of Jesus not for our own sake. Jesus will see us right."

"Yes. Jesus and Perpetua," said Violet in a shock variant that brought them both up sharp. Ever since its beginning, they had supported Perpetuanism for its liberal values but it had hardly changed their conversational ritual, as if it had not quite got into their blood. Clearly now it had.

"Well," said Ronald, "this is one part of the Church's traditions that does not seem to have been affected by all the changes."

"True, but when you think about it, there haven't been all that many changes," said Violet. "At first I thought that there would be many and that we might be forced into yet another of those inner conflicts between what we like and what we know is right."

"I know. Much more than me you feel the pain of changes in liturgy. You once described it to me as candles going out in your heart."

"We plough the fields and scatter," said Violet, in an attempt to get things back onto a regular footing.

"The good seed on the land," said Ronald, trying to play the game, but it somehow did not quite work.

They stood at the top of the chancel steps, looking over the nave altar, down the aisle. Violet surveyed the arrangements of dried grasses and small branches on the pew ends while Ronald concentrated on the symmetry of the pyramid of canned food he had built. Then, as if choreographed, they moved from the centre, Ronald going round the altar on the North Side, Violet on the South. They walked up the aisle together until they reached the back pew and then turned together to look at the fresh produce in the crib bracket below the altar table. They raised their eyes to the flower arrangement on the old high altar and then began to walk down the aisle. Without knowing it, Ronald took Violet's hand. In spite of their inseparability over so many years they had never touched except for the occasional decorous dance at a Parish evening. Violet did not pull her hand away as they went on walking. He became conscious of his right hand in her ringless left but he did not let go as they went on walking.

They stopped in front of the altar and let their hands swing apart as they turned to face each other. "We're the wrong way round," said Ronald. "The bride is always on the North side."

"I wonder why?"

"I don't know. It's probably got something to do with my sword hand."

She looked straight into his eyes, something she had not done since that one time they had got close to a serious discussion of courtship and marriage. He looked unflinchingly back. It was nothing to do with tradition or gender stereotyping that made them both know that Ronald must speak first. It had been he, abandoned by the young woman he loved, who had closed his heart to her all those years ago when he knew that she would gladly have taken him to her, grief and all. She had not wanted a high romance. Her only ambition was to care for him and comfort him until, as she knew he would, he came to love her.

"It is very hard," he said at last, "to say what I must without expressing a deep regret which is not a fitting, but perhaps necessary, prologue to joy. I cannot pretend for a moment that had I asked for your hand some 30 years ago that that would have afforded you a life of bliss, but I am now deeply sorry that I did not give what I could when I knew how badly you wanted my love. I have been selfish and cruel."

"There may be a time when we need to talk this way, to understand each other better and put our different kinds of guilt to rest, Ronald, but not now. There is little I can and should say in reply. Yes, I did love you and longed to comfort you, but you chose a different way and I had to respect that. After all, women and men, by and large, think of love very differently. For you, it had to be pure, perfect, high minded. For me, it had to be practical and necessary. I wanted to comfort you and would have happily foregone the high minded, high blown love that men dream of to give cover to their basic, sexual need."

"I know that now, and perhaps now that we are, in a sense, less woman and man than young people are, and more like people who want to love and be loved in a quiet sort of way, we will be able to understand and think that it were better to do what we are doing now than never to have said what we are saying."

Their looks softened and their bodies relaxed. He walked two paces to a pew end, picked a dry flower from a spray. She bowed slightly so that he could more easily fix it in her undyed, silver-grey hair and as she raised her head he kissed her, not quite chastely on the cheek. She would have been less than human if she had not thought, for just a split second, what that kiss would have been like had it been bestowed all those years ago, but it was an idle thought. She wondered how she had managed for so long to appear cheerful. All those nights alone, meals for one, domestic laughter, and sorrow unshared had mounted up. She had never kept the major issues from Ronald, but there had been so many small joys and sorrows that had gone unshared. She wondered where they would live and whether they would disturb each other's sleep with tossing and turning, and bony elbows.

He could not help, for the same split second, regretting his foolishness in not seeing what they had needed and taking the initiative. Even in the 1970s women of their sort in their mid-thirties did not make the first move. He should have seen her need and his duty. He had only hidden one great secret from her and that was his feeling of uselessness. He had worked, played golf, and served tirelessly in the church, but every time he closed his door he wondered what life was for. He knew that it was supposed to be for God and that had always been his public answer. Not even Violet, he believed and hoped, had seen through the pretence.

As they walked back up the aisle Ronald noticed that a stack of cereal boxes needed straightening. As he adjusted the boxes he noticed a picture of a girl in a bikini and covered it with another box too quickly and awkwardly. "Don't be hard on yourself, Ronald," said Violet, who had seen his distress. "Perhaps the biggest single obstacle to our relationship all those years ago was the muddle in our church over the body beautiful. It tolerates all kinds of silliness and even sauciness as part of the nuptial rituals, but it really is not sure whether it approves of physical relationships. There's a lot of theology against dualism, but a lot of Christian tradition in its favour. I don't suppose we will be tearing each other's clothes off but, still, there's a lot of lost time to be made up. She put her arm round his waist as he finished straightening the boxes.

There was the sound of the first cohort of school children in the porch coming to the Harvest Festival Service. Her first instinct was to remove her arm, but she left it there. The Festival, after all, was about fertility. Indeed, the three great Anglican festivals of Christmas, Easter, and Harvest were all, in their different ways, about fertility. They were also about love and caring and it was pointless to regret their respective childlessness. They would just have to make up for it by loving others and each other even more intensely.

"Accept the gifts we offer," said Violet, invoking the final words of their decades long ritual, "For all thy love imparts."

"And, what thou most desirest, our humble, thankful hearts," replied Ronald. The words had never felt this way before.

The children came into church with additional gifts which Violet arranged as they took their places. These last gifts consisted of toys and games which other children, less well off than themselves, might like, to go along with the gifts of food. Mark was moved by their empathy and enthusiasm. They were always good when it came to collecting for Africa, but then it was largely acting as channels for parental money. He knew these children individually and he knew that some of the gifts that they had brought represented genuine sacrifice.

Fortunately, there were still pictures of Perpetua, including a few taken in schools and a series taken at a computer chip factory. Except for introducing the figure of Perpetua to the crib, this was the first time he had introduced her at a school service and she went down a storm, dressed in her blue jeans and halter top with her hair braided. Mark preached a short sermon on the journey of a can of pineapple chunks from Antigua to the local supermarket, and they sang a new song thanking God for their food and clothes, listing different activities in the supply chain. A few traditionalist parents had been worried, at first, by the Perpetuan development, but it had so improved the children's attitude to Sunday School and RE that the complaints had been short lived.

"In times of change," said Marie to the choir on Friday evening, "some things that we are used to have to be adjusted, so this weekend we have to prepare for two services. The Harvest Eucharist has a new element and some new music, but the Harvest Choral Evensong will be exactly the same except for the blessing which does not affect us. Because we are singing the Lloyd Hereford service Canticles it is not possible to alter the old triune doxology to the new fourfold doxology."

Nigel shifted with just a flicker of discomfort, Scott wriggled nervously on the organ bench, but apart from that Marie's remarks were greeted with contented silence.

The new section of the Harvest Eucharist was a variant of the Sacrament of Response in which members of the congregation would make offerings of useful goods and services to complement the offerings of food. Mark had said that although Walmbury was still set among fields, only a handful of the congregation had anything to do with farming and there ought to be ways to thank God and make offerings to the less well off that were not confined to food. This Eucharist was also the finale of the newly constituted Planet Stewardship observance for September.

The new "Harvest" hymn, already sung by the children, was easy enough and was no worse than many other late twentieth century effort and the choir soon moved on to more traditional material.

Afterwards, at dinner, the conversation did not stay on religious reform for very long. Marie's plans had hardly been changed at all and she thought that the new element in the Harvest Festival made it feel more contemporary. She liked the thought that poor children would receive games as well as a square meal. Scott was not so sure, but playing one new "happy clappy" hymn wasn't too bad. Helen said that the school and the Parish both seemed to welcome the change and, anyway, even without Perpetua it would have been appropriate at the beginning of the twenty-first century to institute a Planetary Stewardship month and September leading up to Harvest seemed right as a way of breaking up the green Sundays. Clement said that looking at creation was a helpful way of remembering our Creator God who was often eclipsed by Jesus. Nigel said that there were all those hymns at the back of the book, written in the twentieth century, about industry and that sort of thing, but they didn't sound like real hymns. Meg said a few words about Kylie's departure and people agreed that it was sad, but would not say much in case it hurt Clement. When Meg mentioned Iris's cure it was as if she was re-telling something that had happened in a doctor's surgery.

Sitting quietly, Clement marvelled at how humanity absorbs change and gets on with living. Superficially humanity seems to be conservative, but it is profoundly unpredictable. You never know what it will accept or fight. It looked, in the long run, as if some elements of the Church of England would more easily accept a Fourth Person of the Godhead—and a woman at that!—than the Consecration of women bishops. Likewise, it was likely that in some parts of the world there would be celebrations for the witness of a gay martyr, but in other parts of the world there would continue to be stiff opposition to gay clergy. He tried to map whether this had something to do with Westernisation, but concluded that it did not. True, many African Christians were suspicious of women clergy and opposed gay clergy, but their views were shared by some of the most Westernised people in the world, in the United States. Conversely, some forms of moral and religious liberalism coincided with Asian perspectives. He wondered how important it was to be highly deliberative about religion. Did it really matter what the origin was, what the metaphors showed, what the ritual did or what the doctrine posited? Wasn't it inevitable that religion would change as science changed, that it should change as science changed? Wasn't the problem that religion had got stuck on a couple of important occasions, causing destructive upheaval? How would it have been if the fifteenth century Papacy had kept its eye on intellectual developments from the Renaissance combined with the development of printing rather than falling into schism and then self-indulgence? How would it have been if Continental Christianity had been more concerned with understanding the 'enlightenment' than holding onto its ancient regime privileges or if English speaking Christians had understood the consequences of Darwinism instead of fighting the theory? "And," he thought, "I am ignorant of quantum physics and theories of the multi-universe or earth's possibility depending on fine tuning. Somehow we really must get away from our primitive obsessions with gender roles, procreation, and what used to be called 'class'. In 50 years there probably won't be gender roles. What will we do without them? Then there's a poor appreciation of philosophy linked with scientific ignorance. If you have a leading clerical opinion former who is ignorant of science, poor at philosophy, and indifferent to beauty, what do you get?"

Helen looked at Clement in her special way to bring him out of his reverie. "We were saying," she said, "that it will not be long before we have to think of Christmas Carols. Marie says that there are two or three which refer to Perpetua."

"Hundreds are written each year," said Scott, "but only a very small number ever make it into the repertoire. I mean, why should Tavener's Lamb lovely though it is, be classed as a Christmas carol? It's one area, though, where I'm not conservative. I think it's all well and good for people in the pub to sing the same ones each year, but in church we should try to find new perspectives. If Mark puts Perpetua into the crib we can't just ignore her."

"She does look odd in jeans amongst the Bethlehem rustics," said Nigel.

"Well I suppose the kings looked odd at one time," said Helen.

Talk drifted towards Christmas, the likelihood of a down turn in spending, and the "phoney war" over inevitable public spending cuts. Clement deliberately forced himself back into introspection to ensure that he was not tempted to intervene in a political discussion. There was nothing he loved more than a good argument, but he knew he must stick to Perpetuan principles and not become partisan. It was one of his most difficult pastoral challenges. "But we probably need to adjust it," he thought. "Christians tend to establish the pastoral paradigm round a power relationship of shepherd to lamb. You get taught how to deal with children, the elderly, the suffering, the confused, and the inadequate, but you never learn how to help the confident and the equal, or even the proud and over bearing. 'Pastoral care' is a euphemism for 'care of the less powerful.'"

Then he sat quietly, concentrating on the red wine and French cheese while Nigel and Scott got into a futile argument about car taxation while Meg, Marie, and Helen went over Kylie's departure.

"I wonder what change in perception about the Godhead—loosely, doctrine—would cause a stir," thought Clement, but there was nothing he could think of.

The following morning, Clement and Helen sat opposite each other at the breakfast table, listening to CD Review on Radio 3 and respectively reading *Church & State* and *The Stylus* before swapping over their second cup of coffee.

"Are we to have a Perptuan weekly paper?" asked Helen.

"I don't know. Max and Gerontius have been thinking about it, but they seem to think it's a superficial response to a communications problem and that it will inevitably talk to an elite about an elite, like the papers we read. Gerontius says, from a management perspective, we need to solve the problem of the relative height and width of the pyramid, so he doesn't want a newspaper for the elite. Christianity, he argues, has got too many people at the top—bishops and so on—and not enough people in the middle—clergy—and definitely not enough people at the bottom—us. He says that if there were fewer at the top or if those at the top conferred their powers on more in the middle, then they, in turn, could confer some of their powers on another layer at a lower level still and that ultimately this would broaden the base at the very bottom, which is your ultimate objective. So, he says, using Christian terminology, you might want six Primates in England, as many Bishops as there are Deaneries and clergy at the parish level whose main job would be evangelisation. That is how we are developing with a small core leadership group, hundreds of Guides and then house group leaders multiplying as groups bifurcate. Max and Gerontius have secured foundation funding for the 'top' and are working to complete it for Guides, but house group leaders will be volunteers. It's as if Christians only agreed to pay their Rural Dean or a bishop at that level. The whole fuss around Stipendiary and non-Stipendiary Ministers is just delaying the inevitable. Clergy salaries are pathetic and pensions are going to be an ever worsening problem. Volunteering should be normative."

"I expect you're right," said Helen, "but at least you have got a stipend."

"Yes, adequate but not more than that."

Helen looked down at her paper. "Have you heard that Ranjit is under attack from a couple of right wing newspapers who say that *Humanity*'s Religious Affairs correspondent shouldn't be a Muslim?"

"Yes, he told me last week. It would be funny if it were not so ignorant. Two newspapers said that he was a Muslim when Ranjit isn't a Muslim name, but the worst of it is that he's a Christian of South Indian origin."

Clement listened intently to a chunk of Mahler and then went back to his paper. As *Church & State* was a much more meagre read than the *Stylus*, Helen finished first and cleared away the dishes. Clement looked up from his reading and said, "I still can't work out whether what's happening is big or small. Neither can most of the serious commentators."

"Well you don't add a new 'person' to the Godhead every day. I mean, the Holy Trinity, as an idea, has stood the test of time."

"About the same time as original sin, but no better for that. What I keep thinking about is the kind of means we need to help us to move religion on so that it stays faithful to what we believe without getting stuck. This goes back to the initial question of what we actually believe. I think, as a word culture, we get far too tied up in precise formulae, applying mathematical procedures to what should be literature. There is some brilliant and beautiful conceptual architecture in the Creed, but most doctrine is inelegant and unilluminating."

"What's elegance got to do with it?" asked Helen.

"Well, it seems to me that the way the world is designed means that if something is not elegant it is not in accord with its nature. I think that what holds true for mathematics and music holds true for doctrine, whereas literature and theology are more concerned with adventure and a more unpracticed kind of beauty which is much more exciting."

"Very interesting," said Helen, not dismissive, but slightly distracted. "We need to go shopping unless you are staying in to listen to the music."

"Not Tchaikovsky," said Clement. "We'll be back before the Bach Cantatas."

They walked down the High street in the late September sunshine, doing more talking than shopping. Helen always had a list of things to ask and added to the list of things asked of her. Clement concentrated on the shopping list and the route to fulfilling it, issuing most of the requests to shopkeepers, but only breaking into conversations now and again when Helen was in danger of double booking herself.

When they had finished, Clement unpacked, still listening to the radio, while Helen went off to meet colleagues arranging events for the Weeks. Clement was up to his elbows in hot, soapy water and BWV 31 for Easter Sunday when the door bell rang. He went to the door reluctantly and was disappointed to find Paul Swayne standing there looking slightly embarrassed.

"Come in," said Clement. "What is it Paul?"

"You won't like it, Clement, but nobody else would do it. They don't mind talking to Helen, but they say you're too fierce."

"Only with the fierce," said Clement. "The trouble with incumbency is that it gets so used to power that it regards disagreement as aggression, but I don't. Anyway, what is it Paul?"

"It's the children. There were some harsh words from parents yesterday afternoon after the Harvest service."

"Let me guess," said Clement. "It wouldn't be Tom and Elizabeth Smiley, would it?"

"How did you guess?"

"O come on, Paul, it's easy. The people who usually get on their high horse about what they think of as the essence of Christianity are usually those who don't go to church to listen to sermons and don't read any religious books. I suppose he didn't like the Perpetua element in the service."

"I don't know about that, but he said that farming was being unfairly cut out."

"But Paul, he's a part-time farmer of sorts, isn't he, with a few novelty animals and a tea room? What else would you expect? For years Harvest has belonged to the farmers. I know they haven't done much about it, but now they have given up on Rogation, Harvest is the only thing they have got left."

"Well he—and some others—say that you have to stop what's going on and that you have to go."

"Well I can hardly do both unless they first want me to stop what I believe in and then abandon it. That is unreasonable, particularly as they don't appear to believe anything themselves."

"Tom Smiley says he's 'orthodox'."

"I wonder what he might mean by that? But don't answer for him, Paul. You can't because he can't answer the question himself. How many others were upset?"

"I can't say."

"So Tom—and possibly, though I doubt it—Elizabeth Smiley, on behalf of orthodoxy, and an unspecified number of un-named others, objects to the Perpetuan element in the school Harvest service?"

"Yes."

"I'm surprised Jennifer let you do it, Paul. If they want to talk to me, whoever they are, they should do it themselves. After all, as somebody who has come round to thinking that Perpetua is rather a good thing, you're really not the right person to send, are you? So why did you do it?"

"Well, because I'm the Sunday School leader they think that I am in a position to speak."

"Which, to an extent, you are, but if there are any parental worries about what goes on in church they belong to Mark."

"Well, according to them—and only them, mind—he's even more fierce than you."

"They might be right, Paul. Have a cup of coffee and don't look so uncomfortable. The radio has gone on to Italian nineteenth century opera, so I'll switch it off. I don't mind talking to Tom Smiley because at least he's allowed himself to be named, but it doesn't seem very sensible for me to pass on to Mark what he's said when he can do that himself. I can't pass on the verbal equivalent of green ink to anyone. I don't deal with anonymous letters so I won't deal with anonymous speech. But, come on, Paul, you know what goes on with the parents much better than I do. What's the real problem?"

"The children want merchandise. Apparently there are Perpetua replica clothes and hair decorations. There's some sort of Perpetua computer game where she overcomes all kinds of demons..."

"I suppose it was inevitable, but it would be a bit drastic to call for the retirement of celebrity footballers because of associated merchandise. This is surely a case of parents blaming somebody else for their problems. On balance, though I haven't seen any of this, I'd prefer little girls in jeans and tops than in more sexualised clothes, and I would prefer boys to play non-violent games so if they must play, I'd prefer a benign heroine. It all sounds pretty tacky to me, Tom, but the Smileys and any other adherents are complaining in the wrong place. If they don't like merchandise their first course of action is not to buy it. If they can't withstand the pressure, they should complain to the advertising authorities."

"Perhaps you would complain."

"I can't really, Tom, even if I wanted to, as I haven't seen the goods. In any case, one of the great tenets of Perpetuanism is that it abhors victimhood and applauds personal responsibility."

"I know, but what should I tell them?"

"Tell them? By all means tell Tom Smiley that he is welcome to talk to me at any time, and I'm sure that Father Mark would be pleased to talk to him. I am tempted to tell him that he shouldn't talk to anyone unless he's pretty clear what he's going to say, having looked into the matter, but don't say that. Tell him that I will pray for him."

"What?"

"Come on, Tom, you're a quasi Perpetuan/Christian, what's so strange about praying for someone?"

"It sounds a bit patronising. He's not sick, or anything."

"I don't only pray for sick people. I pray that people may be happy, or fulfilled or, in Tom Smiley's case, just a little wiser. If I were you, Tom, I wouldn't pass on any message at all, and if I did, I'd ask Jennifer first."

Helen returned from her meeting for lunch and told Clement that she had heard from one committee member that some people were going to stage a protest against Perpetua being forced on the children in school."

"Whatever next?" asked Clement, amused. "First they rig their way into the

Church School by pretending to be devout Christians when they're just church attendance box tickers, and then they presume to give us lectures in theology. The trouble is, they think they can have all the good outcomes from a church school without church, the equivalent of alcohol free beer. There won't be a protest. They wouldn't really know what to protest against. It's just a bit of noise to increase adrenalin levels and self-worth."

Helen sat at her computer and did village and church business while Clement studied and listened to music.

As they were getting ready to go out to dinner Helen said, "I wonder what Mark wants. He never asks us unless there is something important."

"I think," said Clement, "we have crossed a kind of line from being Christians who believe in Perpetua to Perpetuans who value Christianity. I'm not sure. It took Christianity hundreds of years and it's only two and a half since Perpetua was killed. That seems to be where we are. I hope it means that we can get away from doctrinal wrangles, but I doubt it."

◆　◆　◆

Mark was enjoying his usual solitary and silent hour in church getting ready for Sunday. It was not that different, he reflected, from three years ago before Perpetua came into his life. The ritual of frontals, vestments, readings, sound system setting, and so on, were just the same. The Readings were the same except that an extract from Perpetua regularly—and to his considerable relief—replaced the Second Reading from Saint Paul. He had thought of many innovations, but had turned down all but the essentials. The fourfold doxology, the extracts from Perpetua and the Affirmation Sacrament for guides had been recommended very strongly, and except, as Marie had noted, for the problems with choral settings, the Doxology had been observed, the replacement of Saint Paul had been widely welcomed, and the Affirmation of Guides was a popular occasion for celebration and renewal. There had been some guidance, though not quite so strong, on the form of Eucharistic prayers, the plurality of food and drink that could be used and an exhortation to include a more emphatic element of Reconciliation in the Sacrament of Union, but Mark felt less enthusiastic. He promised that he would do something about the Sacraments of Affirmation for "lay" people and Response, but there was no hurry. He had reluctantly joined a house group, but absented himself frequently on the grounds that, as a Guide, he did not want to be seen to favour one group over another. It was like being a Parish Priest without too much paperwork and a bishop. As time had gone by he had begun to miss the Bishop and even the paperwork. People like him with strong personalities, but weak resolve, actually needed a structure. Perpetuanism was Utopian, and the lack of a hierarchy deprived him of a corps of gossiping peer professionals. Even the very liberalism of the movement made him conscious that he was becoming flabby now that he had no real battles to fight about clerical issues.

He looked at the Harvest gifts and they reminded him why he was where he was. If he had allowed the huge variety of children's gifts and promises of time to be part of a Church of England Harvest he would have been thought of as mad or revolutionary, but it seemed quite normal in the Perpetuan context. So many decisions in the Church of England had to be passed up and down the line that it had become clogged. It mattered to him whether he was a Perpetuan, but he doubted that it mattered much to to others. What mattered to them was to have some say in their community institution. Yes, there was the clergyman, but they found the money, designed and filled the rotas, organised events, and supported each other. They were smothered by bureaucracy and frequently crushed by their clergymen. No wonder Perpetuanism was going down well.

For him as a Priest he was shocked to realise that the doctrine had hardly concerned him at all. What mattered was the ability of people to live happy and spiritually rewarding lives. He had made the calculation that his people would be better off with more scope to act even if he was slightly less well off. He had judged that there would be some minor disruption over liturgy, but had judged that what people really objected to was having things taken away, not having things added. It had been a fruitless cruelty—if cruelty could ever be fruitful—to take the Virgin Mary away from the common people at the Reformation, whatever the elite thought, and they would have done much better to keep everything the people wanted while settling the constitutional and ecclesiological questions separate from doctrinal wrangling.

On the whole, then, he thought that his estimates had been accurate and his congregation—no better and no worse than many others—had been pleased. He had kept most of his professional friends although they were not so tightly knit and he could, so to speak, turn the Dean into a kind of episcopal figure. He should have looked up to Clement as the the member of the movement's core group responsible in a loose way for his patch, but he could not bring himself to do it and, fortunately, Clement would not insist. Clement said it was important that they each knew what the other knew, instead of pretending that there was not an issue. That kind of pretence always wore people down in the end.

"Look Mark," Clement had said earlier in the week, "I can see the difficulty of my trying in any way to be responsible for you as a Guide. It's theoretically the case, inasmuch as Perpetuanism has any structure at all, but I was your Reader. You can put up with me as long as I keep my academic side to myself. You don't want me pulling rank and references. I don't want you coming adrift, so stick to the Dean, and I will only be involved if you want, or if there is something serious to handle, such as a critical problem with a house group that you don't want to handle. You must be fed up of the C of E hierarchy telling you that they are a resource and not a bind so I will not claim the same for us. We have our weaknesses, but we are still pretty 'light touch' and people like you can keep us that way."

Mark was grateful. Clement had gone on to say, "I know that I might want to concelebrate with you at the Sacrament of Union, but I will desist. I don't want to break with the Parish, but I will need to be elsewhere quite often. I want you to feel that you are the Guide for the area and I will do what I have to on a sparing basis. Not that I want to deprive people of the kind of teaching you are not very comfortable with, but we can work that out."

Mark took out his Roman Breviary and turned to the page for evening prayer. He did not expect a voice from above nor a numinous experience. If he was lucky, he would be conscious of the peace of the Holy Spirit. Prayer was part of his priestly activity, praying to God in worship, for others and for himself. He had more to be grateful for than he could readily list or express. There had been some near misses, but the Holy Spirit had seen him through and he was now at peace. The warring demons within him were put to rest. The Perpetuans insisted on ethical liberalism, but they were not worried about his liturgical conservatism as long as he kept to the minimum requirements. Love was more important than liturgy, he reflected, as he came to the Psalms for the day. Psalm 22 could hardly have been more apt as he tried to substitute thoughts of Perpetua for those of Jesus as he read.

At the end he said, "glory be to the Father, and to the Son and Daughter, and to the Holy Ghost; as it was in the beginning, is now and ever shall be, world without end. Amen." It didn't sound quite right, but he would no doubt soon get used to it. He did not have similar success with Psalm 23 which could never be anything other than a shepherd but, then, it was a straight prayer to the Lord which did not say anything about Jesus the "good shepherd". He doubted that Jesus could ever be the "good floor manager" or even anything as current as Jesus the "good therapist." He was wandering off. He read the Psalm again and finished with the new four-fold doxology. It was a little easier every time you said it.

● ◆ ◆

Helen dead headed roses as Clement said his shorter-than-week-day Saturday evening prayers. Mark had been a great deal more settled since he had become a Guide. He would never be fully settled anywhere because he wanted structure and freedom at the same time. She thought it must have something to do with his childhood, but she always refused to speculate about things of which she knew not. What she did know was that Clement was finally flourishing in a way she had wanted for him ever since they had met. She would not have put it to herself that what she most cared about in respect of Perpetuanism was that it made him happy. She was not the sort of person who loved and cared at the expense of rigour but, equally, having thought, she loved and cared in spite of whatever results that rigour produced. Her job as Churchwarden had been to keep the parish on an even keel and she had done that, not because she had studied every turn of the controversies, but because she knew enough about each event to keep antagonists as calm as she could by going with them as far as honesty allowed. It had not always worked as effectively as she would have liked, but many parishes, she knew, had had it much worse. On the other hand, after a period of extreme depression from which she, sadly, could not spare him, Clement had found his way without pushing. He had always said that if you did your best and prayed you would end up in the place you needed to be. His loyalty to Bishop James had seemingly led him away from Perpetuanism, but it had ultimately brought him to the centre of Perpetuan affairs.

It did not matter if she gave the appearance of being a docile woman who cared most for her husband and children and spent a good deal of her time sorting out details of community life. She knew how much she had changed the village and how much she had saved it from minor disasters and given it great joy. She took pleasure in Mark's peace and Clement's joy. That was a very good clutch of achievements to be carrying in her basket.

Clement came out to indicate that he was ready. For a man who spent so much time thinking about beauty he was remarkably indifferent to her lovely garden.

"Love," she thought, looking at him, "is allowing the beloved to be honest."

◆　◆　◆

Jane was getting dinner ready. she did not mind catering, it was part of the role of a Rector's wife and she had reduced it to a reliable set of core dishes, taking note to whom she had served what, and a sequential list of activities which resulted in all three courses being promptly served at precisely the right time. Part of this meticulousness had been developed to lower Mark's anxiety when they were entertaining, but part of it was to ensure that she kept abreast of the discussion so that she could head off certain subjects if they appeared to be raising tension. She was, she knew, a little over the top in her application of charm, but nobody stood out against it. "Why do people make such a fuss about meringues?" she said pleasantly to herself. "Only the proud and the mad would make them." She placed half of the cases in a row, painted them with double cream, applied a layer of raspberries from the garden, and then finished them off with a sprig of mint. She then painted the other halves with cream, dotted each with a few spots of black pepper and placed these on top of the raspberries. There would be just enough time for the elements to fuse but not make the cases soggy. "You can be posh for next to nothing if you try hard," she said, taking a look at the gammon rashers. She looked appreciatively at the smoked salmon mousse. "Which," she said, "only goes to show that sometimes processed food is cheaper than unprocessed, as long as you do it yourself. I couldn't do plain smoked salmon for five without buying two packets, as opposed to a single packet of cut-offs. The main thing is, it will be delicious. Mousse is more interesting than plain fish, gammon tastes better than pork, and filled meringues never fail."

Helen came into the kitchen with two chilled bottles of blush which were her new favourite now that her love of New Zealand Sauvignon Blanc had worn off. Clement followed with two already opened "interesting bottles"—a beefy Chilean shiraz and a curious Languedoc Malbec—and immediately left to join Mark.

"I don't mind what they do as long as it doesn't make Mark grumpy," said Jane. "For all I care—and I probably shouldn't say this as 'Mrs Vicar'—they can bundle Christianity with all the rest and have a pantheon."

"Yes. As Clement would say, it's difficult to work out the precise distinction between Jesus and Perpetua as both human and divine, saints and then humble people like us who surely have something of the divine within us. I suppose Our Sister the Spirit dwells in us whereas divinity is Jesus and Perpetua."

"Clement does keep you nicely polished, doesn't he?"

"He says that we've spent too much time on abstruse questions that don't interest people and we haven't thought enough about the things that do. For instance, he says that we shouldn't just dismiss contemporary spirituality out of hand. Admittedly some of it is self-indulgent, consumerist pick-and-mix, but some of it is a genuine search made necessary because the Church has let people down, either through being too middle class or through being intellectually stuffy, or just plain intellectual."

"Well you couldn't accuse Mark of being an intellectual, but he does find relating to people from different backgrounds quite difficult."

"But he's on a house group."

"Only just, really. He tries hard, but he doesn't think that's where he should be. He loves the Perpetuan ethos, but he thinks that his real place is in church, worshipping and praying. But we're losing time. What I wanted to tell you before Brian Sedge arrives is that he's been seen 'going about' with Marianne Gowers."

"No! A nice man like him with that old battleaxe!"

"Yes. He's been smitten by the battleaxe and is said to be at her knees. A bit of a come down from late night assignations at the Palace."

Jane was funny, but Helen's thoughts veered towards the serious and away from the catty. "But does he know what he's in for? He's such a simple man and she tries to keep up with what we used to call the 'County Set'."

"Apparently he thinks that he can change her, but if women can't change men, as they vow at the altar they will, men certainly can't change women. Watch and see if you notice any difference, and say nothing."

Mark and Clement were doing their best to have a stimulating conversation without treading on each other's toes, but Mark soon gave up and relayed the news of Brian Sedge. Clement didn't react. Mark looked puzzled. "I thought you would be fascinated by the prospect of the recently restored archdeacon tying the knot with such a BCP stalwart."

Clement did not know what to say which would neither disappoint nor show him to be foolish. "I suppose Bran really leans towards the BCP although he's been generous when faced with change."

"Oh Clement, you're hopeless. How do you expect to be a good church leader if you don't know what's going on?"

He thought, "I don't think gossiping makes for good leadership", but he said, "well, Mark, I shall just have to improve now that I have moved out of your shadow." He thought he had gone a bit far with that last remark, so he continued hurriedly, "but I'm sure you will put me right." Then he was ashamed of saying it and went quiet. Mark began to fiddle with his computer and Clement looked once more at the small collection of theology books gathering dust on the study shelves. He wondered where it had all gone wrong, as he knew it had, in spite of efforts—no, well, really because of efforts—to maintain normality. Thinking back, Clement sensed that there had always been tension because he was an active student of theology whereas Mark could barely bring himself to read anything serious, which was understandable after almost 30 years in the priesthood. As long as he was accountable to Mark it was just about all right. Now he was technically not Mark's boss, but Mark would see it that way because he needed to. It was up to him to take the initiative instead of continuing to behave as if he were the Reader.

"Mark, I know this may come out of the blue, but don't you think that you should take a break? You need a rest, it will give you time to do some reading, and—this really would help me—I need a bit of time to get used to who I am and it's quite difficult when we've had a previous, quite different, relationship. I don't want to change anything, but I do want to see things through my own eyes."

These were all very good reasons in their way, but Clement thought that the third was the most important and also the most difficult to get across. He counted on Mark's generosity.

"People are always nagging me to take time off, so I will try it. Jane will be particularly pleased, and I can see how you might want to roam around a bit and find your feet. I know you wouldn't consciously do anything to undermine me though, as you know, I am apt to be somewhat paranoid—a terrible problem for a priest—and you will just have to live with that if I can't completely control it."

That, thought Clement, was about as good as it got with Mark. "Well, say what you need to in your own time," said Clement. "I will say nothing."

The conversation was again in danger of flagging when Brian Sedge arrived or, rather, Lady Gowers arrived with Brian in tow.

"Oh Lord!" said Jane to Helen, peeping out of the kitchen door after hearing the strange voice. "How do you turn five smoked salmon mousses and five gammon steaks into six? The dessert's all right because I always make one extra because somebody's always got a sweet tooth and the cases come in sixes."

"Well, as he's got a bit of a Northern accent, she'll never ask Clement to dinner, so he's a vegetarian, and I've just gone off fish, so knock me up a quick salad."

The couple were almost wrestled into the study by Mark, allowing Jane and Helen to re-set the table which was at the West end of their combined drawing and dining room. Mark pressed an over-large sherry into the hand of the abstemious Brian and a correspondingly large gin and moderate tonic, with bitters not lemon, into the hand of Lady Gowers. Clement nursed a glass of 'his own' red and was trying to work out what to say to rescue Mark when Jane came in, oozing her slightly cosmetic charm whose questionable authenticity did not strike Lady Gowers who measured deference by volume rather than by weight.

"I hope I haven't inconvenienced you, but Brian said ..."

"Nothing of the sort," thought Brian, almost too frightened even to think it.

"... you wouldn't mind. Vicars' wives ..."

"... Rector's wife," said Mark not quietly enough to escape detection by Clement, but far too softly to catch the attention of Lady Gowers who never noticed other vehicles when she was driving her own juggernaut.

"... learn to be flexible and to improvise."

"Not six gammon steaks out of five," said Jane under her breath.

"Brian said ..."

"... Oh, what now? ..."

"... that you are a divine cook who can put together a slap-up dinner in no time."

"Slap you!" said Jane to Clement.

Brian edged round a coffee table, trying not to be noticed, until he reached Jane and Clement. "I'm terribly sorry," he risked, although his caution was unnecessary as Marianne was driving her juggernaut straight at Mark. "I hope I—we—haven't put you in an awkward situation. I can't speak for long, but I need help to get out of this. The woman thinks I'm in love with her and she won't leave me alone."

Jane swore, not for the first nor last time, not to jump to conclusions based on gossip. "I don't know how to get rid of her and it's getting desperate. She's not far off measuring for curtains, except that she wouldn't 'lower' herself. I think she's run out of the means to support her lifestyle and thinks that sharing my humble abode will get her off the hook."

Jane thought of suggesting that Brian should just tell her honestly that he didn't care for her, but she knew it would not work.

Clement said, "it's easy, Brian. I'll come and help you. All that you have to say is that you can't abide the Book of Common Prayer and the Authorised Version and that you think we should have rock bands in church. Oh, and throw in something about how much sexier religion is now that we've got a teenage girl as part of the Godhead."

"But I love the Book of Common Prayer."

"Well if you go on loving it," said Jane, "you will have to love her, too."

Clement pulled Brian round the coffee table to where Marianne was treating Mark to a liturgical disquisition. "We're a Prayer Book Church not a Protestant sect. We stand or fall by our Prayer Book."

Mark, accustomed to Marianne's improving medicine, was simply waiting patiently for the call to the table to relieve him when Brian said, "well if we go on with the fusty old thing we'll fall not stand. The Prayer Book shouldn't die with us, it should die before us. We need pop music in church and a big statue of Perpetua looking sexy."

Mark, temporarily stunned, found it hard to suppress a smile. Pastoral experience told him what this was all about. Lady Gowers' trusty vehicle juddered to a halt, coughed, and then spluttered into life. "You turncoat! You traitor!"

Brian began to retreat, but Clement, standing at his shoulder, refused to give. "Take it like a man," he whispered, more ironically than encouragingly.

"And as for you, Mark Price ..."

"... Father Mark Price."

"Father, Father, Popish nonsense. As for you, Mark Price ..."

"... Don't blame him," said Brian, feeling Clement's fist in the small of his back, urging him to bring the encounter to a triumphant close. "I have come to the conclusion, even more fundamental than Father Mark's, that the BCP has poisoned our Church with anachronistic tosh. It's like medicine that's out of date, it's not that it's doing no good any more, but that it's taken with the expectation of results, thus excluding better medicine such as *The Pop Prayer Book* and *Rockin' with the Saviour* which I particularly like."

"But it's the statue of Perpetua in her disco kit—well, not so much kit—that he particularly admires," said Clement.

Lady Gowers, who knew all about dramatic exits, drew herself up to her full cliche and said, "as for you, Jane Price, you're a charlatan putting dinners together out of tins and packets."

Jane curtseyed.

"And you, Clement Sutcliffe, are a northern oik in Reader's clothing."

"By gum, ood a thought it?"

"And you, Mark Price, are just a silly vicar."

"Rector!" roared Mark.

"And as for you, Brian Sedge, you are a heretical little field mouse."

At the end of this judgment she reversed so impetuously, without looking in her rear mirror, that she knocked an occasional table so hard that the tall vase on it began to oscillate ominously. Helen, who was enjoying what she knew she should not, made for the drawing room door, steadying the vase as she went, thus providing Lady Gowers with an attendant for her exit.

"How can I help you? How will you get home?"

"We came in my car. I was only stopping for a drink anyway. If he wants to stay with those people he will have to find his own way home."

"Are you sure you are all right to drive?"

"Of course I am. Only one little gin. Stop fussing, will you!"

Helen calculated whether more good advice was likely to improve her attention while driving or whether it would make her more angry and decided on the latter. She bowed slightly to Lady Gowers and wished her good evening.

Whether Brian's unwontedly large sherry was restorative or celebratory, he mutely requested a refill. Jane was in danger of becoming triumphalist, so Helen drew her over to the table for another re-set.

"Funny," said Helen. "I quite fancy a bit of fish and Clement says he's fed up of being vegetarian."

Jane giggled but saw Helen's caring look and decided that now was not the time. The story would, in any case, be good for years. Clement saw that Brian was comfortable and went to find Mark whom he caught sending an email. "Only to Giles," said Mark, punching the button to send the text off screen. "It never fails," said Clement. "You can say that Lucifer has been granted a transfer from Hell to Heaven United and nobody turns a hair, but if you say something disparaging about the BCP all hell breaks loose. Still, Mark, the poor woman must be pretty—confused?—if she's trying to lure a bachelor Archdeacon to the altar."

"She's been a bit odd ever since the Bishop—Oops, I shouldn't have said that—took her up, so to speak, and put her down."

"It's a pastoral issue, then?"

"So it is, but I'm about to go on sabbatical. Yes, a pastoral issue."

As they sat down to dinner, they all wanted to go over the story, but each of them had a good reason for not doing so. The original idea of the dinner had come from Mark who thought that Clement's new position should be acknowledged in some way and that it would help matters if he and the Archdeacon were brought together, although two and a half years after the death of Perpetua most of the friction had gone out of Anglican/Perpetuan relations. Max had ensured a win/win property settlement, James had got his Commission, and it had become clear as time went by that many parishes with Perpetuan sympathies did not want to break away from old friends and, contrary to Perpetuan hopes, preferred their weekly worship to house groups. The Perpetuan leadership was a little nervous, but unlikely to be aggressive, and the Church of England felt that matters could have been much worse.

"We had two, but now we have three things to celebrate: first, Brian's escape." Jane smiled and then frowned. "Second, Clement's promotion, or whatever it is." Clement who had been ready for this, looked steadily back at Mark. "And, I don't know how to put this, but some kind of Perpetuan crossing the line." Brian looked worried.

"Of the first," said Clement, "the least said the better. As to the second, I am deeply grateful for your generosity given that—and there's no point in fudging it—in some sort of way I've leap frogged you. As to the third, I agree that there has been a significant change of tone recently, so that Perpetuanism can carry out God's mission in harness with more traditional Christians."

"So aren't you separate, then?" asked Brian, hopefully.

"Well, no," said Clement. "We think that there can be some kind of doctrinal settlement at least with Anglicanism. We thought that there might be trouble from more traditional Provinces, but the Africans love it and the Americans can't be seen to be racist. James doesn't see any insuperable obstacles. After that, there will be some shuffling about at the financial and administrative levels, but we've achieved our major tactical objective of not doing to Christianity what it did to Judaism. So what I thought, although I was aware it might cause you problems, was that we should concelebrate."

"It's still the men," said Jane, with just a little edge.

"Not at all," said Clement. "If you come over here we will affirm you as Guides."

The room became wonderfully quiet and comforting as Clement placed his hands on the head first of Jane and then of Helen. Then they made an affirmation of faithfulness to God, through Jesus and Perpetua, in the power of the Spirit.

Clement, as prius inter pares, assembled the elements in front of him and handed out copies of the Great Prayer. "You knew," said Helen. "You planned this and didn't tell me."

"You didn't need me to tell you. God told you."

They said the new Great Prayer together.

"On the night before they died, Jesus and Perpetua took the fruits of the earth, blessed them, and gave them to their followers, saying 'This food and this drink are my body and blood, given for you, as a promise of your eternal life; do this in memory of me.' So now, God, our Creator, look upon your children with that same love in which you sent your Son and Daughter as our Saviours, and send Our Sister the Spirit to be with us, infusing these gifts with your true presence so that they will be to us our spiritual food as we build your kingdom on earth before returning, as promised in the Resurrection of Jesus and the re-manifestation of Perpetua, to be enfolded back into your eternal love."

"That's a bit tortuous," said Brian, when they had finished. "No worse than the original must have seemed, but we've developed it in two years rather than two centuries," said Clement, encouragingly.

They were not quite solemn as they ate, but they were aware that there was a new and unbreakable bond between them. Helen felt blessed. Jane was calmed from her restlessness. Brian felt comfortable in himself. Mark felt the tension temporarily ebb. Clement knew that he would not have to push as the Spirit was guiding him.

◆　◆　◆

Mark could not sleep for worry that all would not go smoothly the next morning, so before the sun rose he was in his study re-editing what he still thought of as the "Mass booklet". He went onto the god4u web site and cut and pasted the new Great Prayer into the booklet, checked all the doxologies and, uncharacteristically, wrote some sermon notes.

Had anyone without a sharp eye and ear for liturgy come to the church two years ago and now, they would have noticed no difference until the Second Reading which was from Perpetua (saved by the Dean). If anything, people were more aware of the novel harvest gifts than the novel Reading. In another modification to the usual routine, Mark asked the children to bring gifts from the back to the altar directly after the Gospel so that they could sit at the front for his sermon which he preached from a chair in front of the nave altar and not from the pulpit.

"Today we are celebrating, strangely, one of the newest festivals of the Church, even though it goes back to the Old Testament tradition of offering the fruits of the earth to the Lord. Going back, in fact, to Cain and Abel.

"You will notice that there is a new twist to the tale in the introduction of modern goods and services to supplement the celebration of farming, and I am delighted to see that the children have donated games and toys and their talents to go with food for children who are less well off. Those of you who keep in touch with the Sunday School will know that this generosity of the children has been sparked by the life of Perpetua.

"In this Parish we have had our ups and downs during what might rather crudely be called the 'Perpetua crisis', but we seem to be emerging from our time of trouble and that is really what I want to talk to you about today. There are, as you know, essentially three major points raised by Perpetua: her Godhead, her sacrifice, and her love. I think that we are pretty close now to gaining agreement on the first point. Perpetuans, like me and many of you, believe that Perpetua was a 'person' of the Godhead in the same way as Jesus. Our beloved Archbishop, once of this Diocese, says that there is no insurmountable hurdle to recognising this truth, and we have already recognised it in our Doxologies. Well, not the sung ones because composers like Marie have to re-set the Glorias.

"The second point follows the first, and again, the area of controversy is narrowing. Even some Roman Catholics now see that the sacrifice of Perpetua, the night before she died and her actual, physical death, in no way compromise or dilute the sacrifice of Jesus. Both are full, but neither is final.

"On the third and most important point, Perpetua—and you can see it today in the children—has revived the idea of community solidarity and care. Yet she says more. She wants us to love one another. Now where have I heard that before?

"Yes, of course Jesus said it in his life and teaching, but now we have a divine example much nearer in time. That is the point. We are the luckiest ever people in th world because we are children of the Resurrection of Christ and contemporaries of the incarnation and re-manifestation of Perpetua. That is fuel indeed for our journey, but that journey is not just caring. It's knowing when to listen, when to shut up, when to let the other just be. That's the most difficult thing of all. We are children of the Resurrection of Jesus and we have lived during the lifetime, death and re-manifestation of Perpetua, our Sustainer and God's Sacred vessel. What more could we need?"

The rest of the Eucharist went on much as usual except for the doxologies and the re-wording of the Great Prayer which only tidied Mark's own previous Perpetuan variant.

Clement, dressed in choir robes, watched from his old position behind Marie. He wondered whether Mark would tell him during "The Peace" whether he wanted the bell, but for once Mark actually greeted him with a sign of peace. Clement settled on six strikes of the bell as two lots of three were no longer possible. Scott was a little worried about the new hymn, *Perpetua walked in the factory, as Jesus walked in the field.* Clement wondered how they would find a rhyme for field, but they didn't. Marie was pleased with the Anthem and Nigel was pleased that he could still sing the solo in *Thou Visitest the Earth* without his voice cracking. Afterwards last minute arrangements for the harvest lunch were being settled as people drank coffee. Violet and Ronald tried terribly hard not to be together. Mark noticed, but said nothing. He had temporarily taken fright after believing the Gowers gossip. Helen, working unobtrusively to see that all ran smoothly, found time to congratulate Mark on his sermon. "Clement couldn't have done better," she said. He smiled.

As the three doxologies were all sung, and as it had been agreed to leave them alone, there was nothing for Mark to worry about at the Deanery Choral Evensong during which there were no references to Perpetua. There was no more worry at her absence at this service than there had been at her presence at the Eucharist. All the BCP regulars were there except for Lady Gowers who had "made it known" that from now on she would be attending Evensong at the Cathedral. Brian, who had "heard" directly about her plans as part of a sustained assault which, to his great relief, began as a catalogue of his weaknesses, but turned out, to his rising horror, to be her particular way of wooing, which he countered in the short time allowed with yet another craven denunciation of the Prayer Book and a Panegyric on contemporary sacred songs, sat safely in his stall.

Afterwards Nigel went down to the Oak to quench his thirst after giving it "a bit of welly".

"I've complained to the vicar," said Tom Smiley, cornering Nigel.

"Have you now? What about?"

"Perpetua."

"What did he say?"

"Well, I didn't exactly complain to the Vicar, but I'm going to."

"As a fervent non-churchgoer I wonder what you have to complain about."

"Corrupting our children, that Perpetua, in her tight jeans and revealing top."

"Not very different, then, from Mrs Smiley," said Nigel, tartly, "but I don't suppose you accuse her of corrupting children. No more would you. She'd have your goolies off!"

Smiley winced, but went on gamely. "It's all right for Mrs Smiley, but not for somebody who claims to be religious."

"No, Tom, that's the Muslims."

"Well, not just religious, but sacred."

"That's a nice distinction."

"Well you can't have an honest to goodness Christian sacred person looking like that."

"But the whole point is that she's not a Christian."

"Got you there. Your very own Archbishop says there will be a deal in no time."

"Well there might," said Nigel, wearily, "but just because we make a deal to fuse Christianity and Perpetuanism doesn't take away from her individuality when she lived. We just have to hope she likes the deal, but I daresay the Holy Spirit will let us know. Don't look so glum, Tom, religion isn't supposed to be a battle ground, it's about love. Have a drink."

He counted the sheep. "I don't know how much longer I can do this," he said as he identified the last of the flock in the gathering gloom.

"Neither free from sorrow, nor yet free from sin. Still, all is safely gathered in."

◆　　◆　　◆

She held her small, slim stemmed, glass of Gavi de Gavi up to the last rays of the setting sun and looked in awe at the goldengreen explosion as the sun sank over Silicon Ridge. She had just returned from a meditation where some 30 people had prayed in front of the harvest gifts, an array of green and gold with highlights of red, orange, and brown. Before she arrived the children had bagged up the tins and packets to be delivered next morning to the poor and the fruit and vegetables would be put on top of each bag just before delivery. In a venerable country church such an array would have perhaps looked something of a cliche, a rather nostalgic retrospective on the days when almost everyone in a village was tied up with agriculture, but the glass and steel top floor board room of SILACT was a striking venue for harvest worship, with its views over the surrounding countryside as far to the north as the southern extremity of the Pennines, so instead of looking at a riotous bowl of yellow chrysanthemums in, at best, the stained glass light of the late afternoon sun, she saw their explosion reflected and reflected in the mirrors in the mirrors in the glass. To an observer it would have appeared to be some form of pagan or spiritualist ritual transplanted into a futurist environment, but the intensely personal strivings for two-way communication with the Creator fused into a numinous silence of peace and light. She had asked them to focus on the Creator in nothingness, the opposite of earth's colours, a kind of blue. A young woman, dressed in blue jeans and a bronze halter top, looking a little like Perpetua, she thought with a tear, asked them to focus on Jesus with bread in his hand. Then a white haired man, dressed in a flowered shirt and yellow trousers, asked them to think of Perpetua with a glass of real ale in her hand. The moss green carpet was so soft that the silence was not disturbed as people changed their position to look out over the countryside from a new vantage point. Light and peace, humanity and nature, Creator and Incarnates, and everywhere the Spirit.

The gold drained away and, at the instant of its last kiss and the arrival of a lip of blue, she saw the bubbles, enlarged, like a galaxy. The colours of the day gave way to the colours of the night, from orange, green and red to blue, pearl and white. Then she realised that the wine would grow warm if she went on watching, so she took a sip and looked out of the window until all she could see in the fading light was a line drawing of life. She hoped for the stars, but a thin haze formed as the earth cooled. It all started here. Without the Creator there was nothing. With the earth in peril it was time for humanity to come back to sacred basics. Jesus and Perpetua were divine incarnates but, in a sense that words could not handle, they could not have been without the Creator. She could grasp the idea of everything in an instant, in timelessness, the chronological equivalent of the geometrical point that has no area, and she could grasp the necessity of earthly space and time as the means to the exercise of free will which made humanity special, but she struggled still with the Creator and us. "Are you there," she often asked, "other than in prayer? I know you're not impassive but what precisely are you to us here?" If the Creator were less impassive there might have been less need for Incarnates. How would a creator "think about" the balance between impassivity and activity and the role of Incarnates? She thought these were really much more important issues to pray about than most of the disputes religious leaders—almost all men—were involved in. It would be better to talk to scientists if only the two ways of looking at things, the public and the spiritual, could recognise their respective merits and limitations. But, then, whatever the state of theology and philosophy, people were needed who could "translate" and carry this, for there was no life that did not depend upon creation.

She thought of the prodigality of it all, the Creator's prodigality and human wastefulness and marvelled at the generosity of the first and the pride of the second. Up in the board room they had valued every drop of wine and every head of grain. If she were to perform a Sacrament of Union now, for herself, would it be a kind of conjuring up of the divine or a humble act of gratitude? She fetched a russet apple from the kitchen which she had brought from the meditation. All was quiet blue as she said the Great Prayer, and then she drank the wine and ate the apple. She poured herself another, unconsecrated, glass and made herself a cheese sandwich. She tried to eat deliberately slowly and then fell into wondering how she had come to where she was.

Her parents were, in their own terms, loving, but her research physicist father and corporate marketing mother had squeezed the Spirit out of her. His proofs and her "bottom lines" had indeed made her young life bleak. She did not know it at the time. She thought that striving for academic honours as a precursor to worldly success was normative. She had absorbed the pressure at school, been Head Girl, won the essay prize in the sixth form and been greatly admired, but, looking back, she had been envied rather than loved. At University it had all gone wrong. There were students far more talented and resilient than she. She had failed to gain the admiration of her peers and lost her own self-respect. Then she had dropped her standards to gain some kind of recognition from the strugglers. Careless of her own prospects, she had helped them to progress. When she left with a nominal third class degree her angry parents had stuck to their blackmail and refused to help her buy a car. She had moved away, sad, but fearless, and got a job at Hypo where she could go on helping the strugglers. Would she have been better off with a better degree and a job in social policy, she had wondered. It was immaterial where she was. Dexter was in danger of going to prison, Kylie had once confided that she would rather die than go on suffering from her obesity, and Jim was a constant victim of bullying. There was plenty to do and although Annie helped where she could, she had been their surrogate mother.

Perpetua had changed her life, freeing her to be a sister. She had grappled with some of the logic that she should have mastered at university and became useful. She even began to read the literature she should have studied. On the missions she had judged with Portia, striven to hold together with Lydgate, mourned Stephanie's death with Daniel and even ventured into the moral entanglements of Ivan Illyich and mused over the more exotic aspects of the human condition with Marcel. She wondered whether her growing love of literature was a substitution for spirituality or a support for it, but with Perpetua's help had learned that beauty was to be admired as one of God's greatest gifts, not worshipped as a God nor feared as a snare, best given its due in tranquility. Brian, quietly overcoming her childhood complexes, taught her the beauty of mathematics and physics and, again, she saw them as a gift. She could see the Creator in their elegance and mystery in their quantum indeterminacy. None of the group had been technically musical nor a connoisseur of pictures, but there, too, she had found elegance and mystery. So, although she had a literary background, she had grappled with Godel, laughed with Escher, and worshipped with Bach. Lately, Clement had helped her with music, explaining that it was scientifically public, but mysteriously sacred. The more she looked, the less she saw conflict between human endeavour and the mystery of God who was its well-spring.

She was about to play some Messiaen piano music when she heard the double chime of an in-coming email. She knew she should leave it, that this evening had been set aside for prayer, but she would never pray wholesomely—and this was her weakness—if she did not look at it. The address was perpetua@phonenet. com and the subject was "doctrine". She opened it and there was former Archbishop Hawthorne's draft statement on Perpetuan doctrine. She automatically saved the file and then took half an hour to read it through. He had done a good job. She had seen it before, but had not read it so carefully. Here, set out clearly, but humbly, was the essence of what they stood for. She read it again more quickly so that it formed a structured shape. She copied it onto an SD card and dropped it into her purse. They had been saved. After months of agonising they had the bones of a future, fuller expression of their beliefs. She was not worried at first about the address because Perpetua had always exercised some power over digital technology, but she now wondered whether it could be some sort of hoax. Had someone kept a copy and sent it to her pretending that it came from Perpetua? It looked simple enough, but it was the very suspicion which began to worry her.

She saw a meeting with the document printed for all the leadership group and the ink markings as words and phrases were added and deleted. She saw Max delivering copies to Archbishop Hall and cardinal Podric. She saw workshops, seminars, conferences, and congresses. She saw the red ink grow denser on some pages and the marginalia denser on others. She saw Damian labouring through the night with track changes and knots of protagonists devising strategies. Would studying this document bring them closer to God or take them further away? She read Hawthorne's warning about the danger of doctrine stultifying theology. She remembered him saying that doctrine was a long way down stream from theology, and she began to see that a massive lump of doctrine like this would cause spiritual indigestion. She saw that the individual quest to know God was primal and took primacy over formulae. Theology was the struggle at the interface between the human and divine and it gave humanity means to try to talk tentatively of God, but she wanted theology to be public as well as private. Even if doctrine was provisional, it so often gave the appearance, created the illusion, of being final. In all likelihood, the divinity of Perpetua would fall at the doctrinal hurdle. The good Archbishop James and the indefatigable Max would no doubt find a form of words on which they could agree but theology was like poetry; it was not there to be reduced to a lowest common denominator. The Christian Churches claimed that the Spirit inspired those seeking to convert their theology into doctrine but she believed that the Spirit promoted harmony, not uniformity. So what was the purpose of this communication? She concluded that it was a temptation.

Perpetua had never really talked in terms of sin or evil, but recognised the temptation to conform and to pass responsibility to others. Doctrine would persuade many that they had nothing to do but mouth it because formulating it was the business of people more clever than themselves. Theology was the duty of every human being, no matter how intellectually challenged. Evil, or sin, was the refusal to pray, to put oneself at the very edge of possibility. If might be one of millions of emails attaching the text but she could not be responsible for others. She deleted the material and inserted the SD card. It was empty. So much for doctrine. Then she wondered whether there was some hidden clue in her being Trina when she was the leader of a movement which believed that the Trinity was not the final, incarnational Word made flesh and dwelling amongst us. No. That would be superstition.

She was so disturbed by the incident that she abandoned her ambition to spend the evening in silence and put on the television. It was one of those rare evenings when almost every channel was carrying material about the desperate state of the human condition—poverty, paedophilia, human trafficking, violence, corruption, injustice, exploitation, famine, flood, fire, earthquake, illness, injury, exile, helplessness, heartlessness, callousness, lying, cheating, delusion, disappointment, obsession, illusion, sleight of hand, humbug, breach of faith, breach of promise, covetousness, and idolatry—and she wondered what she was doing sitting in her comfortable cottage when she should be out there, caring, healing, encouraging, and being valiant for truth. The programmes were not all gloom. There were reports of reformers, campaigners, peace makers, aid workers, counsellors, therapists, philanthropists, and reporters who gave their lives to—and often risked their lives for—the common good. It was not that there were enough to spare her but that their activity of caring was a necessary, but not a sufficient, way of life. There was a deep, qualitative difference between human solidarity and sacred solidarity, between solidarity with the species and solidarity with all of God's children. She thought again—rarely a day passed without her thinking about it—of Nazis hurling Jewish babies into the flames before going home to listen to D960. She thought of the apparent descent from Dante, writing in the midst of civil war, to Bonhoeffer writing during the Second World War.

Then she saw it: humanity, believing, atheist and indifferent—the last probably being the worst—had so abandoned Jesus that he had been sent into the concentration camps to suffer with God's chosen people afflicted by his supposed Christian followers. If humanity had ever believed in the impassivity of God that belief had been shattered by Christ's millionsfold crucifixions on the plains of central Europe. That suffering had been so great an affront to creation in love, to the gift of free will, that God Our Parent had "thought it right" to send a successor incarnate to be the Sustainer, the Sacred vessel to contain, yet again, all that had been done amiss, and to bring new hope. She saw that if Perpetua had not come, the language of theology, so impaired by brutality, would have disintegrated under the weight of guilt, denied and hidden, but fatally corrosive. She saw that she must sit and struggle with Godhead until she was in a position to go out and bring new hope and that this hope would be the most difficult thing of all, for she also saw that what she had to bring would be a denial of the culture of power and judgment and the placing of a realistically low value on the virtue of caring. To be open to the other in a death camp was the hardest thing of all but the most truly human. Not even brave Bonhoeffer had managed it. The unique human capacity for recognising patterns had to be radically separated from the human capacity to impose structures. We must be warned by the indefiniteness of quantum physics against the lure of elegance. Because patterns were publicly verifiable they were too often thought to be archetypal paradigms of society whereas Perpetua had come to nourish the quantum.

So taken was she with this perception that she could not remain seated but paced her tiny living room until it felt like a cell. Then she went out into the dark, still, slightly damp night and walked to the top of the ridge from where she could see the lights of the town, lights that took the mystery out of the night, taming it for human purposes. There was a terrible, paradoxical nervousness about a society that wanted permanent light but wanted so much to be hidden from it. Even great Christian thinkers seemed not to have discerned the decline from the Golden Age of Jesus, of incarnational zenith, through the sunset of Aquinas and Dante into the twilight of faction and the darkness of the supposed enlightenment. God must have "wondered" how bad it had to get and had received a definitive reply from the Somme and Auschewitz, but these people down below, mostly employed in Silact and other hi tech companies, seemed to be living Fukuyama's *End of History*, in the process losing any sense of collective responsibility for its transmission. Most, at best, had only a vague idea about the causes and extent of twentieth century slaughter, but that was an age gone by.

She could, she would, love them all in the abstract, general way of the routine prayer, but it was making that love concrete that counted, not in doctrine, but in a theologically driven community of mutual love. At the heart of it, she thought, there must be sacrifice but that concept, too, had been swallowed by the culture of caring so that it had come to mean giving up something you valued, primarily to improve the life chances of others, something approaching the idea of the in-built drive to save the DNA of the species. Jesus and Perpetua had taught us that the ultimate sacrifice was giving up yourself. That was what love really was, it was paring away at the coarseness that so easily grew on the surface of the individual personality, and that paring she would call virtue. She found it hard to think of the right word for what she meant: impassivity was too arch, fatalism too supine, openness too vague, hospitality verging again on the caring. Then she thought that all these words had some quality of wholeness or competence about them and she remembered when Mark had told her, in an irresistible fusion of enthusiasm and despair, about his own perpetual feeling of brokenness. She would love these people as best she could in her brokenness because, being broken, she was necessarily open. There were some mechanical artefacts that were broken when they were closed, but the human person must be open because it was always broken, created broken, living in brokenness. To think of the human condition as imperfect, the word she often used, was a form of idolatry, being the opposite of perfect which was a term that could only be applied to God. We were not imperfect gods, but broken creatures of the perfect Creator, broken so that we might receive the beloved's brokenness in our own. Those separate, but interlocking, pieces of elusive, modern sculpture, full of strange curves and space, suddenly made sense, more sense than depictions of wholeness. Jesus, perfect God, had been broken on a cross. Perpetua, perfect Vessel, had been broken in the mud. The Christian idea that the human nature of Jesus was perfect had misunderstood. He had never "sinned" but he had been as broken as the rest of us, broken in sadness, broken in suffering, broken in plans gone wrong, broken in expectation of better choices. Over time that brokenness had been morphed back into the perfection of the divine nature, and the idea of intrinsic brokenness had become conflated with the separate idea of sin so that, for many, sin and suffering had become inseparable, the latter being the consequence of the former, not just for individuals but for the whole race. That was why Perpetua had been sent, to restore our concept of the incarnate divine to its radically bipolar reality of perfection and brokenness through which we could live as creatures in our brokenness and not despair even after the Shoah the cold war, the descent from the responsible into the inevitable, the death wish and its necessary accompaniment of hedonism. And then She had come.

"Ich habe genug", she sang, softly, and took one last look at the lights of the town before turning for home.

There would be a right time, hopefully soon, God willing, when she would be ready to go out, to risk the temptation of power exercised under a pastoral disguise, but for now, she must pray. As she walked back to the cottage she saw Perpetua with an ethnic assortment of children in a playground and with a massive leap of her heart which almost made her faint she remembered Julian of Norwich proclaiming Christ as mother, the homely and courteous, the always loving, the perfector of souls with no wrath. Julian who had believed that sin was necessary for learning and would therefore never be punished by a loving God who awaited the maturing of the soul. Julian who believed that all would be saved.

"And all shall be well, and all manner of thing shall be well," she recited, as she put her key in the lock.

VISION

i.

                                                    Moonlight

        the age of
                                                        moonlight

            all colour
                    leeched
                                                    the endless plain
                            like dirty
                        snow
    snow
                                                        moonlight
                        the age of
                                                        moon-
light   answered
by the   fire
dull   glow

                                                          moon
light
                    grey dust
                        and
                                black   shadow
                        A Kind of Blue
                        So What
Ah me!   Ah you!
the cash   the ash
haunted   by ash
                    and an angel's
                                shadow
and did those feet
in   modern   times
turn into ash in Dachau's fire
and was the holy lamb of God
thrown with the infants
                            on the pyre

            Kyrie! Kyrie!! Ky-Ri-e!!!
                Ky-ri-e!
                                    Kyrie
                                    kyrie
            kyrie   kyri
                                kyrie
                                                    Ky
                                                        k

                                                              y-ri-e

The ash of Auschwitz is not
cold Baleful the moon frowns
in Her reflected
light   Downward
   they claw   for
phosphorus   and
gold To assuage
the gloom of never   -   ending night

                              Shoah!
                          Shoah-Shoah!

                                                        Kyrie

The flames   flare
chemical   burned
brick   Glass
blue and   green
that nature never
saw   The Somme
lives on   beyond
arithmetic As stooges and apparatchiks
feed the   maw

                                        Somme

                                  Sommm-omme Som-omme

                                                    Eleison

Forged to rake the
ravaged plain Where
jungles fell beneath
the bomb and axe The
towers of Babel stock
and bond the   slain
The glittering Levis
of the faceless tax

                          Dollar!

                                Dollar Dollar!

                                      Dollar vobiscum!

Grain smoke chokes like eating
coke The   time   of glaciers
quickens towards the dam   The
mighty Indus jerks from rage
to croak The Gaia meters   stretch
off-screen and   jam
                          Fire!
                      Fire-Fire!

                                              wa-ter

                          Veni
                      Veni-Veni!

They seeming
playful   scorch   the page
Which monks illumined   Dante graced   and
Proust Enlarged sparks
swallow reference   in a rage Of   aimless
scorn   against   structure
and   trust

                         Chaaar-lus
                                     Creator
                                                    Spiritus

Bach's   score settled   seductively
With naked   flesh flare-lit to
sell cigars   And Mahler's
last extended threnody
Crazed into ring-tones
plangent   in
singles'
bars
                              Genug!
                         Genug-Genug!
                                                    Kyrie

Plato   and Aristotle   adieu!
Facts are hacked   adrift
from history   Only
the will I know in   me
is true   Truth   chaff
for the   bonfire
of mystery
                              Chaff!
                         Chiff-Chaff!

VenI!   Veni!
                                        Veni Creator
                                                    Spiritus!
Kyrie!   Christe!
     Kyrie!   Christe!
              Kyrie!   Christe!

Veni!   Veni!   Veni!
                    Creator Spiritus!

                                                    Kyrie
                              Kyrie!
              Kyrie!
Eleison

Elei

                                             son

where did the sun
                    go
when did the colour
                    fade

          I see them
          bright as Poussin
          in a grand parade
          as strange as stories
          of the knights of old
          and wizards turning
          iron into
                    gold

                    Ivan!
                    Ivan-ho!

where did the
                sun go
when did the
            colour fade
            as elegant as Manet
            figures dancing in
                            a glade

                    Ma-net
                    Manet-Monet

so many different kinds of
                            light
                                        and
                                                    shade
of ways of seeing
where did the movement
                    go
the way the Venice water seems to
                                flow
shadow on
            water shadow on
                            grass
                                shadow of a

b   r   i   d   g   e

on water
as they seem to
                pass
through the
            shadow on the
                        grass

```
where did the sun
                    go
where did
          the sun                                      go


shadow

light and shadow
the different ways
we used to know

kyrie!
  Kyrie!
   Kyrie!
       Kyrie eleison!

             if we have feeling left
             let us weep for cut flowers


             cut
                flow
                     ers

             if we have feeling
             left let us weep for
                                   cut
                          flowers

             if we have feeling
             left - a shadow
             of imagination - let us weep for cut
                                                   flowers


             Mary
             flower of flowers

                      Maria!
                      Ave-Maria!

             if we have feeling
             left let us weep
             for Mary's flower
                             cut

             if we have a shadow
             of imagination
             let us remember
         the sun
```

              when did the
                        sun go
                                leaving us in the
                                              moon's

                                              shadow

              where did the col
                        our fade
                                leaving
              a kind of light
              and a kind of shadow

baleful   the moon frowns in Her reflected
light downward we claw for phosphorus and
gold to assuage the gloom of never-ending
night   the ash of Auschwitz is not   cold

Shoah!   Kyrie!

glass blue and green   that nature   never
saw the Somme lives on beyond arithmetic
as stooges and apparatchiks   feed the   maw
the flames flare   chemical   burned brick

                    So-o-o-ommmme!

                    Ora!
                  Ora-pro
                Ora-pro-nobis!

where jungles   fell   beneath the bomb and
axe the towers of Babel stock and bond the
slain the glittering Levis of the faceless
tax   forged   to   rake   the   ravaged   plain

                    Dollar!
                  Dollar-Dollar!
            Dollar   vobiscum!

                    Miserere
Mise   re   re
  Mise   re   re   mei!
    Mise   re   re
                                                             mei!
mei

the   time   of glaciers quickens towards the
dam   the mighty Indus   jerks   from rage to
croak   the Gaia meters   stretch   off-screen
and jam grain smoke chokes like eating coke

                                                        Fire!

Fire!
                                Fire!

Veni

                        Creator Spiritus
                                Creator

                                                Creator Spiritus

                water of life
                water of death

                                Water!
                                war-ter!

what monks illumined Dante graced and Proust
enlarged they swallow reference in a rage
of aimless scorn against structure and trust
s p a r k s seeming playful scorch the page

                                Char-lus
                        charred
            burnt alive!

Veni
                        Veni-Veni!
                                Creator

                                        Creator Spiritus!

with naked flesh flare-lit to sell cigars
and Mahler's last extended threnedy crazed
into ring-tones plangent in singles' bars
Bach's score settled   seductively

                                Genug
                                                                Ich

                                habe
genug
        Miserere
                Miserere   mei

facts are hacked adrift from history
only   the will I know in me   is true
truth chaff for the bonfire of mystery
Plato and Aristotle   adieu!

                                chaff
                        chiff-chaff

                                        El-e-i-so-o-on

phosphorus and gold
all that glistens is but cold
gold is the fool's sun
clawed from the ground
in the dead of night
glittering in the phosphorus light

                                                                    Me I

strange to tell
as we exchange sad stories
on the road to hell
the sun buys no bombs

the sun buys nothing

            where did the sun
                            go
            when did the colour
                        fade

the moon frowns
            in Her reflected light
            who might
                    She be
            who lights that frowning face
            if   not   God

        if   IF   If
    IF!   IF   IF
            If   IF   IF!   IF   if
                                                            if

            I see him raging radiant and lush
            as rich as Rubens in a velvet cloak
            with napery's gleam more pleatly than a mole
            and milliard stitches in his cambric stole
            as strange as stories of fire without smoke
            blazing within the calling of a bush

and did those feet before our time
walk upon Horeb's mountain bare
and did the holy fire of God
burn for his servant cowering there
and did that countenance divine
fly past as Moses turned away
and was the Covenant etched in stone
to trumpet blast and ram's horn bray

                Shoah
            Shoah-Shoah!

                                            Kyrie

who lights that frowning face
                              baleful
a dull metallic light
bricking the flame
greying the ash
   until
       it seems that all its
                                   flames are
                                                       dead

       yet it is not cold
       it will burn beyond the
                       time
       that we grow
               old
       the ash of Auschwitz is   not cold
       who might She be

                                   Miserere Mei!
the Somme lives on   beyond   arithmetic
as Wittgenstein and Russell
count no Moore
glass lurid blue and green
that nature never saw
casts deathly light on faces cruel past death
as rough and sharp as brick
baked by the maw's breath

       I hear the octet opening its eyes
       and see the trout glide in its whispering
       stream but our death is that there is no
       surprise when D960
                   morphs
       into a
s-c-reeeeeeeeeeeeeeeeeeeeeeeeeeeeeeeeeeeeeeeeeeeeeeeeeeam!!!!!!!

Miserere

O miserere

  O miserere

    O Miserere   mei
how have we
         come to this
more treacherously foul
than a Judas
         kiss
             Miserere

                                   Kyrie

and were those feet in modern times
force marched to Dachau from the Somme
and was the holy lamb of God
dismembered by a road-side bomb

                    I see him desperately grey
                    a bunch of Lowry twigs bound with barbed wire
                    all colour faded texture worn away
                    a withered posy of the world's desire
                    and the world's
                                        decay
                    a bouquet of   cut   flowers
                          t   d
                        o   e
                         s
                            s
                    on a fire
              where did the words
                              go
              when did their
fear   and   beauty
fade
              when did the cattle truck
                                                            replace
              the cavalcade
                          Princip!
                                        Princip Imperator
the shortest distance
                          between
two   points
is not a straight line
but
      a
        cr
              a
                 a
                       aa
                            b
                           b
                              b

                                        g

in the slime
gagged by the glass blue green
that nature never saw
and the phosphorus from the cannon's maw
men as mad and brave as horses
for the lion and the eagle claw
praying as they swore
on their way to the Chankly Bore

O   far
                                                        far
                      and few
                         and few
their heads are green
and their hands are blue
                                                        far

                      and
few
blue and green
should never be seen
as the mill owners walk on the prom
to the pleasant play of the sea
and the ROAR of the
                              distant
Somme
                         Princip!
                         Imperator!
                         the lion
                         and
                         the eagle's
                         claw

and back in blighty
names inscribed
                    in stone
begrimed by factories
were all that had been salvaged
for the girls
               made yellow widows
bewailing their virginity
with their fellows
as they hurried ammunition
                         to the front
with the contagious schizo/phrenia
of the ruined child
only the bridal feather
was
    undefiled
as the reaper smiled
thirst sated
then suffocated
          ceased to
          smile

                         the lion
                         and
                         the eagle's
                         claw

                    Imperator!

                    such a strange
                                                        palate
                    I never saw
                    not even Gericault could hint
                    at the deadly tint
of the gas shells
                                                        green
                    and
                                                        blue
                    and the
                                                        gold
                    of the phosphorus glint
                    and the
                                                        grey
                    of the men
                    and the
                                                        red
                    of the dying fire
                    and the
                                                        black
                    of the drying   blood
                    and the colourless mud
                    sapping desire
                    and the
                                                        yellow
                    girls
                    and the village
                                                        green
                    with the
                                                        pink
                    of the new recruits
                    signing up for their
                                                        khaki
                    suits and their first ever
                    pair of shiny   brown
                    boots and the
                                                        cream
                    virgin war plaque
                    and the feather
                                o so
                                                        white
                    and the
                                                        black
                    of the silk hats
                    on the Brighton shore
                    and the
                                                        purple
                    of the Emperor

                            Imperator

                                                    were
                                              you
                                        there

          O where were you
          most of the time
          they could not even see
                              the moon

          where was She
and did those feet in civic times
walk upon England's village green
and was the holy lamb of God
in England's pleasant barracks seen
and did the countenance divine
shine forth upon Kitchener's bills
and was the war to end wars builded here
among the never quiet mills

          where did the sun
                          go
          when did the colour
                          fade
          where was

                                                            She

                    Princip!
                    Imperator!
               the lion & the eagle's
                    claw
          Where were   you
I was singing a newly minted hymn
by Spring-Rice to a tune by Holst
which is terribly nice
and a tune about those feet
composed by Parry
happy as Larry
making do and mending
jazz   forgetting
making do

          where were you
     when
          they crucified my Lord
          were you there
     when
          they laid him in the tomb
          were you skulking in
                          the upper room

          where were you
          where was   She

somehow
we lost track
a shot

                                                        in Sarajevo
kcab gninrut on
and then there was all the deranged arithmetic
    of Paschendale
and the Somme
and the Spanish flu
and something dreadful in Armenia
and the excitable Italians
and frightening Bolsheviks
and shouting Germans
and then war
but this time we knew
    what it was for
and Stalin's gulags
and Hitler's camps
and millions of refugees
and strange tales from the few
    soldiers who could talk
    of horror beyond arithmetic
    of the empire
    of the stooge and the apparatchik
and as I try to turn away Pol Pot
    hits me between the eyes
and to tell the truth
    it isn't a great surprise
and countless
    atrocities in the Congo
and God knows
    where else

                    they shall not grow old
                        blood and gold
                        gold and blood
begins   and   ends
in   mud
and splintering wood

                    I can still hear it in the entartete dread
                    from Schulhof's rag to Krasa's dying note
                    more frightened now perhaps than those who
                        wrote
                    and are now
                            dead
                    their strange and murdered hope
                    and
                    reminding us of our collusion
                    that the civilising force of art
                    is an
                        illusion

and did those hands in
                        Hitler's time
play in a band in
                        Theresienstadt
and did the holy lamb of God
walk
        naked   to   the   anthropomat
and did that countenance divine
lose all its innocence in the fire
and was
            Jerusalem
                            razed

                                                        again
a monument   to   dark   desire
                                                                        Silence
                                            silence
                        silence
Silence
is the   only   response
                                        to such   catastrophe
                                        to
such   collusion
but I
cannot bear the   silence
                                                        silence
                                    silence
                        silence
perhaps
in the   end
we who are poor in
                        spirit
cannot bear the necessary
                            guilt

we have inherited
and have resorted to the
                            noise
of money and the
                    stirring
of cheap
        desire
and   i e
str-a-a-ange   f r w
                                    o
                                    rk

                                s
                                                                    dna

the dying
        fire

the fire made
                    brighter
by the impending   death
of the   moon

where has She gone
will She be coming
                                        soon

higher   &
higher
the Babel
towers
climb
towards   the moon
above
            the streets that never
                            rest
above
            the crowds of restless
            speculators digging through the
                                                        nights
with the aid of a million   lights
at once
                        collaborating
                             &
                        competing
in a single tongue
ringing through the global bazaar
                                                        dolar
                                                        dolar

                    Dollar vobiscum

where napalm failed the chain saw
takes the strain as verdant jungles
                                    turn
to corn then dusty plain bones
                                    turn
to bonds and axes
                                    turn
to gold and taxes
                                    turn
to bones and Dollars
                                    turn
to flesh and flesh to
                                                        dollars

                dollar Dollar DOLLAR

on every screen there is speculation
and   pornography
and   homicide
       forged
       by the cyber alchemists who
                                        turn

       everything into gold
       every thing can be bought
and   sold a woman for heroin
and   a child for cocaine
and   a country for a crate of beads that

ex   pl   ode
in a shower of toxic
rain the acid rain
falls mainly in the plain
                    somehow
the damage results in a tidy sum
Dolar vobiscum

from   New York   to   Shanghai
from   London   to   Mumbai
the waves of Dollars
come   and come   and come
forged by a ratchet spasm the
rapist orgasm the
ever swinging axe the
death tax the
bones of the slain the
dry bones on the
dusty plain

          where did the sun
                    go
          when did the colour
                    fade

          I see them in the Caravaggio light
          a short step from Hitchcock
          all in seeming black and white

and did those feet in distant climes
walk through the cities of the plain
and was the holy lamb of God
scarred by a shower of acid rain
and was the countenance divine
cast into shadow by the light
and was Gomorrah builded here
a place of ceaseless restless night

                            screen flash
jungle slash

                                                           no escape
gold
and   rape rape
and   gold bought
and   sold bland
and   cold

                hope I die before I get old

           when will She come
           when will night   tur
                                                          otni n
           day
                              miserere
                          miserere mei

                                                     somewhere
a butterfly dies
and the weather   changes   forever
they say
you could set your calendar and watch
by Caribbean rain
but
                                                     never again
the rain
comes early
                                                              or
the rain comes late
and
the climate has   turned
                                                       otni
weather
and there is no telling
what will happen
from   day   to   day
and
another
lump of ice
           f
           a
           l
           l
             s
              into
                 Lago Gray
and the popsicle icebergs
                                          float
                                                        away

and   the river roars
and   the river dies
and   a star shell
                          sh   att   er   s
and   She shuts Her
                      eyes
and   nobody cries

tears are souvenirs

and   all that is left is GDP
and   a poisonous sea
and   tales of what used to be
      in the land of the fair
and   the free

                              dollar dollar
                               Dollar Dollar
                                 Dollar! Dollar!
                                          DOLLAR DOLLAR!
                                      follow
                        follow
come   come
                       dollar vobiscum

from blood
shot pearl to blood
shot pearl   across   the   barren
plain the beautiful
people fly with their bronzed limbs and
lycra libidos as if
they can defy
the fact that they will   die
to
new Babylons of barbed wire and
burglar alarms where the beautiful
people feverishly dress and undress
in their unreal world
of unreal charms of wealth
and   success
and   the barely suppressed
fear that the press of a button
and   half the world's Euros   t
urn   into Dollars
and   then   in
to Yen
and
                                            kcab

again

the fruits of ploughing and planting
                                   nothing tu
                                   nr
into air miles
and   another plane to
      another pearl
and   another trade
and   another girl
      from   blood shot pearl
      to   blood shot pearl across the dying sea
and   when the bough breaks
                  the cradle will fall
                  down will come babies cradles
and

                                                         all
but
the traders in their towers
and   the girls with their flowers
                            t
                          nru
their backs as the cradles
splinter for kindling
                  in the bleak midwinter
when the bough breaks
it's always another
who falls to his death
in front of his mother
it's always another
who is told to behave
as a friend and a brother
even though you have stolen
his job and his lover

            I remember Mesa Verde in the snow
            the improbable
            architecture of hearth and cliff and
            the stone in the meal
            of life and death and we
            would not have it so but
            in Monument Valley the people
            drank
                  and

                  sank

                                                     so
                                                     low
            having seen pictures
            of Babylon they could not
                                       let   go

and were those feet in Babylon
put on a treadmill in the gym
and was the holy lamb of God
put on a plan to make him slim
and did the countenance divine
shine forth among the movie stars
and was Jerusalem builded here
in jacuzzis and cocktail bars

splash   cash
            cash   dash
            on the descent you
            can see the wounds
            of neon in the pearl
            in the dull pearl show of
            the marble towers in
            the moonlight glow where
            did the sun
                        go
            when
                did the colour
                            fade
            where
            has She gone

                                                            higher
                        and
higher
the Babel towers climb
            to the light of the silvery   moon
above
the never resting streets
above
the crowds of restless
prospectors digging through
the nights with the aid of
a million lights
at once
collaborating   and   competing
in a single   tongue
                        ringing
out through the global bazaar
to the slave
and   the con
and   the star
                                                            far
and   near
        near
and   far
Dolar Dolar

Dollar vobiscum

where
  napalm failed the chain saw takes
  the strain as verdant jungles
turn to corn
  then dusty plain
  somehow bones
turn to bonds and axes
turn to gold and taxes
turn to bones
and on every screen
  there is speculation
and pornography
and homicide
  forged by the cyber alchemists who
turn everything into gold
  every thing can be bought
and sold
a child   for cocaine
a woman   for heroin
a country   for a crate of needles
         that impale the skin in
a shower   of toxic brain

the acid rain falls mainly on the plain
                    in the brain
somehow
the damage results in a tidy sum
        dolar vobiscum
from   New York   to   Shanghai
from   London   to   Mumbai
the   waves of Dollars
come &   Come &   COME
forged by a ratchet spasm
the rapist's orgasm
the ever swinging axe
the death tax
the bones of the slain
the dry bones
on the dusty plain

   where did the sun
        go
         when
  O when did the
      colour fade

  when will She come
  when will night

```
         turn into day
                              miserere
                          miserere mei


             I remember
             seeing the golden heads
             of grain in the slightly
             undulating plain of Picardy
             with sun flowers glowing in the
             gold and elms in water
             as if
             van Gogh              and                    Monet
             were calling          across
             the water gardens of Amiens
             before the guns sounded at Mons
             so bright the virgin grain
             in the flowered
             plain
and thousands
of miles away another lump
of glacier
          falls
              into
                            Lago Grey
it is impossible
to say
where the line is to be
drawn
                         between
the natural                and                    the industrial
corn                     between
the agricultural           and                      the military
smoke                    between
the river's                and                    the soldier's
rage                     between
the farmer's               and                    the soldier's
croak                    between
the lions                  and                       the hyenas
that made the meters
jam                      between
the pesticides             and                       the napalm


                         fire fire

sparks fly
savage
as if
in play
lighting the fires                                    at the end
of another             sunless                        day
```

```
        Oh!                                                    o
        where did the sun                                     go


                        FIRE!


perhaps
it was the sheer                                    devastation
of    land      and   spirit
of    position  and   orientation
of    purpose   and   direction
                          which                            cut
us
                                                          loose
from any sense of                                          form
from any sense of                              responsibility
perhaps
we lost
or
did we throw                                               away
the map
or
did we
think
always supposing such a word is not an exaggeration
there was no way                                           back
to an unwritten reciprocity
of feeling
of fair dealing


                                                        attack

                               Attack

                    Attack!
              ATTACK
ATTACK!!!


            I remember
            the shock of the shallowness of the
            White Rhinoceros after
            the blighted gravitas of former days
            for his  obtusenesses still  I could
            attach a part of me to pallid Soames
            against the lurid charms  of Michael
            Mont for notwithstanding  dull  self
            consciousness  of style and eminence
            there was something of the solemnity
            of the dance                          over
nwo                                               rht
```

by the

                                          tan

                                            g

                                              o

but
it would be unfair to think
                    FIRE
                        ATTACK!
this frivolity totally without
foundation as liberals made sacrifices
and still smiled
but
                something
                    snap- ped

and   the Greek
and   the Latin
and   the illuminated monastic manuscripts
and   the illumination of Dante
and   the forensic skills of Shakespeare
and   the classical necessity of Racine   lost
      purchase in
                a single generation
           a concern not primarily curatorial
but   moral not in the judgmental way
but   in the matter of sensibility
and   what started as satire is now
      a firestorm
                    ATTACK ATTACK!
                        FIRE
                  !erif
    amid the desiccated tinder of our traditions
sparks supposed playful
are lethal
having turned on each other
                    on the Somme
we have come to turn on ourselves
they   seeming   playful
are scintillatingly
savage   aggressive

        not self referential
        knowing that ultimately
        there is nothing to say about Charlus
                Charlus
                Charlus Charlus!
        only to understand the lived
        experience the sense of being
      inextricably bound with time and a tradition and to
        each other
                fire fire!

fire
     against tradition
                          fire
                          against structure
                                        against trust
the blaze of the referential is the most catastrophic
                                                    leaving

                                                    only
the surface   the shallow sense
     of the syntax
and   then there is the ultimate
     the destruction of trust

we are all alone
                    now
        all alone

the words have lost
their sap and are dried to   nothing
               we are
                    as it were
               unclean
               we are   faded
               like a leaf
               our good deeds   torn
               like rags
dried to nothing we
are the husks that are left to blow
in the hostile winds of the plain
          O
          where has She gone
          that it should come to this
          that we have been   left
          after Dante's
                    setting sun
          with the moon
and   our dying fires
and   a traitor's kiss
and   the ruin of what is left of our self
absorbed desires we have been left
to hate ourselves
                         for not knowing what
we ought to know
          O
          the moon glows dim
          on Mrs Porter and her daughter they
          wash their feet in sparkling water wondering
          what love will bring when there is
          no Sweeney in the Spring

                    wondering
                    how long
                    the diamond clasp will
                    hold will somehow
                    bring a sense of purpose to
                    growing old
                    wondering
                    how they might reclaim a sense
                    of themselves more substantial
                    than a stole
                    or an exquisitely manicured
                    hand on a golden
                    bowl

and   then
      the scene shifts when
we came back why
did you give us
              nothing when
we came back and
were not unduly demanding why
did you give us
              nothing why
were we sent back
                  to
our various degradations
                        as if
we had done nothing and
                    when
the second time they promised
us a land fit for heroes we
half believed and they
more than half
kept their promise of
cheap
     houses and
cheap
     televisions and
cheap
     cosmetics and pasta and
cheap
     credit   and   cars   and   rock'n'roll   and
endless movie stars and
then without noticing it the stuffing went
out of our books and
                  our conclusions
sparks   play
            sparks   play   sparks
     play   sparks   play
                        FIRE!!

```
                                                                    fire
                                                          fire
                                              sparks play
                                    sparks play
                          play fire
                play fire                                            fire
fire


now
there is self parody instead
of parody and self
consciousness instead of consciousness and
I watch you watching me watching you watching me watching me
waiting to
        die
but hating that prospect more
than any other building up
a stock of lonely treasure
in the                    passing           passing        away
pleasure


and did those feet in troubled times
walk upon England's new laid lawns
and was the holy lamb of God
counted among the countless pawns
and was the countenance divine
made up to draw the camera's glare
and was Jerusalem erected here
amid a shock of pubic hair

fire
                              desire
                                                          higher
                                                             and
                                                          higher
forget
     the trust
now
   we have lust
the spark ignites
the archives in the dark Greeks and
Romans go away Dante and
Proust have turned to dust we
are betrayed we are
afraid they have left us with
nothing
but mistrust                                           miserere
                        miserere mei
mei
```

                    Longtemps
when Swann was dashing and Odette
wore violet in the dark time
that to us seems to hang heavy
perhaps allowed for a certain
degree of discrimination for a way
of looking outwards as well
as inwards before we exchanged
the microscope for the telescope and
Freud for Jesus when we knew
the names of birds and plants and
could see the stars and when
perhaps we were a little less
moralistic and a little more moral
when Bergotte was writing at his best before
the time when he was better at seeing the patch of yellow in
Vermeer
than his own pen when moonlight
ruled the romantic mind we had
a kind of coping strategy
for the bright day's end and the long
night of the body and the soul
knowing ourselves to be in
age of silver far past
the age of gold
in the dull glitter of pearl and pewter and
the heavy comfort of damask and velvet
when we made a virtue of the domestic self
consciously distanced from the rustic
longtemps
we dipped our biscuit and wondered
if that bar of Vinteuil's Sonata was
quite as it should be
but with the gas and the shells and
the gas and the piles of shoes
it is hardly surprising that our laborious
discrimination collapsed
into brashness as
our heavy bourgeois trappings went up
in flames

to be replaced by virtual fun and games when
the evening gown gave way
to the bikini and the requiem dwindled to
the ballad
longtemps longtemps
longtemps
longtemps

---

                time present and
                time past are both
          perhaps present in time
                           future
          on the Starnbergersee
           you gave me hyacinths
               first a year ago
          against the mountain
             snow snow on snow
                       long ago
        I only have eyes for you

             Charlus! Charlus!

                  's View of Delft
                      and roses

             A Kind of Blue
          Te lucis ante terminum
            lighten our darkness
        the dangers and perils of
                     this night
           for a manger-bed

                   underground

                      longtemps
               as I wandered
           every good boy
          deserves favour
                        datta
             da dayadhvam
            da damyata
        London Bridge is falling down
      these fragments I have shored
           against my ruins

                    fire! fire!
             girls and boys
              go out to play
         I did it my way
      shantih shantih shantih

                              amen

```
there is
no time     to mourn
just buy    a card and a teddy bear and
            a bouquet then cry a little
                                                    and forget
no time     for cantatas and serenatas
now
            we have the beat from the street    in our feet and
no time     for extended improvisation
now
            we test our reflexes
            at the play station
no sense    of the learned gesture
when        we are assaulted
            buy naked flesh
not that we are different from
            any age in wanting sensation and money
it is just that we are
less frightened     of God and
less aware          of ourselves and
more wanton
more careless       than sinful
```

genug genug!

```
Schlummert ein,                   close your careworn eyes
ihr matten Augen                              in sleep
Fallet sanft                        soft and blissful
und sellig zu!                       tension eased
Welt, ich bleibe,               world you have nought
nicht mehr hier:                     I would keep
Hab ich doch               since that part in you
kein Teil an dir,                   has ceased
Das der Seele                 that might live
konnte taugen.                   my soul in me
Hier muss ich                    here my lot
dass Elend bauen                is misery
Aber dort                    but there, up there
dort werd ich schauen             I long to be
Sussen Frieden,                     at peace
stille Ruh.                 in hushed tranquility

Ich habe genug                    it is enough
Da entkomm ich            then shall I escape
aller Not,                          to mirth
Die mich noch               from the prison
auf der Welt gebunden.          of the earth

Genug!                              enough!
```

and did those feet in velvet
times walk through the drawing room
with grace and was the holy
lamb of god accorded proper pride
of place and was the countenance
divine reflected in the golden
bowl and was Jerusalem appointed
here far from the fumes
of lead and coal

        O where did the sun
                            go
     when
         did the colour
                 fade
  O
       will She ever
         come!
                                                  ewig

the torment
      in the note
the torment
      in the girl
the torment
      in the temps perdu
Ah me!   Ah you!
      the impossible climb
  towards the   sun
      suffering
      from the Sisyphian gravity
      of the Faustian pact
      living within eternal
                gloom
      explicit
      in the greed for
      the artificial
             light
      Faust
      the cleverest of fools
      where did the sun
             go   we know
      when did the colour
             fade we know fade where is She
      is She coming
          soon   god knows
      all we have is the
          moon
      we are playing with the
      spark we are frightened of the   dark
      genug
                        kyrie

it is almost over
                        now
all is   chaff
                        chiff chaff
to be   thrown
on the bonfire of   mystery
                        chiff chaff
the end of   history
Plato and Aristotle   adieu
              I can no longer be with you
          on the hard road   with the long view
      adieu adieu

what is truth   truth chaff for the bonfire of mystery
I will therefore I am only   the will   I know in me is true
history is bunk   facts are hacked   adrift   from history
now is the time to say   Plato and Aristotle adieu
goodbye   adieu
farewell
adieu
exegi monumentum aere perennius
no longer stands and serves
the immortal few
so much
so few
so many

always on   crazed into ring tones plangent
in singles bars
before the Anschluss   Mahler's last extended threnody
                             I could have danced is played
all night   with naked flesh
to sell cigars
on a G string   settling Bach's score seductively

                    genug genug

                                                    genug

Derrida derides   against   the legacy   of form   and trust
Foucault plays   sparks swallow reference in a scornful rage
Lyotard scoffs   what monks illumined Dante graced and Proust
fire down below enlarged they seeming playful
                                        scorch the page

                    Charlus Charlus
                      ewig ewig
              where did the sun go
              when did the colour fade
                    from the intensity of Caravaggio
                    to playful and languid rage

men may come   the Gaia meters stretch off screen and jam
and men may go   the mighty Indus jerks from rage to croak
but I go on   the time of glaciersquickenstowards the
forever   dam grain smoke chokes like eating coke
and ever
Alleluia! Alleluia   king of kings
forever and ever   and lord of lords
                         alleluia! alleluia!
and He shall reign   forever and ever
but   where did His sun
                              go   where did his Son
          if you have borne him away   go
          tell me   when did His colour
          that I might bring him back   fade
                              veni
                         creator spiritus

my vineyard   the glittering Levis of the faceless tax
what have you   in towers of Babel stock and bond the slain
done to   where jungles fell beneath the bomb and axe
my vineyard   they forge the tools to rake the ravaged
and the rough places   plain
                         Dollar vobiscum

dollar   vobiscum
               I remember when
               we walked the Autumn   leaves
               woods moved by the final blazing fire of life
               more lovely and necessarily   as desperate
               as Spring is hopeful
               and crunching the leaves
               as if they had
                         fallen   for our pleasure
                                                before

               the men with tractors
               came and the way
               every flower and bird and lichen
               had its name and
               what made life   eternal
               was the   promise of
               the returning   flame

               where has She   gone

all animals   as stooges and apparatchiks feed the maw
are equal but   the Somme lives on beyond arithmetic
some are more   glass blue and green that nature never
equal than others   saw The flames flare chemical burned
thick as a   brick

                         Shoah

Kyrie

                                                                miserere
miserere   mei

in a cadenza of hubris and fury we
have
      fallen from ritual
            and mystery to
from people to   explanation and system
                  process from
                        the holocaust to
from   the shoah
      Marxism to
                  the dynasty of
                  North Korea from
                        language
                                          to
                                                silence

                  to assuage the gloom of never ending night
lead   downward they claw for phosphorus and gold
kindly   baleful the moon shines in Her reflected
light   the ash of Auschwitz is not
                                                      cold
                  kyrie
                                          miserere
haunted
by ash and an angel's   shadow
                        A Kind of Blue
ah me   ah you
            where did the sun go
            when did the colour fade
            when will She come
            O when
            is there a glimmer in the   East
            or is it an   illusion
            is it a cloud or has the   moon
            grown pale
            it is nothing we can   remember
            but an idea
            which has not quite   died
                                          of roseate
                              dawn
                        and a new
                  morning
            O
morning star
Veni   creator   spiritus

veni creator spiritus

and did those feet
in desperate times
willingly walk
the extra mile
and did the holy
Lamb of God
disperse the darkness
with his smile

and did that
countenance divine
subdue the Dollar
and the gun
and was Jerusalem
promised here
with a new rising
of the sun

veni

bring me my thread
of constant prayer
bring me a word
of fond regret
bring me my past
oh age unfold
bring me the strength
not to forget et

lest we forget

I will not cease
from endless faith
nor shall my love
sleep in my hand
till we have built Jerusalem
where hope will rise
and She will stand

Moonlight

amen

                                        gaudete
                                          veni
                                   veni creator
                                          veni
                                   veni creator

                                     Agnus Dei
                                     qui tollis
                                 peccata mundi
                                 miserere nobis

                                     Agnus Dei
                          qui tollis peccata mundi
                               dona nobis pacem
                                 the holy city
                               a new Jerusalem
                                 decked as a bride
                               for her bridegroom

                                        gaudete

                     te ergo quaesumus famulis tuis
                        subveni quos pretioso
                        sanguine redemisti
                     nunc dimittis servum tuum
                   Domine secundum verbum tuum
                               in pace in pace
                     lumen ad revelationem gentium
                        gloriam plebis tuae Israel

                                        shoah
                        dimitte nobis debita nostra
                                miserere nostri
                    fiat misericordia tua Domine super nos
                     quemadmodum speravimus in te
                                in te Domine speravi
                        non anfundar in aeternum

                     Magnificat anima mea Dominum
                                          Amen

                                        AMEN.

II.

                              round

                  and   and

r   r
o   o
u   u
n   n
d   d

                  and   and

                              round

the mill wheel
grinds   SMALLER   smaller
              &
round

                                                    &
                                                        round

                              &
smaller
                                        &
                                                        smaller
the mill
                      wheel grinds
salvation   into   powder
            'tis not the mills of God
            that grind exceeding
            slowly and exceeding
small for if
            God has wheels
they do not grind at
all but carry us His
children to where we may hear
His call   but
            the wheels of man
            who thinks he heeds
                      God's   call
            be-cassocked
                              humpty-dumpties
            of salvation
                                                    &
                                                        the
                                                        fall

            meanwhile

```
                    in a dingy street a widow
                    feeds a neighour
                    widow's child
                                        not
                    because she will gain another
                    scruple of salvation
                    powder                                    from the
                                                          m   i   l   l

                    but because
                    it is hungry young
                    and cold and she
                    is                                            only
                    hungry cold and
                    old
                    kindness                                       for
                                                                   its
                                                                   elf

                    the sense of who
                    we are                                        made
                                                                    to
                                                                    be
                    imperfect so that we might be                good

round                              &                           round
with a threatening
sound as if                                                 nothing
        had changed                                    since
        the publican and the pharisee                  since
        Jesus was killed
        by authority                                   since
        Peter and John stood                           before the
        Sanhedrin                                      since
        Stephen was stoned
perhaps
it was Paul who brought
the end of innocence                                        half
in love with love                                            and
                                                            half

in love with sin but
it was always a foregone conclusion which
would win
Jesus the gentle
pharisee out-written by Paul
the mad
        slaves and soldiers in
        the catacombs always
        needing orders
to maintain                                        the borders
        for their own good something
        understood then
```

```
       the fine people
       arrive with just a hint
       of purple
and    after a                                        somewhat
                                                      fractious

       Eucharist the elders are seen whispering
       in a corner with an architect
and    as they climb
             ds      ds
         war &   war
         up   out
from
                                      catacombs and kitchens
and    the clandestine paraphernalia
       of a police state
to
       churches how-dyou-do
and    liturgy the women lose their place
and    the slaves know just where to sit
and    the elders know just
       where to stand for the greatest
       effect with the bread raised high
       in a manicured
       hand       the body of the Lord          is broken
                  just for you at the end
                  of a queue unless
a Jew by command
                  of the Senators of Christ            then
the trumpet sounds                            and the dead
and The Cross                                 shall be raised
at the Milvian Bridge                         incorruptible
and   we shall be                                    saved
as    The Cross and the Eagle
seal the Empire's                                     fate
as                                           Christ triumphant
servum servorum                                        dei
stands with his keys at the city                      gate
The Cross                  &                      the Eagle
The Eagle                  &                      The Cross
                                              Eagle & Cross
Eagle                      &                          Cross


and    the realm of noble near-miss               Polycarp
and    the dew                                    of Jesus
       on the Celtic hills are
       swallowed by edgy alliances
and    outbreaks of unimpeded power
and    the trade of Lydia
                      between
                  Pope & prince
```

```
and                                                     Jesus lives
        in palaces
and     the officers mess with servants
        bearing silver dishes
and     estimates of marble to be
                              re    con
                              fig ured
from         Apollo                    to            The Virgin
and     orders of service
and     council minutes
and     the latest tracts                        on hypostasis
and     the latest bulletin                          on Arius
and     as
                    the canon & the Creed
and       the schools and the rules
and                   the bitterness and the schism
and       the pomp and the pride and the governance
and                   the structure and the hierarchy
and       the process and the product

                                                   are forged
                                                        on
the Papal                      &                 the Imperial
                                                      anvils
Martin                         &                    Nicholas
fight                          &                       preach


and


the peasants                   &                    the slaves
the craftsmen                  &                 the gentlemen
        look for sweet Jesus in the days
        of dying freedom before
                        the Councils and the Vandals
          the Emperors and the Ostrogoths
                  the Patriarchs and the Visigoths
        prepare respectively
to      imprison
and     destroy

                        the quiet lake              Byzantium
                        of Galilee                  Byzantium!
                        the Mount of Olives        seven hills
                        the carpenter            a marble mason
                        His smiling face          an icon gold
                        His simple words        the binding book
                        His self                   a doctrine
                        His life                    codified
                        He only lives               because
                                                    He died
```

                life debris   in His
                                                           passiontide

then
in a moment of desperate
denial of self responsibility which
will recur with Luther Descartes and Rousseau
Augustine of Hippo productises sin in a way
that would have puzzled Paul even more than
Jesus in the concept
of the fall born
                            between
excrement   &   urine
we hardly look at all as if
we were created by a loving
God more like a hanging
judge who sentences each
of us   and His Son
and leaves us   in no doubt
of our brokennness
with the sack of Rome
crushing us   against
a tottering wall where   we are
but for that Jesus   lost
who died for our sins   who died for us
                        all
we who can do   nothing at all

                        Kyrie
                        eleison
miserere   mei

we have   moved
from the bread of the body
broken in fellowship   for me
miserere   mei
to the blood that flows to
wash   away   my
                                                        sin
which lets the clerical   brokers
                                                         in

                as the hordes of Visigoths and
                Vandals sweep the sumptuous
                plains those that are out
                of earshot of the slaughter offer
                refugees a little bread   and water
                before the news they hear
                makes them equal to those
                they have just fed
                        miserere

and   away
                    from the battles   and bishops
                    the fathers   retreat
                    to monasteries in the Egyptian   desert
                    who see that the alliance
                                between
the Eagle   &   the Cross
has been a failure for
                    each leaving the See of Peter to pick up
                    the Latin pieces
                    while in   Byzantium
                                                          Byzantium!

                    fusion
                    has politicised religion and
                    deified politics as
                Emperor   &   Patriarch
                    uneasily rehearse a   dance
                                &
the gentilisation   &   gentrification
                    of Jesus are   complete
                    He is a
New Roman   and an   old Greek
                    now heaven reaches
                    down to the high
                    altar of Hagia   O wisdom
                    Sofia and although   O Sapientia
Jesus is far away   God is very near
we are lost
                    we are all lost
                                but are we not saved
            and how are we saved
                                and who is saved
            and how do we know who is saved
                    perhaps   we are
                                                        all lost
                                        but we are not
                                                        all lost

for out of the Celtic mist
emerges a sketch   of a plan
of a mighty salvation engine
as a monk in a humble
cell tabulates the tariffs
for escaping   hell
and so
the holy mill   begins to grind
exceeding   small
and exceeding   slow
                                round
&   &
                                round

                                                                          and
in the name of Jesus
the mightiest enterprise   that ever was
mightier than the Empire   of Alexander
mightier   than Rome
is built to feed   the mill
with   chapels
                    &   chantries   &
     cloisters &   cathedrals   &
         pieties   &   pardons
&   prayers   &
         penances   &   sacrifices
to feed the mill to
placate our God who   somehow
made us needing to
do it like savages   but
with a more certain outcome under
written by the Holy See which
hit upon the ingenious device of translating
salvation   into   money
and Infidel
blood   into   salvation

but   where were you
           as the peasants toiled with their sinews
           snapped and their wives
           despoiled
and   where were you
           when the streets of Jerusalm ran
           red with the blood of the Chosen
           People
and   where were you
           when your people sacked
           Byzantium
and   celebrated the treacherous
           catastrophe by singing the Latin Te
           Deum in God's name in Hagia
           Sofia preparing for the Infidel
                                     collecting the rents
                                     protecting the rich
                                      riding to hounds
                                      jousting at court
                                      counselling kings

           minding   the mill

                                          oh yes
                                      minding the mill
           a millennium of   minding the mill
           building and   minding the mill
           Oh yes   minding the mill
           Oh yes   minding the mill

the shadows lengthen   and the colour fades
with the setting sun   and gloom pervades
the nights grow longer   and the blackness claws
as the Summer fails   at the weakening
for all its faults   day
that earth which smiled is
dull

the pious folk who bought
indulgences at your behest buy
Bibles mark and inwardly
digest and worry
your worries and suffer
your power and find
no stillness in the twilight
hour
and   the lust for gold to allay
the gloom brings death
from slaughter
and   disease to Indians past anything
inflicted on the Infidel or
the Byzantines clinging to the Blessed
Virgin
and   in a small town
in Germany the misery
of Luther is so intense he
takes a hammer to the mill   the mill
and in three decades smashes   the mill
leaving nothing but
abject dependence on God back
to the drudgery of miserable
earth
no sun but man
toiling in the dark with
only
the moon
for light   fire!
the days grow
shorter
and   the nights grow
longer
God is only seen
now
in the moon
sin is past
remedy out of human
hands

moonlight
moon light

```
but man must build                                      must build
must build must
begin again                                              to build
rival mills the Roman                                        mill
more modest than its predecessor                              yet
mechanically much improved with clerical                  custody
to care for it and
all other believers                                     relegated
to supplicants the other in Geneva                      pitiless
lacking even the guise of                                    self
sufficiency spawning                                   capitalism
enslaving
                  body and soul
in grinding out                                              time
the elect                                          grinding down
the non elect
                  body and soul


          and we the saints
          watched poor souls
          unsought for Christ's Kingdom
          on earth only sent
          salvation vouchers                          from Rome
and       production vouchers                        from Geneva


                                                             oh

where were you when I called
                for unity when
                penitence was forgotten
                in the name of orthodoxy when
                doctrine tore you when
                you thought that I was more
                like something from Euripides than
                a Galilaean child a
                child of Abba
where were you when Luther nailed his theses to
                the door and the councils and
                tribunals sat in pallid
                reverence to the ghost of Byzantium when
                broken bread was fought over by
                scholars and the horsemen
                rode out to kill
                in my name when
                half of Europe slaughtered for
                the Cross and
where were you when Galileo no more radical than
                Alfonso the Wise or Hildegard considered
                the heavenly bodies too proud to
                look up too
proud                                                   too proud
```

                  Oh

where were you

              in the beauties
               of the broken
             pearls seduced
             by beauty blind
            to babel hearts
            warmed by art's
             allure too rapt
              to walk
               away

far

    from the people set
    fast in Rome and
where were you when the Genevan mill
    strengthened by the wits
    the Father gave you to
    build the Kingdom
    not blot out
      the sun and
where were you when millions of bewildered
    peasants laboured in the smoke and
where were you when the ships' maws
    opened and shut with
      slaves & sugar
      sugar & slaves
    the sweet scent
    of gold and the sour
    reek of corpses

         bowing to the golden
        monstrance inveighing
          against the

      gold & sugar
      sugar & gold

         that we bought
         and sold blind
         to brotherhood
        thinking you were
         white deaf to
       the cries for freedom
        in the Barbuda
          night
           and
where were you when the crops failed and
    the plague ravaged

       some of us laboured
       for the poor and
       sick but the times
        were against
         us

                                                          the Bastille
                                                               fell

                        with my name smirched
                        in the name of   hell
when   you somehow thought
                        you were doing   well
                        no wonder the Bastille   fell

thus   Rome   the home of Peter
and   Paris which gave the Angelic Doctor home were torn
and   Paris   which the Angelic
          split apart   Doctor called home
          no matter that Descartes and
          Pascal still
          struggled to believe   but
          the sheer ignorance and intransigence of dignity and
          let in idiot delusionist self   dogma
          indulgent will
                        what had been built   with careful
                        with high   hands
                        though flawed intent   broken
                        razed with the logic and   wit
                        sarcasm of an age made
                        new as bad old mother
                        church with narrowing narrowing
                        eyes averted   from the Jesus
                        wrote her own   of Julian and
                        epitaph   the mystic wisdom of
                        in gold leaf   the sensus fidelium
                        as if it had taken the golden
                        calf and plated the Sinai
                        tablets and
                        set them up in the marbled
                        atrium of the corporate
                        mill
                                        round
                            &   &
                                        round
                        a clerical replica
                        of the dark
          satanic mill bells
and   whistles clocking in
and   strict observances
and   punishments
and   sackings
excommunications
and
                                    &
                        round   round
                                    &

```
      the                                                golden
      thurible
and   the                                              jewelled
      monstrance
and   the                                          oppression of
      the confessional
but   always
      the mill


poor creatures with precious
little bread and precious
little pleasure in
their intimacy
driven by survival and the                      terror and
relentless turning of the                     degradation of
mill and                                       hard times and
the mine                                            Germinal
such small sins for
such crushed people with
such burdens of guilt and
such sorrow and
such fleeting              fleeting                      joy
once
   when I was young between
       the beatings at school and the beating of
                   the drum before
           I was condemned to live
                    forever underground only
     solaced by beer and an occasional
                 coupling when I had the energy
                             more in hope
              of children to sustain us than
              in pursuit of pleasure
                          I thought I was in heaven
              for an afternoon
           when the sun shone on the ripening
                  corn and a lass and
   I bathed naked in a stream as if
           in Eden moved by awe to look
                        too wondrous to touch and then
       too weak to soldier I
drove the children in the mine and she
was raped by a foreman and
was found with child to save
his shame she was given up like Uriah
to serve at the most dangerous
front and both were
soon


                                                      dead
```

where were you when the common
                  man rose to defend his family
                  life to bring the unbalanced bond
                  between labour and capital back
                  into balance to
                  feed children and
                  keep them off the streets
                  as beggars or worse or
did you think   that revolution was an alien
                  atheist sport did you
not think   that you had left a
                  vacuum
                  through your
                  indifference

                                    we were fending off
                                        the revolution
                                          preserving
                                    stability and good
                                        order keeping
                                           on good
                                    terms with the judge
                                           eternal
                                       suffering God
                                     knows the lesser
                                        to prevent
                                       the greater
                                       ill minding
                                    the mill minding
                                          the mill

where was your sense of Jesus in
                  the struggle and
where was your interest in healing
                  the sick the science
                  of healing and hygiene seeming to
                  forget Gregory the Great
                  up your ultramontane
                                             affairs of
                                       state affairs of
                                         state keeping
                                     a grip on the terms
                                         of debate and
where were you when the gates
                  were locked against the just
                  cause   fighting
                                              revolution
                                          in the House of
                                                  Lords

yes you were   there   in the margins
                Christian Socialists fighting the
                Church as much as the capitalist
                powers leaning on
                each other for mutual
                support then came the war
                credits and the death
                of Jean Jaures but
                it would all be over
                by Christmas
                        across
            the broken
              ground
            as I
                lay dying I
                     saw or thought
                            I saw an angel
                                        beckoning
                                     me home
                                     back
                        to the Christmas hearth and the
                             tiny church where the rustic
                        choir most of whom are lying
                             with me now sang
                                            carols
                             and the Winter
            evenings shivering at our bedsde
                 prayers to gentle Jesus but
                 then I remember how I had
                                        walked away
                             from childish things
                                 to where angels
                             were no more than
        decorations in fine pictures or golden mythic wings
            to shelter mythic or mystic
                 Jesus whom I never quite
                                    forgot and
                 I made my own way to manhood and
                 to this
                      so
                     what or who is this angel
                          no
                          nothing
                     but an illusion
                left behind
            by a church for children or two-
              faced a church of barren abstract talk of concepts
                                            outside
the life that I then
lived

                    the angel faded and
                          my light went
                                    out
and
   as I hover over the blood
and mud the smoke and gas I can see
   a splintered church where no child
           might crouch no
       choir boy sing all
                  prayer gone and wonder
                  if fairness is a part of being God or
                          whether it's only a foolish
                                  human ambition
                              an illusion God
                  knows when I was small they
                  promised hell if I did wrong and
              I have just died in it for
                          doing very little of any sort I
                  cannot believe that
walking away
and being a man
     merited what I've been through
                 and
where were you in body and spirit
                  spirit as the presses rumbled and
                  the newsreels skittered and flickered
                                          defining the fact
                                      refining the message
                                      maintaining the mill
                  ah yes! minding the mill
                                      discerning God's will
                  too far away to know how you
                  the rich are different
                  from the slum and the bare
                  feet and the babies and
                  the landlord and
                  the debt collector and the pressure
                  to test the boundaries
                  of what you would call moral by
                  the rich and powerful whom you
                  by your silence at best
                  implied were moral and
                  where were you when false prophets arose
                  ranting about the irrefutable
                  arguments of concrete and steel and
                  converting disciples into the proletariat
                  almost a century of rhetoric and you were still
                  unready   minding the mill
                                          for good against
                                                      ill
                  ah yes   minding the mill

yet   it was they
                           who brought the good news
                           of justice and bread of
                           the straight back and raised
                           head of the dignity
                           of humanity not a figure
                           kneeling to the Lord but to
                           the foreman totally
                           in thrall to mammon and driven
                           out of the kingdom and
where were you when the train arrived
                           at the Finland Station not
                           of the welcoming party but
                           at the Winter Palace shoring up
                           a despot
                                        we would have
                                 followed
                           the Czar
   for so little
     for such few
       concessions but
         as it turned out
                      we would have followed the Czar
                 if he had asked for more
                            had we known what was coming
                                      but we thought
                it was the end
                                          of war   not
                                   the beginning
                                        of the grimmest
                                            mill yet
                             that man had turned
                                    to sell a kind
                                        of salvation
               the cruellest ever
               doctrine of the elect murder
               in the name of freedom
               thousands died for no apparent
               reason and hundreds of thousands more
               were the victims of paranoid megalomania
                           and yes you had your sufferings
                           like us
                           but you could do nothing once
                                          you lost
                                          your mill
                     no tenderness
                     no risk
                     no suffering   too harsh
                                 with us
                                          too harsh

                                                           no
            even in your disintegration
                    you are too self satisfied
        without Hitler the Soviet
        epoch would have been the worst
        that befell humanity
                                            but we only knew
                                            that later
        spirits over the gulags and the collective farms and
                    some say
            without the dictatorship of the proletariat or
        rather the dictatorship of the secret
            police we could not have triumphed
                    over Hitler but I say and
            my comrades say we would have been better
    off fighting for freedom than fighting out of fear
                            we kept our icons
                    secret
            longer than you dreamed but
        the church of Mother Russia   disintegrated
        splintered dismembered a rotten
        husk trampled   smashed
        under foot by the irrefutable   brutal
        arguments of concrete and steel
        the inevitable   catastrophe
        culmination of the brutalising
        of serfdom
        the hierarchy
        of terror the genealogy
        of vice
                which you promised
                    to break
        but you brokered a merger   a merger
        between church and state   of mills
        after which you were   pulverised
        ruthlessly disimissed and
where were you as the barriers rose and
        the moderate social justice
        of 'revisionists' was driven
        out by extremists   counting
why were you   still supporting the ancient   the silver
        regime when the centre   counting
        cried out for help   the commas
        before it was engulfed   minding
        by the pincers of   the mill
        Czar and Emperor
        Stalin and Hitler
where were you when we all colluded
        in the Shoah while pretending
        to be different

what was   the necessity
              of the long term deliberative stance which over-
                    came passion and   compassion
                    feeling and   action
                    O such little gain for so much   time
                    two thousand years of   stewardship
                    come to nothing more than a   tottering
                    self regarding institution there
                    is little to say so   little
                    to say other than to   mourn
                    the ruthless extinguishing of the Johannine
                    spark which plunged us   back
                    into the dark
                                  it was only in early
                    adulthood that I laughed
                          at Tom Lehrer freed from
              the routines of the relentless mill
                          of rosaries
                    & novenas
                      processions
                              & stations
                      genuflections
                              & elevations
                    of incense
                    & ash
                    of vestments
                  & jewels
                    of the nice
                      distinction between the venial
                  & the mortal
                      penances measured out
                  in Hail Maries
                like lines handed out
                              in a purgatorial
                      class room and
        behind   the mill
                          the harshness
                        & the violence
                        & the manipulation
but
    there was an unforgettable day in May when
      we processed through the green corn behind
        the plaster virgin with the moon
          in the deep blue Marian sky balancing
            the setting sun when I thought that I was
                      walking to heaven
but

                              it was the illusion
                        of the ritual
                      over the generative

a mantra of
well being
and although
aspects of ritual comfort remained
into maturity such as
the benign addiction to
The Eucharist
I have never felt engaged in anything spiritual
               that verges on the moralistic
meanwhile what of the Church of England by law
established to support the great and
the good the doctrinal   opposite
of Roman doctrinal obsession
wasting its tradition in benign
indifference and
trivial faction only
a sad

                                               footnote

but

the danger was not in the brutality and
the carnage the
incomprehensible purposeless slaughter of
                                     the Somme
not even in the calculated horrors of
Stalin & Hitler
supposedly the most
sophisticated civilisations the world had ever
                                         seen
bent on slaughter playing
Schubert on the off shift from Belsen
bad enough but only the result
of something bigger
              but in presiding over the steady
              decline into darkness
              moving steadily away from
              Anselm
              to Schleiermacher
after
       Dante and Aquinas
       we were plunged into   darkness
              only
moonlight
and   the dull red fires
       on the blighted plain
       the ash of Auschwitz   has never
the culmination of   died
       a church of measurement and calculation
       a church that has run
                                        its course

              a church that had run its own mills
              for so long that other mills in
              the camps and the gulags strangely
              familiar conflating
              salvation with behaviour
              not seeing that salvation is   beyond
              and goodness   is
              our nature and our created
              purpose and thus
              we were plunged
              into the   mill inevitable
              inexorable smoke and
              dull flame and sooted
              brick and tainted
              gold   moonlight
&   ash

                                                            let me
                                                   let me introduce
                                                         myself
                                                   just a little
                                                   diffidently as
                                         you have formed a false
                                             impression of my
                                             person and purposes
                                                  I
                           who would have worshipped
                                   Him forever but
                           for his absolute obsession
                     with the personal and abhorrence
                           of the structural always
                                   love
                                   above
                                   duty
                                                        was
                           allowed
to roam   the world
                                                    but
                                                 unlike
                                           caricatures
                                        of me that are all
fire
                                   I am quintessentially   cold
                           what God could not stand
                           was hierarchy & command
                                                       he
                                        wanted to be
                                        close I
                                        wanted to
                                        obey

                        to stand in my place
                        to see things done
                            tidily & well
before my crime of uncovering
the catastrophic conspiracy   of the Son
                        which is when
                            I
                        switched sides
            which is why again contrary
            to popular iconography
            hell is the best organised
            place you have ever seen
            naturally better than
            the earthly enterprises which turned
            to it for inspiration
            why else would
                    I
            have orchestrated empires
from   Babylon   to   Byzantium
from   Rome   to   Washington
from   the Winter Palace   to   the Vatican

            empires   have been my way
            of defying a God who
            emptied himself   of power
            which is why
            my greatest triumph and my best
            joke was the Church with Joker
            Constantine which in turn
            is why the Christians barring
            a few in monasteries the early
            friars and a handful
            of subversive mystics
            have got it wrong preferring
            Deuteronomy to the
            Sermon on the Mount or on
            the plain have opted for the
moonlight
                        not
                                                the sun
            since when
                    I
            have had much of my own way
            in the matter of governance
from   relational   to   organisational
from   attachment   to   detachment
            assisted by a massive programme of
            distraction helping
            them to build imitation hells
            through the turning of their   mills

grinding away   at the cost
sapping the strength   of the personal
anything to attack   the intimate
the reflective   culture of praying
O far from what you might imagine   Pater Noster
                              I   qui est in caelis
did not mind indeed   Hail Mary full
                 I   of grace
rather liked the liturgies and   Glory be
the liturgies as they were in my   Alleluia
line of business rather courtly   Salve Regina
in a self regarding sort of   Mater misericordiae
way   Dies Irae
closer to art than   O Salutaris
prayer   Tantum Ergo
the wonder of it was that after
Gentle Jesus they turned domestic
fellowship on its head and
founded a Church if ever
there was celebration in hell it was
for Constantine left
to Peter Christ might have prevailed but
my friend Paul ensured that he
failed

                                        it was the Bible
                              it was Law and ritual
                                       not what He
                                         meant by
                                        Word and
                                       Sacrament
and
    I
    simply loved the cathedrals and
the collective pieties which made   good Christian
the faithful   folk
the heirs of Babel
meanwhile
the greatest damage that
                 I
                        ever did was
to persuade them all from Paul
onwards to abhor the intimate
           in God's name
           instead of mine
thus
distancing Christians from   the intimate
                                    the vulnerable
                                    the courageous
                                    the sublime
enterprise of   love

never did the mill turn more briskly
            than when the sins of the flesh were
            excoriated O
            blessed irony O perfect
            mortal Saint Augustine given the place
            of honour with a statue in
            Hell's portal for
            turning humanity's nearest
            act to God's creative power into
            a sin O
                        what tenderness destroyed
                        what beauty blighted
                        what guilt ingrained
                        what scandal excited

                their one great gift
                their one chance of delight
                their route to prayer
                            wrecked
where were you   o they
            when we were so traduced   were there
            so destroyed   for good or ill
            we were too late to undo   minding
            what you had done   the mill
            yes   minding the
                                                      mill
        how I loved their   mills their
                    sin mills and their
                    wool mills and their
                    cow mills and their
                    war mills   I
        even
            I
        was incredulous when
        all the supposedly liberal democracies
        lured millions of young men
        to voluntary and later compulsory
        slaughter for what for
        organisational necessity for
        the good of   the mill
        but
        my greatest triumph even
        greater than the Somme
        is
                                    sound the fanfare
                                    of trumpets

                the bling mill

                design to kill

never   never

  was luxury so cheap so
  accessible so   alluring
  corrosive
  the ultimate   distraction
  which left the holy millers
  courtesy the glitzy millers
  with only a husk of Easter   rabbits and
  all Passion spent   hot cross buns and
  Resurrection disowned or   chocolate
  unknown Christ   eggs
  pressed back into the enclave
  of Christmas then   Jingle Bells
  inundated   Santa is coming to town
  by a tide of self   Rudolph the red-nosed
  indulgence   had a very shiny nose
  admittedly the red hatted cardinal of the chimney
  ritual has a quality of manic
  competitive generosity
  a small consolation

but

  you would be wrong
  if you think
  that all this wanton consumption will result
  in diabolic ranting and
  punishment   O no
    I
  simply assert the superiority of
       organisation over spontaneity
       certainty over risk
       assurance over vulnerability
       duty over love
  still bent
  on giving God his due
  without the untidiness
  of humanity which
  Christ crystallised overthrowing
  the beautiful formality of the Book
  of Revelation
       of thrones & kingdoms
       hierarchies & gradations
       angels & archangels
       saints & sinners

  I
   have been held
  responsible for what is God's folly
  in Christ

             exit
            silently

I enter quietly with fire
   aspect of God cold Satan feared
      to name the agency of the Creator
         the core of Christ within you
            falsely invoked to justify the Church
            of which I am the chief tormentor lover
           of mystics and the unconsidered thrall
            I engrace those who follow where I
             call in crooked ways where love is
           found not in the ordered landscaping
         of ground but in a garden wild
        where once a child in obscure
         Palestine as partner in my power
         overturned the stilted YHWH
           picture that our Chosen Ones had
            fastened on learning a graven form
          in words that broke The Law in
         a way they would not recognise as
          worshippers of the word and like
          the Jews good Christians have
           anthropomorphised the divine and
          forgetting their creaturely
          humanity of fragile love and
          the life of goodness they
           were made to be distinct
           from our salvation which all
         will see have distanced
          their God from Christ losing
         hope and thus all labour wasted
        they have resorted to the dross
      of gold and phosphorus all that
     is left to light the ashen plain
     a state made rigid to inflict and
     deaden pain but all things must
       pass and on earth all things must
      change so that free will's writ may
     be re-launched after the horror of
    the Somme and Auschwitz O
    what surprise in store they cannot
     hope to see for they irrationally maintain
    that God is dead or at least
     in some way static so that
    the God of love has shrivelled
   to a God of judgment and
  that the Christ of love healing and
peace has been overcome his supposed
once-for-all redeeming gesture rendered
obsolete but its fullness did not imply finality so
  I will renew the love of God as surprisingly now
as I did in parenting Jesus

wait

                              and

                                              see.

                                        the horizon

clinging to

                                            cloud
                                          roseate
                                            tiny
                                          a

                        of dawn
              hint
    the slightest

III.

                                        not to be denied
                                        burgeoning
                                        insistently
                                        colour gently but
                                        before reviving
and then   reverse and   fade
                                        to stop
and yet   it seemed
                                   of day
                                  the idea
                                  stirring the memory of
                                the grey
                              rose enlightening
                        a hint of
                        disclose
                           beauty that the curators could
                       beautiful than any
                  comprehend more
                cramped world could
                anything the grey
            momentous than
          new star more
          any new planet or
        foretold more spectacular than
      improbable that no seer
  a circumstance so

                                        of the new dawn
                                    and my intimation
                                  down my prayer
                                they could not close
                            rose but
                        because I had imagined
                    of all my books
                and deprived
                to an asylum
            had been committed
            Damian
            and I
          raving
          as mindless
              their hope had been dismissed
          moving but
        who had felt the Spirit
excommunicate who said
            there were a few mad mystics
        books of prophesy
        warning no
      of Jesus there had been no
    that unlike the birth
  it was later said
and although

                                        promised by the Lord's
                                        Spirit for the new dawn
                                 waiting in the gloom in the
                                by a river but a watcher
                                I am no John Baptist inveighing
                                to say that I was a forerunner
                                for whom it would be too grand
                                than I will come
                                greater
                                one
                           when
                             I will be useful
                              when
                                that the day will come
                                a way but know
                             which has not yet found
                             I am only a signpost
                             obscure
                             the shape of which are still
                            in advance of great events
but I said   I am only a witness
                   mad but I said
              drive the people
            to put them on general view would
           view them for it was feared that
          only the elite were allowed to
         thought to be so dangerous that
        incomprehensible curiosities
     in an archive of
     of a bygone age trapped
    decoration all the colours
    despair wrapped in gaudy
    threatening the status quo of
  of prophesy
they said I had delusions

me alone to await the dawn
                    hope and in the end they left
        confining us to the ruins of our
                    deep that could resist God's love
            no church so strong no despair so
        this being so there was no gloom so dark
        and
        love
            can do to impair divine
        that there is nothing humanity
        his Crucifixion standing as a pledge
        we tried to shake him off
        us no matter how hard
        he would never leave
who said
son

come

had

SHE

          I saw a face so radiant that I knew that
      in Spring
      one day
     then
     and

                that the day had come
           so bright that I believed
        generated by the cities of neon and glass
      there were fantastic illusions
       and often

          forever alight on the plain
          a reflection of the dull fires
          was a trick of the light
           the tingle of blood in the grey
           false dawns when
     there were
     as there will be
     and

                                                    the promise of light.
                                                    the dusk and the dawn,
                                                and light, day and night,
                                             Day, were created darkness
                                           from which time, on the First
                                        away,
                                        and hurried soundlessly
                                     with barely a shadow
                                  in the almost dark
                                           turned
                                        of dying. Then She turned
                                     will make sense of my manner
                               an experience which, in a strange way,
                                     of Jesus My Brother,
                                     you were standing at the side
                                     for you will live as if
                                  do not despair
                                  for it, nonetheless,
                                  and will be murdered
                                  will live in love
                               even though I
                               and
                                           from different perspectives
                                  seen
                                  are the same though
                                  God's will which
                                  and
                                of humanity's ambition
                               the summit
                            before we reach

                         ranking liking over loving
                         self indulgence
                         callousness
                         egotism
                         conformity
                         indifference
                         inertia

                      the seven barriers of
                      For we must overcome
                      hell.
                      to heaven out of
                      have to come
                      and we, like Dante, will
                   hard and long
                 for the climb will be
              say: Damian! Prepare
          I heard Her
    As the rose intensified

new
memory
freedom
tyranny
revolution
time struck me
until that
and what had
the people rise
the spirits of
city and I felt
looking down upon the
and I stood upon a hill
the ancient stars came out
of golden light
and as the sun set in a blaze
across the plain
and rivers roamed their way
and springs of sparkling water broke
on ground parched for centuries
and then a gentle rain fell
and I saw clouds gathering in the West
back in its natural place
with a crescent moon
in perfect balance
the rising sun stood
on the Third Day
And
and the Spirit was with me.
on my watch
that glimpse of day but I stayed
And the darkness overcame
we dared to hope.
in the light and
looked derelict and fragile
suddenly
and the black hearted, all pervading mills
and the monstrous towers of bones and glass
sank low
arid plain
of the smaller fires on the outer edges of the
to lose the fierceness of their glow and some
plain I saw the fires flicker and falter and begin
the West; and as I looked down upon the fearful
that the darkness faltered and flinched towards
the curtain of clinging grey, shining so bright
tentative at first, broke through
on that Second Day, the rose light,
which we would learn again to call morning,
And on a blessed time,

incarnation would bring earth into balance with its God.
of Christ had so lost its traction that only a
let alone the means to engineer escape. And I saw that the
so profound that it had lost the capacity to contemplate
which would free humanity from centuries of self-imposed
as a cosmic evolution was now revealed to me as a human

                                                        And
                                          the heavenly chorus
                                             stood silently
                                             behind the new
                                         prophet praising God
                                         for bringing new hope
                                         to a struggling earth
                                                        and
                                          when the sun rose
                                     there was a mighty anthem:

                                                   alleluia!
                                                   Alleluia!
                                           Glory to the Lord
                                                  most high

                                                    Glory!
                                                    Glory!
                                     Glory to the Lord most high!

cumquat mulberry and plum
redwood sycamore and palm
squirrel marmoset and lamb
granite malachite and lime

    bluebell daffodil and rose
    coffee lemonade and wine
    falcon mockingbird and goose
    parsley sage rosemary and thyme

        make we merry
        dance and sing
        for the earth's
        awakening

        ruby amethyst and pearl
        saffron hyacinth and mauve
        snowflake glacier and frost
        melon tangerine and pear

            sing and celebrate
            the way
            sun and moon
            and night and day.

                                    only been
                              returned more
                           on the Fifth Day,
                    And
                 for the revelation of another
               my watch, held there, mostly in
            thanked God for sending Her to save
         of joy and thanks faded gently, without
        the more they emerged as individual souls
        the more sharply they emerged from the dark
        And, in the paradox of Christ and His beloved
     as the whole earth took courage until union was
   the choirs of heaven stayed silent for the space of
  but sublime, outpouring all the pent-up vigour of God-
 and, from a sustained chord, broke into mighty song, so
then all the voices, maintaining their individual lines,
 and then the people began to shout and sing, discordantly
  pounding and crowds cascading out of their bone and glass
a low, distant rumbling from beneath the earth and the sound
on the Fourth Day when it seemed that the brave new time had
and

                                                      view.
                                                  the mind's
                                                  the joy of
                                              away but for
                                              bear to turn
                                            I could hardly
                                          our humanity; and
                                      which celebrate
                                    to make the colours
                                  must pass
                            through which God's light
                          that we are glass
                    saying
                    I remember Her
                    and

                  creation:
                  could contrive to represent and celebrate
            of every colour that nature and human artifice

          shell and fur
          wood and stone
          sea & sky
          leaf & fruit

            light and shade, of every colour of
          moon, now there was an infinite range of intensity, of
        worst of all, the suffocating grey of ash and the obscured
      brick; and the rank brightness of gold and phosphorus;   and,
      the ugly blue and green of war; and the dull red of fire and
      rich than any record of the archivists. Where there had
      colour, in all its grace, variety and abundance,

      dawn.
      but still with a hint of fear, waiting
      us all from ourselves; but I would not leave
      fear, into the on-coming night, I
      with creaturely purpose. And as the sound
      drudgery of uniformity into the light of freedom
      half an hour; and it swelled
      Sister, the more they were in union
      restored between heaven and earth.
      created life, that
      sweet and wild, untutored
      became harmonious
      at first, but
      prisons
      of feet
      come there was

And
spell.
the sad
to break
strove
and so I
of good cheer
me to be
encouraged
but She
forgotten
would be
that the lessons
and I worried
of the people
in the hearts
was alive
and She
and the laughter;
and the faces
in the movement
of hope
but an abundance
no hope of perfection
no universal love,
And there was no universal peace,
with their God.
and to communicate
and to listen to
to create
so that what the people needed was
was at an end
and that the age of oppression
knowing that my vigil was finally over
into the city
And I came down from my watch
in houses.
and broke bread
and repented of their power
and prayed in the streets;
came out of their fortresses
in the church who cared
and those who were left
and the fires were put out
and the mills were torn down
by voluntary consent
was established
the order of plurality
on the Sixth Day
And

on the Seventh day   there was peace.

IV.

And
    after Her great manifestation
    in a quiet voice, the earth
    breathed with new life.
And I bear witness, as She
    would have me bear it, not
    to condemn but to warn and to
    encourage, to recall how
    She wanted to keep all things
    simple and unadorned and how
    She warned against imitation of what we abhor;
and so, beware not that which is obvious, not
    that which comes from the source, but
    that which infects: fear not
    the rage of the ignorant and those
    who manipulate them, in the name
    of God, for their own purposes; fear not the mob
    in Karachi crying for Christian blood; fear not
    the bombs hurled at Christians in Iraq,
    at Copts in Alexandria; and fear not
    the homicidal maniacs who shoot at Perpetuans
    in the name of God. Yes, all these things
    are to be regretted but
    suffering is integral to truth.
    The fundamentalists of Islam and Christ will rage, they
    will hurl explosives at us and line us up
    in the cross hairs of their rifles; but
    the danger is not in persecution but
    in imitation. Beware
    the simplistic in the face of the mysterious,
    the fundamentalist pronouncement from the Vatican or
    a God-Channel fastness. It is easy to condemn
    the Fatwa and the outrages of perceived
    victimhood but learn to see ourselves
    in them. Learn to see history
    repeating itself. Let mystery reign
    in our hearts and, reflected from them, in
    our institutions, such as we must have; but
    let us not make clerics to compete
    with clerics; let us not make theologians
    to design munitions; let us not train
    seekers to be soldiers. Let leaders
    clear mines, make peace, promote
    diversity, discourage victimhood, promote
    personal responsibility, open doors, explore
    possibility, refuse to close or to
    condemn.

For we who are so close to Christ,
given a renewed heritage by His beloved Sister, are
in danger of repeating that from which
She came to save us: we
crave churchdom and organisation; our Guides
itch to be leaders. Our critics accuse us
of being amorphous; of failing
to provide a focal point for dialogue; of
not knowing what
we stand for. But these aims
are vain, reducing the Godhead to
anthropocentric politicisation.
There is no leadership but God;
there is no focal point but God;
there is no leadership, only service;
there is no negotiation, only faithfulness;
there is no formula, only mystery.
There is no magic, only Her
          new way and the warning
      of history.

                  It is so wearing, although
                  who am I to be weary? It is
          so monotonous, though who am I
                  to complain? The same
                  mistakes again and again.
                  How can the Tea Party so easily
          abdicate humility? How can
                  prelates claim to imitate
                  Christ? How can public relations executives
                  represent Perpetua? O how,
                  O how have we come to this, so soon
                  after Her demise? How
                  have we become so enslaved by our
                  individual psyche and collective
                  history?

Let us, then, beware,
let us be cautious in our claims,
modest in our celebration,
faithful in our imitation,
sceptical of human accretion,
remembering that it was not Christ's life,
nor Perpetua's life, that present any complication,
but only those who would own these lives
and use them as a means of social
organisation, political oppression and sexual
suppression, taking the flesh
out of God, God out of Christ and Perpetua
out of the flesh.

It is not the headlong dash nor the rash act,
it is not the fiery pen nor the surgical analysis,
it is not the lust for riches nor the grab for power,
it is not the restless feet and the feverish brain,
it is not the burning of desire nor the smouldering of
resentment, it is not even the building and climbing
of Babel, the towering pride, that most offends
but the inertia of the complacent
that obscures humanity's destiny with God.
For, even after the blessed cataclysm of a new salvation,
we are lured into a sense that our chief objective
    is comfort,
that we need do nothing but allow a myriad objects
to adhere to us, insulating us from thought and decision.
It is not the luxury in itself, although that is bad enough,
    but the loosening of the hedonistic inhibition
    and the perfume fogged myopia, the way
    truffles bring unfought contentment,
    the way of the thousand olives and the ease of silk.
There are many who would say that our God is perversely
    opposed to the beauty of the world of creation
but it is not the beauty in itself, not even the love
    of beauty for itself,
that mars, but the distractions of beauty that allure us
into a deadly timelessness which presumes
that heaven is on earth,
that we need say nothing,
do nothing, go nowhere,
but sit in our palaces of ease as if that were enough,
without reflection or contemplation.

And
She came to remind us of the bliss and dangers of ease
but we have already begun to forget,
to be allured into inertia by the same sweetness
that cloyed and clogged the arteries of our outwardness
so that, ultimately, what was sweet became too easy
    and therefore addictive.

She brought back beauty
so that we could renew our worship and
our understanding of God within us,
not so that we would again be imprisoned by our own
    preoccupations.
The terror lies in the inertia without reflection
    or contemplation,
self induced vacuity, leading to boredom and a temperament
    of want beyond content;
but there is the worse prospect
of the violence of ennui.

Forwards, forwards, ever forwards
The people are mad and the reasons are obvious
The world can be mine and all things mine
There is no rest for nothing is settled
There is so much I want; and so much denied me
Higher and higher! We are masters
of the universe for God is a delusion
The folded hands and half-closed eyes
Nothing is at stake but our gentle comforts
Time to go, only a show
There is nothing to be gained from effort
      but more time to rest
All necessities for a fully empty life
A chocolate, a rug, a diamond, sparkling water
      carried in blue/green glass from a country far away
      a knife for figs, a knife for cheese, a knife for steak
      and duck, a fork and spoon for oysters,
      a spoon for grapefruit, a spoon for deep-glassed sorbet
      the paraphernalia for eating snails
Puritan dualists, weighed down with gold and guilt,
      consoling themselves in the mall
The taper of a stem, the curve of a vase, the
incomprehensible beauty of humanity's romance with the tulip
the wide embrace of static narcissism
The endless, golden afternoon
All ye know and need to know
That silence is golden is more than a cliché
Perchance to dream
To return from the exile from Eden
      untroubled by the tree of knowledge of good and evil.

The proximity of ecstasy and madness
Necessarily frightened of burnt fingers
Prey to our age-old addictions
Helping the medicine go down
The strange safety and solemnity of cold blue steel
      and sweet fire
Shadow of lady release.

All things bright and beautiful
God be in my head
No man is an island
It tolls for thee
Life as a series of clichés in water-colour
      of collecting without collating
The victimhood of plenitude
The oppression of the oppressed
Welcome, welcome
      into Bluebeard's castle.

Then
there is the beauty of the settled way:
in liturgy, the meticulousness of the familiar, that point
    when the sublime emerges from what otherwise
    might be repetitive;

in doctrine, the hard-fought settlement of old scores
                    worn smooth into venerable grandeur, intoned
        in fine words which convey the absolute balance
        of the proposition, far from the rawness
of the multiple theological encounters
        which were its necessary precondition;
in governance and structure, the suffocating temptation
        to prize the avoidance of controversy above
        the search for meaning.
All these, Christianity has suffered and now
I warn the houses where bread is broken:
Do not succumb to the inertia of the safe and the pleasant,
        the beauty of the settled way.

How easy it is
for inertia to metamorphose into indifference,
from not seeing to not caring,
from staying still in the moment to assuming
a sense of superiority over the external,
where all is complete in our ordered world
and the mess outside is beyond our comprehension
and beneath our intervention.
How can mission flourish in stagnation?

How can compassion grow out of indifference?

How can humility grow from superiority?

How can solidarity be built from division?

As there is a kind of beauty in the melancholy
        of the dwindling Autumn light,
so there is something hypnotic in the minor,
a peculiarly decadent form of self indulgence
        which turns the suffering of the world
into morbid entertainment,
the long night of the soul encapsulated
in the shallow mourning of celebrity:
Tears for souvenirs;
Teddy bears for tears.

The path well trod, the ancient wisdom known
The splendour of the Benediction,
    the drama of the Elevation,
    the blending of music, Word and light
    building a mysteriously calm foundation
    for the numinous
Credo in unum Deum, patrem omnipotentem,
        in unum dominum Jesum Christum filium dei unigenitum
        et incarnatus est de Spiritu Sancto ex Maria virgine
        homo factus est ... et in Spiritum Sanctum dominum
        qui ex Patre Filioque procedit

Leave well alone, the Bull and the Quadrilateral,
    the Threefold Ministry and its degree,
    priority and place set down in Scripture.
In our glorious heritage lies the way:
    defend what we have; the age of the Prophets and
    and divine intervention ended with Jesus;
    there is nothing left to say.

Like the changing from major to minor,
from the pleasant to the plangent, from the mellow
    to the mordant.
We have polished our shrine
We have honoured our words
We have built temples to beauty and peace
    which surpass all previous architectural invocations
    preserving us from distraction
We have laid out ways and built safe houses
    for pilgrims
The world goes as it must on its wicked and untidy way
Nothing ever quite clear
    Never quite explicit
Always a slight whiff of scandal seeping between the satin
    curtains
We are properly suspicious of the venal
    and must beg to be spared the detail.

The schadenfreude of lost love
The addiction to adrenalin
The pull of the prurient
The activist turned commentator
The being and not being separated
    by glass
Self-indulgence in the name of the impartial
Excitement for feeling
The corrosive detachment
    of doing from meaning,

For religion, for politics, as for the individual,
   the return of innocence is impossible,
the supposed transparency smeared and warped
   by exploitive experience,
the wilful and then subconscious
   manipulation of motive into self justification.
What a child's eye sees clear and true in its morning
   becomes a fiction in the high noon of self indulgence
and then a deep perversion
   as the light fades into decadent night.
Watch yourself watching
   the girl that passes in the mirror in the glass,
an innocent rolling in the grass,
   a circus girl turning cartwheels on the sand,
before the puberty of knowingness,
   the opening and shutting of a sun flower.
What starts as watching in innocence
   becomes love and then obsession,
the abandoning of self possession
   and the jealousy of possession.
All such change is part of the discourse of generation,
   of learning the meaning of inter dependence,
the balance of control and letting go,
   the search for a word and the acceptance of silence;
but to pretend that suffering is a re-birth of innocence
   is a betrayal,
to see love turned into obsession and self destruction
   is not a childish pastime for the bored.
There are more kinds of pornography in human relations
   than the erotic, notably the romantic;
in politics the pornography is ideological,
   the separation of reality from aspiration;
and in religion it is the separation of the sacred
   from the profane,
the perverse detachment of the Godhead
   from creation.
And although in this last case the customary 'sin'
   is supposed to be a recourse to the physical
and a flight from the spiritual,
   the greater sin is
the flight from the physical,
from the incarnational,
contempt of the flesh
   in favour of the vicarious but,
worst of all, is the perverted invocation
   of innocence to disguise indifference,
the safety of not knowing, in the name of purity,
how things really are "out there".

The artifice of the simple
  and the artifice of the insoluble
are both alike the artifice of denial,
  a plea for mitigation.
How easy it is to take and view a photograph,
  how much more complex to read reality
in a handful of spare, telling lines
  or the elusive allusion.
God is not a settled way of being
  but a call upon the imagination,
a ceaseless winnowing of experience,
  an unremitting cycle of love and repentance.
Beware that which is said to be completed,
  the charm of the museum,
the settled position,
  the affixing of the seal.
I saw her walking in the garden of turbulence,
  in the radiance of incompleteness,
a new rainbow promise that would shine
and fade;
and Oh, so much like the forgotten Jesus,
  the friend of the uncertain,
the guardian of the unsettled,
  the pilgrim on a journey,
the victim who paid the price
  of stooping.
How pallid we look in the light,
  how distant from ourselves,
as we look in the glass
  and through the glass
to where we know we will find nothing
  to inspire but only contain.
The last, the ultimate, secret, is not in the journey,
in the struggle or the climb, not in the hidden treasure,
  the sealed box and the locked room,
not in the icon of the container, the illusion
  of redemption in the discovery of the complete,
the disjunction between the object and its context,
  the end of pilgrimage and history
but in absolute vulnerability and openness.
She saw it all
  and now
so soon after Her new foreshowing,
  our new redemption,
we are not earth that nurtures the plant
  but glass, refined
to see and be seen through
  and broken.

How easy it is
for indifference to metamorphose into conformity,
the quiet cowardice,
the avoidance of embarrassment and loss,
risk aversion,
the failure to stand up and be counted.
Beware the delusion of free speech, the assertion
of liberty masking oppression,
the control of the capitalist in the 'free market',
the control of the progressive in bland consensus,
the marginalising of Christmas in the return
      to the Winter festival,
atheists who legislate in the name of Islam or Krishna,
who say what can and cannot be said,
whose respect is vacuous.
Consensus should arise from and not anticipate negotiation
for compromise depends upon the understanding of otherness,
the social imagination, the valuing of the unattainable,
the understanding of the variety of gifts
      and the impossibility of possession,
the commonality of creation and the unorthodoxy of beauty.
Then there is the paradox of individualism,
the apparent choice which results in conformity,
the choice of a thousand pastas, the rise of the olive
      and bottled water,
a retreat from the chromatic,
a shying away from the question.
An olive for acquiescence, new pasta for pragmatism,
the flatness of managerialism and suspicion of leadership,
the silent driving out of the controversial,
the polite withdrawal from dialogue.
All such denials of self deny individual responsibility,
the essence of democracy, the core
of what She taught about community and solidarity:
      the disinterested principle,
      the courage to campaign,
      the necessity of the egregious,
      the leaven of experiment,
      the rewards of failure,
      self identity in sacrifice.
Her way of 'being church' was individual responsibility
      not conformity:
stay faithful to theology,
confront your God with courage in the face of mystery;
and only conform to doctrine in the way
you conform to literature,
as a means of exploration,
where otherness is honoured,
the unpredictable recognised
and the lone voice heard:

accents
amateurs
Angostura bitters
Antiguan Moravians
aphorisms
Arjuna & Krishna
assonance
baked alaska
Berio
black swans
Bolero
Bosch
bread
bric a brac
catastrophe theory
causeways
chilli chocolate
chromaticism
claret
collage
community radio
cooked eggs
consecrated gin
crèmes brûlées
crown green bowls
crumbs
D960
dancing
dialects
diaries
dice
Eco
ee cummings
elastic
elections
emerald skies
Escher
exceptions
experiment
explorers
faith
feathers
fingerprints
fractals
fuzzy logic
gargoyles
gems
geodes
Gesualdo
Gandhi

ghosts
glass
Godel's
  Incompleteness
  Theorem
Gorecki 3
grapes
the Grateful Dead
haiku
hair
Heisenberg
Helen's wart
heretics
heroism
Heston Blumenthal
holy fools
home cooking
hope
honey
humility
humour
hypotheses
identity
improvisation
infinity
inhabited planets
innocence
intuition
journeys
jungles
kaleidoscopes
Keith Jarrett
kittens
knots
koalas
Kung
laughter
lefties
Liquorice Allsorts
litanies
long odds
love
the Magnificat
magnification
Mandela
marbles
market stalls
the Master
  Carpenter
mercy

micro breweries
mirrors
Mr. Toad
mongrels
more gruel
  for Oliver
Monet haystacks
mystery
opals
optical illusions
Ovid
paradox
peppered
  strawberries
Perpetua
Picasso
pinball
pinch hitters
plastic taxonomy
poetry
pomegranates
possibility
potential
praxis
prayer
presents
prophesy
puzzles
quarks
questions
Don Quixote
rainbows
red hail
remission
responsibility
reverse swing
rivers
rum punch
sacrifice
sails
saints
sausages
scandal
secrets
Sgt. Pepper
shuffling
solidarity
stars
stories
surprises

Thus, the strange migration of
        difference,
        discord,
        chromaticism,
        heroism and
        leadership
from the public world of discourse
to the incommensurable private worlds of
        leisure and
        hedonism,
        self indulgence,
        the frisson and
        the adrenalin shot,
        the fantasy of violence,
        the miasma of romanticism,
        the degradation of pornography,
mere shadows of the deep,
unrequited dream of something better,
the failure of individual nerve and, therefore,
the failure of collective democratic responsibility;
the failure of conscience and church,
the failure of the soul.

Paradoxically,
how easy it is for conformity
to metamorphose into egotism:
the lack of discourse engendering a lack
        of credible comparison,
the lack of dialogue diluting the collective,
the licence to promote the self without a comprehension
        of limitation.
Meanwhile,
with the bread and circuses well set, leaders
        detach from reality,
        ignorant of history,
        routinely overlooking the obvious,
believing their toughness will outstay
        indifference
and then,
through them, the egotism of the nation,
        the racist fantasy,
        the effortless superiority.
And
behind all this,
the abandoning of person for the self.
Of all the vices that I warn against,
the ego is the most obvious
and the least needful
of dissection.

Time Regained
theology
Toxic Times relents
Tristram Shandy
trust
truthful Cretans
tulips
typefaces
The Unanswered
  Question
underdogs
unfairness
Vincentian bananas
volcanoes
vulnerability
weather
whistling
wild flowers
yeast
York Minster
  rood screen
&c

The Big Society
'bottom up'
The dictatorship of the proletariat
Divine Augustus
each will sit under his own fig tree
the end of an era
the end of boom and bust
the end of spin
grass roots
Home by Christmas
a land fit for heroes
a land flowing with milk and honey
Land of hope and glory
liberty, equality, fraternity
life, liberty and the pursuit of happiness
the market
a new dawn
the open society
Peace in our time
there is no such thing as society
things can only get better
This royal throne of kings
self reliance
the Second Amendment
the thousand year Reich
a war to end all wars
we will apprehend them and bring them to justice

and yet
perhaps
the greatest danger is the collective ego
        of the new enterprise,
the new dawn of the converted.
Beware, those who break bread, that we do not fall
        into the same temptation
by claiming that we have learned all the lessons
        of Christianity,
that our new way is so superior
        that it does not require vigilance.
Beware the illusion of the novel and the exciting,
        of the yet untried,
        of the shiny and the malleable.
We will be tried more by our ego than our enemies:
        discard most of what you have;

        relax the body and open the heart

        keep silence

        examine your life;

        survey your community;

        open your arms to the world;

        reject the baggage of history;

        tell the new story of Perpetua and you;

        abandon victimhood and embrace responsibility;

shun the ego and cultivate humility.

Religion is no guarantee of virtue:
        we are creatures of necessary imperfection
                for which we should therefore not be punished
        the conflict between genetics and holiness is
        a conundrum from which we cannot escape;
and those who lead us are as we are,
                sharing our imperfections
yet, as we were created to do good for its own sake,
        let us persevere.

How easy it is
        to metamorphose from egotism into callousness:
        the separation of self from person;
        of persons from self;
of persons from humanity.

the sky so bright, the darkness gone away,
        all is before us,
The Third Testament, the new way
falling back into hierarchy and doctrine
        the mind for the heart
The mill! The Mill!
        The Salvation Mill!
She has made all things new
        She has set us free
        How fresh Her smile
        How bright Her memory
        How sharp Her message

the loss of possessions is not simply a traditional
        but a necessary enterprise
relaxing the body and opening the heart are more than
                the trade of the coach and the psychotherapist
chatter is not a contribution but an escape
        from the essence of our purpose
            In the privacy of our own heart,
        nothing is beyond further exploration
The House Group
        and the street
For, it being in our stewardship,
        it is our responsibility
Most of the baggage of life, the assumptions,
        the habits, the pronouncements, are moribund
A mysterious story, not a bald history,
        of making no claims, of letting go
Everything we know is our responsibility
        every situation demands a decision
self assertion is unhelpful to others
        who need to be helped to help themselves

Peace on earth
Goodwill to all men
Love your neighbour as yourself
Thou shalt not covet
Lord, I am not worthy
Wounded healers
God is love
        and our way of loving reflects that love.

Cogito ergo sum
Imperator
Vermin!

Beware the complacency that says that
     Hitler,
     Stalin,
     Pol Pot and
     the rest
               - the obscure names of the murderers in
                    Rwanda,
                    Burundi
                         and
                    the Congo
          do not readily spring to mind;
          and
          of the endless degradations of Latin America
          only Pinochet stands out from the military crowd;
          and,
          surely, we think, there is more to mass torture
          and
          killing in Asia than Burma -
          were somehow, themselves, lower than human,
that they were what they accused their victims
of being,
     mad,
     sub-human,
     animals
     somehow radically separated
     from humanity's common
     experience
     which is why they laughed,
for they, like us, were
created in love to love.

And
do not think that it is all over,
or that it will ever be all over
for, as She spoke,
the supposedly civilised, lovers
of the free, in miscellaneous jurisdictions,
traded in torture and secrets
for the greater good.
Let us say that Guantanamo Bay
is simply an icon,
the overground excrescence of a subterranean
labyrinth of calculated cruelty.
As She spoke,
     the systematic practice of slavery
          did not cease.
     Exiles were returned to death.
     Refugees were scorned.
     Families were dismembered.
Children were imprisoned.

The rhetoric of inferiority and sub-humanity
were never far away.

She urged personal response and responsibility.
But
as She said that it was not for Her
to fix what humanity had been given
tools to fix, what
are we doing now in our quiet
house groups where bread is broken:
the flotsam of desperation washes up
            on our more prosperous shores,
            unless it may be allowed
            quietly and decently to drown;
            when doors are barred but when,
       for those who evade capture
                     - how desperate
                     they must be to commit themselves
                     to prison -
       the cells are crowded;
and
       in far-away places
       the torturers extract intelligence
       in the name of peace
and
       we buy newspapers which demonise
            the children of Allah.
We shrug when we are warned
that there is a progression,
neither uniform nor predictable,
depending on propensity
       not predestination,
on the failure of self awareness
       not original sin,
but tending in a predictable direction:
       the child who mistreats a fly;
       indifference to sadness;
       disregard of a neighbour's grief;
       the shrugging off of family obligations;
       the desecration of public space;
       the dismissal of strangers as nuisance
            or obstacle;
       the construction of a hierarchy of means
            to satisfy cravings;
       sexual objectification;
       rape;
       the assumption of victimhood;
       the excusing of addiction;
       the declaration of helplessness;
       the washing of hands.

And then,
following the destruction of the individual,
at the collective level:
    the ranking of ends above means;
    the prosecution of the abstract cause
        over individual human flourishing;
    the separation of the deserving from the undeserving;
    the taxonomy of racism;
    the invocation of collective self,
        rather than collective humanity,
    behind the seven deadly mantras of:
        state
        religion
        purity
        peace
        piety
        prosperity and
        survival
in no particular order.
And
all this time, while
countless bodies writhe under the assault of
    the lighted cigarette,
        the electric shock,
    water boarding
and worse, all
perpetrated in our name, or
in the name at least of the deadly mantras,
we separate ourselves from, even
protest against, the process
in which we are complicit.

She, above all else,
made us
responsible for who we are and
what we do. Created
to do good we
warp our natures
because we value:
    hierarchy
        as long as we are near the top
    segregation
        as long as we are superior
    meritocracy
        as long as we are clever
    uniformity
        as long as we are the yardstick
    respectability
        as long as we are normative.

Democracy is not enough; and
often choosing is too   much.
She called for solidarity and sacrifice;
     but we are falling short,
     falling back to our old ways.
We are not great sinners
     in the sense of the first Covenant and
     the First Testament:
we are not gross idolaters
     except in the sense that we over-value the material
     but it is unfair to say that we worship
     what we own;
we are not great blasphemers
     although we can be careless with language
     and tend to assign all manner of bizarre and cruel
     acts and statements to God
     which suit our individual and collective purposes;
we do not worship graven images but,
     again, we sometimes care too much for objects;
we do not go out of our way either to honour nor dishonour
     our parents
     but the languishing of the aged in residential homes
     speaks of the way the obsession with privacy
     metamorphoses into isolation;
we are not murderers
     but we are indifferent or careless
     in matters of war and peace;
we are not serial adulterers but
     who can honestly say that they have not erred or,
     more likely, wished to err;
we are not great thieves but
     we deny the poor their due
     which is a public theft;
we do not seriously covet anything but
     we are vaguely discontented with our lot and
     are too concerned with yesterday and tomorrow,
a kind of wishful thinking which devalues action
     in the present.
We are the generation of the soft sin,
     of distributed responsibility,
of the collective shrug;
we consume our massive variety of goods,
and our self indulgence kills at a distance
     where we never see the corpses;
for every evil there is a scapegoat,
     for every disaster there is a culprit;
for every accusation there is a get-out clause.
For all our passions are turned
inwards, muffled in a smothering sophistication.
We are neither hot nor cold.

Our vices are many but mostly, outside personality, subtle:

alcopops	excess	poker
affluence	exaggeration	polarisation
anthropomorphising	fantasy	pornography
animals	fashion	postmodernism
astrology	fast food	prowess
bankers' bonuses	flippancy	prurience
binge drinking	Fox-TV	publicised
bling	Milton Friedman	philanthropy
blogging	fur	racism
boasting	gambling	reality television
body piercing	game theory	relativism
BOGOF	gas guzzlers	romanticism
bottled water	glitz	Rousseau
bullying	gossip	sarcasm
George Bush	grandstanding	saturated fats
Caligula	greed	self
callousness	gyms	sentimentality
cadenzas	Harry Potter	servants
Canary Wharf	haute cuisine	sexualising
celebrity	hearsay	children
chewing gum	hedonism	sham
chocolate	humiliation	showing off
Jeremy Clarkson	hypocrisy	slimming
Claridges	indifference	slogans
Max Clifford	Jordan	snobbery
cocktails	kitsch	social networking
computer games	kung fu	sports cars
compassion fatigue	laddism	spin
competition	lifestyle gurus	spitting
contracts	lycra	substituting
cosmetics	mock tudor	possibility for
conflating	monograms	probability
contingency &	narcissism	superiority
causality	net curtains	superstars
consumerism	Nietsche	superstition
cowardice	nostalgia	surrogacy
Simon Cowell	obsession	swearing
cruelty	obesity	Switzerland
designer babies	George Osborne	tabloids
designer labels	Sarah Palin	tanning studios
Disneyland	panic	tattoos
display	pastiche	tax avoidance &
dogs	performance	evasion
donkey sanctuaries	plagiarism	television chefs
doilies	plastic surgery	Thatcher
ego	platitudes	tomorrow
escapism	pre-nups	the Toxic Times
	private schools	tweeting

veneer   vigilantism   waste
victimhood   vulgarity   &c

and our virtues are fewer and less heroic

Abreu	fairness	plain English
aptness	faithfulness	polished wood
Aquinas	forgiveness	praxis
Aristotle	fresh produce	prayer
art	generosity	preparation
Jane Austen	glass	proportionality
authenticity	God	Proust
Bach	Godel	Psalms
bees	grace	responsibility
Beethoven	harmony	restraint
Eduard Bernstein	hay	Oscar Romero
bread	George Herbert	sacrifice
Breughels	heroism	Saint Benedict
bridges	humility	Saint Francis
Byrd	Jesus	of Assisi
care	John XXIII	seasons
chess	Jonah	self discipline
choral evensong	Julian of Norwich	Amartya Sen
claret	kenosis	service
clowns	lambs	shame
collaboration	landscape	Socrates
commitment	laughter	solidarity
compassion	C S Lewis	George Steiner
contentment	linen	string quartets
courage	love	theology
craftsmanship	Saint Luke	thoughtfulness
cricket	Magnificat	Titian
Dante	Nelson Mandela	trees
decisions	mercy	truth
dedication	Mobius strips	trust
detail	moderation	unknown soldiers
Dickens	modesty	virtue
eccentrics	natural fibres	vision
economy	now	walking
editors	objectivity	water
empathy	passion	wisdom
evidence-based	patience	Wittgenstein
decisions	Perpetua	Zola
exegesis	personhood	&c
	Picasso	

Do not wait
for a crisis to stir
you into action, to cure
what might have been prevented, and
do not count on your catastrophe
being dramatic but, rather,
beware
the subtlety of temptation, the plasticity
    of the postmodern,
not that the mechanisms of modernity
    were any better
- and were, perhaps, in some ways worse -
but return to the mystery and
in Her witness
re-kindle
the passion for responsibility.
We are neither hot nor cold.
Warmed by self satisfaction and sophistication,
far from the fire source,
pampered by temperature control,
our windows sealed against the world,
our machinery quietly whirring,
the catastrophes of flood, earthquake and Tsunami
in Brisbane, Christchurch and Japan
sad curiosities,
we sink into marshmallow contentment.
We are neither hot nor cold,
neither passionate nor fearful,
we have lost the heavens and the earth and
live in a pleasant purposelessness,
in a green and pleasant land
prone to unjustified resentment at minor malfunctions,
more resentful of inconvenience than injustice.
For all Her suffering and death,
for all She said,
for all we know of Her,
for all the truth She held,
for all the truth She told,
clear beyond speculation,
clear as Jesus but more contextually familiar,
how soon we are in danger of reverting
to our former situation,
to our limp response to the world's weariness.
Can we, in one short generation,
become as indifferent to Her as our predecessors
    after two millennia became to Jesus?
Can we really waste this subsequent incarnation?
I look at Her triumph and our failings
and am almost too frightened to ask
    the prophetic question.

Procedure leaves scant room for prophets.
A Godhead sanitised leaves little need for sacrifice.
Sacramental production lines leave little room for risk.
And risk aversion leaves little room for vulnerability.

Beware!

V.

SONG

Yellow is the promise
of a happy day
shining out between the threatening clouds of grey
the promise
of a friendly smile for a face that's down
the promise that the clouds will blow away.

Purple is the prospect
of our life journey
stretching out further than earthly eyes can see,
the prospect
of a struggle to the journey's happy end,
the prospect of a shared eternity.

Red is the experience
of a fatal pain
calling out for words of fellowship in vain,
the experience
of a threnody for a cause they say is lost
the experience that a chance will come again.

White is the Resurrection
of the faithful heart
reaching out to all who yearn for a new start
the Resurrection
of the hope that our new lives have now begun
The promise that God and man will never part.

Yellow for the promise
purple for the way
red for the sacrifice
and white for the new day.

BEGINNING

God is the self in the other
and the other in the self
The children in the Parent
The Parent in the children
God is the Spirit in the children
the children in the Spirit
God is Jesus and Perpetua in humanity

and humanity in Jesus and Perpetua
the life of four in one.

God is the self in the other
the baby in the mother
the mother in her child
God is the self in the other
the space for the lover
the verb of four in one

God is the point of intersection
The perfection of perfection
connecting everyone
God is the love that makes the circle
the circle without limits
enfolding everyone

God is the self in the other
love is the space for the lover
God is love.

PRAYER

God, you who is inestimable
and outside the language of space and time
yet is with us now,
not in our intellect,
although that informs,
nor in our works,
although you inhabit them,
but are with us in Our Sister the Spirit
Here with us now
in this humble home:
Bless us as we pray to you in the four ways
in which you have revealed yourself to us thus far:

PARENT

O Parent God made child
we thank you for our touch:
abide with us in all beneath our hand
in rock made flesh
in rough wood made to shine
in patterns in the sand;
in the joy of the dance
and the skill of the game
in stone and steel

the wilderness and the wheel
that we the monarchs of all we survey
may be good stewards for today
and for all children and all tomorrows
in rosebuds and in lips
and in the baby's hand that grips,
abide in us in everything we touch
for us it means so much.

O Saviour God of truth
once in bread and wine,
in the golden grain
and fruitful vine
- now sacrificed in everything you gave -
who gave for our delight
the chilli's tang
and the sweetness of meringue
all herb and spice
for pasta wheat and rice,
we thank you for the chef's art
and the cunning confectioner
for the miracle of yeast
in bread and beer
for the oil that gladdens
and the wine that cheers:
may we offer our skill
in field and farm
to nourish all your children
with your food
through sacrifice
as well as greater yield
in thankfulness and for the greater good;
as all is yours
may we not eat in haste
but saviour what you give
in the Sacrament of the earth;
and thank you Lord for everything we taste.

As we take our ease
near the end of the day
drowse us with incense and apple wood
with the perfume of the fashion house
and the scent of fresh flowers
with the sharpness of the new book
and the pungency of parchment

ravish us with coffee
entice us with cognac
poke us with lavender
solace with night scented stocks
bless us with the sour sweet of hay
near the end of the day.

Creator God who split the day from night
shine in the radiance of created light
in the artlessness of nature and in art
in beauty painted in tranquillity
and in the restless insight of photography
in the trick of the light and the innocence of sunrise
in the vocabulary of gesture
and the language of the eyes
in reflections in water and reflections on water:
shine for us in every subtlety of green
and in the brave colours of children:
be in our eyes and in everything they see
in riotous array and harmony.

God of love
who sent a choir of angels down to earth
to sing our Saviour's birth,
sing in every song
we sing along
smile in the lamb
uplift in the bird
warn in the drum
plead in the violin
cry freedom in the rap
and praise in the hymn
whisper in seashells
thunder in the choir:
that what you made in earth
might yet aspire
to offer what you gave
above desire.

With all our senses
may we thank and praise
the way of God
made rich in human ways:
the way of nature
and the way of art
the way of skill

as servant to the heart.
The mystery that Word Made Flesh was sent
to be alive with us in Sacrament;
Perpetua and Jesus, loves divine,
enabled by The Spirit, in the sign.

SOLEMN CHANT

It's the sign that counts
It's the sign that counts.

SONG

It's the sign that counts
the glass we see through and shatter
the bread we offer and break
the gifts we offer and take
the ash we gather and scatter:

It's the sign that counts
it's the sacred sign
it's the joining hands
and the broken line
it's the space we dance in
but we never own
it's the love we fashion
in word and bone.

It's the sign that counts
the dance of passion and danger
the working and weaving of fragments
the sound of laughter and laments
the fire of warmth and anger:

it's the sign that counts
the kiss bestowed on a lover
the sex unwanting and open
the child born of emotion
the smile that says it's forever:

It's the sign that counts
the melody that bends its line
the bridge that crosses a river
whatever brings us together
it's the sign

It's the sign that counts.

BROTHER

First we thank you for your mother
Mary brave and bright with love
whose conceiving cry for justice
ringing down the generations
was renewed by God our Parent
in adored Perpetua.
Thank you mother for the heartache
thank you for your weeping at the cross
in a life of humble service
bearing Jesus for our loss.

Next, we thank you for your coming
born among the poor and needy
dozing in the prickly hay trough
in the noisy Kataluma
not in comfort nor display
lighting all the saddest corners
lighting feet along the way
God incarnate in kenosis
living wholeness in the other
helpless child
creation's lover.

Then we thank you for your healing
love above the law's abrasions
gentleness where judgment postures
openness where closure threatens
shepherd's flock beyond all number
Jew and gentile without favour
fed and comforted together
love above our race and gender
love beyond our way as lovers
love beyond the flaw and fracture
love beyond our broken passions
you who loved our imperfection
necessary to the creature
feeds us with your truthful presence.

Next, we thank you for your suffering
undergone to show the world
that God's love is beyond limit
past the worst that we can do;
we who could not stand perfection
killed you for the space you made
but we know from what you showed us

that your love is beyond limit
even killing God will never
part you from your broken creatures.

Last, Lord Jesus, friend and brother
shining bridge of Resurrection
praise must end in penitence
for the way your word was doubted
for the guile that turned your message
from a church into a prison
from a dialogue into a doctrine
from the joyfulness of risk
to the meanness of the certain
from the kenosis of vulnerability
to the greed for certainty.

We are sorry for turning away
but, Jesus, if we are honest,
it is a strange grief
because it brought Perpetua to us.

As Jesus emptied himself
we commit ourselves
to personal and collective kenosis.

SONG

All of the time I waited,
All of the time I cried;
Crowded with those who hated,
Empty the hour you died:
O Jesus, son, you came to save
But left me in a living grave.

Pierced by Simeon's warning,
Pierced by every nail;
Struck by the early triumph,
Struck by your will to fail:
O Jesus, son, with so much given
You left me when you entered heaven.

Strong in the face of weakness,
Weak in the face of power;
Days when you were victorious,
Lost in that final hour:
O Jesus, son, I need your love
But you are living far above.

Rose in a field of thistles,
Crowned with your own blood thorn;
Flesh for a world in torment,
My flesh so sharply torn:
O Jesus, son, I should feel free
But languish in your agony.

Through the tears I followed in the crowd
Through the taunts I struggled to be proud
And saw your smile in the rain
And saw it flicker through the pain
O Jesus, son, I pray to see it again:

Then you sent down the Spirit
Sent down the power of grace;
Helping us face the future
fire in your wounded face:
O Jesus when the Spirit came
the Easter spark burst into flame.

SISTER

Sister, Perpetua:
born in obscurity
Reared in poverty
schooled in conformity
who yet
smiled in adversity
championed responsibility
lived in solidarity and
died in humility
let us not forget the core of you
as so many have forgotten the core
of Jesus your brother.

Parent God
we thank you for sending Perpetua to us
our Sister in the hard times
of softness and affluence:
thank you for making her lively
for making her so sexy
for giving her the body and the word
for the dance and the hymn
the kitchen table and the altar;
thank you for bringing yourself,
through her,

back to the people,
away from the trappings of wealth and power
away from rituals
which have taken the liturgy,
the work of the people,
away from the people;
and thank you
for re-uniting the physical and the spiritual
into each of us, your children.

Perpetua,
mystery of creation,
Sister of Jesus
Sacred Vessel
who absorbed all our wrong choices
so that we might know
the possibility of creating space
in absolute vulnerability to the other,
do not leave us now,
even though you live through your Sister the Spirit,
be near to us in the image and the word
so that we shall not so easily forget you;
spare us the few remaining records
and help us to use them properly,
to remain open to God in encounter,
wary of the pride of the unchecked intellect
and of the slide from personhood to individualism:
stay with us,
particularly in the new Sacramental way.
We are sorry
We are sorry for killing you.

SONG

She is God's own Daughter and we love Her
when She rose again we ran to Her forever
She had been so kind
She had won our hearts and minds
We gave all that we could find to show we loved her:

And She came in a blaze of glory
yes, she came in a blaze of glory
the sacred babe in Her own love story
in a blaze of glory She came.

Such a start, such a start
When She gave her sacred heart
such a sense of failure turned to glorious fame
such a gracious space when She came to us in grace
when we promised Her that we would bear the flame.

And She came in a blaze of glory
yes, She came in a blaze of glory
the sacred babe in Her own love story
in a blaze of glory She came.

We live in the brightness of the day
With its sweet and mellow curve
In the gentle light of hope, the space of love,
With the sound of silent prayer and such radiance in the air
when She said She had come back again we knew it.

And She came in a blaze of glory
yes, She came in a blaze of glory
the sacred babe in Her own love story
in a blaze of glory She came.
She is God's own daughter and we love her.

SPIRIT

O Holy Spirit
universal sister,
who brought inexhaustible consolation
to those whom Jesus left behind,
bring us consolation now
for we still remember Her,
we feel Her death;
we know it was necessary, inevitable,
but we feel it keenly;
we know you are with us
in never-ending love
but we need to feel you more:
strengthen our faith
so that we may feel you more forcefully
feel the searing of your solace within us
so that we may think less of our misfortunes
and more joyfully carry Her word into the world.

Sacred fire within our hearts
discipline within our brains
protector of delayed gratification
patron of the open space

guardian of vulnerability
giver and receiver
channel of all love
guarantor of grace
the self within the other
the other within the self
the inspirer and product of kenosis
source and realisation of unity in diversity:
help us to proclaim
the innocence of love
against the knowingness of calculation
so that we may never be afraid to be vulnerable
in the sight of humanity and God.

SONG

O force that makes the waters flow
O fire that glows all gloom away
O strength of grace no limits know
intensify your comfort now, we pray.

Our hearts with joy and sorrow filled,
Her death and rising harsh in us collide;
She left and now we pray uncertain still,
need even more the Spirit as our guide.

As days go by the wonder fades,
Praying is torment, guilt in every vein;
Where there was love now only pained restraint:
Come Holy Spirit, save us once again.

Water of life
Fire of the spirit
Fill us with grace
Beyond all limit.

PENITENCE

Parent God
we are sorry that we killed Perpetua
We are sorry that we killed Jesus
We are sorry for our acts of unkindness and selfishness
but more sorry for our indifference and cowardice;
we are sorry for abusing the space of others
but more sorry for not making space for others:
forgive us for, in our indifference,
we are the dictators

we are the torturers
we are the embezzlers
we are the masters;
forgive us,
together with those whose wrong choices are more salient
and therefore seem more serious;
and give us the strength
to refrain from the silence of cowardice.

PSALM

1. Lord, we have lived through turbulent times:
     we do do not know whether to cry or to rejoice;
2. Your daughter Perpetua has been so recently taken from us:
     and we do not know where to turn.
3. We felt the guilt of our treachery:
     we, the ambassadors of humanity who stood by at Her murder;
4. And we had hardly come to know Her again after
          Her miraculous manifestations:
     before She left us, apparently forever.
5. Lord we are hard pressed, we are hemmed in on every side:
     the tide of consumption rises as the lot of the poor worsens;
6. Our missions of friendship to your Christian people are insulted:
     and we are either ridiculed or, worse, ignored.
7. We have Her image before us:
     but it is fading already;
8. We are desperate to keep Her before us:
     so that we may know Your ways.
9. We worship You as our Creator and we revere Jesus Your Son:
     forgive us our favouring of Your Daughter
          Perpetua as Your sharpest presence.
10. Praise to the one God in Parent, Jesus, Perpetua and the Spirit:
     and in Your manifestations in other places, and times before and to come.

READING—LUKE

A lawyer (though today it could have been a journalist) stood up to trap Jesus.

"Teacher," he said (perhaps with a hint of sarcasm) "What must I do to inherit eternal life?"

Jesus said: "What is written in the law? What have you seen there?"

The man answered: "You shall love the Lord your God with all your heart, and with all your soul, and with all your strength, and with all your mind; and love your neighbour as yourself."

And Jesus said "Yes; you have given the right answer. Do this and you will be saved." But, wanting to retrieve his dignity, the man countered: "But who is my neighbour?"

READING—JACK

Somebody shouted: "Keep our country Christian".

"One day," said Perpetua, "two tough guys in white vans were involved in a minor accident on the main road a few miles outside Stumpy Knoll. They jumped out of their vans and started punching each other. One of them was knocked bleeding to the ground and the other one drove away at high speed, leaving his victim lying between his van and the road in full sight of the traffic.

"An off-duty paramedic drove past but did not want to get involved in case of troublesome insurance claims. An officer of Neighbourhood Safety drove past but he could not become involved because he had an important meeting scheduled with the police. A Curate drove past but he was too frightened to become involved; he was worried that the victim might be carrying a knife. He looked like a very unpleasant customer; it was probably his own fault anyway.

"Then a Muslim taxi driver stopped at the scene. He saw the National Front badges on the man's clothing and the swastika tattoo on the back of his right hand. But he got a cloth and cleared away the grime and blood from his wounds and bound them up with a couple of clean rags. He hauled him awkwardly into the back of his taxi, sent a message to Control and headed for the A&E Department.

"When they got there, the man was abusive but the Muslim and a couple of Filipino nurses managed to calm him down. They dressed his wounds and discharged him. The young man, still confused, moaned about his fate and hurled abuse at the Muslim. The taxi driver took him to the nearest Wayfarer Lodge and offered a swipe of his credit card as surety. The Manager, who disliked the look of both of them equally, bridled but, in the end, still grumbling, agreed to take the man.

"Next day, the victim, feeling a lot stronger, threatened the Manager with violence if he refused to give him the cash for a taxi against the swipe the Muslim had left. He phoned and asked for a white taxi driver and was re-united with his vehicle and drove away. The Muslim paid the bill and said nothing."

CREED

We affirm the mysteries:

that God who is love
created everything out of love
and created humanity as imperfect
so that we might freely love God
in a personal relationship
and love each other;
that in love God Our Parent sent a Son, Jesus Christ,
and a daughter, Perpetua, The Sacred Vessel,
as God to share our humanity;
by such sharing they brought new hope
but their perfection was too much for humanity to bear

and so we killed them;
that they absorbed all humanity's wrong choices
and gave us new resources to love
through our consciousness of our Sister The Spirit
who is God within us,
who gives us Incarnational Perception
and attunes us to God's self-communication in love;
that by their re-manifestation Jesus and Perpetua confirmed
that, because no wrong choice,
including killing them, can ever limit God's limitless love,
all humanity will be enfolded back
into the Godhead
from which we came.

We affirm the mysteries:

of our earthly purpose
of living a Sacramental life
of physical encounter with the divine
through the life with each other
and we accept the privileged responsibility
inherent in that encounter
to bring the news to all humanity
that it will be re-united in God.

PRAYERS

We who are imperfect,
who make wrong choices
pray, through Jesus and Perepetua,
and in the power of Our Sister the Spirit,
for the imperfect:

» For organisations raised in your name
   which have lost their purpose
   through the perils of clericalism,
   dogmatism, intolerance, the exercise of power and pride
» For dictators, torturers, exploiters and defrauders
   who are the living crystallisation of all our own fears,
   our lack of confidence in You
   and our pride in our own power
» For those too frightened to make space
   for the love of the other
» For those who can give but cannot take
» for we who stand by in indifference
   while the world suffers,

    thereby making us torturers and murderers
    in our own right
»   For those who make the sacred trivial
    and make the trivial sacred;
    for all idolaters.

SONG

As we sit around Your table
ready to enjoy Your feast
offering our gifts for blessing
each a supplicant and priest:
offering the things we value
to be pooled in sacrifice,
given back as You within us,
in our earthly paradise.

Here we recognise your kingdom
in the food and drink we bring,
to be offered in The Spirit
to become Your offering:
Your true presence here among us
four in one without an end,
Parent, Christ, Perpetua, Spirit,
maker, sibling, lover, friend.

GREAT PRAYER

As we, your priests, sit together
offering thanks and praise
for Your creation,
for Your physical presence with us
in Jesus and Perpetua,
and for Your presence with us
now in the Spirit,
we bring to mind,
as best we can,
the mysteries of Your loving creation,
Your incarnation
and Your true presence with us;
we call to mind our necessary imperfection
and our constant need for penitence;
and we commit ourselves in Your presence with us
to our earthly work
of collective and individual kenosis,
in imitation of Your children,

Jesus and Perpetua,
so that love may flourish
in Your kingdom on earth.

We unite ourselves in prayer,
within Your blessing,
to all those who have been
brave in the cause of love,
unsparing in their reception of others,
tireless in the fight against apathy,
unstinting in the creation of unconditional space;
and we unite ourselves, too,
with the creation from other times
before and to come,
and in other places and spaces
in the whole universe, or universes,
with all those who have known Your creation in love;
and we unite ourselves with Your children
who showed to us imperfect creatures
that Your love is beyond limit,
even the limit of humanity's murder
of Your children.

On the night before we killed Jesus and Perpetua,
two millennia apart,
each took food and drink
made by our hands,
thanked You
and offered them to You
in the power of Our Sister the Spirit
and promised,
in their respective Second and Third Testaments,
that when we offer food and drink in their names,
recalling our murder of them,
that they would be truly with us.
They, as we do now,
took food and drink,
blessed them
and gave them to all who were there,
saying:

"This is my true presence with you.
Do this until you are enfolded
eternally into God's limitless love."

In offering food and drink we,
in the power of the Spirit,
live their final offerings to You once more
in the paradoxical knowledge
of the certain mystery
of their presence with us now.

We return to you
your gifts of fruit and wine,
knowing that you will,
through the Spirit,
bless us with the true presence
of Jesus and Perpetua among us:

Christ died
Christ returned to us
Christ will never leave us;

Perpetua died
Perpetua returned to us
Perpetua will never leave us.

Through Your blessed children,
with them,
and in them,
and in the power of Our Sister the Spirit,
in union with all those
before, now and in the future,
here, and in the whole of Your creation,
committed to sacred kenosis,
the epitome of divine and human love,
we welcome Jesus and Perpetua
who are with us now.

Amen.

FAMILY PRAYER

Parent God
other yet within us
we bless Your name;
may Your kingdom be
as near on earth to You
consistent with our creaturely imperfection.
Give us the strength to steward what you Created
and acknowledge our limitations
as we acknowledge the limitations of others

in love;
and help us to make space
rather than to close it down
so that our kenosis may be worthy
of your sacred children.

THE SACRED MEAL

As we give each other
what You have given to us
in the form of food and drink,
we commit ourselves to loving communion
in Jesus and Perpetua,
being with them in the brokenness
of their bodies,
broken for us in this sacred food,
poured out for us in this sacred drink.

THANKSGIVING

Loving Parent
we thank You for nourishing us
with the true presence
in food and drink
of Your Son and Daughter,
Jesus Christ
and Perpetua, Your Sacred Vessel;
through them we offer back to you
all that we are,
which you gave to us,
in tribute to Your goodness;
may we leave this house
to be fitting witnesses and imitators
of Your divine kenosis.

PRAISE

Glory to God in the highest
and peace to all creatures
made to love:
Lord God, lover of all,
the ultimate self-giver,
we worship You
we give You thanks
we praise You for Your presence.
Jesus our brother,

Son of Our Parent,
Perpetua our Sister, Daughter of Our Parent
Lamb of God
and Sacred Vessel,
symbols of our aspiration,
help us to bear our imperfection;
help us to be more open:
for You are our holy ones
You are our sacred guides,
You who took flesh are ourselves
in Our Sister the Spirit
through the love of God Our Parent:
we worship and thank You,
Creator, Lamb, Vessel, and Spirit.

Amen.

SONG

Out into Your world we travel
in the starlight and the gloom;
offering ourselves in service,
willing as Our Lady's womb:
open to the taunts of strangers
lashing out in abject fear,
vulnerable to the dangers
that in striking bring You near.

As we stretch to almost breaking,
vulnerable in Your space,
risking ever more for others,
generous in the harsh embrace:
we look to Your own Kenosis
God poured out in human form
Lamb of God and Sacred Vessel
firm in imperfection's storm.

God, the source of all creation
pouring out Your love for all
emptying Your flesh and Spirit,
healing wounds from flare and fall
yet in mystery absorbing
all wrong choices in your name,
showing that Your love is endless
in the Vessel and the Lamb.

BLESSING

The Godhead outside time and space
bless us
in the being of Our Parent
in the Lamb and in the Vessel
and in The Spirit. Amen.

LITANY

Daughter of Our Parent
Sister of Jesus
Sister of the Spirit
love incarnate
Sacred Vessel
fountain of responsibility
stream of serenity
consolation of the imperfect
epitome of the divine mystery
pattern of openness
icon of kenosis
guardian of risk takers
support of the weak
stronghold of solidarity
guide of the helpless
liberator of the addicted
haven for the frustrated
hope of the desperate
healer of the cynical
light of the sceptical
vigour of the apathetic
softener of the callous
comforter of the frightened
champion of the second chance
prophet of peace
woman most holy
woman most earthly
woman most sexy
woman of all women
woman of all people
steward of sunrise
Patron of the vulnerable
child of God.

EU GPSR Authorized Representative:

LOGOS EUROPE, 9 rue Nicolas Poussin, 17000 La Rochelle, France

contact@logoseurope.eu

www.ingramcontent.com/pod-product-compliance
Lightning Source LLC
Chambersburg PA
CBHW030914050726
47498CB00003BA/728